Laura Wright is passionate about romantic fiction. Though she spent most of her life immersed in acting, singing, and competitive ballroom dancing, when she found the world of writing and books and endless cups of coffee, she knew she was home.

Laura lives in Los Angeles with her husband, two young children, and three lovable dogs.

Visit her online at www.laurawright.com and www.twitter.com/ LauraWrightRom

Also by Laura Wright

MARK OF THE VAMPIRE SERIES:

Eternal Hunger
Eternal Kiss

Eternal
CAPTIVE

LAURA WRIGHT

piatkus

PIATKUS

First published in the US in 2012 by Signet Eclipse,
An imprint of New American Library, a division of Penguin Group (USA) Inc.
First published in Great Britain as a paperback original in 2012 by Piatkus

A CIP catalogue record for this book
is available from the British Library.

ISBN 978-0-7499-5638-7

Typeset in Sabon by M Rules
Printed and bound in Great Britain by
Clays Ltd, St Ives plc

Papers used by Piatkus are from well-managed forests
and other responsible sources.

MIX
Paper from
responsible sources
FSC® C104740

Piatkus
An imprint of
Little, Brown Book Group
100 Victoria Embankment
London EC4Y 0DY

An Hachette UK Company
www.hachette.co.uk

www.piatkus.co.uk

To you, my readers, who love these boys just as much as I do

Glossary

Balas—Vampire child.

The Breeding Male—A *paven* of purest blood whose genetic code and structure has been altered by the Eternal Order. He has the ability to impregnate at will and decide the sex of the *balas*. He is brought in by Pureblood families and/or to repopulate one sex or the other in times of dire necessity. He is uncontrollable, near to an animal, and must be caged.

Credenti—A vampire community, ruled and protected by the Eternal Order. Both Purebloods and Impures live here. There are many all over the world, masked by the Order so that humans barely notice their existence.

Duro—Tender word for "brother."

Eternal Order—The ten Pureblood vampires who have passed on to the middle world, yet make the laws, punish the law-breakers, and govern every vampire *credenti* on Earth.

Eyes—The New York City street rats who run the sales of drugs, blood, and body to both human and vampire.

Gemino—Twin.

Gravo—Poisoned vampire blood.

Imiti—An imitation vampire, one who can take on the characteristics of a vampire if he or she drinks blood regularly.

Impurebloods—Any combination of human and vampire. They have no powers, a heartbeat, and can live in the sun. They only have fangs when blood is consumed. Males are blood castrated, their sex drive removed through the blood by the Order. Females are blood sterilized and the inside of their thighs are branded with *Is*.

Meta—A pureblood female of fifty years, she can still remain in sunlight, but needs the blood and body of her true mate.

Mondrar—Vampire prison.

Morpho—A pureblood *paven* of three hundred years; as powerful as a *paven* can get. He is sunlight intolerant, and the need to find his true mate becomes impossible to deny.

Mutore—A Pureblood vampire shape-shifter. A Beast. A child of the Breeding Male gone wrong. Is considered less than trash, and a bad omen on the Breed. Is usually killed right after birth when they shift for the first time.

Paleo—The Order's secret location where Impures are blood castrated.

Paven—A vampire male of pure blood.

Pureblood—Pure vampire. Powerful, no heartbeat, will go through Morpho and Meta and find their pureblood true mate.

Puritita—One who is chaste.

Sacro—Dirty.

Similis—The Impure guards of Mondrar.

Swell—Vampire pregnancy.

Tegga—Nursemaid/nanny/governess.

True Mate—The one each Pureblood *veana* and *paven* is destined for. Each shares an identical or complementary mark somewhere on their skin.

Veana—A vampire female of pure blood.

Veracou—The mating ceremony between two pureblood vampires.

Virgini—Virgin.

Witte—Animal.

Prologue
The Breeding Male

Scotland
1872

Titus Evictus paced in his iron enclosure, his fangs fully extended, his pale eyes dilated, his long, heavily muscled body nude save for the painful iron cup that imprisoned his cock. There were moments in his miserable existence, brief and gleefully hopeful, when he felt less than rabid, when his mind attempted to clear away the fog, when the scent of blood was not ever-deep inside his nostrils—and when the call of a warm, wet pussy didn't send his body into spasms of painful arousal.

That day, however, was not today.

A *veana* was being led into his pen by two short *pavens* with long braided beards. Her kin. He recognized their scent from the night before. The *veana* struggled and grunted and breathed heavily, the scents of peat smoke and the spray of the sea escaping her skin. Though his nostrils flared and his mouth filled with saliva, Titus kept his back to the iron wall and his eyes down. After so many years of this delectable, tortuous labor, he now refused to look at the faces of the *veanas* that were brought before him.

He found their fear impossible to resist.

As her kin released her and quickly left the pen, slamming the iron door behind them, the *veana* stood stock-still, her fingers fisting around the gray fabric of her gown, the key to his iron prison dangling from the middle finger of her right hand. True to his nature, Titus wanted to leap upon her and take what was his, but his chains wouldn't stretch that far. Like all the others that came before her, she would have to yield and come to him. It was how it was, how it must be. Until she submitted, gave in to her fate, she would remain captive, hungry for blood, and desperate.

And the longer she waited, the more rabid Titus would become. It was better for her if she came to him, unlocked him, lay beneath him within the next hour.

"Breeding Male?"

She spoke clearly and without tremor.

"Look up, Breeding Male."

Titus's chin twitched at her voice, her calm, determined tone. Normally it took hours, days for the *veanas* who were brought before him, caged with him, to give in, give up, and beg for a gentle hand.

"Now!" she said, so sharply it caused his fangs to descend. "Look at me!"

Titus couldn't help himself, not with such a bold, impassioned tongue before him. His eyelids flipped up and he took in the daring Scottish lass, the one who carried no scent of fear on her skin or in her blood. She displayed fine curves and a heavy bosom. Her neck, though burdened with a thick strip of purity cloth, was the whitest, most luscious thing he'd ever beheld. And just a few inches north, long ringlets of honey blond hair framed a pale, pleasing face. But it was her pink mouth and her eyes— green flecked with black, staring straight into his, brazen as a demon goddess—that had his fangs dropping farther.

She lifted her chin and regarded him. "What say ye, Breeding Male?"

Titus could form no words. Instead, he growled at her.

The *veana* grinned at his animal-like response, flashing her own set of needle-sharp fangs. "That'll do fer a start," she said, her brogue rich and throaty as she looked him over.

His cock pulsed inside its iron prison—the one that kept his hand away when he was blindly desperate to mate—the one that preserved his seed. Never in Titus's long life, in his capacity as Breeding Male, had a *veana* ever spoken to him in such a manner. Once beneath him, there were moans, yes, and cries, both in fear and in pleasure ... but never this. This calm, this curiosity, this nearly lusty excitement ...

"It has taken me quite some time, Breeding Male," she said, walking toward him, her hips swaying gently beneath her simple gown, "not to mention great effort, to find myself here. I have heard the tales of ye, and those who were in fear of yer touch—but I am no silly lass. Aye, I may be *virgini*, but I have prepared myself for ye." She smiled. "Many nights, many times."

Fire raged through Titus and he strained against his chains, the clash of metal echoing throughout the pen enclosure. His nostrils widened with every step she took, eager for more of her scent. How could it be? he thought desperately. There was no fear in her scent—not even a trace. It was impossible and yet it was how he had always wanted this moment to be. Just once. He despised himself every second of every day—but not today, not this moment. In this moment, the reflection staring back at him in her green eyes was not of the monster Breeding Male.

It was of a desired *paven*.

He ran his tongue over his fangs as she moved to within a foot of him.

The words of the *veana*'s father to Titus's master last eve made sense now. She was six months into her Meta and in that time there had been no appearance of her true mate's mark. Her father had claimed that she was unconcerned with retaining her purity, remaining outside in the eve without the watchful eyes of her kin. And just three nights ago, she had been found on her knees in the family barn, servicing an Impure field worker.

Disgusted and terrified that they would be burdened with the stain of an Impure *swell*, her kin had thought it time the *veana* visited the Breeding Male—time she had her womb filled with his Pureblood seed.

Titus watched hungrily as the *veana* stripped the purity bands from her wrists and neck, then started to work the buttons of her gown. He didn't need clothing removed to do the job he was required to do, only the quick lift of her skirt, but as she slowly revealed her skin to him, each pale inch, he understood the true feelings of lust—pure, not purposeful, lust.

"I would be content with a wee *paven*, Breeding Male," she said, stepping forward, taking the key she had been given and unlocking the iron cup between his legs.

Her hand shook slightly in her work, but it was not from fear. He knew this. He scented this.

He let loose another feral growl as his rod sprang free.

She licked her lips at the sight. "But dunna be quick about it. They willna come for me until daybreak. We have much time together."

Stripped bare, she lay down on the hard stone floor before him, displaying her pale, young body, her long legs, her glistening cunt to his ravenous gaze.

His cock stood straight up and ready, and as she opened her legs for him, the cry—the howl—that erupted from his throat

4

could be heard all the way to Edinburgh. He was Titus Evictus *and* he was the Breeding Male. In an instant, he was on top of her, his fangs striking into her shoulder as his cock slid deep inside her hot, willing body.

1

Mark of the *Veana*

Boston
Present Day

Her fangs had been inside him only once, and yet they had left an unseen mark on his skin, his blood, even his breath. In consuming his blood she had consumed his very soul and now—every day, every moment he existed, she moved inside him, her unending hunger deafening as she searched and slithered through his veins, circled his muscles, squeezed until his brain threatened to explode.

Lucian Roman sat perched, as he had for the past seven nights, on the snow-crested roof of Bronwyn Kettler's brownstone. Still and menacing as a gargoyle, he ignored the vibration of his cell phone in his coat pocket and stared without purpose into the heavy snowfall, which dropped bride-white over the silent Boston *credenti* landscape. An hour ago, the streets had been alive with Impures running about, adorning the doors of their master's dwellings as well as the gates, fences, and lampposts leading up to the Gathering Hall. The tasteful bunting and subdued winter flowers were a testament to how the Boston

7

community viewed the binding ceremony of its true mates—
with serious and reverent celebration.

Now the streets were empty and silence reigned, as did the
snow, and Lucian sneered in appreciation as the decorations for
tomorrow's Veracou were quickly being buried in heavy white
frosting. Would a blizzard annul the binding ceremony between
Bronwyn and the *paven* who claimed her mark? Lucian thought
not. But he would remain, affixed to the roof to watch. To wait.
To see the binding done and over. Or—if his blood had its
wish—to see Bronwyn run from her true mate, reject her body's
choice.

As another wave of longing, of desire-ladened torment pulsed
in his bones and brain, Lucian's fangs slowly descended and the
blade in his fist trembled.

There were only two ways to stop this madness.

Fuck her or kill her.

And yet he could do neither and remain free. The former
would turn him into a Breeding Male one hundred and seventy-
five years before his time—a rutting animal with no conscience,
no control, only a hunger to claim. While the latter would send
him to Mondrar, the vampire prison, for all eternity.

Again he felt the vibration of his cell phone and again he
ignored it. He knew Alexander would never give up looking for
him, and in fact had seen his brother walking the streets below
once already this week. But the eldest Roman had never looked
up, and down below had found only snow and the censure of a
community who reviled anything with a matching set of
Breeding Male brands.

A sudden rush of sound, a faint cry, like air released from a
balloon, stole Lucian's thoughts and left him with nothing but
a raw, feral craving. He sprang to his feet, his entire body going
forest-fire hot as a growl sounded in his throat.

Damn her. With one bite, she had made him into this, this animal, this creature of destruction, and though perhaps it hadn't been her intention to ruin him, he would make her pay.

His hand fisting the knife, Lucian moved like a panther down the pitched roof and over the edge, dropping to the small balcony attached to her room in near silence. The window was a large square, and in the handful of times he'd stood there watching her sleep, he'd surmised rather easy to maneuver through.

Darkness blanketed her bedroom, the only light coming from the streetlamps below. But to Lucian's keen gaze, it was enough to make out the furniture, the artwork on her walls, and the *veana* lying in her bed. As usual, she was on her back, her dark hair spilling out over her stark white pillow. In nights previous, she had slept soundly, unmoving, like the princess Lucian had insisted on labeling her.

But tonight, she moved.

Leaning closer to the glass, his insides still blazing with heat, Lucian narrowed his gaze on her lower half, specifically on her legs as they stirred beneath the white coverlet. It was as if she were running a race in her sleep, and yet, as his gaze trailed upward to her thighs, to the outline of her hips, he realized that the race she was running was the one that ended in climax.

Madness splintered his mind once again, and instead of pushing away from her window and returning to his rooftop perch as he normally did, he quietly broke the lock on her window, eased up the frame, and stole inside her room. Instantly, the scent of her yet unclaimed orgasm washed over him, and he flew to the bed and coiled over her like a snake, any last shreds of stability he may have had upon entering now dead, drowned, forgotten.

The white coverlet blinded him from the act she performed,

9

but Lucian could imagine her hands working her core, just as he could scent the dance of her fingers inside her cunt.

He snarled softly at her, at the pale, perfect face that was framed with long black hair.

No veana had the right to be this beautiful.

No veana had the right to hold him captive.

Held in her own state of captivity, Bronwyn's eyes remained clamped shut, but her cheeks held the delectable stain of desire, and her pink lips were parted just enough for the ragged breaths of her building passion to escape. Like a dog in heat, Lucian leaned in and took one long sniff.

The mistake of it hit him instantaneously.

His fangs dropped to needle sharpness against his lips, and all he could see was blood, and all he could taste was sex.

All he could do was place his blade to her throat.

Bronwyn's eyes slammed open at the feel of cool metal. "You."

"Not who you were thinking about, Princess?"

Her arms shot out from beneath the covers; her fingers wrapped his wrist. "What do you think you're doing?"

"Don't move."

"Get off me, you bastard!"

The scent of her fear did nothing to stall him, only pushed his madness further. "Don't talk. Even your breath on my face makes me want to scratch at your skin to get inside."

Her gaze narrowed on his. "What's happened to you? You look—"

"I said don't talk!"

"If you're here to kill me," she said, her nails digging into his skin, "don't expect me to die easily or quietly."

Her lips pressed together, fear tensing her jaw and the skin around her eyes—though the scent of arousal still lingered temptingly in the air.

10

The blade still held to her throat, Lucian's fangs dropped even farther as he uttered, "I hate you."

She stared up at him, unblinking, her nostrils flaring as she breathed in and out. "Hate me or yourself?"

He leaned in closer. "You've turned me inside out," he whispered near her mouth. "Do you understand that? I can't feed. I can't fuck." His head began to pound, his muscles too ... Damn it, he wanted her mouth under his, her blood rushing over his tongue—her death on whatever was left of his conscience. If he pressed the knife just a hair closer, he could have it, have it all ... "That night you came to me—"

"I didn't plan it, Lucian," she interrupted fiercely. "Goddamn it! I didn't plan to feed—"

He cut off her words, pressing the blade nearer to her throat. "Another word and I will be feeding from you."

"*Release the* veana, *Lucian. Now.*"

Before Lucian even had the chance to respond, the knife was ripped from his fist. For one brief moment, the cold metal hovered in midair, then shot past his face and disappeared behind him.

Lucian whirled around to face the intruder, in the back of his mind hearing Bronwyn slip from the bed, taking her freedom. But his gaze, his focus was pinned on the hooded figure lurking in the shadows near the window. He snarled, "What do you want?"

"To keep you from harm," replied the ancient *paven*.

Lucian sneered at his father, the Breeding Male—the Order. "Too late."

"It will be if you continue on this path." Titus raised his hooded head toward the corner of the room. "I am sorry for this, Mistress Kettler."

Lucian turned and narrowed his eyes on the *veana* who, even in her fear, stood tall and imperious.

"I thank the Order for its help in this matter," she said,

11

nodding at Titus. "Now, pray, get him out of here before my parents awake."

"Come with me, Lucian."

Instantly, Lucian felt the pull of his father, magnet to iron. It was a solid yank, and yet Lucian was immobile, his eyes locked on Bronwyn. He uttered a pained, "I cannot."

Bronwyn turned to look at him.

"She is to be mated in the morning," Titus said tightly. *"She will feed from another and he will feed from her."*

"Shut up!" Lucian roared.

"Your torment will pass."

"My torment has only begun!"

Lucian's gaze caught on the mark near the base of Bronwyn's thumb. The *paven*'s mark—her *paven*. Feral rage slammed through him, and he shot across the room, forcing her deeper into the corner. She belonged to him. Her mouth, her gaze, her neck, her vein, her voice, her cunt. He grabbed her hand and pulled it to his lips. But just as his fangs entered her marked skin, he was yanked back, slammed into the one who had given him not only life, but the curse of the Breeding Male.

No blood met Lucian's dry tongue, but Bronwyn's cry of pain ripped through his black soul as Titus flashed him away.

Bronwyn stood in the corner of her now-empty bedroom, her legs shaking from both terror and unfulfilled desire—her mind already spent with questions she wasn't entirely sure she wanted the answers to.

But they came anyway.

How long had Lucian Roman been watching her? How long had he been perched on her roof? Just today? Tonight? Or many days? Lord, how many times had he seen her tears, her worry— her hands travel south to her core?

Groaning, she turned and faced the wall as her parents had forced her to do many times as a *balas* when she was a disagreeable force in their home. The coolness of the plaster felt good against her cheek and yet it did nothing to cleanse her fear.

Though the wound registered most unpleasantly, she didn't want to look at it. She didn't want to look down, at her hand—where that menacing vampire, that terrifying angel, had bit into her flesh.

She shut her eyes and prayed, as if those two actions could will away the crisis before her. This was truly her nightmare come to life. Lucian's fangs inside her skin, inside the mark of another.

Tears pricked her eyes, but she dismissed them and pushed away from the wall. She went over to the bedside table and lit her lamp. Slowly, she sank onto the mattress. Where moments ago she was writhing in a state of frustrated, hopeful pleasure, now there was only pain. Deep, aching pain running through her, riverquick. What was Lucian trying to do? Bleed her? Drink from her?

Punish her.

With a deep breath, she dropped her gaze to her hand. Blinking, she studied the white skin, the dark mark. The animal brand on her thumb—the one that marked her as taken, as the property of her true mate—appeared uninjured. Yes, Lucian's fangs had ruptured the skin, but there seemed to be no permanent damage done to the brand itself.

Her sigh of relief was so strident she nearly laughed.

She hated the effect this *paven* had on her—hated that even after weeks away from him, she could still taste his blood—not on the tip of her tongue where she might get rid of it with rations, but at the back of her throat. The sweetest blood she'd ever had, and God help her, the only blood she wanted in her veins now. She hated that ever since she'd drunk from him in his

13

bedroom in the house in SoHo, she could never make it to orgasm. No matter how long and how hard she tried. It was deeply frustrating, not to mention humiliating. It was as if he'd granted her his blood, and had broken her in return.

His words, his accusations—his declaration of hatred as he'd hovered menacingly above her minutes ago—echoed in her mind . . .

Perhaps they'd broken each other.

As the snow began to fall in the darkness outside her window, Bron prayed that her mating would kill this bond, this need, this ache between them. Because if it didn't, she had an eternity of misery, regret, and unclaimed passion to look forward to.

She lifted her thumb to her lips and was just about to blow on her skin, use her powerful *veana*'s breath to heal her wound, when her hopes were utterly destroyed before her eyes. Was it an omen? she wondered sickly. Or the beautiful albino mocking her from wherever he was perched now? She didn't know, and really, did it even matter? There, on her thumb, the ink that had been implanted under her skin to fool her parents and the Order bubbled to the surface, inching toward the two pinprick holes, then slowly leaked out like oil from the ground.

Panic swelled within her, ballooning in her chest. Forget Lucian Roman and her unending need for his blood. She had a far greater problem.

She jumped up and scurried over to her desk, grabbed her cell phone, and dialed. She had to get to Synjon before the next eve's Veracou ceremony—their ceremony. She needed to get beneath his needle once again, and let him carve his mark into her skin before anyone discovered the truth.

Synjon Wise came out of hiding for no one. Nicknamed the ghost, the only vampire *paven* to ever serve as both an elite

Special Forces officer in his native Britain and as an American Navy SEAL, he regarded his current existence as a spy, an assassin, and a bounty hunter for the Eternal Order as bloody perfection. With no family, no mates, no strings of any kind, he received his orders and carried them out without any chink in the reserved armor of the breed. It was a simple and satisfying existence to one who craved danger—an existence he could sustain for many centuries.

That is, if he'd chosen to ignore the call of one very surprising voice from the past.

Gunfire erupted below. Nothing sinister—not yet. Just the target practice of four human males who foolishly prided themselves on being amateur vampire trackers, irritating buggers, and *credenti* infiltrators. The pulse-bearing pack stood side by side on the ground, shoulder to shoulder over their low-flamed desert campfire, argy-bargy, knocking off shots into the black night. Less than three miles away was the Southwest Texas *credenti*, their target. Synjon had been following them for two nights through the Chihuahuan Desert, and he listened now as in between quick bouts of gunfire they decided on the best way inside the secret compound.

On top of a small desert hill, tucked behind a thick grove of ocotillo plants, Synjon silently checked his weapon supply. His orders were to interfere only if the four wankers attempted entrance into the *credenti*, but he wasn't keen on letting them get that far with the amount of weapons they had on them.

His cell pulsed against his leg, announcing a new text message, but he made no move to get it. In fact, as he watched the group below stamp out their fire, his instinct was to ignore the call completely. In the past, he'd carried only weapons, no communication devices. He liked it that way. Brilliant, old-school warrior mentality, that was. Once he received his orders, he took off, became invisible, unreachable. But things had changed since the phone call, since *she* had come into his life.

Yes, she was an exception to all his bloody rules. Beautiful, brave, and unflinchingly moral, Bronwyn Kettler had saved his sorry life—and his soul, once upon a time. Granted, he had known her for only one summer when his family stayed with relatives in her Boston *credenti*—but one summer had been enough to alter him completely. Synjon had been one sorry bloke back then; thin as a bowie blade with a head far too large for his frame. And the lisp ... shite, the lisp that had nearly ended him before his time. The torture, the beastly knocks from the other *balas*, had been unrelenting and unbearable—until Bronwyn Kettler had stepped in front of him and taken on each ugly jab with her own brand of brilliant weaponry.

Syn grinned at the memory. That *veana* was a brick, wielding words with the same deadly accuracy as he used to shoot cherries from a tree at a hundred paces. Just thinking about her censure, her dressing-down of those who had sought to injure what little was left of his boyhood pride, made him want to love her in the way a *veana* should be loved, deserved to be loved—in a way he would never love again.

She had remained by his side all summer long, just as she had remained in his heart—not as a lover, but as the truest of friends ... forever. Synjon had grown to appreciate her, to rely on her over the many years into his *pavenhood*, most especially when the woman he loved, the one who had slept by his side and was his true partner, though not his true mate, was killed, her body stolen before he'd ever had a chance to give her over to the sun.

It had been Bronwyn who had comforted him, who had helped him to grieve. She was the only vampire he trusted, and when she had come to him requesting a favor, he hadn't even blinked before agreeing.

Movement below caught his attention once again, and he watched as the four human males shouldered their weapons and set out across the desert for their three-mile trek to the *credenti*. Again, the cell at his boot pulsed. This time he snatched it up. No matter what his position, he couldn't ignore it. He wasn't a ghost anymore, and if it were her, she may have need of him.

His eyes dropped, roamed over her text. *Bollocks ...* That albino *paven* again. Syn's fangs dropped. Lucian Roman would leave her be. After tomorrow, he would leave her be or find himself good and wasted.

Sudden gunfire stuttered the still night air and Synjon's chin jacked up. He replaced the cell back in its case on his bootstrap and leaped off the bluff onto the smoking fire. As a morphed *paven*, he could be there for her in an instant, but tonight she would have to wait a moment longer. Fifteen minutes perhaps. That would be sufficient time to halt, question, and dispose of the four human donkeys before they ever reached the *credenti* walls, he thought, flashing from the smoke of the fire in the soft silence that was his trademark.

2

He could still walk in sunlight, still breathe the unbound air, and if all went well, in about ten minutes he'd have the use of his cock for something far more satisfying than just pissing.

"What are you doing, Lucian?"

Lucian remained where he was, didn't even blink as he registered the voice behind him. "What does it look like I'm doing, Pops?"

"It looks as though you're marking your territory," said the male, his tone concerned.

As night reigned overhead, a dome of black and diamond stars, Lucian finished his golden shower against the brick wall of the building that housed Bronwyn and her true mate, then zipped his fly. "What do you want, Titus?" he asked, turning to face his father.

Under the deep yellow glow of the moon, Lucian saw that the aged *paven*, the Breeding Male, the ancient Order member, had his head uncovered. A rarity for Titus, but it was clearly a sign that the *paven* was alarmed. "It looks as though you have an obsession that won't be contained."

Lucian grinned at the near mirror image of himself. "Well, I suppose that makes two of us, then."

Titus said nothing, but his silence illustrated his confusion.

Lucian's grin turned to acerbic laughter. "You're on my albino ass 24-7. Methinks you've got quite an obsession of your own."

Titus's pale eyes locked with Lucian's. "I am only trying to help you. Guide you." He dropped his chin. "Warn you."

"Well, don't," Lucian said flippantly. "I'm good. Soon as my *veana* walks out—"

"You have no *veana*," Titus interrupted briskly. "You have no true mate. You will never have. Breeding Males are not destined for love."

Lucian's fangs descended, like a razor-sharp elevator to hell. "As soon as the *veana* walks out of this Veracou hall," he spit out, "once she's bound and mated for eternity, it's done. This . . . " He spread his arms out, looked down at his far-too-lean frame. "This . . . *fuck*! Whatever it is that has consumed my brain and body will end. It has to end."

"I hope so," Titus said darkly, his eyes shifting from Lucian and moving over the Boston *credenti* landscape. It was quiet and devoid of all Pureblood community members, as most were inside observing the Veracou. "Because if it does not, you are in great danger."

Lucian snorted. "Tell me something I don't know." He gestured to the door of the hall, where Bronwyn and her true mate were at that very moment pledging their undying and untamed love for each other. It was enough to make a *paven* puke. And yet Lucian prayed it would grant him some relief. He had to believe that, had to believe that once the commitment was sealed it would break the hold this *veana* had on him—on his blood, on his bones, on his mind . . . Because even now, he could still feel the need for her pounding through him, searing him.

Fighting a groan, he glared at his sire. "Shouldn't you be inside, Daddy Dearest? Giving your blessing to the happy couple, and all that horse shit?"

"I will go inside when you leave the *credenti*."

"And I will leave after I see her."

Eyes narrowed, Titus said, "You do not need to see her!"

"Wrong," Lucian growled, his index finger nearly in his father's chest. "Her eyes will tell me she is mated. Her mouth will tell me it belongs against his. If they are truly one, her body will pull closer to his as she moves down the steps of the hall. Then my fucking renegade blood will know if this hold she has over me is done."

"And if you don't see these things?" Titus asked, the wind picking up around them. "Feel these things? Will you go after her again? Will you risk your freedom, your very existence for one moment of pleasure?"

"Get the fuck away from me, Pops."

"Because that is all it will take. Her blood is inside you. The change has begun. Will you truly surrender to it? Will you risk turning into the Breeding Male—turning into *me*?"

"I will never turn into you," Lucian returned sharply, a deviant grin playing about his lips.

"Don't be so sure."

"I will die first. Off myself. Drain all the pretty red stuff. Get it?" Lucian tore away from the side of the building and headed around to the front. Shaking his head, he cursed inwardly. Fuckity fuck, fuck, fuck. What *was* he doing here? Was it truly something rational and understandable and necessary, or was he just acting out Stupid Move #78?

He came to a halt at the bottom step of the Veracou Hall and looked up. It barely felt like winter tonight; the early scents of spring were light in the air and the snow was melting off of every surface it clung to. Maybe his piece of shit pops was right. Maybe he shouldn't be anywhere near this building. Maybe he shouldn't be anywhere near *her* and the *paven* who would take her sweet, willing body under his tonight. And yet he had to see for himself that she was done, over, taken. He needed to see the evidence, to force his traitorous body to accept that Bronwyn Kettler was forever out of his reach.

Gone.

Untouchable.

Titus was again behind him, silent in his breathing, yet heavy in his unease.

"Lucian ... "

"I will know it is over between us."

"It should never have begun."

"Enough!" Lucian's head came around so fast Titus gasped. His voice was low and deadly as he said, "You need to fuck off right now before we end up taking a father-son bloodbath together."

There was a moment of flared nostrils and heavy breathing, a moment when the elder *paven* remained immobile, his eyes nearly unseeing as he stared at his *balas*. They were both so still, and then Titus reached back, grabbed the edges of his red hood, and placed it over his head.

With fangs extended and eyes narrowed, Lucian watched him ascend the stairs and disappear inside the Veracou Hall. For a moment, he wished to crawl under the steps like a rat to wait— wait for her scent to grow stronger, for the feel of her footfall overhead as she descended the stairs with her true mate, feel the death of his eternal soul as he watched her leave with the one who would feed her body in all the ways he couldn't.

Then he would get lost.

Maybe for a week, maybe forever.

Maybe between the thighs of the entire New York Jets cheer-leading squad.

Inside the Veracou Hall, dressed in her scarlet mating costume, Bronwyn stood before Synjon Wise and tried to breathe. The room was still, no sound save for the monotonous *drip*, *drip*, *drip* of the thousand white candles hanging from the ceiling. It was a gift from the Order—who sat before them in a long row, their hoods hiding their faces—a hope for a thousand years of eternal happiness for these true mates.

Bronwyn fought the anxiety in her chest, shifting her weight from one foot to the other in hopes of sending the fear down and out. If they only knew who stood before them. If they only knew two friends, not true mates, stood before them in this sacred hall. If they only knew a lie had been constructed—a fabrication—all to avoid the one primal fear that Bronwyn had lived with, worked to stop, and prayed would never befall her.

The rape of the Breeding Male.

His seed forced inside her womb.

His *balas* growing within her.

And like her sister's fate, more *balas* than her body could contain without giving out, giving up—her blood unable to cease flowing until she no longer breathed.

Just as the guests were doing, the Order sat as still as the stone walls. They were waiting for the final agreement to be given. They were waiting for Bronwyn to say her final word—the one word that would bind her to this *paven* who stood beside her at the podium, his hands clasping hers, his ocean blue eyes fierce but steady.

Bronwyn gazed up into the face of her dear friend. Movie-star handsome, with an athlete's body and the loyalty of a gracious god, Synjon Wise had grown from an awkward *balas* into the six-foot-six, broad-shouldered *paven* of every *veana*'s fantasy. He had been her friend longer than any other, and she loved him—could want him if they took it slow. Not in the way her body craved another, like air to her lungs—not in the way he had cared for his deceased lover—but in the ancient way of long years and care and commitment.

Synjon said nothing as he stared down at her, but raised one black eyebrow. Not in censure, but in concern. He knew the truth of her heart just as she knew the truth and tragedy of his, and as the friend he was, deep and unbending, he would protect her, even in this—even if it meant his own ruin and embarrassment.

He was the eternal catch, this male, and with that one word uttered, he would belong to her forever. God, it was so simple, Bron thought, and yet all she wanted to do was break from his hold and run from the Veracou Hall, to the blood that called to hers.

She blinked, her breathing shallow in her lungs and throat. She knew he was out there, waiting. The pale one, the one that had given her his blood. Every instinct she possessed warned her that he would not leave her alone until he saw that she belonged to another—that she had given herself to another.

Squeezing her hands gently, Syn smiled down at her. *Get a grip then, love*, he was saying in that gravelly British accent of his, his eyes wicked with humor, but also filled with understanding.

Bronwyn opened her mouth, and in that second her gaze caught on her mother and her father. They were seated just behind Synjon. Pure love fairly burst from them both. They were so happy, so relieved she had found her true mate, and yet Bronwyn knew without a doubt that if she hadn't found Synjon, even with all of that love in their eyes, her parents would have gone to the Order. It was said by the Order, and by many, that

23

all the Breeding Males had died out over two decades ago, but Bronwyn knew better. Though they were a very rare entity, not every son was being tracked or watched for signs of Breeding Male status. And Bronwyn had current DNA samples from vampires in the western United States that proved a Breeding Male had sired within the past two years. It was only a matter of time before the Order found this information, if they truly didn't have it already, and she couldn't take the chance of her parents discovering it too. Because if they did, they would have her taken to him before the month was up, just as they had done with her sister many years ago. Her beloved sister, who had died with the Breeding Male's twin *balas* in her tired body just six months into her *swell*.

Jerking her gaze back to Synjon, to the safety of her friend, she did what she had to. "Given."

The word exited her mouth loud and clear and committed, and for one second, silence hovered in the air. Then the room seemed to expand, explode with cheers and laughter, and the hoods of the Order, save one, were tossed back and the brick-red fangs that demonstrated each member's completion with the act of drinking blood were displayed in wide, delighted smiles.

Another Pureblood true mate pairing had come to pass.

The celebration had begun.

Sensing her mood, Synjon led her out of the hall and into a quiet passageway, keeping her close to his side. To Bronwyn, every step was heavy, like walking in sand; every image in her head was still of him.

Him.

It would go away ... It would lessen in time.

It must.

"You all right, love?" Synjon asked once they were away from the crowd.

24

"I'm fine," she managed, licking her dry lips and forcing her gaze up to his.

Though she wasn't privy to the details, she knew what Syn was—that he worked undercover for the Order in all manner of dangerous and exotic places. She knew what he was capable of, his talents with every kind of weaponry, how close to an assassin's life he lived, but as he looked down at her, there was only softness in him. And perhaps a trace of sadness. He too had lost the promise and hope of love.

"You had me wondering there for a moment, Bron," he said with a gentle huskiness.

She shook her head, fighting the heavy sense that she had made a mistake in all this. But she knew she hadn't! She knew she had done the only thing she could. And, God, she'd be good to Syn; she'd help him forget as he would help her. "My nerves got the better of me for a moment. That's all," she said.

His eyes homed in on her face, his hands warm with concern around her fingers. "That all it is?"

She thought about lying, but this *paven* was trained to see all forms of deception—and truly, what was the point? They knew each other's pasts, every painful bit. She released a weighty breath. "I feel him outside. I feel his blood. Still."

Synjon's eyes turned from liquid to ice, and his tone was deadly as he spoke. "I'll take care of it."

"No," Bron said quickly, almost desperately. Foolish *veana* ...

"He has no right to be here, Bron—to be anywhere near you."

"Please, Syn. I don't want a fight. Not today." She lowered her chin, let her gaze speak to her intense feelings on the subject.

After a moment, Synjon's eyes softened and he grumbled, "All right. I'll keep my fists to myself today. But only today."

Bronwyn nodded, gave him a smile. "Noted."

25

He chuckled softly, brought her hand to his mouth, and kissed it. There was no passion in the act, but Bronwyn was thankful for that. Thankful there was no pretense between them, no charade. It would've been impossible if he felt true love for her.

"I'm not sure if I've told you this tonight, my dear," he said, granting an easy smile. "But you look smashing."

She smiled, thankful once again for his control and patience. "Thank you, *Paven*."

His gaze tracked over her. "It's a damn fine getup, that."

She dropped his hands and turned slowly in a circle. The dress was a deep merlot silk, as were the bands on her neck and wrists—all were tied securely, but ready for her *paven* to unwrap his gift.

She stopped twirling at the thought, saw the night to come in her mind, and her belly grew tense. Her blood, her virtue was now Synjon's, even if her unbeating heart belonged to another. Her breath hitched in her chest as she caught that last thought—that traitorous last thought.

"I think I'd like one in my size if you can manage it," Synjon was saying, pulling her back to him, to the present—what was real and true.

She forced a smile. "You'd like a Veracou gown?"

He nodded. "In blue, of course. To match my very fine eyes."

Bronwyn laughed at that, at him, so grateful for his lightness, for his teasing, for the fact that they were friends and she would always be safe with him.

"I'll get started first thing tomorrow, *Paven*," she said, moving closer to him, ready to follow him into this land of light and easy.

"Good," he growled. "See that it's done in time for tea."

Again she laughed and let him twirl her around, let him

continue to brighten her mood, let him take the memory of the one whose blood scent remained imprinted on her senses.

It was on the third twirl, the third manic, crazy spin when she spotted something down the corridor. Not something, she realized when she came to a stop, but someone. Someone who made her insides jump and pulsate.

Calm and immobile as a stone, the *paven* stood there watching them. Waiting.

How long had he been here? she wondered. And—God help her—had he brought anyone else with him?

Synjon had noticed the *paven* too and his mouth drew close to her ear. "Friend of yours, love?"

She couldn't help herself. It just came out quick and worried. "Nicholas Roman."

A growl unlike anything she'd ever heard before erupted from the *paven* beside her. The sound was otherworldly and terrible and she'd never want to be on the other side of it. "The Romans have no place here," he said. "I will let him know this."

"No."

Syn paused at her fixed reply. "I brought no weapons, Bron. I promise I will only explain his unwelcome state with my fists."

"No, Syn." Her eyes implored him. "He is a good *paven*, kind. The one Roman brother with tact and sense. Please. Let me talk to him." With a quick breath, she moved past him.

"I'll come with you."

"No." She touched his chest, hard as stone—just like his expression. "It'll just take a minute—I swear it."

"Ever stubborn, Bronwyn."

The words were said to her back as she walked down the corridor toward Nicholas. She hated disregarding Synjon's feelings just as she hated the deep curiosity that pulsed inside of her. What was Nicholas doing here? Was this about Lucian? Was the albino *paven* outside waiting ... or had he finally given up, gone away?

Bronwyn approached Nicholas with a soft smile and a shrug. "If he asked you to stop the Veracou, you're too late."

The *paven* moved deeper into the shadows. "I was asked nothing in regards to the Veracou," he uttered, then glanced back at the open door he'd no doubt entered through moments ago and the dark landscape beyond.

"Then why are you here, Nicholas?" she asked, noticing the snow melting off the eaves behind him.

"Do not scream, *Veana*," he said, reaching for her, pulling her out into the moonlit night. "It will only hurt more."

Bronwyn noticed the diamond eyes, the claws, and the lack of two circle brands on the *paven*'s cheeks too late. This wasn't Nicholas at all. She screamed silently as she was flashed away.

It was her captor.

3

Cruen stared at the thing he'd created, had stolen, had harbored. He wanted to feel sorry for it—for her—but all he felt was appreciation for the beauty of suffering.

The Order would think him cruel—a butcher, a sadist. They wouldn't recognize the artistry at work. But then, they never had. It was well and good to be rid of them. As a whole, the ruling ten thought the Breeding Males were animals, uncontrollable and better left extinct. But to Cruen they were works of art—the perfect extension of Pureblood vampire. And with his assistance, guidance, and a thick leash to control their every movement, they would replace the Order as the ruling class.

He moved closer to the cage. It was one of many in the secret laboratory he'd had built over seven centuries ago in the Sacri Monti—the Sacred Mountains of Italy. It was where he'd created the first Breeding Male, and the second and third, and where he'd raised his own five *balas*—his Beasts.

"Please . . ."

Cruen smiled at her as she writhed in her cage, her skin glistening with sweat. For so many years, he had not believed in her existence. The rumors were strong, yes, but he knew—as their creator—that females rarely survived after their sixth year of life. It was an anomaly in their genetic structure he hadn't been able to correct. But he would. With this female, and the Boston geneticist by his side, he would fix the problem.

She looked up at him then, her pale lavender eyes peeking out from yards and yards of wet blond hair. She was begging for relief.

"It won't be long now," Cruen said with a gentle voice. "His body will please you and his seed will calm you."

Her head dropped forward and she whimpered, her hands covering her core.

Cruen nodded, smiled with the deepest of pleasure. She was the elusive diamond, priceless, and she would be the mother, the dam—the queen of a new class, a new order.

Vampire royalty.

The Breeding Female and the Breeding Male: a union of purest blood. And Cruen would be their adviser, the mind behind their actions, just as he was their creator—their god.

All that remained was turning *paven* into predator, and Lucian Roman was nearly united with his prey.

4

The soporific sounds of happiness and celebration dissolved inside Synjon's head and were replaced by a hard, rhythmic pounding. Like a hammer smacking thick, steel nails, one after the other. He'd seen her go, seen her being ripped out the back door and flashed away in less than five seconds. The flash—the fucking flash, like a firecracker in the night—and Synjon had nothing on him to protect his *veana*. No guns, no blades—nothing but his goddamn legs.

He ran at hyperspeed down the corridor, but by the time he hit the open door, there was nothing but *credenti* landscape, melting ice and snow, and night air heavy with the scent of Pureblooded *paven*.

Synjon wasted no time. Once outside he flashed: to the back of the building, to one side, then the other, searching for that piece-of-shite Roman brother who had the bollocks to take someone who didn't belong to him.

Lucian had sent his big brother, Nicholas "soon to be dead" Roman, to do his dirty work for him—Synjon just knew it. Christ, to steal away the *veana* who'd refused him. What a sodding git. Both Romans would be husks of dried skin when Synjon caught up with them.

Again he flashed, this time to Bronwyn's house—dark and empty—then back again to the front of the Veracou Hall. His eyes moved over every inch of the *credenti* landscape. Not that he expected that Breeding Male mongrel to be hanging around anymore, but Syn would make sure. Just as he'd make sure he flashed to every square inch of earth until he found her.

He was just about to hit the airway when his eyes skidded to a stop. Ire flared within him, and in that moment, the Boston *credenti* winter wonderland went from wide-angle-lens landscape to pin-prick-hole focus. And in the very center of that hole? Leaning back against a tree that was as white as the *paven* himself?

Lucian Wanker Roman.

Synjon growled low in his chest and flashed directly in front of the *paven*, his arm already yanked back, his hand already clenched into a steely fist.

Crack. Right across the *paven*'s jaw, nothing but power and pain.

Lucian's head snapped back into the tree and he cursed loud and dirty.

"Where is she, arsehole?" Synjon demanded.

Lucian heard nothing inside his rapped skull, but he sure as shit saw red. Blood red—and the sudden death of this vampire who had sucker punched him like a little bitch. Recovering quickly, he shoved the *paven* back, followed up by pummeling him with a quick set of jabs to the abdomen, then one clean, hard shot to the face.

Pow. Crack.

The *paven*'s dark head snapped back and he staggered a couple of steps like a drunk. *That's right, dickhead,* Lucian mused blackly, his nostrils flaring with deep intakes of breath. Fall down, drop to your knees, and take a few more knocks to the skull like a good little bloodsucker. But the vampire wasn't into taking. Clearly the giver, he shook the fog off and leaped in the air, just a few inches, cocking one knee back. Before Lucian could sidestep the coming blow, a foot shot straight into the flesh below his left knee.

Fuck.

The pain exploded inside him, and the blow sent him flying back, past the tree. He dropped like a stone on his back, disabled for a moment. But a moment was all the black-haired *paven* needed to get down and dirty. He dropped on top of Lucian, his hand clamping around Lucian's throat. *Oh, hell no,* Lucian mused, recovering quickly and reaching up to lock his right hand around the other male's thick neck. Grinning, he squeezed with all the built-up rage he had inside himself for this pretty-boy vampire who had claimed his princess.

Both breathing heavy and feral into each other's faces, like animals after a hunt, the blue-eyed *paven* chose to speak first. "You know who I am."

"Got a good guess," Lucian uttered, his chin hard as he fought the *paven*'s grip. "But since your dick is pressing against mine, maybe we should introduce ourselves proper-like."

The grin Synjon Wise flashed him had all the charm of a snake. "Where is she?"

"Who?"

"Don't play games with me, Frosty."

"Are we talking about Bronwyn?" Lucian laughed darkly. "You lose your *veana* already, Brit Boy?"

"Only one *paven* who lost something today, and I'm looking at him, mate."

In under a second, Lucian released Synjon's throat and

shoved the base of his hand up and straight into the *paven*'s nose.

"Ahhh, fuck you," the male cursed.

"Another time," Lucian said, grabbing Syn by the arms and rolling them both over. He had the black-haired bastard on his back now, blood streaming out of his nose like water from a hose.

Synjon glared up at him. "That was a mistake."

"Maybe so, but I don't really give a shit at this point."

"Tell me where she is and we can end this play."

"I don't have your precious mate," Lucian returned with ice. *Never did. Never could.*

Synjon's tongue emerged and swiped at a pool of blood near his upper lip. "Your brother showed up a moment ago inside the hall. Bronwyn went to have a bit of a chat with him." His brow arched. "She never returned to me."

"Maybe she ran back home. Maybe she had second thoughts. Maybe it's all that cologne you're wearing." Lucian said the words with all the sarcasm he could muster, but something inside him started to churn at the words Brit Boy had just uttered. It wasn't anxiety, but it was close.

"She's not at her home," the *paven* said, his eyes serious as a heart attack to a human now. "I checked. Your brother took her—flashed her away. I saw the bloody sparks."

"Not possible." But he pushed off the Pureblood and stood up. He was antsy now—like he hadn't had blood in a week.

"Where is your brother?" Synjon asked, snapping to his feet too and meeting Lucian eye to eye, grave stare to grave stare. "Where is Nicholas Roman?"

"None of your motherfucking business," Lucian snarled as his brain squeezed inside his skull and his ears rang with bells that clanged the march of death.

"If you care for Bronwyn at all, you'll answer me," the *paven* said with controlled venom as he wiped the last drops of blood from his nose.

Lucian wanted to tell the guy to fuck off and die, wanted to tell him he didn't give two shits about Bronwyn and never would—but those words wouldn't come out easy or true.

"Nicky's in France, all right?" he said tightly. "Has been for three weeks."

Lucian barely had the last bit out before Synjon grabbed him, hauled him into a tight embrace, and flashed him from the cold, hard ground outside the Veracou Hall.

As soon as her feet hit sand, Bronwyn screamed and started flailing her arms, punching at anyone or anything that held her. But nothing did. She was alone. On a beach—the sun setting impossibly and beautifully all around her. From cold, snowy Boston to gentle breezes and warm sand—it was a complete shock to her system, to her mind, and she couldn't catch her breath.

Where was the *paven*? she thought, panic clinging to every cell, every inch of her skin as she turned in circles, making herself dizzy. Where was the monster who'd abducted her?

Her eyes scanned a section of beach, the water, then darted right to a stand of palm trees and beyond that a hill, green and lush, its very top kissing the sky.

Paradise.

Perhaps it should have calmed her. Perhaps that was what it was designed to do. But she just stood there in her Veracou costume and felt the salty breeze caress her terrified features. What the hell had happened? Where was she?

She heard something behind her. Or was it in front of her? To the right? Damn it! A rustle.

Maybe just the wind tossing the palms.

Maybe not.

Her feet dug into the sand and she ran. She ran hard and fast down the water's edge until her lungs ached, until her body forced her to stall. *Nicholas*. At first, seeing his frame in the hallway, she'd been so sure. But it wasn't Nicholas. It was something wrong and unearthly.

Her chest hurt, struggled for breath, but she couldn't get the air in.

What did that *thing* want from her? Why had she been taken from her home, from her Veracou—from Synjon?

Oh, God—Syn—he had to be losing his mind right now. She belonged to him, and he was old-school protective that way.

Something flashed directly in front of her, dark hair, diamond eyes that lifted at the corners like a cat. *Him!* She knew it was him. God. *Please,* she silently begged no one in particular, but anyone who might be listening. As her feet refused to move, her manic gaze ran up and down him, taking in his thickly muscled frame. Back in the hall he'd looked exactly like Nicholas, but now ... Now something had changed—something had changed him. Morphed him into this half vampire, half monster. He was male in form, yes, but his face was covered in scars and had an animal's shape to it—almost like a lion.

He reached for her. Bronwyn screamed and tried to turn around and run again. But he had her now, held her to face him, made her look up into his ruined face.

Breathing heavily, forcing her mind to calm down and think of a way out, a way to claw and kick and bite herself to freedom, Bronwyn stared into diamond eyes and the scared, ravaged skin of an animal, a monster.

"Calm yourself, *Veana*," he said, his voice low and gravellike. "We want no bruises on you."

Bronwyn found her voice through her fear and whispered, "Who are you?"

36

"A Beast," he uttered. "A defender and servant to my father, and the *gemino* of your Nicholas Roman."

As soon as they landed, Lucian smashed his elbow into the *paven*'s neck and pushed him off. "You are a motherfucker."

"No. I am Synjon Wise, Bronwyn's true mate. And I will have her returned." He said the words with deadly calm. "Now, your brother? He in Paris, then?"

"No," Lucian said, glancing around at the city lights against the night sky. "But we are, and I'm about to stick the Eiffel Tower up your ass!"

Synjon ignored him. "Where is he?"

"My brother's been in France for days," Lucian countered, despising this *paven* and the power play he was working on Lucian's body and mind. But he couldn't shake the fact that Bronwyn was gone, taken—in the hands of someone who wouldn't treat her kindly. He may have been the biggest asshole on the planet, but he wouldn't have that. Wouldn't ever have that. "It's impossible that Nicky took her. He's with his mate, and has no interest in yours."

Synjon snorted, uttered a terse, "Well, at least that's one Roman brother not interested in Bronwyn."

Lucian snarled, his blood reacting with anger. "Whoever you saw was not Nicky. Just another vein for your new bride to suckle at."

Synjon moved so fast Lucian didn't have a second to block the punch to his neck.

"Fuck," he gasped, tasting his own blood, dislodging his fangs from his tongue. "You are going to pay for that, you piece of *sacro* ... " Lucian's voice trailed off, his words and his threat too, because in that split second of time, of pain, it hit him—it hit him hard and sick.

Who might have Bronwyn.

He looked up at Synjon and the dread in his eyes must've been blatant. "Wasn't Nicky."

Synjon cocked his head to the side and said slowly, "Bronwyn said—"

"She didn't know." Lucian spat blood. "Wouldn't know. Not until she got close up anyway." His gut clenched and rolled. This was serious now, not just busting the balls of Bronwyn's mate.

"What the bloody hell are you going on about, Frosty?" Synjon said with harsh impatience.

"Call me that again and I will gut you," Lucian spat back. He needed to think, to plan—to get to his brothers. Shit, Bronwyn had to be scared to death. Why would that *paven* take her—?

"Wake up!" Synjon glared at him. "Do you know where Bronwyn is, or not?"

"I know who she's with."

"Share with the class, please," Synjon said through gritted teeth. "How big of a problem are we talking?"

"We need to get to my brothers. Now." Lucian stepped right into the *paven*'s face. "They're in Provence. Touch down near the center of Lorgues. Go!"

"You'd better have answers as soon as we drop." Syn's arms wrapped around Lucian and they were gone from Paris, the Tower, and the blinking city lights in a flash of time and color.

Shaking, sweating, and terrified, Bronwyn stood with her feet buried deep in warm sand, facing the Beast who had ripped her away from her Veracou. "You're Nicholas's twin."

"You should know that," he said, his diamond eyes flat, contained. "You were the one who discovered and announced my existence, were you not?"

How did he know that? Bronwyn wondered, her breath

38

coming fast in and out of her lungs. How did he know what went on in the Romans' home? Or hers? Her eyes moved over his face. "You are like your brother and yet . . . "

"There is no brotherhood," the Beast interrupted. "The *paven* and I share DNA, nothing more."

In her fear, Bronwyn fought for understanding, but there were so many questions in her mind, and none more important than this one: "What is this place?"

"A reality."

Reality? Her mind spun back, gathering and circling information—things she remembered from her research, from all of her years of study. Realities were the territory of the Eternal Order. Were they behind this madness? What the hell was going on? "Why am I here? What do you want with me?" The panicked trill in her voice was evident and she hated it. It wouldn't do to have a breakdown or show this animal her tears. She had to fight—fight her way off this reality and get back to her own.

"You have a purpose, *Veana*," the Beast said to her, still holding on to her arms—not painfully, but solidly, resolutely. "You have been brought here to lay with the one who will be the next Breeding Male."

Bronwyn's face drained of blood. "What?"

She mentally shook her head against his words. She hadn't heard him. Hadn't heard him . . . This couldn't be! She'd mated with Synjon! She belonged to him—only to him. Did her parents or the Order—someone in the *credenti*—find out that she'd tricked them? That Syn wasn't her true mate?

She locked eyes with the Beast, and for one brief moment she swore she saw a trace of humanity in his gaze. But it was gone in an instant.

"The Breeding Male will come for you," he said without a trace of emotion.

Air left Bronwyn's lungs. She tasted bile in her throat, felt blood thunder in her ears. Pounding, pounding the march of terror and madness. This couldn't be true. Couldn't be happening. She started to shake so violently that her knees suddenly lost their ability to remain solid and strong.

"You will be his way home," the Beast continued, holding her steady as he described her nightmare come to life, "to his creator and the one who waits for him."

She shook her head, tears burning her eyes, spilling down her cheeks—she couldn't do a thing to stop them now. Just as she couldn't seem to escape this nightmare. "I don't understand any of this."

He nodded. "You will."

Then her adrenaline hit—flooding her body with the need to fight—and she struck out at him. Again and again, she struck, arms, fists, feet. Like an animal going to slaughter, she struggled. "I want off this beach, you bastard! I want off this reality! Let me go—NOW!"

The Beast held her without effort, his lips flickering up, showing off his long white fangs. "Not until you have done your duty."

She wasn't going out this way—going down this way. "I have a mate, you asshole! It—"

"It matters not," he finished for her.

"I will not lay with anyone but my mate!" she screamed into the sea air, into his ravaged face. "No one will force me—"

"No." Smug certainty coated his voice. "No one will force you."

She stilled for just a moment, trying to process what he'd said.

But he was looking her over now, her Veracou costume, and his brow grew tight. He sneered. "No. This will not do. He

40

would not find you appealing like this." Without another word, he released her. And with a wave of his hand, Bronwyn's Veracou gown and everything beneath it disappeared. In a mere breath of time, she stood before the monster naked and vulnerable.

Gasping, she groped at herself, trying to cover her body.

The Beast's diamond eyes leveled her. "Lucian Roman will be inside your tight cunt, Mistress Kettler. I suggest you prepare yourself for him."

And with that, he flashed away.

5

As soon as they hit dirt, Lucian broke out of Synjon's grip and starting running, hauling ass up the moonlit road, away from the village. His head was heavy, his chest constricted. Maybe it was the air, which was colder than it had been in Paris. Or maybe it was just that he despised himself—despised the fact that he couldn't flash on his own—or maybe it was the fact that the *veana* he shouldn't give two shits about was out there somewhere and he couldn't get to her.

"Hey!" Synjon yelled after him.

Lucian kept eating up cold, wet ground. The *paven* behind him didn't exist. It was only road and moonlight and heavy breathing, and the roofline of his brother's villa in the distance.

"This is bollocks and a waste of time," Synjon growled, flashing in front of him every other second. "Stop, you daft bastard! I'll flash us to the front door."

"No, you won't," Lucian said, picking up his pace, the world around him growing darker as he moved farther away from the lights of the town.

"What are you playing at, Frosty?" Synjon demanded, sprinting with him up a hill and into a grove of olive trees.

Lucian remained silent, focused, weaving in and out and around the barren trees. Once free of the grove, he sprinted forward, only about ten feet, then stopped abruptly. Synjon was right beside him, keeping pace, and without a warning, and with far too much momentum going, he hit hard—*smack*—right into the invisible fence the Roman brothers had magically installed around the perimeter of the villa.

Lucian saw the *paven* fly back, heard him land on his ass somewhere in the ice-cold grass. "I warned you not to call me that." He bared his fangs and bit into his wrist. This was a Roman brothers' *credenti*, and Lucian let the blood run down for a moment before swiping it against the invisible lock.

He felt the heat, the vibrating energy of shifting powers, shoot through him as the concealed gate evaporated.

"Let's go, Brit Boy," Lucian uttered, coating the last two words with as much smugness as he could manage.

"Could've warned me, mate," Synjon grumbled, coming up beside him.

"Now, why would I do that?"

"I dunno," Syn said as they cleared the gate and headed toward the house. "Maybe you're really a decent bloke under all that thin, pale skin."

Lucian snorted. "Try again."

"For Bronwyn, then."

Lucian's gaze snapped right and his lip curled with irritation. "Not sure your life really means all that much to her."

"You have no idea."

The words died in the air, but were not forgotten as two massive *pavens* flashed directly in front of Lucian and Synjon. They both looked surprised, but not unhappy at the unexpected guests.

"It's about time you came out of hiding." Alexander Roman put a hand on his brother's shoulder. "Good to see you, *Duro*." Nicholas turned his attention on Synjon, one eyebrow raised in amused curiosity. "Interesting choice of playmate, Luca."

"No playing here," Synjon said blackly.

Lucian eyed Nicholas and nodded. "The *gemino* has taken Bronwyn Kettler."

Perched on a hillside with fifty acres of beautiful grounds, olive trees, and no curious neighbors to deal with, the eighteenth-century villa that Nicholas had bought for his true mate and their nephew now catered to a group of angry, arguing male vampires and their eye-rolling true mates.

Though there were dozens of rooms to choose from, two kitchens, a cinema, and a gym, the three Roman brothers, their irritated British guest, and both Alex's and Nicholas's true mates had congregated in the massive dining room. All six coiled around the table like knights disagreeing on their plan of attack.

"Can we discuss this like civilized *veanas* and *pavens*?"

Sara Donohue Roman, the mate of Alexander, the eldest Roman brother, stood at the head of the table and called for calm among her family, and from the stranger who had blustered in, demanding information on the whereabouts of his true mate. He was displaying the expected irrationality and dominant behavior of a true mate, Sara knew. Alexander, too, had been out of his mind when her life had been threatened by one of her patients several months back, so she sympathized with Synjon. And truly, they were all worried about Bronwyn. The beautiful *veana* had come to the SoHo house at the same time as Sara, and had thought herself Alexander's mate until the truth had revealed itself to them all. She was a good, intelligent female, and Sara wanted nothing to befall her.

Sara felt Nicholas's mate, Kate, sidle up next to her as the group of *pavens* continued to go at one another around the table.

Synjon leaned forward in his chair and snarled, "We're wasting time."

"Then, go," Lucian said fiercely. "We don't need your sorry British ass here. Or is it arse?"

"You look in the mirror and tell me," Synjon returned, eyebrow raised.

Lucian growled at the *paven*, a warning, a promise.

"Easy, both of you," Nicky began, though his eyes remained fixed on his little brother. "This back-and-forth bullshit isn't helping."

Synjon ground his molars. "All I want are answers; then I'll be on my way."

"Good!" Lucian uttered. "Can't wait to show you the door all personal-like."

"Hey!" Kate shouted, clapping her hands, her brown eyes fierce as she addressed each one in turn. "Zip the lips, boys, or lose them."

All four male vampires froze and turned to look at the female, eyes wide with surprise.

But Sara had eyes only for Synjon Wise. "Our family has been in France for weeks now, Mr. Wise. If the vampire you saw—the vampire who took Bron—looked like Nicholas, then it had to be his twin."

Synjon turned to glare at Nicholas. "Another sodding Roman brother. Perfect."

"Watch yourself," Alexander warned, running his hand over his shaved skull. "You're in our home. Don't make us forget you're a guest."

"I'll forget," Lucian growled. "Hell, I'd love to forget."

"Hey," Synjon began with irritation. "I wouldn't be here at all if someone in your family hadn't nicked my bride."

"He's not family, Brit Boy," Lucian countered. "We barely even know the *paven*."

"Well, let's get to know him," Syn said, his blue eyes wide with ferocity. "All of us. Let's go have a bit of a chat with him."

"Not that easy," Nicholas said.

Synjon pushed back his chair and stood, frustration evident in his corded muscles. "And why the hell not? Bron is mine! She wears my mark!"

"This is going well," Sara said, shaking her head.

Kate chuckled beside her. "I'd say so."

"We've only just learned of his existence," Nicholas said, his own frustration barely contained. "It's why we came to France. To track him down."

Through gritted teeth, Syn asked, "And have you?"

"Not yet." Nicholas shook his head, his eyes dark with ire. "We've moved on every tip we've received, but the *paven* is . . . slippery."

Synjon sneered. "Brilliant. And by that I mean, what a sodding cock-up." He glanced at Lucian. "Why did we come here, then? They have nothing to offer me."

A hiss erupted from Lucian's throat. "No one invited you anywhere. Screw this twin bastard brother of ours. We'll find Bronwyn ourselves!"

"What do we know about this *paven*?" Syn said, ignoring Lucian as though he'd said nothing at all, and eyeing Nicholas again. "Why would he want Bronwyn?"

The dark-haired brother shook his head. "I don't know. She's Pureblood—she's your true mate. Perhaps you should ask yourself the same question." He narrowed his eyes. "Perhaps this is about you, your past—your enemies."

Syn cocked his head. "Bugger off, all right, you stupid git. Bugger the fuck off."

"Oh crap," Kate uttered, turning to Sara. "Here they go again."

"Would anyone like something to eat?" Sara asked, in a tone meant to gentle the air in the room. "Blood, perhaps. It may not be straight from the vein, but—"

"Blood!" Lucian said the word, rising from his seat and pointing at Synjon.

"What the hell are you doing?" Synjon asked. Shooting his gaze around the room, he demanded, "What the hell is he doing?"

Nicholas shrugged. "It's not always clear."

"You and Bronwyn have mated," Lucian said, his tone threaded with disgust. "Have had your Veracou."

"Yes. Do you have a point, or are you just reminding yourself that I am Bron's mate?"

Lucian ignored the barb. "You should be able to find her, track her, know where her blood is. Isn't that right, Alexander?"

Alexander nodded, his eyes suddenly graying over with thought. "It is."

"There's no need for any of this," Lucian said, his voice rising, his fangs dropping. "Let's go. Let's go and get her."

But Synjon didn't move. "Stay where you are, Frosty. I haven't taken her blood. She was nicked from me before we could have our consummation, both in blood and in body."

Lucian growled fiercely.

"Chill out, *Duro*," Alexander warned in an almost parental tone.

Sara felt for the youngest brother. Everyone knew that he was denying his feelings for Bronwyn, and she was pretty certain Synjon suspected the truth and was enjoying torturing the *paven*.

47

"The bond is unshakable," Nicholas said quickly before another kind of blood was shed. He glanced up at Kate and gave her an easy, loving smile. "True mates should be able to find each other even if they haven't—"

"Wait a moment," Synjon interrupted, pointing at Lucian. "You've taken her blood, haven't you?"

Everyone in the room turned to stare at Lucian.

"She drank from me," he clarified, his chin lifting just a fraction. "Not the other way round."

Synjon's lip curled.

"And she drank quite a lot, as I recall," Lucian said thoughtfully. "Nearly drained me dry."

Synjon slammed his arm into his chair and sent the bit of wood flying across the room, his growl low and feral.

"Alexander!" Sara called to her true mate with both her voice and with her gaze. This was getting out of hand. Time was ticking by and they were nowhere nearer to finding Bronwyn than when they'd started. She knew the moment had arrived to spill the secret she and Alexander had been carrying around for far too long, it seemed. It was something her mate had never wanted to admit to his brothers, especially to Lucian, but there was nothing for it, and by the look on Alexander's face, he was thinking the same thing. Sara pressed harder. "Please, Alex."

His merlot eyes lifted to hers.

"Tell them," she urged with fierce determination when he appeared to resist. "It is time."

"Tell us what?" Lucian said, fangs low and eyes on Synjon.

Nicholas's brows drew together. "Alex, what's going on?"

With a sigh, Alexander turned to both Lucian and Synjon. "Will you two be cool?"

"Cool about what?" Lucian said uneasily.

"I have drunk from Bronwyn."

The room went silent, as if breath and time ceased to exist. A servant walked in, and no doubt sensing the rabid tension around the table, walked right back out again. Suddenly there was an audible snap, and both Lucian and Syn dove across the table at the eldest Roman brother, landing on top of him with a crash of heavy bodies.

Kate sighed. "Oh, God. Are we really going to do this *balas at play* thing, *gentlepaven*?"

"Stop it!" Sara yelled at the mosh pit of fists and furious curses. "Stop it right now. Goddamn idiots! Nicholas, stop them!"

But Nicholas wasn't aware of her plea. He sat, unmoving, his gaze pinned on the wall behind the group of fighting *pavens*.

"The Order," he uttered with pure hatred. "They have her ... "

The *pavens* froze, bloody and bruised and with fangs extended, and turned to look at the message scrawled on the plaster.

Bronwyn Kettler will be given over to the sun unless Lucian Roman comes for her by daybreak.

"I'm going with you."

As he strapped on a Glock and two blades, Lucian schooled the *paven* standing beside him in one of the villa bedrooms, which had been turned into a weapons hold when the Romans had moved in three weeks ago. "It says Lucian Roman on the wall out there. Not Lucian Roman and his punching bag."

"I don't give a right good shite what the Order wants," Synjon sneered, helping himself to a few weapons.

"Did you not get the part about Bronwyn and the sun? Or do you not care about your mate's longevity?"

"The Order is full of empty threats. Trust me—I know."

49

All geared up, Lucian stepped into the *paven*'s eyeline. "And sometimes they're not. Trust *me*."

Alexander stuck his head in the doorway. "I've had no luck locating her through my blood—maybe it's been too long." He lifted his chin. "You'd better get yourself to the Hollow, *Duro*."

Lucian gestured to his brother. "Look at those morph brands on my brother's pretty, pretty face. The Order wasn't blowing smoke up our asses with those threats. We didn't get Ethan Dare first time around and Nicky got more of the same."

For the first time since they'd met him, Synjon said nothing.

"Stay here and wait. I'll bring her back." Lucian followed Alexander out into the hallway, and was in the entryway and on his way outdoors when he felt the *paven* on his tail. Again.

He whirled on the Brit. "What the fuck don't you get here? The Order wants *me*!"

Syn didn't even blink. "And the *veana* wants me."

Lucian's nostrils flared, in fury, in disgust, in desire. A memory, quick and uninvited, jerked into his mind. Her touch on his arm, his wrist. Her mouth against his skin. His blood going into her, inside of her, where it belonged, where it thrived.

Synjon said simply, "She is mine to find and fight for."

Lucian felt Alexander's arm on him, pulling him outside, into the cold night air. Melancholy and pain rippled through him. The truth of this bullshit situation was that even though he could never have a *veana* of his own, he wasn't about to let Bronwyn die—even if it meant bringing her back to the piece-of-British-shite in front of him. Bitterness rose up and threatened to choke him, but he plastered on his fighting face and said, "That's real sweet, Brit Boy, but the Order doesn't care who she belongs to. Clearly." Lucian glanced over at Alexander and raised a brow. "You my ride?"

Alexander nodded.

"Let's go."

As Bronwyn hovered below the water, flashes of her past and her sister's short life competed with the rays of the sun overhead.

Farrah had been in her Meta for just under five months when their parents discovered she'd fallen in love with another *veana*'s *paven*. Not certain as to how long the relationship had been going on, or how far it had progressed sexually, they kept her under close watch. It seemed the pair hadn't been intimate yet, but both Bronwyn's parents believed it would happen soon. They didn't want the Order to find out. After all, an affair with a mated *paven* was grounds for time spent in Mondrar, the vampire prison, and the last thing they wanted was to see their child behind bars.

Better beneath the Breeding Male, Bronwyn thought sadly. How wrong they had been.

Farrah spent only one night with "It," and had returned a different *veana* than when she had left. After confirming her *swell*, she'd remained in her room, refusing to be seen by anyone but Bron. Over the next several months, her belly grew—so large she had trouble breathing. It was in her sixth month that her blood began to run.

It had never stopped.

With no care for her small frame, the Breeding Male had placed two *balas* inside her. But what could be expected from such an unfeeling, rutting animal? Bronwyn had studied their genetic structure for her private client, and it was as though their cells commanded the animal response from them.

The soft, warm ocean water lapped gently at Bronwyn's shoulders, as if Farrah were somehow trying to comfort her.

But it was no use. Bronwyn had sworn on the day of her

sister's death that she would never let the same fate befall her. And she had done everything she could to make sure it didn't by finding her true mate before her parents could make the same demand of her. For even though her parents grieved Farrah's loss, the humiliation and shame of a daughter pregnant with a mated *paven*'s or an Impure *paven*'s child was far worse. Her death was, at the very least, an honorable one.

Bronwyn would never share that "honor"—never lie beneath the one she feared above all others. Yet that one was supposedly coming to this reality to do just that.

Lucian Roman.

She dropped her head back, accepting the full false sun on her face, and sighed.

Lucian. The next Breeding Male? Why hadn't she seen this on her data? Why hadn't she pushed to get his DNA results before the other Roman brothers—why hadn't she looked at his blood work for the Breeding Male marker? Yes, she'd known it could happen after the morpho of any of the Roman brothers. But according to her research, morpho for Lucian wouldn't occur for a very long time.

Unless the Order had premorphed him too . . .

God. Had that happened? Is that who had sent her here? The Order? Did the Beast work under them? If they did know the truth about her and Synjon, why would they bring in the Breeding Male? Syn was Pureblood and unmated. Wasn't that all that mattered to them? To her parents?

Her skin felt weightless and smooth under the water. As if it knew it was protected. She'd looked everywhere on the beach for something to cover herself, but there was nothing. Nothing but the ocean.

The Beast had said that having sex with Lucian would be his final step into Breeding Male status. If so, if it was just about having sex with someone, he'd have been the Breeding Male long ago, wouldn't he? He was no *virgini*—of that she was sure.

Maybe the Beast had been lying. Maybe this was a way to control her or scare her.

Maybe he was just a monster with a cruel streak who liked to torture *veanas*.

She placed her wet hands together under the water—the water that blocked her nudity from anyone who would be coming to this reality—and prayed that was true.

She would not give her body to a Breeding Male, no matter who he was.

And yet her core trembled.

6

Lucian and Alexander hit the ground near the Hollow of Shadows with more weight than they'd started with.

"You jackass." Lucian pushed the unwanted *paven* off of him. "You piggyback on me again and you'll be lying on a platter with your eyeballs gone and an apple in your mouth."

Synjon looked unfazed at the threat as he processed his surroundings: the lush green forest, the rocky caves, the deep, rich scent of earth that always permeated the air in the Hollow. "Save your threats for the Order," he said evenly. "This is my right, my claim on my mate."

"Your mate," Lucian scoffed with an edge of suspicion. What the hell was going on here? he mused, his gaze as challenging as his tone had been. What was he missing? "Why is it you have no sense of where she is? It's impossible."

Squaring his shoulders, Synjon leveled a brick-wall stare at Lucian. "We won't be connected until she's inside me, and I haven't taken her blood or her body." He raised a brow and tipped his chin up. "Yet."

Lucian's growl was fierce and feral. Hot coils of possession unraveled in his gut, and the need to rip this male apart, then find and take his mate, was unrelenting inside him. He didn't know what to do with these feelings, and goddamn—he refused to name them, but if the *paven* before him wanted to live, he'd better shut the fuck up about Bronwyn's blood and body.

"Luca has a point," Alexander said, stepping between the two *pavens*, his tone the very essence of calm as he eyeballed Synjon. "The true mate bond is impenetrable and uncomplicated. Whether you've taken her blood or not, you should know where she is. Unless—"

"Unless by taking her blood *you* screwed something up," Synjon accused him severely.

Alexander snorted. "Get serious."

"This whole thing is screwed up," Lucian stated with ire, stalking around Alex and getting in Synjon's air space once again. "You're hiding something, Brit Boy. I can scent it, along with that cheap cologne you're wearing. What is it?"

Quick as an intake of breath, Synjon reached out and grabbed Lucian's gun, but just as the weapon slipped from the holster, Lucian was flashed from the Hollow and away from both *pavens*. In seconds, he felt both heat and sand, and even though he knew exactly where he was, he stumbled for a second to find his balance.

"Goddamn Order," Lucian muttered as he righted himself and slid his gaze over the table in front of him.

As usual, the ten ancient ones were dressed for success—otherwise known as "Please, assholes, be intimidated by us." Each wore a red monklike robe, had a black circle, a perfect O, branded around their left eye, and each *paven* had a full beard. But—he squinted, there seemed to be a robe missing. His eyes searched the line of bodies, landing on his father at the end, head covered with his red hood. Only nine accounted for.

Cruen.

The mastermind, the evil one among all the other evil ones who had defected to places unknown. Sounded like a good trick. Maybe the others would follow his lead. Lucian sniffed at that. Maybe not. The Order had yet to find Cruen and bring him to justice for what he had done with Ethan Dare and all those Impure fools who had been destroyed and manipulated in the name of progress, but no doubt they were working their own schemes to find him.

Of the three *veana* members, the one with skin the color of clay and waist-length hair the color of snow spoke first. "Good evening, Lucian Roman."

Lucian didn't have time for making nicey-nice—even if he thought the old assholes before him worthy of it. "Where is she?" he said with undisguised menace.

The *veana* looked confused, the skin between her brows wrinkling. "Who do you seek, Son of the Breeding Male?"

Oh joy. He cocked his head, narrowed his eyes. "Are we really going to play this game? Because if we are then I'm going to need one of those BarcaLounger recliners and a snack."

"We play at nothing," she said quickly, seriously.

"And by snack I mean blood; preferably from a female and over ninety-eight degrees."

Her lip curled with distaste. "It is you who have sought us this eve, Lucian Roman. We felt your presence in the Hollow, pulled you in, and brought you here before us."

This bunch of relics was working his last goddamn nerve. "That's bullshit and you know it," Lucian said, heading to the table like they couldn't incinerate him with just a thought. "I just came from a wall with your scrawl on it. Bronwyn Kettler and the sun. Ring a bell?"

The *veana* turned to the others at her table. "Did one of you call for Lucian Roman?"

Beyond irritated now, Lucian's gaze shot to his father, who, like the others, shook his head in response.

"We sent no message, Son of the Breeding Male," she said, her tone rife with confusion and concern as she turned back to face him. "Bronwyn Kettler has mated. We all witnessed this mating. She is no longer a concern of ours."

A low growl started in Lucian's throat. He had no idea what was going on here, but he didn't like it. "The Order cannot open their mouths without deception bleeding out."

A *paven* beside the white-haired *veana* hissed. "This censure is uncalled for."

"Lucian, Son of the Breeding Male." It was Titus now, his hood unmoving, his voice an even thread of calm and reason. "We have made no call to you."

Jacked up on both irritation and—fuck it—a pretty heavy dose of concern for Bronwyn now, Lucian sneered at his father, and was about to open his mouth and say something ugly and obvious when the *paven* spoke inside his mind.

"Do not reveal my identity. I beg you."

"Beg all you want, Daddy," he mused, lifting his upper lip as he stared at that hood. *"This is about Bronwyn now. Your secret is not mine. Your life, your future—none of it is—"*

His thoughts, his ire, his near reveal of the *paven* who had given him life, were interrupted by the white-haired *veana*. This time her voice demonstrated its own version of irritation. "There is another who has the power to call upon you still."

As the low rumble of concerned chitchat ebbed up and down the long wood table, Lucian felt the pulse of understanding jar his mind. This game was a sick one, a cruel one—and clearly it wasn't stopping here.

"Cruen," he said, his pupils dilating, his skin retracting over his bones—ready for flight, ready for fight.

The *veana* nodded, her eyes glazed with the anger of one who thought that up until a moment ago they had all the control.

Welcome to my world, Veana. Feels pretty shitty, don't it?

"So," Lucian began, having a seat on the Order's illustrious wood table. He ignored the quick intakes of breath from either side of the *veana*. "Why would that menace to our breed have a need to call upon me?"

"It seems he has a special interest in you," she said evenly, though beneath her cool exterior there was more than a sliver of unrest. "We didn't know it when there was the original call on the Roman brothers. We think Cruen may be trying to draw you in, draw you to him—wherever it is he hides from us, from justice." She lifted one pale eyebrow. "Did you know that Cruen was the one who created the Breeding Male program?"

Lucian's gaze shot to Titus.

"Yes, I knew."

"His main goal was to morph you," the female continued, "to send you into Breeding Male status."

"There is another place for us to speak of this, my son."

Lucian could barely contain his anger, his questions, could barely keep his fangs from extending. Betrayal—ever present when it came to this *paven* who sired him—surged through his blood. Had his father known about Cruen's intentions and given Lucian no warning? Piece-of-shit bastard ... Using his mental gifts to get inside Lucian's head, planting ideas and maybe even a little bit of softness in there while he was at it. And now the old *paven* expected Lucian to keep Titus's secrets?

The growl that left his throat was meant for the lot of them. They were all fucking with him—it was their greatest pleasure to fuck with the Roman brothers.

"Wasn't that the Order's goal?" he said, his tone accusing and ugly as he jumped off the table and headed down the row to stand in front of Titus—who incidentally refused to look at him. "Getting me morphed, sending me into Breeding Male status?"

"No," the *veana* confirmed more passionately than she no doubt intended. "We only wanted Dare found and destroyed. Cruen wanted the Romans premorphed. He wanted to see which one of you might have the gene."

The intensity of Lucian's ire at that moment threatened to tear his sanity apart. These self-righteous wannabe gods created monsters like him, like his father, and reveled in their abilities, then acted offended and disgusted when the animals didn't heel the way they wanted them to. And now they pretended to care about his pale ass, pretended they hadn't fated him to an existence where he was either utterly alone or lost inside the mind and body of a beast in heat ... Because—let's get serious here—those were his only options as he was allowed no true mate in his future.

Well, screw the Order. Screw dear ol' Daddy. He needed to get off this plane—find that ancient bastard and get the girl back where she belonged.

With him, a voice deep inside his blood uttered maliciously. And just to make things real nice and brutal, the ancient *veana* with the white hair and clear, gentle voice said it—the thing that was meant to kill his insides and make him beg.

"There is one other thing, Son of the Breeding Male," she began tentatively. "We have reason to believe Cruen may have an antidote for the Breeding Male gene, something that could possibly turn off the need to breed."

Lucian didn't move. In fact, nothing inside him moved—not his blood, his skin, his muscles, not even a twitch as he processed the words thrust upon him. Words that had to be a lie, a manipulation ...

His gaze burned into the unseen face below the hood, his father. He waited—waited for confirmation, something inside his mind. But nothing came.

He chuckled, dark and sick. He was a descendant of cowardice. Shit, that was unfortunate.

"How convenient this all is," he said, walking toward the *veana*. "And how timely."

"Perhaps if you help us," the *veana* began, her Order status forcing her to use the serendipitous moment to her advantage.

But Lucian wasn't biting. Hell, he wasn't even hungry anymore. Time was being wasted ... If Cruen truly had Bronwyn, they were in some serious trouble—she was in some serious trouble. He needed to jump on that, not sit here and lap up juicy bits of possibility. Life didn't run that way for him. No hope, no girl—no happy ending for Lucian Roman.

"Gotta go, boys and girls," he said, backing up from the table.

"If you bring Cruen to us," she continued as he moved back, "we will force him to halt the Breeding Male gene inside you."

Shaking his head, Lucian laughed with centuries of bitterness. "Go fuck yourselves. All of you."

"Lucian."

Not a chance, Pop.

"Go! Now!"

The alarmed tone inside his head had Lucian stuttering with sudden panic. What the hell was going on?

"You must go! He knows. God, he wanted you here—wanted you to come here."

Lucian stared at the male in the robe.

"It is the one place he can latch on to you. I should have realized ... I cannot send you back myself—"

For the sixth time that day, Lucian was yanked away, flashed out of one reality and deposited into another. But this time, he was on his own and where he landed looked nothing like the Hollow of Shadows, SoHo, or France—and everything like his jail.

His eyes sliced over the endless scene of blue.

Oh shit.

And her jail . . .

"Don't come anywhere near me, Lucian Roman," she called out, terror in her voice, in her eyes.

7

She wanted to feel no fear. She wanted to pretend that what she'd heard, and understood, and had been threatened with, was all a lie—a sick joke by a sick Beast. But as Lucian appeared out of nowhere at the water's edge, his eyes finding her in an instant, she buried that hope deep within herself. She was no automaton, no female warrior ready to take on her enemy. She was just a simple *veana*, a *veana* who was deeply and profoundly afraid of being taken against her will.

Especially by this *paven*.

This beautiful, terrifying angel of blood who had given her strength once upon a time when she'd needed it, and had given her shit many a time when she hadn't wanted it. This one who had ruled her thoughts, her dreams, and her fantasies every night for months. She didn't want to ever be afraid of him.

Her lip quivered and she bit it. Hard. What would happen now? Would he swim out to her as the animal that her abductor had claimed he was? And if he did, would she have the guts to fight him completely? Would she have the heart to be sickened by him and what he wanted from her?

He moved then. Stepped into the water, lifted his hands expectantly, and called out across the calm sea, "Having a swim, Princess?"

The dark humor that resided in his tone—that always resided in his tone—made her release the breath she was holding in her lungs. There was no feral animal there—not yet anyway. It was him—the him she knew, the one who taunted and teased her.

"Come out of there, *Veana*," he called, louder this time. "We have no time for bathing."

"No," she called back. "Can't."

He tilted his head in curiosity. "Why the hell not?"

She hated to say it—say it out loud, admit it. But what was the choice? "I have no clothes on."

He made a grunting sound, deep in his throat. "Sure hope not. You're in the water."

"I'm in the water *because* I have no clothes on, Lucian," she shouted.

His pale brows shot upward. "Is that right?"

"Yes," she said quickly. "So just stay there. We can talk this way."

"No. Hell no." He pulled off his shirt and tossed it onto the sand. "I'm not going to caw back and forth like two parrots."

"Wait . . ."

He pulled off his pants.

"Stop!"

Oh my God, what was he doing? She shifted on the large rock that held her weight and kept her comfortably above the water, and tried desperately not to stare at his long, lean frame as it became more and more exposed. Her eyes darted from him, from skin, hard muscle to the hill beyond, the palms and the endless stretch of beach.

"If the princess won't come to the asshole," he called, "then the asshole will have to come to the princess."

She backed up a step. "Don't you dare get in this water."

He grinned as he walked straight into the sea toward her, only his bottom half covered. "Don't be shy, Princess. I've seen you all wet before. Remember?"

Her face went pink and she lifted her chin. "If you're referring to your nightly stalking routine, then you should be ashamed to even mention it."

"Hey. Not my fault. You take a *paven*'s blood, you get his prowl."

"I was ill, starving," she said stiffly. "It was one moment in time, and you *did* offer it to me. Let's never forget that."

"I don't," he uttered, just a few feet away now.

She put out a hand to stop him before he got close enough to touch her. Before he got close enough to touch. "That's far enough."

His pale brown eyes looked clear. Cocky—but clear. "Nothing to fear from me, Princess. You're a mated *veana* now. Your body belongs to another. As does your skin, your unbeating heart, your pu—"

"Stop that," she warned him, trying desperately not to stare at the smooth crests and valleys of his wide, muscular chest.

He inclined his head. "My apologies. I am a self-confessed heathen. But my point is, your body will only want to give to him. And his mark, his scent, will turn me off—so there's nothing to worry about here—between us."

Inside of that moment, Bronwyn felt the breath leave her body and shoot off into the perfect sunset. He had no idea why they were here—or why she had been placed here, nude and scared. Just as he had no idea that the mark on her hand was made, not out of true love, but out of ink and deception.

He was staring at that mark now, his jaw tight. "Nice brand."

She swallowed tightly. "I think so."

"I met the *paven*, by the way," Lucian said, water lapping at his neck, his hard jaw. "Seems like a huge dick."

She lifted a brow and quickly jumped to Syn's defense. "Haven't seen it yet, but I'll let you know."

Lucian's lip curled.

She shook her head. "This is foolish. This back and forth. We have a serious problem here."

"I'd say it's more of a predicament."

"Come on, Lucian. This is far more than a predicament."

His shoulders seemed to grow broader, more powerful under his self-assured gaze. "I'll take care of it."

"Really? How?" She'd been desperately trying to find a way out for hours. And her only solution so far was to hide in the water.

"At some point, someone will show up—maybe even my half brother," he added with a sneer, "and tell us what they want."

"Wait. What?" She stared hard at him. "You knew," she accused him fiercely, her stomach clenching as her mind processed. "You knew that that monster was the one who abducted me?" She released a shaky breath. "Please tell me you didn't have anything to do with—"

"Hey!" he interrupted her sternly. "Don't even go there, *Veana*. This kind of thing ain't my style." His gaze flickered with heat. "No matter how into you I may be—or have been," he corrected himself. "I don't take what doesn't belong to me."

She wondered if he really believed that. She sure as hell didn't. Lucian Roman had absolutely no moral compass or code. He was a heathen of the first order, and a *paven* who took whatever he wanted without a thought to consequences. It was unfortunately one of the many things she found attractive about him.

"But you knew about Nicholas's twin," she said, pushing that last thought aside.

"Only after your male friend said you were abducted by Nicky." He cocked his head to the side, the ends of his white hair licking the water's surface. "Didn't take long after that for me to realize the *gemino* was at work."

Hours of fear and wondering when Lucian was going to show up, and how he was going to act when he did, erupted inside her. "He took my clothes."

All humor and easy manner evaporated from him. "What?"

"The *gemino*," she said. "That's why I'm out here ... like this. Stripped them right off my body with his magic," she continued with passion.

Lucian growled. "I'll kill him."

Her gaze faltered. "I stood there naked before him while he told me to prepare myself. Told me you were coming for me. That you were coming to ... " She stopped. She couldn't go on, couldn't say it. Not to his face. No matter how familiar he felt in that moment, in that unfamiliar situation and landscape, the words would not leave her mouth.

Momentarily stunned, Lucian just stared at her. She'd seen him angry, disgusted, arrogant, but she'd never seen him horrified. She'd never seen him with even a trace of fear in his eyes. Until now.

"Lucian?" she began.

"I'll get us out of here," he said quickly, his eyes darkening as the skin around his muscles tightened with strain.

Bronwyn bit her lip. "And then ... "

"And then I'll slit the throats of everyone responsible for putting you in my path." He lowered his chin and said slowly and blackly, "Stay in the water."

"Where are you going?"

"To find a way out of here." With that, he turned and dove under the water. With great speed and precision, he swam toward the shore.

Two hours later, after investigating every inch of the "island" and finding nothing but vegetation and more water, Lucian stood on the sand, his chest exposed to the warmth of the false setting sun, his white hair shifting in the manufactured breeze, and faced reality. He could no longer act cavalier and brazenly confident about his ability to get them off this plane.

This was Cruen's doing—this exquisite prison. It was obvious and purposeful and undeniably worrisome, and as night slowly descended around him, and Bronwyn continued to exist in the sea alone, standing on her rocky perch under the water, Lucian fought for calm inside himself. He was growing weary from hunger, and the scent of her—even with the mark upon her hand and the sizable distance between them—was demanding entrance inside his nostrils.

Control was a funny thing. When you had somewhere to run to, to escape the call of blood, the need was no longer fierce. But without the escape hatch, desire chased you like a demon.

The flickering jabs of ferocity unnerved him, sobered him. He wouldn't allow her to see his concern or his hunger. Just as he wouldn't allow her to tell him what the Beast had said, what he'd predicted would happen to her, even though he had a pretty good idea.

He walked to the water's edge. She was still out there, her unclothed form hidden beneath the water's surface. Safe from his gaze, his need. For now.

She had to be getting cold.

He cupped his hands around his mouth and called, "Come out."

"Can't," she called back.

"You can and you must. It's growing dark." He could practically hear her thoughts, her concern. "You can wear my shirt. It'll cover ... everything." He took the extra-large button down and spread it out closer to the water, then walked away and kept his back to her.

She was silent for a good minute; then he heard her swimming, coming toward the shore.

It wasn't his way. Chivalry and thoughtfulness. In his many years of life, Lucian Roman had considered only Lucian Roman. For the most part. But this *veana*, the princess, she needed his care. Even if it was done sparingly and cautiously.

"Lucian?" she said after a few minutes, her voice closer now, perhaps just a few feet away.

"Don't worry, Princess," he uttered. "Eyes down."

He wouldn't look, but he wanted to. Hell, he wanted to so fucking bad he ached from nose to nuts.

She was quick putting on the shirt, and in under a minute, she called out, "Okay."

He turned around, keeping his eyes off of her and those legs peeking out from under the white cotton that not so long ago covered the skin of his chest.

"Why don't you sit?" He gestured to a huge chunk of palm he'd ripped from one of the trees. "It's not the lap of luxury or anything, but it's something. It'll keep your ass off the sand."

"Thanks." She did as he offered, then pushed her knees up inside her shirt for warmth. And yet she continued to shiver.

"You're cold."

"It's okay," she said softly. "I'm fine." The quiet defeat in her tone bothered him. Bothered him more than it should. She was cold and scared—and fuck, he wasn't going to touch her.

"Are you hungry?" he asked.

She shook her head. "Not yet."

Good. Feeding her would be absolute hell. But he'd do it. If he had to, he'd do it.

"I'm just tired," she said.

He felt her eyes on him, and he made the mistake of looking, of meeting her gaze. As always, her beauty was lush and undeniable, and had a strength he couldn't relate to.

"You go to sleep," he said, turning back to the water, scanning the horizon, the length of beach, for anything that threatened. "I'll keep watch. See if that brother of mine shows his face."

Bronwyn did as he said, lying back against the long strip of palm. She was quiet for a while. Then out of the growing dusk, she whispered, "Lucian?"

"Yeah." He glanced down at her, couldn't help himself. Just as he couldn't help the way his eyes moved over every inch of her: smooth legs under white cotton, the curved outline of an unbound breast, the delectable peak of one nipple pressing against the fabric of his shirt.

And the face, he mused with the grief of a captive *paven*—that face held such exquisite beauty marred only by the strength of worry . . .

"It's not a predicament," she said, her dark eyes on his.

"No, it's not," he uttered.

"It's bad."

Her distress tore at his gut. "It ain't good."

She curled her arms into her chest, her hands under her chin. "We're stuck here, aren't we?"

He scoffed, then shook his head. "Can't be, Princess. Can't be. Because if we're stuck here, it's only a matter of time before I turn into the Breeding Male."

8

The son approached the father and inclined his head. It was as it had been decades ago when Cruen had gathered his young Beasts around himself and revealed to them how and why they were living inside the secret laboratory of an Order member. Cruen grinned as he recalled how each one had dropped his chin in submission and understanding—and most important, in allegiance. It had been a proud moment, nearly as glorious as the day he'd created the first Breeding Male. There had been no questions about the ones who had given birth to them, who had then thrown them away like so much rubbish. To each Beast, he was their family.

"Father." Erion came to stand beside the metal table in Cruen's laboratory, his size unnerving, his form that of a vampire. "It is done. They are together. Trapped. Ready to fulfill their destiny."

"Very good," Cruen remarked, returning to his work, his eyes pinned to the Titan 80-300 Cubed microscope and the blood samples beneath. "It won't be long now."

"How will you know when the event has occurred?" Erion asked.

"I will feel the shift. I have always felt it."

"The shift into Breeding Male status."

"Yes." He glanced up into the cold diamond eyes of the child who was not of his body, but of his creation. "I will call for you when it does. The moment they are released from my reality, you and your brothers will seize them."

"You want both the Roman brother and the *veana* brought here?"

Cruen nodded. "Where their purpose will be revealed to them."

"And if they refuse?"

"If they refuse, put up a fight or play dead," Cruen said, repressing his annoyance at these questions. "Just bring them to me."

A slash of heat moved past Erion's eyes, but he said nothing—merely nodded.

"You have work, do you not?"

Standing stiffly, Erion gave a sharp nod. "The caged one must be fed."

"Let her know she will have her needs taken care of very soon." Cruen grinned, then turned back to his blood sample. "Very soon."

Bronwyn slept not. Her eyes refused to stay closed for longer than a few seconds. They either swept over the landscape in search of the one who had snatched her from her Veracou, or over the *paven* who sat immobile and vigilant beside her.

The darkness of the Beast's reality was not the same darkness of the real world. It was as though a lavender haze coated the sky and made all who sat beneath it ever wary.

Even Lucian Roman.

Especially Lucian Roman.

Sitting back on his heels, he was as alert as a bat, his body poised and ready to fly at anything or anyone who threatened them. It was strange to feel safe and protected by the very *paven* she should fear.

"Aren't you tired?" she asked him softly.

Lucian glanced down. "I don't sleep."

"Me either. Well, not lately anyway."

"Too much on your mind, Princess?"

"Something like that." The sad seriousness in his expression no doubt matched her own, and she expelled a heavy breath. "We need to talk. About why we're here, what they want, what we need to—"

"No." It was a solid and direct response. But it hardly deterred her.

"Lucian, come on."

He shook his head. "Not yet. Not ever if I can get us out of here."

"I'm beginning to believe that's impossible. The thing that brought me here—"

"You may refer to him as 'Dead Meat.'"

"Nicholas's twin," she said with a small smile. This was growing more difficult by the second. His attitude and unwillingness to discuss a course of action was making her more anxious. Did he think *she* wanted to talk about it? About what the monster had said to her?

She stared at his pale, beautifully startling face with all its sharp angles and fierce expressions. God, was it better to bite her tongue and wait like he so obviously wanted? Or would waiting only make it worse.

She swallowed thickly, knowing it needed to happen. Knowing she should just let it rip. They needed to work together, be honest with each other. Now more than ever.

Sitting up, she braced herself on her arm and faced him fully. "He told me that you will be the next Breeding Male."

The words left her tongue and hovered in the air. She watched him for a response, for his eyes to change and his lips to curl back. But there was none of that. In fact, he chuckled. But the sound wasn't exactly merry. It bordered on bitter.

"Oh, that." His jaw twitched and she felt him shift an imperceptible amount away from her. "It's not like you didn't suspect it."

"I know. But I thought it couldn't happen for another hundred years or so."

"And it won't." He returned his gaze to the sea.

"Then everything is fine?" she said, her muscles softening slightly with relief. "The Beast was lying, trying to scare me—"

Refusing to look at her, he said, "It's not exactly fine, Princess."

"But you just said . . ."

"There was one thing in my long life that never attracted me. One thing I never allowed myself to do, to give. Perhaps I had a built-in deterrent. Perhaps I was just the selfish bastard everyone thinks I am. Until . . . " His eyes shifted to her mouth. "You."

Bron didn't understand at first. Her mind shuffled through memories and thoughts, confused and searching. Until one stopped her cold. One night in Lucian's bed, sick and starving. "Oh, God." She licked her lips involuntarily. "Your blood."

His gaze remained fixed on the water.

She shook her head. "You've never given your blood to anyone else before?"

"No."

It all made a terrible kind of sense to her now. You give, you get . . . It was the law of nature, be it a good outcome or a bad one. "Your cells changed when you fed me, didn't they?"

He nodded. "But only halfway."

Her eyes narrowed. "What do you mean only halfway? What does that mean?" Her mind reeled and wavered, tried to focus in on what she knew as a genealogist. "Are you saying that the change into a Breeding Male has two parts?"

He nodded.

She never knew, never suspected this. "One part blood and one part—?"

He turned then and his gaze raked down her body. "Sex."

He said the word so quickly it stuck in the air, but after a moment it began to swirl, circle around Bronwyn with heavy intent.

"The Beast," she whispered as the false sunlight broke through a false cloud and warmed her skin. "He said you would come here for that, for sex. He said you would plant your seed inside—"

"Cease!" He cursed under his breath, slammed his eyes back to the water. "I have the gene, okay! The change is inevitable, but as long as we don't have sex, you will remain *virgini* and I will remain myself for another one hundred and seventy-five years."

"But you clearly have the urge—"

"I have the urge with every female, Princess," he said flippantly. "You're nothing special."

Bronwyn would never have expected to feel such a profound pain slice through her with his words, but she did. It was her sad truth. She belonged to Synjon in word and promise, but her body, her unbeating heart ... Well, unfortunately, they both seemed to want to belong to Lucian Roman.

She lifted her chin and pretended a meat cleaver hadn't sliced her in two. "Maybe I'm not special to you, but your blood is inside me and that makes me special in a whole other way."

74

His jaw tight enough to crack a couple of teeth, Lucian stood up. His strong, muscular body was momentarily bathed in sunlight, making him look like a god carved in marble.

"Nicholas's twin said you would go after me," she continued. "That we would ... have sex here. That we would breed and you would begin your destiny."

"It won't happen," he uttered with ruthless defiance.

"I'm glad you're so sure of yourself."

"Go to sleep." He started walking away, toward the shoreline.

"Because I'm not all that sure of me," she called after him. "Hey! Hey—I'll admit it. Right here, right now, in front of you and whoever is listening or watching." When he didn't stop or turn around, she jumped up and ran down to the shoreline, grabbed his arm, and yanked him to face her. "My body and my blood want it—they want you."

"Try telling them both to fuck off—that works for me."

She wasn't listening to him. "But my heart ... "

"Doesn't beat, Princess. Just like mine."

"Must you always be so cruel?"

"You enjoy my cruelty."

"No, I don't."

"It's what makes your mouth water and your pussy cream."

She gasped, dropped his arm, and slapped him hard across the face.

He didn't even flinch. "Oh, please do that again," he whispered, his nostrils flaring.

Shaking now, her eyes filling with tears, Bronwyn slapped him again.

"More," he hissed, his eyes blazing down at her as his body closed in. "One more time, Princess. Just to make sure I understand."

Bronwyn didn't move. She just stood there, her mouth trembling, her hand tingling from the double contact with his cheekbone and jaw. She couldn't do it again ... didn't want to ...

"Fine, I'll shut us both up." He pulled her to him and covered her mouth, kissed her hard and hungry until her lips were bruised and she whimpered.

Tears spilled from Bronwyn's eyes as he eased back just a fraction of an inch. She should've had the urge to ram her knee right up between his legs, push him away, tear at his lower lip with her fangs. But her body betrayed such thoughtful, protective instincts. Instead, her skin pleaded for more, her breasts ached for his hands, his fingers, his mouth. "You disgust me," she whispered, her tone fraught with passion and fear and desperation.

"Good," he returned harshly, but his mouth trembled too. "Then you won't be tempted to run after me again."

As he backed away, turned, and headed down the beach, his dark and dangerous scent following after him, Bronwyn stared, unblinking. She'd gone after him and tempted him, tempted the beast within him. Why? Why would she do such a foolish, harmful thing unless she was asking him to take her—asking the Breeding Male buried within him to take her ...

That thought broke her soul in two.

"You disgust me," she'd said to him, nearly against his mouth.

As she watched him advance farther down the shore, she wondered just who those words had truly been meant for.

Were they really aimed at Lucian Roman?

Or herself?

9

Alexander returned to the villa just as the light was changing. As expected and hoped for, his true mate stood anxiously outside the massive front door, her blue eyes sweeping over him, checking for blood or bruises—anything to explain his long absence.

Sara shook her head. "It's nearly dawn."

"I'm sorry, my love." He gathered her in his arms and kissed her temple. "I couldn't leave until I had some news."

"News? What do you mean?" Her expression changed again as she noticed who wasn't at his side. "Where's Lucian? And the other one ... Bronwyn's mate?"

"I don't know." His jaw tightened. "Lucian never came back, and no member of the Order popped down to the caves to fill me in. I'll return at first dark."

"And Bronwyn's mate?"

"When Lucian didn't return, Synjon decided to go look for her on his own."

"I don't like this," Sara said. "Luca being held. I don't want you going back to the Hollow."

"He is all right, my love. I would know. I would feel it if he weren't." Alexander shook his head. "But I have to find him. Just as you could not abandon your brother, I must help Lucian."

Sara appeared tense, but she nodded her understanding.

Giving her a soft smile, Alexander asked, "Is Nicholas here?"

"He just returned as well," she said, urging him forward, inside the house. "Come on, before the sun claims us both."

Keeping her close to him, Alexander stepped into the entryway. "The sun will never hurt you, my dear."

"Make no mistake, *Paven*," she said, settling into the crook of his shoulder, "if it claimed your life, it claims mine as well."

Alexander's gut clenched with feeling. Time couldn't be spared, but he was a *paven* in love, a *paven* who was trying to create a family, and this female was ever reminding him of how lucky he was. His arm curved around her waist and he pulled her close and kissed her.

"I love you," he whispered against her lips, his forehead touching hers.

"I love you," she whispered back, then tipped her chin up and ran her fangs across his top lip. "Always."

He groaned at the erotic, possessive sensation. "Not fair."

"I know." She laughed softly. "Come now."

Again his mouth claimed her, hard and demanding.

She laughed and tried to pull away. "Alex . . . "

"I'm only doing what I'm told."

"I know, and I appreciate your obedience," she said with a grin. "Your brother's in the library."

He nuzzled her cheek. "I don't give a shit about my brother."

"Yes, you do."

"Yes, I do." He dropped his head and sighed. "Fine. Let's go, but later . . . "

"I am yours. Every inch."

"But not too much later."

She laughed again and took his hand. "I'm not going anywhere. You will always have me."

In a low, gravelly voice, he demanded, "Swear it, my love. Swear you're mine now and forever."

"Cross my heart."

"I hate that saying," he grumbled as they walked down the hall.

Nicholas was behind his desk when they arrived in the library, his eyes running laps over the computer screen. He didn't even look up. "I didn't hear any fighting outside the door, so I assume Lucian and his new playmate aren't with you."

"The playmate went off on his own," Alexander said, heading over to the desk. "Lucian is still with the Order."

That made Nicholas look up. "What?"

"I'm going back at first dark."

"With you, Nicky," Sara said, sitting down on the couch. "God only knows what the Order is up to now. You're stronger and more effective together."

"I don't need backup with the Order, my love," Alexander stated flatly and with a touch of arrogance.

"Good," Nicholas said. "Because I have a meet."

Sara released a weighty breath. "Then you will contact Dillon, Alex. All right?"

"Dillon is freezing me out," Alexander put in with irritation. He'd attempted to contact the bodyguard to a human senator several times in the past two weeks to assist them in finding Nicky's *gemino*, but his old friend wouldn't even call him back to tell him to fuck off. Wasn't like her. Wasn't like her at all.

Sara shook her head. "Just as Gray is avoiding me."

"When they are done acting like *balas*, they know where their true family lies," Alex said, tightening his hold on his true mate, then turning back to Nicky. "Who's the meet with?"

"The Eyes," he said. "They hooked me up."

"With whom?"

"A *paven* who used to run odd jobs for the Order when he was a *balas*. They paid him in blood."

"Of course they did," Alexander uttered darkly. "And were you able to extract information on the *gemino* from this *paven*?"

Nicholas's fingers paused over the keyboard. "I found out that he was given away at birth."

"Why?" Alexander went over to stand behind him.

"He had a deformity," Nicholas said so quietly and without emotion Alexander wondered what the *paven* was thinking.

Behind him, Sara inhaled harshly. "Your mother gave him away because of a birth defect?"

Nicholas nodded, his eyes lifting to meet hers. "Perhaps she was not in her right mind. It is the only excuse, isn't it?"

"It's pretty rare for a vampire to have a defect," Alexander stepped in, trying to switch the focus in the room from pity to purpose. "What did he have? Blood disorder? Limb missing?"

"No." It wasn't Nicholas who spoke, but Kate. She walked into the room and went straight over to her mate. "Just got Ladd to sleep." She sat on his lap and curled into him, gave him a kiss on the cheek. "Nicky, just tell them."

Alexander glanced over at Sara, then back at his brother. "Tell us what?"

With a weighty breath, Nicholas said, "The *paven* said that our brother is a *mutore*."

"*Mutore?*" Alexander repeated, then burst out laughing.

Nicholas nodded. "That's right."

"He's lying to you. I hope you did not pay him."

"Wait a second," Sara said, confused and curious. "What is this? *Mutore*?"

With a snort Alexander replied, "It is only a fairy tale, my love."

"More like a ghost story," Kate added.

Sara shook her head. "I don't understand."

"A *mutore* is a vampire who is genetically wrong," Nicholas explained. "Born with more than a birth defect. They are mutants."

"I've never heard of such a thing," Sara said, her gaze moving from Nicholas to Alexander. "Are they vampires? Pureblood? Impure?"

"They are nothing," Alexander put in with tight assertion. "They do not exist."

"They are Pureblooded vampires," Kate said, then paused for a second before adding, "and shape-shifters."

"Shape-shifters?" Sara cried. She looked around the room for confirmation, explanation. "What kind of shape do they shift into?"

Alexander chuckled, but it was a bitter sound. "I have never seen one. They don't exist."

"I have heard they are Beasts."

It was Nicholas who spoke, who tightened his hold on his true mate with one hand, and returned to the computer keyboard with the other.

"I have heard they have claws instead of hands, scars instead of skin. But tonight"—he nodded at Alexander—"as you go after one brother, I will find out the whole truth about the other."

Lucian had no idea what time it was, but he'd been walking up and down the beach for hours, his eyes as watchful over the *veana* as he could manage without causing excessive strain and need within himself. That kiss had been a mistake—as had the goading her into hitting him, inciting her anger, her passion. Both had been proof positive of how strong his desire for her continued to be. It didn't take a genius to realize that if he was to remain sane, he must also remain calm.

As he passed by her pallet once again, he saw that she had taken to lying down. Her arms were wrapped around her torso and her legs were pressed together. He moved away from the water and trudged up the sand to the closest palm tree. He was a damn good climber and it took him only minutes to pry a soft, green frond away from its host and drop down to earth again.

Quietly, he walked over to where Bronwyn was lying, and with supreme gentleness he spread the wide leaf over her. It wasn't much of a blanket, but it was the best he could do. All he could do. No way was he using his body as warmth, as a shield to her skin as he wanted to.

He was about to walk away when her voice caught him and held. "I'm growing in hunger, Lucian."

It was the worst thing he could hear at that moment, and yet his reply, his own admittance could be far more damaging.

"And I grow in animal."

She sighed. "What are we going to do?"

"Think of your true mate," he uttered with disdain.

She sighed. "I'm scared."

"I know."

"I don't want to be a coward."

On a heavy breath, he turned to see her watching him, her eyes so exquisite and tortured in the false light of the new morning. "That is the last thing you are, Princess."

"You don't know . . . " she uttered so softly he could barely hear her.

"What?"

She shook her head.

He stopped himself from pressing further, from forcing her secrets from her. They would do nothing but complicate things more. "Try to sleep," he said. "It'll help with ... everything."

"Lucian?" she said as he turned to walk away, get away—keep away.

"What is it, Princess?" he said, glancing over his shoulder.

She smiled softly. "Thank you for the blanket."

The ache inside him squeezed and clawed. "It is all right?" He was a fool, a dangerous *paven* because in that moment he almost hoped she'd say, *No, I need you.*

But all she said was, "It is well and good," saving him from himself once again.

10

His ass to the sand and his back against a palm, Lucian had shut his eyes for only a moment. But a moment was all it took for him to dream.

This time, he was in the ocean, standing upon a rock, not cold but shivering nonetheless. On the shore stood a goddess, dressed in nothing but her long dark hair and an expression of such intense desire he would've drunk the entire sea to get to her. But his body wouldn't move. His legs were affixed to the rock and if he struggled any farther to reach her he would fall into the water and, unable to swim, drown.

She smiled at him then, her fangs descended, and she called to him, "Lucian! Lucian, come to me."

He couldn't resist her plea, her need of him, and he dove under the water. But his feet remained affixed to the rock and with the power of his dive, he curled under and into himself and smashed headfirst into the stone beneath his own feet.

"Oh, God, Lucian!"

Blood spread in the water like gathering thunderclouds and his eyes went dark. Yet still he heard her calling him ...

"Lucian! I'm begging you."

Fuck . . . Would he forever hear her calling him . . .

"Please, you have to wake up . . . It hurts."

He came awake with a jarring lurch, back into the reality that was really no reality at all. Something heavy was on his chest, something sweet burned his nostrils and made his cock stir.

"Shit, no!" Oh, God . . . Bronwyn was on top of him. "Not good, *Veana*." His fingers gripped her upper arms and he eased her off of him and onto the sand. "What are you doing? Are you trying to send us both to hell?"

On her knees beside him, panting, her tongue lapping at the tips of her fangs, Bronwyn stared at his neck. "I . . . I need you."

The scent of her supreme hunger hit him—hit his nostrils, the back of his throat, the heavy organ between his legs. "You need blood."

Her lids flipped up, and her dark eyes pinned him where he sat. "Your blood."

His cock pulsed against the thin fabric of his boxers. This was bad, dangerous . . . delectably dangerous.

"The hunger," she moaned, her eyes glassy now. "It really hurts. It's been too long."

Lucian stilled. "How long?"

"Weeks. I waited until the Veracou."

"No." The word came out in a rush of heat and regret.

"I thought . . ." She shook her head. "God, I don't know what I thought."

Lucian cursed again, dark and loud and angry. "You and your primitive ideals." He smashed his fist into the sand, which was growing warmer by the minute as the morning progressed. "*Virgini* foolishness. Where do they get you when you're in trouble?"

She let her head fall back. "I was trying to stay pure."

"For him," Lucian growled. Her pain and need were eating at him, making him rage with the desire to shake her and then take her. "He is not pure. Why must you be?"

With another moan, she crawled atop him again, lay against him, belly to belly, her face in his neck. "Lucian, please—"

He didn't stop her. How the hell could he? "So I am to feed another *paven*'s true mate, then?"

His cock was hard as stone now, like the stone he'd bashed his head against in his dream—and he knew she could feel it, pressing against her stomach, warning her. Goddamn it! Didn't she get it? If she put her fangs in him it was over!

"Lucian ..."

"Don't beg, Princess, Christ!" he snarled, her breath doing a sensual dance against his skin.

"Why not?" she uttered. "Does it make me look weak, desperate? Good, because I am!"

He took her by the arms and lifted her off him once again. "No, it makes you impossible to resist. It makes you a challenge I will not lose." He forced her gaze to meet his. "We should wait to feed ..."

"I cannot." She sounded close to tears.

"Fuck!" This was bullshit, impossible, and the most delectable need he'd ever felt. He shoved his arm toward her, offered her his wrist. "Fine. Do it. Take it. Take what you need. But come no closer and control your thoughts."

"Why?" She grabbed his wrist.

"Because the hotter you get, the more impossible it is for me to not take you."

At his words, her scent rose up and slammed into his nostrils. Arousal. Sweet, heady ...

"Like that," he growled. "Goddamn it. Stop thinking about anything but the blood."

Her eyes on his vein, her tongue lapping at her dry lips, she whispered, "You flatter yourself."

He yanked his arm away from her and challenged, "Tell me you're not thinking about getting fucked right now."

She inhaled through her teeth, her fangs. She was about to dive for him. "Maybe I am, but maybe it's not you I'm thinking about."

"Since when?" he uttered and thrust his arm back under her waiting lips.

She closed her eyes and inhaled deeply through her nose. "I'm sorry. That was a terrible thing to say."

"Not to mention a huge motherfucking lie."

"Stop it, Lucian."

"Hey, you can always wait for him to show up with the blood."

Her answer to that was a swift and hearty strike into the flesh of his wrist.

"Ahhh, God ... " Lucian uttered, his mind going black, his eyes widening as he watched her feed, watched her drink from him. Again. It was beautiful—she was beautiful, and rabid, and hot as the sun.

Goddamn, he wanted to moan, cry out as she drew on him so heavy and hungry, her fangs working him like the best fuck he'd ever had.

Turn away, he warned himself. *Turn away before you mount her and take what has always belonged to you.*

Oh, those fangs, moving in and out of his vein. They were dangerous and luscious and would surely lead to his demise— but wasn't that true perfection for a dickhead like him?

A low growl sounded. For a moment, Lucian thought it was himself. Then, when he realized it wasn't, he looked to Bronwyn.

She lifted her head. "What is it?"

His blood dripped from her lips, teeth, fangs, and all he wanted to do was bare his tongue and taste himself on her. But then the growl sounded again. In the distance, but close enough to set off his instincts.

He pushed Bronwyn behind him and stood. "Don't move," he commanded in a whisper. "Don't make a sound."

An animal, he thought, hearing it again. That was no human or vampire. An animal was in this reality with them, and it sounded feral.

Fucking Cruen. When Lucian got ahold of him, he was going to wish he had a feral animal on his ancient ass . . .

Lucian's thoughts trailed off as something came bounding out of the forest toward them. On four legs, tan with spots and fangs like a saber-toothed cat. It was trying real hard to scare the shit out of them, but Lucian knew it would never hurt them— Cruen wouldn't ruin what he was protecting, saving . . . Problem was, Bronwyn didn't know that.

She screamed and took off running, away from the beach and into the forest.

"Bronwyn!" Lucian shouted after her. "Goddamn it!"

The animal slowed, waiting. It was a panther or some type of cat hybrid. Its blue eyes watched Lucian to see what he would do next, his mouth nearly curling up in a grin.

"What the fuck are you, kitty?" he said with a snarl.

With that, the animal growled again, then turned tail and ran after Bronwyn. Something clicked inside Lucian, like a flipped switch of blinding ferocity he had no idea he possessed. Animal to animal—predator against predator.

Same prey.

He took off, running at top speed into the forest, the forest he'd checked out several times during their stay here. Over small peaks, past palms and other trees he didn't recognize but scented. His awareness ratcheted up, he scented everything now, intensely, including the cat and the *veana*.

His blood jumped and pumped in his veins as he ran, as he slowed—as he spotted the cat through a stand of trees, running as he was running. It was like he was competing with this fur asshole for Bronwyn. Something his rational self would never do. He knew it and yet he couldn't stop it—stop himself.

The sounds of speed echoed in his ears—*whoosh*, *hiss*—and he took off again, running toward her, her scent—and the scent of his own blood.

The cat swerved in front of him, cutting him off, and Lucian reached out to grab it, haul it to the ground, but he missed, his hand grasping at air. He growled in defeat and the cat cried out in triumph as it got lost once again in the woods.

Lucian picked up speed—pure instinct now—leaping over a stream and heading down a hillside. Bronwyn was close; he could feel it, feel her. And her scent ... God, his mind and body were reeling from it.

Then, from overhead, the cat leaped from a rock and onto Lucian's back. Nails dug into his skin and he went down. But only for a second. With sudden fierce strength, he reached around, grabbed the animal, and tossed it off his back, his flesh ripped and bleeding and stinging like a motherfucker. But he didn't care, didn't slow. The thing went rolling away and Lucian prepared for another battle. Then he saw Bronwyn. Down in the gully, near the creak. She'd fallen over a thick root in the ground, and was on her hands and knees. Her bare ass exposed, his shirt nearly up to her neck, ripped apart by branches or whatever had barred her way as she'd tried to escape the animal.

Or him.

He was down the hill and on her in seconds, rolling her on to her back—initially out of protection, his eyes shifting every which way to search for the cat.

But it was gone.

That animal was gone.

The one that remained, however—the one that raged inside of Lucian wanted what he'd caught. Snarling down at her, he ripped the rest of his shirt off her and bared his fangs, ready to strike—ready to have her.

MINE. Panting with hunger and the need to claim his kill, Lucian hovered over her. *Mine,* he thought wildly. *Do it! Take her now!*

Breathing heavily, Bronwyn stared up at him, her eyes wide with fear and excitement and hunger. She licked her dry lips.

Fuck.

Oh, God ... Oh, shit. He shook his head, tried to clear his mind, force it to think, to process—to reason. He knew, understood what was at work here. The animal—whatever it was—had been sent here to push him forward, torment him, get him inside Bronwyn Kettler once and for all. With or without her consent.

But he wasn't the goddamn Breeding Male.

Not yet.

Panting and cursing, Lucian closed the fabric of his shirt as best he could to cover her, then pushed himself off of her.

For a moment, he sat there, his chest rising and lowering, in deep pain—his cock harder than it had ever been, his balls twin rocks of misery.

He heard her sit up beside him, the scent of arousal encapsulating them, making it nearly impossible to breathe.

He uttered a pained, "I'm sorry, Princess."

"I shouldn't have run," she said, her own pain evident in her raspy tone.

"I may be an asshole of epic proportion, but I'm no rapist."

"Oh, God, Lucian." Taking a deep breath, she said softly, "I wouldn't have resisted."

He turned to her, saw her cheeks flushed. "Don't say that."

"Why not? It's true." She shook her head miserably. "My body wanted it. Still does."

Her words tore at him, dug into his need to make her his. Every second, every moment they remained on this island was borrowed time.

"You know it and I know it," she said. "We're never getting out of here unless ... "

"Don't say it, goddamn it!" he begged harshly.

But she didn't have to. As they each took their next breath, the truth was carved in the rock before them.

No way out for the Breeding Male but to breed.

11

Bronwyn's blood pounded the beat of destruction and desperation inside her veins as she stared at the rock. But her blood also pounded for the one beside her, the one whose life force kept her mind clear and her body sated. He had sustained her—twice now—when she'd thought she would go mad from hunger. He was the *paven* she had desired since the first time she'd plunged her fangs into his skin when she'd come to the Roman brothers' house in SoHo.

As the heat of the sun abandoned the forest floor and the island was overtaken by clouds and stormy skies, Bronwyn knew they had lost the battle. Problem was, even though she desired Lucian, this wasn't how she wanted to surrender herself to him.

"Why does the Order want this?" she said out loud, more to herself, not expecting an answer. Almost not wanting one.

But Lucian spoke swiftly and with an almost eerie calm. "It's not the Order."

"Of course it is. Look at that." She gestured to words carved into the rock. "Only they can manifest their will in such a way."

Lucian's gaze was filled with regret. "It's Cruen."

At first she wasn't sure she'd heard him correctly. "The rogue member of the Order?"

He nodded. "He's ex-Order now, mastermind of the pre-morph of all Roman brothers, and the one who is clearly plotting our downfall."

His words sank in slowly, and she looked down at her hands. They were shaking. "But why?"

"He wants me morphed."

She looked up at him, but said nothing.

"He wants my Breeding Male gene to kick in." Lucian's pale eyes flashed with heat. "And if you and I have sex, it will."

Like a battering ram to the brain, everything became crystal clear. She saw her room in the Boston *credenti*, her office, her work—all the e-mails from that private client who had never revealed himself but had hired her to research Breeding Male lineage, Breeding Male descendants and their possible true mates. Her hands went to her face and she shook her head.

Lucian moved in closer, touched her hair. "What? What's wrong?" A low, fierce growl erupted from his throat. "Did that cat touch you, hurt you?"

Her eyes lifted to his, her head just kept shaking—she couldn't stop it. She was horrified. "This is because of me." Cruen was her private client—had to be. She found the Roman brothers for him. This male before her had risked himself, his future, his captivity for her hunger, and *she* had outed his genetic structure to the monster who wished to destroy him.

"Hey—"

She moved away from him, stood up. "Oh, God."

"Don't—"

"I started this!" she cried, turning and heading over to the rock that bore their fate. She couldn't tell him, couldn't tell him

93

she'd been the cause of all of this. First with her research, then with her blood.

"Come on, now." Lucian was already behind her. "Don't start whipping yourself over something that cannot be changed." He took her shoulders and turned her to face him. "Self-flagellation's not your style, Princess."

"Neither is trapping *pavens* into sleeping with me," she said with disgust.

He grinned at her then. It wasn't a happy a grin, but pointed. "There is no one less in need of trapping a *paven* into sleeping with her than you. Get serious."

She sighed. "You know what I mean, Luca."

He cocked his head to the side, and she realized that she'd called him by his nickname, what his brothers called him—his intimates. Something she was not. But the look on his face could not hide his feeling.

He liked it.

"Make no mistake, Princess," he said, brushing a strand of long, dark hair off her neck. "It would be an honor for any male to slide slowly between your thighs."

She didn't even attempt to scold him for his crass words, because inside her, just below her belly, a shiver of lust had been ignited.

"If we want off this reality," he was saying, "there's only one way."

"No," she whispered, shaking her head. "I won't do that to you." She wouldn't change him, be responsible for bringing on the animal, taking away his cutting humor and wicked gaze— any more than she already had.

"It is not your choice, *Veana*," he said at last.

"Of course it is. I'm not sending you into Breeding Male status before your time—and for God's sake, I'm mated to

94

another." Her mind kicked; her gut too. She hadn't thought of it, of him, since Lucian had landed on the island. Synjon. The one she supposedly belonged to. Her friend, her savior, had been buried under the weight of Lucian Roman in her mind, and she should be ashamed.

She wanted to pull away from Lucian, but she didn't—couldn't. There was something so addictive about being in his space, his eyes on her, his chest in full view, his mouth close enough to imagine it on hers, the taste of him consuming her. Around them, the woods scented of earth and coming rain, and between them the air was electric.

"No one can break in or out of this reality," Lucian said, an edge to his tone now. He placed his hand on the rock and cursed into the empty woods. "How long shall we wait? How long before the cat comes back and provokes us again? How long before either one of us is so hungry—"

"I can wait!" she said quickly, too quickly.

His eyes flared with raw, aching hunger. "I don't know if I can."

She died a little at the look of desperation in his eyes. "For my blood?"

He closed his eyes and sighed. "God, for your blood, your body—the need is the same, the desire is the same." His lids flipped up and he took in her features, one by one. "You know how I've been affected—infected—with you, with your scent. I won't be able to control myself forever." He stepped toward her, closing the gap between them, thrusting her back against the flat surface of the rock. "At least now," he whispered, eyes on her mouth, "this moment, today, I can give you something close to gentle."

Tears sprang to her eyes. She hated them, hated herself in that moment. She was about to destroy a *paven* she cared for more than she ever wanted to admit. "I will be your downfall."

95

He reached out, brushed his thumb across her bottom lip. "Stop."

"You'll never forgive me." *I'll never forgive myself*.

He stared at her then, his chin down, his eyes clinging to hers. Then his lips tipped up at the corners and he chuckled softly.

"What?" she asked.

"Do you really care? Do you really care if I forgive you, Princess?"

Something pinged inside her, where her heart should be, where her heart should beat—but she forced a smile in return. Not because she was agreeing with him, but because if she didn't, he'd know—just by the look on her face—that his opinion mattered to her, that there was nothing she wanted more in that moment than his forgiveness for ruining his existence.

Nothing, that is, but his touch.

She reached up, took a bit of his white hair in her hand, and played with it between her fingers. So soft, nothing like him. His hair fell against his tight jaw, his slash of a cheek, and she touched those too. She knew in that moment what it felt like to want to own another being, declare them as yours.

Lucian's hand came up and covered hers, as his eyes implored her with their ferocity. "I feel the animal within me emerging, Princess. It's raw and uncontained, but it wants to please you. If we wait ... " His chin dropped, his voice too. "I cannot hurt you, do you understand?"

Did she understand? God, she wanted to weep with her understanding. He was about to claim an out-of- control life, about to set free the animal he feared so desperately—that she feared so desperately.

And yet what was the choice? In the moment, this impossible moment, what was their choice?

None.

But each other.

Her eyes pinned to his, she fought back the anxiety within her and slowly opened the ripped shirt that barely covered what was left of her modesty, let it fall from her shoulders onto the ground.

A rush of air picked up around her and hit her skin, but it was nothing to the sound that exited Lucian's throat or the feeling of his predatory gaze. His eyes moved over her skin, taking in each inch, each curve of shoulder, each slope of breast, each nipple that hardened in the cool forest breeze. The groan of lust escaped his full lips then and he looked up into her eyes.

"I fear I will die before I've had the chance to live," he said, the scent of his heated blood entering her nostrils.

She licked her lips, hunger assaulting her, but anxiety staying with her. "Will you go slow?" she asked, shivering in the cool air—or was it the anticipation of his touch?

He nodded. She was glad he knew what she was, how her body had never taken a *paven* into it. And as he said the words "As slow as you want," she released the held breath inside her lungs.

"And will you kiss me before you do it?" she whispered, a bit more urgently this time. "So I know you're with me, really with me."

"I will kiss you before, during, and after," he promised, his arm going around her waist. "For as long as we are together, my mouth will belong to you just as yours will belong to me."

For weeks, months, Bronwyn had wondered what this *paven* would feel like, what his skin would feel like, smell like, taste like—what it would be like to look into his eyes as he kissed her, as he spread her legs apart with his thighs and sank deep inside her.

Now she would know all.

Her breath caught in her throat at the thought—and at the truth of why she would have her fantasy realized. She hadn't wanted it this way—not out of necessity. She'd wanted him to want her, God—to really care for her. She'd wanted him to take her, make her feel what he felt; his rage, his lust, his sadness—his endless sadness.

She'd wanted to be the one to kill that sadness within him, not add to it.

"Stop thinking." His lips brushed against hers. "Stop thinking and kiss me."

"Oh, Lucian," she uttered.

But her regret was lost as his mouth claimed her hard and possessive, his body too—melting so tightly against her now that she could feel the waves of his chest muscles, the curve of his lean stomach and his thick, marble-hard shaft at her belly.

God, she wanted to see it, see him, fully naked and aroused. In her mind as his mouth moved sensually against hers, she imagined what his cock would look like, how it would feel inside of her. So many nights in her bed, she'd wondered if it would be like its master: hard, experienced, demanding.

Lucian's hands gripped her back as he suckled her lower lip, then moved down over the curve of her buttocks.

Yes, she'd bet it would be.

He captured her mouth again, thrusting his tongue inside and she met him, tasting him as she arched her back and pressed her lower half closer, grinding herself against him. He tightened his grip on her buttocks, his fingers spreading to take all of her as he angled his kiss. Breathing was near impossible now, but it didn't matter. She had his air to take into her lungs, just as she took his tongue into her mouth and played with the tip. He tasted like the forest somehow, fresh and earthy and cool, and it was intoxicating.

Granted, she wasn't experienced, had kissed only a few *paven* in her fifty years, but she had the imagination and fantasy life of a courtesan. For the past several years, her nights had been consumed with mental images of skin and hands and tongues and fangs in places that only a true mate should know. But over the past several weeks, there had been a face attached to those images, a face between her trembling thighs.

And then that face, that mouth, tore away from her and stared down at her. He looked enraged, desperate, starving, sexual, as his eyes traveled down her body, his breathing so heavy she felt a trace of concern.

"What?" she uttered hoarsely. "What's wrong?"

"Look at you. I want to consume you. Feed off every inch of you and leave nothing." His gaze flared again. "God, look at your breasts, your nipples."

She glanced down, her eyes searching for what he saw, what made him so hungry. Her breasts were as they had always been—large, full—but her nipples, her nipples were the hardest she'd ever seen them, and so dark, the color of wine.

"Mine," Lucian growled, releasing her buttock and reaching around to cup one heavy globe, feel its weight in his hand.

Bronwyn sucked air through her teeth, then moaned. His skin on hers felt so good, so right—just as she'd imagined it. He took what he wanted, reveled in it, placed one turgid peak between his fingers and rolled it gently, then squeezed.

Bronwyn cried out, the sound echoing off the trees. Not from pain, never from pain. But from pleasure, the sweet pleasure streaking down her chest to her very core.

"And this one," he uttered darkly as he dropped his head and licked her, swiped his tongue across one stiff peak.

Moaning like an injured animal, Bronwyn felt her cunt weep.

It wept for him, for her—for its emptiness, for the longing it had to be filled.

"Damn you, Princess," he uttered, his face a mask of desperation. "I've wanted this for so long, wanted you forever, it seems. My mouth on you, every wet, delicious inch. My cock against your belly, then up inside your tight, hot pussy." His mouth covered her nipple and he suckled the peak deep inside again.

The sensation nearly blinded her, made her legs quiver, made her core flare and shake. And God, where was the air? There was no way to breathe. No way to cool herself, control herself. Lucian's control was slipping too, but hers was already gone, and she grinded her wet core against him, telling him in the only words she had that she wanted his hard shaft inside her now before it was too late—before they both died from the wanting of it all.

For weeks, since Lucian had fed her his blood, Bronwyn hadn't been able to come—no matter how long, how intensely she'd touched herself. And as the heat built inside her now, just from his mouth on hers, from her hips working his cock, she wondered with hope and excitement if she'd finally have her ending.

And then his teeth nipped at her, and she wondered if the earth would shatter inside her now, while she watched him bite and suck and lick her nipples like a hungry *balas*.

His hand, the one that had been clutching her backside began to move, down, through the crease of her buttocks. "Are you ready for me?" he hissed against her wet nipple, making her shiver. "You'd better be ready. You'd better be so wet I'll be sliding all over the place—my fingers, my cock." When he reached her, the opening to her, he groaned and lifted his eyes to meet her. "Ahh ... That's my good little princess." He circled her entrance slowly with his finger. "I'll slide right in. And I think I'm going to right now."

Bronwyn gasped as his finger plunged deep inside her.

"You're so tight," he said, coming up and taking her mouth under his again as he thrust his finger in and out, working her cunt gently until his hand felt slick against the insides of her thighs. "I swear to God I don't want to hurt you, but I may. Fuck, I just may."

She shook her head, the blood in her veins pounding and pleading. "No, stop talking and kiss me."

He chuckled against her mouth, then kissed her fiercely. It was the first time Bronwyn had ever heard Lucian Roman, the terrifying angel, display anything close to genuine happiness. It brought tears to her eyes as they continued to kiss—a clash of tongues and teeth and demands as he eased another finger deep inside her wet core.

The mad, uncontained heat that was building, rocking her foundation—the heat that was quaking like a world upset and upside down—now began to plead for release. Her growing climax was pleading with her to beg him. She needed him—the real him, the hard and strong shaft that mocked her belly—inside where he belonged, where he could take her and die happy.

"Lucian, please ... " she uttered as his fingers thrust into her, stretching her, filling her, all while his mouth kept its promise to kiss her, before, during, and after.

After.

God, no. *Don't even think about after, about what that means—what that will look like.*

"I can't stop," Lucian growled, his lids at half-mast, his fangs fully descended over his lower lip. "Don't ask that of me now. It would be torture."

She lapped at his tongue, his fangs. "I don't want you to stop. Ever." She cupped his face as he kissed her and she kissed him, angry, repentant, all-consuming. "I want you inside me right now—inside me always. You belong there, Lucian. It's not what we planned, or what's right. But you belong in me."

"Fuck it!" His growl was fierce as he reached around and grabbed her buttocks, then lifted her up.

Bronwyn wrapped her shaking legs around his waist, but her mouth continued to work his. She felt him between her thighs, the head of his shaft at the entrance to her cunt, playing, kicking against the wet mound of her pussy.

"Oh, God, yes," she cried, grinding against him in utter submission, total abandon. "If we're going to lose this war, let's lose it good and hard."

With a cry of hunger, starvation, he let her fall nine inches, straight down on his cock, utterly impaling her. Bronwyn gasped, her limbs instantly stiffening as she fought the deep sensation of pain and pleasure. It ran up her belly, to her breasts, up her neck, deep in her throat, and caught there, causing tears to form. For several seconds she just breathed, and then, like a warm blanket of comfort and love, the heat, the sweet delectable heat, began to move and coat her insides.

"Oh, there it is," Lucian whispered against her mouth, his tongue lapping at hers.

"Don't go slow," she called out as she started to move, her legs tightening around his waist now as she rocked her hips back and forth. "I know what I said, what I asked for, but it was before I knew ... before I knew what you would feel like in me!"

Lucian took a few steps, found his balance, gripped her tight, and anchored her against the rock. "And what do I feel like, Princess?"

"Perfection," she uttered. "And disaster. And everything in between."

He grinned. "Yeah, you too."

Her arms wrapped around his neck and she squeezed her legs and drove her hips upward. The buildup, the desire they'd shared, yet tried to hide for so long, exploded, and they just wanted to screw.

Lucian slammed into her, making her moan and shake her head against the beauty of it—the painful, pleasure-filled beauty of it. He was inside her, Lucian—finally.

"This is it!" he called out fiercely, his hands gripping her buttocks as he drew out slowly, then slid back in. Over and over he did this, relentlessly pressing against the walls of her cunt, driving her insane, making her shake. "The only time I'll ever be inside you. Goddamn it!" His mouth covered hers and he kissed her hard and deep and with as much meaning as he could manage. "I'm going to make you explode, Princess." He bit her upper lip and swiped at the blood with his tongue. "I'm going to stay in your tight little cunt until you come over and over again."

He crushed her to him, and the slap of hot, wet flesh was all that was heard for a moment. "You won't forget," he uttered. "You won't forget."

Her mind reeled as her body quaked. She was on the verge of orgasm—her first since she'd taken his blood. She wouldn't forget. Ever. But did that mean he would? Oh, God . . . Would he forget her? . . . Would he forget this?

Her fingers pressed into his neck and she wanted to bite him. When she came, she was going to bite him.

He pumped his hips into her, slapping against her—hard, delicious wet slaps. "It's done, Princess. I fucking hate it. When we come, it's done. I'm done. You'll never see me again."

Anger rocked her insides, warring with the coming climax. She reached up and dug her nails into his skull, her eyes locked with his and she cried, "Maybe I won't come, then."

"No!" He held on to her ass with one hand, slid the other between them. "You're coming hard and long and loud. I'll see to it. Right now, I'll see to it."

His fingers found her core, slipping through her wet lips to her swollen clit. The second his thumb brushed over the hard bud, Bronwyn bucked. Oh, God ... oh, God ... His hands ... masculine and unyielding. She was giving herself over to him now as he pumped slowly inside her, as his finger worked her clit like it was the sweetest gift she could give him.

Breathing hard, her mind went blank, completely lost to the hot tremors climbing up from her feet, to her ankles, legs, thighs.

"Oh, God, Lucian," she uttered as her hips pumped and pumped against his hand, his thick cock tucked so tightly inside her. "No," she begged, "Not yet. Not until you ... "

Her words died as her body keened, then exploded, shattered. Madly, she bucked her hips, moaning, crying, shaking her head against the beauty of what a climax truly felt like under this *paven*'s touch and power.

Clenching his teeth, Lucian held her as she quaked and quivered, all the way until she trembled with the last waves of orgasm. Almost snarling at her, he declared, "That was your first, Princess. Now hold on, second one's coming up."

Her arms wrapped around his neck, gripped him tighter, even though she felt weak as a *balas*. But even as her insides clenched with the end of her orgasm, they shimmered with the burgeoning need for another.

His mouth covered hers again, and as they kissed and bit at each other, Lucian held her buttocks in his hands and guided himself in and out of her drenched core in a steady rhythm.

Looking at him, into his eyes, Bronwyn felt something inside herself break. Not in body, but in feeling. She didn't have a beating heart, so it couldn't be that.

Could it?

"Wider," Lucian whispered into her mouth as the speed of his thrusts intensified and sweat broke on his brow. "Open wider for me."

The broken thing inside her squeezed, and she panicked. She left his mouth and found his ear. "Don't come," she said stupidly as her skin tightened and her muscles began to convulse. "I don't want you to leave me!"

Oh, God. Was that it?

"Too late, Princess," he uttered savagely. "You're coming again, and I'm on my way."

He battered her hard and she writhed against him, the heat tormenting her again, the fire growing out of control. His hands squeezed her buttocks, his fingers moved down, moved purposefully down and between the crease, until one long digit eased gently into a narrow passageway where she never thought a *paven* should go.

And yet it was her ruin.

Her breath jumped, her body spasmed uncontrollably. Bucking against his cock, against his gentle hand, she cried out as climax slammed her over and over in its brilliant, glorious waves. Without thought, she turned into him and licked the inside curve of his ear, then bit down on his lobe.

Mine.

Lucian was too far gone now. All that came from his throat were male cries of torment and ecstasy, and all that came from his body were four last savage thrusts into her tight cunt.

In the final moments, the final thrusts, final pulses of release, he held her so tightly she could barely breathe, his mouth finding hers.

Before, during, and after.

One final kiss, as he'd promised.

12

Lucian sat with his back against the rock, Bronwyn curled in his arms like the sweetest fucking thing in the world. It was a momentary blip of time, of bliss, and he couldn't help wondering, as the wind blew cool air around them and the skies threatened rain, if he would be able to remember it when his soul died—if he would be able to remember her.

He leaned down and kissed the top of her head, breathed in the scent of her hair. This wasn't him, this tender *paven*, and yet it was—at his core. Clinging to each other in Cruen's reality felt like the last moments before death; you did things and said things you wouldn't have the balls to do and say if your life was guaranteed. For one second of time, Lucian was almost thankful for his fate because it had called on him to recognize the true feeling of affection for a female.

He drew in air, quick and hungry, as she stirred against him, as she turned her head into his chest and nuzzled him.

"How long?" she whispered, her breath warm on his skin.

"I don't know," he said.

"Do you feel different?"

Yes. But not in the way she meant. "Not yet."

She kissed his collarbone, and he wanted to tell her to stop, tell her to stand up and run—get the fuck away from him before it was too late.

And then she tipped her head back and looked at him, her face flushed, her lips swollen from his kisses.

Fucking *veana*. Didn't she know what she was courting here? . . .

"He's won, Luca," she uttered, her dark eyes the color of wet bark.

Lucian's nostrils flared and his fangs dropped. "Only round one, Princess." Cruen would suffer greatly for this—all of this. Lucian would strip him—not only of his life, but of his skin, inch by inch. "It will be his only victory, I swear it."

She reached around him then and cupped his neck, drew him down to her, to her mouth. God, her sweet, perfect mouth. A wet, warm sheath, not unlike her cunt, that he could get lost in for days. He kissed her, a kiss so filled with desire and despair he nearly cried out in her mouth. But the sudden cry that was wrenched from him, the debilitating cry that echoed throughout the island, had nothing to do with emotion and everything to do with the bone-shattering pain that had just slammed into his gut.

"Fuck!" He tore away from her mouth. He was on fire—but from the inside. Everything burned—his bones, his organs, even his teeth.

Bronwyn scrambled off of him, her eyes wide and fearful, her hands trying to find an inch of skin that wouldn't hurt at her touch. "Oh, God, no . . . not yet . . . "

Doubled over, Lucian howled like a wolf caught in a steel trap. Every inch of him felt as though it were being crushed beneath a semi truck, every happy feeling he'd had from a moment ago bled right out of him.

"What can I do?" Bronwyn begged beside him, her voice panicked, terror-filled. "Lucian. What can I do? Please tell me!"

"It's coming," he uttered, shaking his head—against the pain, against the future. "He's coming. For me. Nothing to be done . . . " It was the pain of the world on his shoulders, the pain of the world reviling his presence—the pain of an animal that was dangerous and sick in the mind and needed to be put down before it bit again.

The only reason he didn't end it now, stab himself in the neck or smash his brains in with the very rock that had ended his life with its cruel message was that he'd meant what he told Bronwyn—animal or not, he would get revenge on Cruen.

"Let me help you," she begged him, her arms wrapping around his shoulders. "Can I hold you? Anything, please!"

He pushed her off. "No. Get away!" The pain was too great, as was the fear of what he could do to her. Fuck, her scent was already stronger in his nostrils.

Where was Cruen? Why hadn't he grabbed his white ass out of this reality and got to work on whatever scheme he had planned?

Bronwyn hovered over him, unwilling to heed his words. "Lucian, please!"

"Swear to me," he grunted over a new wave of pulverizing pain. He felt it . . . he felt it now . . .

"What?" she asked, tears in her voice.

He looked up, blinked through the endless suffering, saw the grief and guilt in her eyes for the *paven* he was barely holding on to.

"As soon as we arrive," he uttered, his fangs . . . they were moving inside his mouth . . . growing . . . expanding.

"Arrive? Arrive where?"

The rain began. Tiny drops on his back. But they were

109

anything but soft and soothing. It was like shards of glass entering his skin, over and over.

"Promise me you'll run!" he cried, cursing—at the pain, at Cruen, at the one who bore him and the one who'd made him.

"I don't understand." She shook her head violently, trying to get close to him, but he kept moving away.

"When we get ... out of here ... Promise me you'll run away!"

"From you?" The rain started falling heavier now. "No! Lucian, you're not like that! I won't believe—"

His eyes flipped up and she gasped at his face. "Oh, God, you have the brands. On your face. Circles, empty."

"The Breeding Male!" His voice. It had changed, an animalistic howl echoing through his brain.

He saw Bronwyn reaching out to touch him; then her eyes went wide and she disappeared.

"Princess!" he uttered hoarsely, then collapsed on the ground, his call met only by the sound of rain hitting the forest floor before he too was flashed away.

Synjon Wise stood before the Order and demanded payment of another kind for his years of service. "You owe me."

"Take great care, Lieutenant," the white-haired *veana* warned him, her lip drifting upward to display a fine pair of bloodred fangs.

"Snarl all you want to, love." He walked forward, didn't stop until he hit table. "My life has belonged to you for decades—"

Her gaze was cold. "That was your choice, not ours."

Since Cruen's defection, it seemed that this *veana* was now in charge. And while she played the game in a far fairer fashion than her predecessor, she was anything but sympathetic or trustworthy.

Hell, none of them were.

"I find it odd," he began, his gaze moving down the table of wine-colored robes, black circle brands, and ancient flesh, "that with all your great wisdom and power, you cannot find one Pureblood *veana*."

"It is unfortunate," she agreed, looking thoughtful. "Cruen's powers have been underestimated by the Order before. We cannot let this continue unchecked."

The members nodded in unison.

She fixed her dark eyes on him. "You will make sure that it does not."

Syn chuckled. "I came here for your assistance, not the other way round."

She joined him in laughter, as did a few of the others. Not surprisingly, it was far from a joyful sound, but something one would hear before the blows of death were upon him.

Which meant, Syn realized quickly, that these sodding bastards were going to try to work out a deal with him. They were going to barter his mate's safety. And if he didn't pucker up and kiss arse, he was either screwed or on his own.

"Cruen has taken something that belongs to me," he said brusquely. "And I want it back."

More than something that belonged to him really. Bron was the closest thing he would ever have to a friend, a real love of the heart, and he would protect and care for her with everything that was in him—for as long as life remained in him.

The *veana* placed her hands on the long table before her and asked in a soft, curious voice, "Does she belong to you?"

A growl shot from Syn's throat, and he leaned on that very same table in a brazen, didn't-give-a-shite-about-his-own-life sort of way. "Careful, *Veana*."

Her brow lifted. "After what has transpired this eve, I am

beginning to have doubts about your union with Mistress Kettler."

Heat started in Synjon's chest and starting churning until it spiraled out of control. What was it they thought they knew? Whatever suspicions they had, he dared not show uncertainty. "She bears my mark. She belongs to me."

"I hope so," said the *veana*. "For everyone's sake, I hope so."

Synjon leaned in, feeling the magical weight, the supreme power of the other Order members surrounding her. "Make no mistake, love. I will defect right along with your previous leader if you dare to question or interfere," he returned with venom. "Do you have another like me in your political arsenal? One who will kiss, kill, or capture at the drop of a hat?" He raised both black brows. "I doubt it."

Up and down the table came hisses and low, angry chatter, but the *veana* in charge sat back. She spread out her arms and called for calm. "It would be grave to lose you, Lieutenant."

He sniffed and stepped back.

"But." The word jumped in the air between them and remained. She arched one white brow. "We would manage."

His snarl cut into the desert heat of their reality. "Send me back."

"Not yet," the dark-skinned *paven* beside her interrupted. "We have a job for you."

"You've got to be kidding!"

"We do not 'kid,' as you well know, Lieutenant."

He shook his head in disgust. "You arrogant sons of bitches. Oh"—Syn pointed at the white-haired *veana*—"that goes for the daughters too."

She barely registered his insult. "We want Cruen."

"You and me both," he uttered. "And if I bring him to you?"

She took a breath, touched her face thoughtfully. "Well, then. Bronwyn Kettler, as far as we and any who are controlled by us are concerned, belongs to you."

He fixed her with a challenging stare. "Who the hell else would she belong to?"

"Lucian Roman, of course." Before he had a chance to reply, she lifted her hand and waved it over him. "Now, get to work."

Cruen had felt the surge of power even from the depths of his laboratory belowground. *The Breeding Male.* It was as if a switch had been turned on, as if the world had colored and beamed, and he instantly walked away from the table and the blood samples he was testing and went over to the four caged ones along the wall.

With his eyes closed and the many strings of his mind unleashed, he locked on to the pair of new lovers in his reality and summoned them home. To him. To their new life.

The fifth cage was ready for Bronwyn Kettler, just as the female was ready for Lucian Roman.

The chants that flowed from his lips were thoughtful and pure, and they needed to be. It was no easy feat summoning Purebloods to an interior location, and even more difficult the deeper into the ground you attempted to call them.

But Cruen let the dark magic flow through him, the darkest of blood magic—it was his greatest ally, and after several moments, he felt the floor below him shift and shudder like an earthquake. He grinned at the surge of power inside and beneath him, then chuckled as the Pureblood tester rats before him held tight to their metal bars and cried out in fear.

His eyes flipped open. He inhaled sharply, expecting to see the shocked pair in the empty cage on the far wall, the large cage—big enough for two. But there was nothing, no one. Fear scuttled through Cruen as the chemical scents of the laboratory suddenly grew thicker, harsher in his nostrils.

He moved to the cage, empty—*EMPTY*!

A growl escaped his throat, wicked and unearthly. Where were they? Where were his two prize rats?

He slammed his eyes shut. He could not lose them. Lucian's seed was vital to his plan, and the Kettler *veana*—she had all the genetic information he needed inside that thick brain of hers. He would try again. Then again, if necessary.

Heat suffused his limbs, his organs, and he reached out to the reality and tried to lock on to their scent, their heat patterns—anything . . .

Fuck!

He growled again, low and deadly. How was this possible? How was it that he felt nothing? It was as if they never were—had never existed—as if they'd been erased from the planet.

He slammed his eyes open and called to his eldest son.

The Beast flashed to his side in under a second, towering over his father like the Pureblood son of a Breeding Male that he was. "You have need of me, Cruen."

Shaking with rage, with bewilderment—with failure—Cruen slammed the bars of the empty cage and commanded, "Take Lycos and find them."

The Beast's diamond eyes flickered with confusion. "They are not here?"

"Do you see them here, Erion?" Cruen said caustically. "My magic has been severed."

As the captive ones behind him fell silent, listening, curious, Erion's voice bordered on wonder. "Someone interferes."

"Someone dares to play with me," Cruen said viciously, pushing away from the cage and quickly heading for his worktable. There, he picked up a syringe. "A dangerous, foolish game."

"Who would make such a grave mistake?" Erion asked.

Cruen cocked his head, pulled back the plunger on the syringe, and said with deadly calm, "I believe I may have the answer."

Erion lifted his chin. "Shall I send Helo to execute this hindrance?"

Cruen's anger turned thoughtful for a moment. "No. The interloper will pay, but not in death." He flicked his chin at his son. "Go now. Time is of the essence. The female will be ready to breed in four days' time. We must have her male ready."

Cruen watched Erion flash, then stalked over to a sleeping Pureblood in one of the smaller cages. Without care or sympathy, he thrust the needle into the *paven*'s throat and withdrew another vial of blood.

Bronwyn landed naked and cold on the only drift of remaining snow outside a massive villa. It took her a second or two to get her bearings, to question where she was and why—and to realize just how exposed she was. It was day and the sun was bright in the blue sky above her, but still she shivered. Not from the cold, but from fear. Lucian was no doubt following her here— wherever this was—at least, that's what she hoped, and as he was the Breeding Male now she wondered plaintively if he was also morphed. In her genetic studies, there had never been a clear answer on the morphing process for Breeding Males— some did, some didn't. But she didn't want to risk it with this one. Unlike Meta for females, morphed *pavens* couldn't survive in the sun, and if Lucian had undergone the change, the moment he hit the wet spring earth, his flesh would burn.

Completely unconcerned with her nude frame, Bronwyn jumped up and looked for something, anything to cover him. All she needed was a moment, to cover his skin before she could flash them closer to the villa, closer to shelter. But like the island, there was only plant life to be had: leaves and bark, rocks and olive trees. Her gaze slid up to the villa, the massive castle on the hill with its tentacles of vines on the exterior walls, and the windows that looked like eyes. Could she flash there, beg the occupants for a blanket or something and get back before Lucian arrived? Did she want to risk it?

The popping sound that had accompanied her entrance into this world sounded once again, and when she saw Lucian appear nude and writhing in pain on the ground a few feet away, she ran at him and covered him with her body, tried to use her nude frame as a shield. But the *paven* was fast. In under a second, before she could get to him, he ratcheted up to a standing position and shot out his arms.

For one brief moment, Bronwyn sighed with relief. His skin was the same, beautiful, hard angles, jutting manhood. No sun had harmed him. He wasn't morphed—and she wondered if he ever would be.

But then he opened his mouth and hissed at her and she abandoned all thought, all the questions in her mind.

His eyes huge, his fangs extended, he whispered in an ugly, animal-like voice, "Another step, Princess, and you will face your truest fear—a Breeding Male's pleasure."

Lucian felt the innocence in her expression, perhaps even the beginnings of love, die before his eyes. But there was nothing for it. He was already halfway to hell, his mind shifting in and out of consciousness, his senses looking, searching for prey—female prey as the drive to breed fought for control of his mind.

He hadn't completely turned Breeding Male yet, but the change was coming, and coming fast . . .

As her gaze moved over him, it took all of his remaining self-control to keep himself from running down the hill and into the woods—away from her and in search of more female flesh.

Goddamn, he was like a mad wolf.

Gripping his belly, his hands clenching and unclenching like claws, he uttered a terse, "I need to get up there, to my brother's."

"That's your brother's house?"

He nodded. "And you need to get to your mate."

Her expression of sadness, of fear, of anxiety fell even further. "I can help. Let me flash you there."

"No."

"Lucian—"

"You can't touch me, damn it!" he snapped, backing up. "Fuck, I've got to get out."

She stepped toward him. "What do you mean?"

Why couldn't she get this? Why did she continue to come at him like she was going to be the one *veana* in the world to tame the wild beast that raged inside of him?

"I've got to get away," he told her, his skin growing thicker, his muscles getting tenser. "Before I can't control myself any longer. Before this thing, this gene—whatever it is—takes over my sanity completely, and I find and rape any female who has the misfortune to cross my path."

She shook her head, refusing to listen. "You won't."

His eyes drilled into her. "You know I will. You of all people know that."

In his one hundred and twenty-five years, Lucian had felt deep hunger. He'd felt uncontrolled lust. He'd felt impending insanity. He'd felt sorrow and hopelessness come over him in thick waves of fog. But never in his life had he felt them all at once. This wasn't morpho—he was never going through morpho. This was the pain and agony of changing into the Breeding Male.

117

His gaze dropped, moved over every inch of her exposed skin. Through gritted teeth, he uttered, "Flash up to the house. Tell my brother—tell the guards—to come and fetch me." A low, brutal sound exited his throat. "I fucking despise that anyone must see you this way. But better them than me."

Another lightning rod of pain, just like the one on the island, ricocheted through him. His nostrils flared, his fangs dropped. Pure hell on earth.

He caught her looking at him. Fear, pity, and something else in her eyes—something he didn't want to see ever again. And yet he knew he would, over and over.

A trace of disgust.

His gaze shifted up, past her head. He spotted something, someone, perhaps a guard at the top of the hill. He shouted over the pain ringing in his ears, "Hey! We need some help! Get down here."

But as the male drew closer, Lucian saw that it wasn't an Impure guard. This *paven* was tall, broad, and moved like a bull charging a canvas of red.

"Lucian, that's not—"

The *paven* flashed directly in front of them. Lucian heard Bronwyn gasp and utter the words, "It's him. The one who took me. The *gemino*," before he lost his mind altogether. Suddenly, the Beast reached out for him, tried to get his arm and neck, but Lucian slammed him in the face with his fist. The Beast dropped back, his nose dripping blood, his eyes flashing hate.

The intense amount of new and unexpected strength Lucian possessed surprised him, and he didn't block himself when the *paven* came at him again.

"No!" Bronwyn screamed, grabbing Lucian out of the imposter's reach and thrusting him against her.

She flashed them away just as the *paven* called out, "Run and hide, little mice. But I will find you."

In the villa library, Nicholas was hard at work on his laptop. Pissed off at the contact who had been a no-show the night before, he was trying everything he could think of, contacting everyone he knew, to get this guy back on his radar.

He needed answers. Ladd needed answers.

As if his thoughts could actually summon the boy, Ladd Letts, his seven-year-old nephew and ward came running into the room, his eyes wild with excitement, his white hair disheveled as if he'd been at play. The boy had no idea that the mother he'd loved and lost a few weeks ago to the deadly hands of ex-Impure leader Ethan Dare had once unknowingly given herself to Nicholas's twin brother—and Nicky planned to keep it that way for as long as possible.

Kate was following at a brisk pace behind Ladd, but her beautiful face and dark eyes lacked the enthusiasm of the boy. Her expression was heavy with concern.

"We saw them," she said, her tone just as agitated as her expression.

Nicholas put down his BlackBerry and asked, "Who, sweetest one?"

She shook her head, started rambling. "At least I think it was them."

"Oh, it was them!" On the couch now, Ladd jumped up and down, a big grin on his face. "They had no clothes on, Uncle Nicky. It was weird and kinda funny."

Turning from the boy, Nicholas raised his brow at his true mate. "Have the peasants in town been bedding in our hedgerows again?"

Kate lifted her gaze, shook her head. "It was Lucian and Bronwyn."

Jumping to his feet, Nicholas demanded, "What! Where are they now?"

"Gone," Kate began. "I told you, they flashed away. I don't know who it was, but another male approached them, and after a moment they flashed."

Nicholas's words were grave. "Another male?"

"He flashed too."

The toxic scent of fear moved slowly into his nostrils. "Where are the guards now?"

"Two of them were knocked unconscious; the others are checking the perimeter of the grounds," Kate told him, her eyes and expression stronger now. "They're looking for Bronwyn and Lucian—looking for anyone who would want to do them or us harm. But they did try to catch whoever it was. They were nearly on his tail when the threesome flashed."

Nicholas didn't wait for anything else. He crossed the room and left the library. The first servant he encountered he stopped and demanded, "Find Alexander Roman and bring him to me immediately; then round up the guards and send all but four to us."

The servant bowed and was off.

When Nicholas returned to the library, he went straight to Kate and Ladd and asked in the calmest voice he could manage, "Now, tell me again exactly what you saw."

13

In the split second of her flash, Bronwyn had been forced to pick a location that would be safe and familiar to them both. Boston was out—couldn't risk her family knowing the truth or tattling to the Order. Middle of the ocean—been there, done that. That left SoHo—the house where she and Lucian had met, where it had all begun just a few months ago.

They landed near the back door, Bronwyn's body still covering his as they pushed their way inside. Darkness enclosed them in its comforting way, the electric shades already dropped on every window in the entryway.

"Why did you do that?" Lucian muttered, stumbling inside, moving through the kitchen.

Bronwyn followed him, completely unaware—or was it uncaring—about their nudity now. "Do what?"

"Flash me out?" he barked, his voice hoarse. "Why the hell did you do that?"

"Is this a trick question?"

"No."

"I don't get you."

"You should've left me there, goddamn it!" He kept moving, past the living quarters and into the massive entryway, stopping only when he hit the stairs going up to the second floor. He gripped the banister, his knuckles white as he breathed heavily—too heavily.

Bronwyn hesitated to go near him. He seemed so unstable, talking nonsense—so on the verge of a change she'd never heard about or witnessed. But why was this change so different from morpho or meta? she wondered. Why was it so drawn out and painful?

In the near darkness, the only light coming from a pale yellow motion detector above them, Bronwyn watched Lucian cling to the banister, his bloodshot eyes lifting to hers, his voice gravel-like and devoid of calm emotion. "That 'brother' of mine, the *gemino*—he would've taken me back to the mothership."

Bronwyn felt the blood drain from her face. "You're saying you wanted to get caught?"

"That's exactly what I'm saying."

She shook her head. "You're insane."

"Yes! Glad you're finally getting that fact, Princess. Christ!" His hand slid from the wood banister and wrapped around his waist as he doubled over in pain. "I should just off myself right now."

Bronwyn felt so helpless standing there in the middle of the entryway. She wanted to run to him, pity him, comfort him—but Lucian didn't respond to that. Or wouldn't. She forced down her own agony at seeing his suffering and fixed him with a glare. "If getting back at Cruen is your goal, then offing yourself—as you put it—defeats the purpose, I believe."

His gaze flickered up.

She continued. "Cruen wants his mild-mannered undead prize, undead."

The grim line of his mouth twitched. "Smart-ass."

"Yes, well, it takes a smart-ass to recognize an asshole."

In that moment, that brief moment in the darkened entryway, she saw him—just a hint of the bad boy, the smart-mouthed *paven* who had always teased her to the point of exhaustion. Her heart ached for that *paven*, her body too . . .

"My brothers," he began through gritted teeth. "They'll come here."

"Good. We need all the help we can get."

He pushed away from the railing and hobbled past her, over to a window. With great effort, he yanked down one beautiful tapestry window covering and tossed it at her. "Here. Cover yourself."

"Embarrassed by me, *Paven*?" she said, wrapping the fabric around her shoulders, grateful for the warmth even as she chided him.

"I wish it were that." Pale and exhausted, he dropped right where he stood, his backside hitting the hardwood by the front door with a smack, his body slumping against the wall.

Bronwyn started to go to him, but he growled at her and shook his head. "It's hard enough just having you in the same room. Nude, smelling like me, like sex. The more aroused I get, the less sanity I can hold on to."

She swallowed and closed the fabric even tighter around herself. The last thing in the world she wanted to do was torture him—not anymore, not in this way. "I'll get some clothes for you too."

He laughed bitterly. "What's the point? Animals wear only their fur."

"Well, since you have no fur as of yet," she said, fighting for calm as she turned and headed up the stairs, "I'll get you some clothing."

"Fine," he uttered, too tired to argue now.

She didn't like that—the quick way he acquiesced. She needed to keep him mocking her, teasing her—she needed to keep him *him*. Again, she forced the light, playful sound into her tone and called over her shoulder, "And try not to feel too sorry for yourself while I'm gone."

Lucian felt like a slab of steel that was being crushed, then flattened out, then crushed again. It took every effort to lift his head and watch her go. An effort he shouldn't have bothered with. The curtain had shifted, and wasn't covering her ass completely. He could just make out the twin curves of both smooth, soft cheeks. A surge of animal-like lust roared through him, but the weakness in his limbs forced him to remain where he was. Thank God for small and short-lived favors, he thought, his tongue lapping at the tips of his fangs as he watched her delectable heart-shaped ass move and sway in her hurried stride.

Fuck, he was in no position to stare at something he could never have again. But he would always remember. Remember it, remember her in his arms, that sweet, supple backside tucked in his hands as he pumped in and out of her body.

His teeth ground together. He'd give anything for another round—hell, for weeks and weeks of rounds. But it wouldn't be him holding her, touching her, moving in and out of her body. It would be the Breeding Male—the thing she despised, the thing that raped and hurt and could make only one reasonable decision—create *paven* or *veana*.

The shock of that thought weakened him further and he dropped back against the plaster wall and wished for death to take him. But the sound of a door smashing open and heavy footsteps on the hardwood had him pushing himself to stand.

His brothers stormed into the room, their faces masks of concern even in the dim light, their eyes taking in his nude frame, the hard cock between his legs, the pathetic, pain-filled fighting stance he was in.

"What the hell happened?" Alexander said, getting to him just in time to catch him when his legs gave out.

Dropping down on his haunches, Nicholas touched his shoulder. "Are you all right?"

Flinching from the touch, Lucian uttered a terse, "Fuck no, I'm not all right."

Nicholas dropped his arm, concerned frustration coating his words. "What happened, *Duro*?"

Lucian fixed his gaze on the far wall. "Doesn't matter."

"Like hell it doesn't," Nicholas said.

"It's done!" Lucian returned with as much force as he could manage.

Alexander leveled him with a hard stare. "We need to know exactly what went down to help you, to fix this."

He didn't want to look at them, didn't need to see the disgust-laden pity that would shadow their eyes when they realized the truth. "You don't get it, *Duros*. There is no fixing, no help. I need to be chained up or destroyed now." He turned his gaze on them. "That's the only *fix* there is."

"Good, you're both here." Bronwyn hurried down the steps, dressed in jeans and a black sweater, her dark hair swirling about her face. She went straight to Alexander. "We were taken, sent to Cruen's reality, and forced to ..."

"Stop!" Lucian barked, then waved their concerned looks away. "What's done is done."

Cursing, Nicholas turned to Alexander. "That's why they offered up a safe haven."

"Who?" Bronwyn asked him.

"The Order," Nicholas said, his voice a mass of despair as he put it all together—island, blood exchange with Bronwyn, sex,

Breeding Male. "When we found out you both had returned, and that someone was after you, we went to the Order." His gaze shifted to Lucian, the old anger riding his words. "But we were never pulled in. A certain member came to us in the Hollow, told us to get to you immediately."

Titus. Lucian sneered. The one who had started this whole fucking mess with his seed! He slammed his hand back against wall. Damn! Felt good—that kind of pain, the self-inflicted kind felt good. "Too bad our father didn't contact you while I was on the beach in Cruen's reality."

Bronwyn had given Alexander a bundle of clothes and the older *paven* knelt in front of Lucian, his eyes trying to connect with his younger brother as he helped him tug them on weakly. "No one could get to you, *Duro*. We all tried."

Titus could have gotten to him, Lucian thought bitterly, the clothes feeling like sandpaper against his tender skin. But why hadn't he? Why was he always on the fringe of helping, but never fully committed? Hell, Lucian thought blackly—because he was just another seed spilled while he'd been in the grip of the breeding animal.

No matter what that *paven* had said in the past, Lucian was no son to him.

Bronwyn was speaking then, and her words brought his attention back to the moment. "What about Synjon?" she said, her eyes on Alexander. "Is he with you? Did he come with you?"

"He went off on his own," Alexander told her. "To look for you."

Nicholas shook his head. "He should know where you are, should feel where you are. I know exactly where Kate is at this moment. I don't get it."

Like a tidal wave, indescribable pain flowed over Lucian,

126

blanketing him in its misery, and he screamed like a dying animal.

Beside him, Nicky stared at Alexander for answers. "What's wrong with this? Why is the transition to Breeding Male so drawn out?"

"Why isn't it like morpho?" Alex added. "Quick pain, over and done. It's like fucking torture!"

"I believe it was designed to torment," Bronwyn said, her tone a grand attempt at sounding professional. "Throw the new Breeding Male into a maelstrom—into a pain so unyielding that his mind would shut down. A way of destroying any resistance to the gene taking full control of his actions."

"Good," Lucian growled. "Shut me down before I turn into a fucking raping monster. I don't want to know—don't want to be aware of my actions or their outcome." He gripped his skull as racks of pain went through him.

Nicholas put his wrist in front of his brother's mouth. "Drink, Brother."

Lucian swiped at the arm. "Get off."

Again, the wrist was before him. "Titus said it would ease the pain while you go through the process. Like morphine to a human."

"Fuck no."

Alexander stepped in and threatened, "Do it before I hold your lily-white head down. Do it before that Beast of a brother of ours—that *mutore* I never believed existed—shows up here and tries to get past the enchantments on our property."

"He could drink from me."

Lucian looked up at Bronwyn, at her sincere and worried expression, then quickly jerked away from the searing temptation. He wouldn't stop if it was her.

"Do it, damn it," Nicholas urged.

With a curse, Lucian bent his head and promptly bit down on his brother's vein. Blood flowed into his mouth, onto his tongue river-quick. It wasn't sweet and satisfying like Bronwyn's blood, but it was strong and rich and he took deep pulls into his throat.

After a few minutes, he disconnected and lifted his head. He waited for the pain in his head, belly, cock, bones to recede—even a fraction. But as the moments ticked by, pain continued to slam him from all sides.

Help the pain, my ass, he thought. It was like taking baby aspirin for the migraine from hell.

Barely took the edge off.

"We need to talk," Nicky said, his expression dead calm, dead serious.

Lucian wiped his mouth. "So talk."

"The Order has offered you safe haven until Cruen is caught."

"What does that mean?" Bronwyn asked. "He's under their protection?"

Nicholas nodded. "At a *credenti*. He will be"—he shook his head, the words coming slow and painful—"contained. He'll have the blood he needs, everything, until we can—"

"I don't want their help," Lucian interrupted blackly, trying to stand. "I'll get to Cruen myself."

"Look at you," Alexander said, gesturing to his *balas*-like attempt to get on his feet. "You can barely stand, and you're shaking like a junkie."

"Is that right, Nicky?" Lucian rasped, gripping the wall for support.

Shrugging his shoulders against the bitter dig regarding his past addiction to the vampire blood drug, *gravo*, Nicholas said, "Hey—you have my permission to be the biggest asshole on the planet right now, little brother."

Baring his fangs, still bloody from their meal, Lucian uttered, "Oooh, yum—*pity*. My favorite snack next to dog shit."

"The *gemino* will find a way to get to you if you're not protected," Alexander said, then shook his head. "I still can't believe a Roman brother would work for the enemy, betray his own."

Nicholas grunted. "He is no Roman brother, *Duro*." Then he turned his gaze on Lucian. "You can't stay here."

"Who says I am?"

"What is your plan, then?"

Standing now, Lucian attempted to move away from the wall. "Get myself lost."

Alexander turned away, cursing. "I don't believe you. You'll be caught within a day."

"That's exactly what he wants," Bronwyn added quickly. "He wants the *gemino*, the Beast, to find him and take him to Cruen. It's like a double death wish—Cruen's and his own."

Lucian glared at her. "You're a real peach, Princess. You know that?"

She shrugged dispassionately, but her large, expressive eyes told a different story. "They deserve to know the truth."

"You're fucking nuts!" Alexander raged. "You know that?"

"Yes, I've heard," he snarled.

"Luca, clearly the Order knows what's happened," Nicholas said in typical Nicholas fashion. Trying to reason with the unreasonable. "They are deeply grieved—and I'm quoting them on that. I don't use that kind of bullshit language."

"Are they?" Lucian said with venom. "I must've missed the condolence bouquet and card. They sent it here? 'Sorry for the loss of all reasoning and control.'"

"Lucian, you're being a stupid ass, but more disconcerting is that you don't seem to give a shit about anyone else's feelings but your own."

"Well, get used to it!" he raged, glaring at them all. "I am the Breeding Male!"

Alexander and Nicholas stilled, their eyes glued to their little brother as the truth in his words slowly sank in. It was a sobering moment for all of them.

"Take the safe haven, Lucian."

They all turned to Bronwyn, who blushed, but didn't look away from their gazes. "Please."

"I want no safe haven," he uttered, then sucked in a breath as pain hit him square in the chest. "If I have to live in chains, then I'll be the one who decides when and where and who gets to have the honor of engaging the lock."

Bronwyn sighed, her frustration evident.

He gritted his teeth. "Cruen is mine to destroy. I will be the one to take him down."

Alexander shook his head. "Not possible."

"Says who?"

"Your skin, your eyes, every twitch in your body. You're unstable as hell, and the moment you get in his presence, he'll have you captured."

Nicholas took over. "And then whatever plan he has for you will be on."

"Fuck that," he rasped. "I'll die first." Shivers, cold and pain-laced stuttered down his back, gripping each vertebrate, tugging, ripping ...

Watching him, Nicholas sobered, asked in a soft voice, "How bad is the pain, *Duro*?"

Through gritted teeth, Lucian managed to say, "Living inside a volcano."

Nicholas put a hand on his shoulder, begged him to listen with his eyes. "We will track him down. Alexander and I, and Dillon, if we can get to her. The Order said that Cruen may have a cure to stop the Breeding Male gene altogether—kill it dead. If he does, we'll find it."

Lucian despised the flare of hope in his chest. "They told me that too. I call bullshit."

"You call nothing," Nicholas said, as behind him Bronwyn leaned back against the opposite wall and shook her head in frustration. "If there's even the slightest chance we can save you, we're taking it."

Alexander nodded. "Give us a few days. Stay in the *credenti* the Order is supplying; stay hidden until we come for you."

Lucian was about to deny them again when he looked over at Bronwyn. Big. Fucking. Mistake. The heat of need slammed his balls. It was bad enough he could smell her, but he could also register the scent of every female in their neighborhood. If he went on the run, it was only a matter of time before he truly became his father's son.

Forcing his gaze back to his brothers, he said, "I have to be chained. Have to be monitored and fed and controlled. There's no telling when I'll lose my mind and my judgment."

"That can all be done," Alexander assured him, looking relieved as hell. "If you don't want to use the Order's guards, we'll use our own."

Lucian groaned as another wave of shattering pain gripped his bones. "The eunuchs will not step foot in a *credenti* ever again."

"They will if I say they will," Alexander retorted. "And you will have Bronwyn's help as well."

"What?" Lucian barked, his gaze shifting to Bronwyn, who looked momentarily shocked.

Alexander nodded toward her. "She must go too. Out here in the world, unprotected, she is just another way for Cruen to get to you, draw you out." He shrugged at Bronwyn. "We cannot watch over you if we are tracking Cruen and his Beasts. And your mate is nowhere to be found."

She nodded. "I understand."

"Unless you wish to return to your *credenti*, under the protection of your family."

She shook her head. "I wouldn't bring danger upon them."

"No!" It was the only word Lucian could utter, but it echoed throughout the house.

"I'll go." Bronwyn walked over to him, and they all turned to stare at her.

"I won't . . . allow it," he rasped.

She eyed him. "You don't get to make that choice, *Paven*."

"You bet your sweet ass I do, Princess," he said. The pain in his throat mirrored the pain in his entire body. "I won't go after her if Cruen takes her . . . " He couldn't finish that statement, that promise—and every part of him knew it. Maybe he wouldn't go in search of her as himself, the rational *paven*, but for some reason he knew deep in his gut that the Breeding Male would.

She refused to look at him, her jaw tight. She addressed Alexander and Nicholas. "If he is chained and we have guards, I'll be safe."

It wasn't a question, but Alexander nodded anyway. "I believe so."

"Then, I will do it."

"You have a mate," Lucian hissed at her. She wasn't doing this—wasn't throwing her life away for him. "Go back to Boston. Keep the home fires burning."

"Synjon will find me when he's ready," she said, ignoring the snort of disbelief around her. "You need help. And I owe you my help."

"I don't fucking want it!" Goddamn it! He'd made the deal, agreed to be chained, fed blood like a *balas*, watched like a

132

prisoner; he wasn't having this *veana* beside him the whole god-damn way! He couldn't bear it—Christ, couldn't bear for her to see him as he disintegrated into an animal. He just wanted her to remember him as the *paven* who had played with her, teased her—pleasured her.

Bronwyn got that stubborn look—the one that was impossible to reason with. "It won't be forever, Luca. Just until they've found Cruen and discovered if there is an antidote or not. And maybe I can help with that. Maybe I can do some testing on your blood in the *credenti*, see what changes have occurred—"

"You both need to leave. Now," said Nicholas, going to the window. "Sun is almost down and our *mutore* brother will be coming for you."

Lucian gripped the railing.

"Come, Luca," Bronwyn said, holding out her hand.

He faced her, leveled her with his pale gaze. "It will be the ugliest nightmare you've ever seen. It will be what your sister faced—what you never wanted to face." He lowered his chin. "Are you truly ready to face that animal, Princess?"

She paused, her eyes moving over his face as her nostrils flared. Then a look of sudden and absolute determination rolled over her. "I will face anything to keep breathing, keep us both breathing."

"Foolish *veana*," he whispered, his strength waning.

Alexander and Nicholas took Lucian under his shoulders and they walked across the entryway and down the hall, heading for the back door. The very moment the sun went down, they would all flash to the caves to await the Order's transport.

Alexander gripped Lucian tightly, lovingly.

Nicholas did too as he whispered into his little brother's ear, "Please hold on to your mind, *Duro*."

*

Erion stood outside the villa in the small French town, a town similar to the one where he had been born—and where he had been tossed away like the unwanted refuse his dam had believed him to be. As he watched the very last rays of the sun disappear into the horizon, his brother Lycos moved to stand beside him. The wolflike *paven* didn't get too close, didn't drop a hand to Erion's shoulder as brothers of blood were known to do. After all, they had not been raised to care for each other in such a manner.

"You let them go, didn't you?" Lycos said, his voice a near growl.

Erion said nothing, his gaze still and uneasy as he watched the windows. Would the automatic blinds lift as they normally did around this time, or would the fortress remain sealed up and quiet now that they knew he was after them?

"Father's orders must be met without question, Erion."

Erion turned, eyed the Beast, his brother. Lycos's wolfish features were particularly sharp tonight, his dark eyes watchful, always watchful. "I know all about our father's orders."

"And yet . . . " He raised his dark eyebrows.

Erion inhaled deeply, his lungs filling with air and the scent of the many in the town below. "Things are different with them."

"Different." Lycos sniffed like the dog his own mother had called him when he exited her body and, like all *mutore*, instantly shifted into his Beast-like state. "Nothing is different. We serve our father. The one who rescued us from the flesh seller when we were only cubs, the one who resurrected us— who gave us a home, freedom, purpose."

"Yes." Erion nodded, returned his gaze to the villa. It was the way his mind worked too, what he believed to be his truth, his motivation for everything.

And then again, he had started to see a different kind of life, a different kind of freedom in the Roman brothers. There was a small part of him that felt envious. It was why he had stolen his twin's identity that night in Vermont, laid with the *veana* Mirabelle Letts—Nicholas Roman's trick. She had touched him, reveled in his touch. She had looked at him like a Pureblood *paven*—not as a freak of nature.

It had felt good.

Yes, he was devoted to his master, the only father he would ever know, and yet there were questions inside him. Questions that persisted no matter how hard he tried to suppress them. The first being, if he wasn't as truly free as they were, what was he?

"An indentured servant." He said the words aloud, causing Lycos to coil around him like a snake.

"What did you say, Brother?" he asked.

"Do you ever feel as though we have no choices, no excuses, no impulses or emotion?" He knew he should cease this line of questioning, yet he could not. "Do you ever feel we are weapons and nothing more?"

The look in Lycos's eyes said it all.

One word.

Never.

Before him, the window shades of the villa lifted, but no light flickered on life inside. Erion gestured to his brother. "Let's go." And the two flashed out of the French countryside.

14

Ever since morpho hit, Synjon had enjoyed the feeling of flashing. Flying in wind, the rush of air and speed, going anywhere he wanted—just as long as the sun wasn't out. But as he moved from one country to the next, one city to the other, in search of his bride, he began to despise it. Bronwyn felt as far away as a lost thought now, and the tiny scraps of information he'd been able to gather from his many sources regarding Cruen and his whereabouts had made his mood foul, to say the least.

He touched down in a London street near Big Ben, hitting the pavement and walking away so fast that the mere mortals around him saw nothing but a breeze ruffling a few stray bits of garbage into the street. He was meeting with a female contact—an Impure he'd known for several decades, who was in the spy game like him. Most vampires looking for information went to the Eyes, but Syn didn't trust those rats anymore. They were greedy little peckerheads with no sense of loyalty.

He spotted her on a park bench reading the *London Times*, her long red fingernails grasping the paper with a fierceness he understood. He slid down beside her and heard her inhale slightly.

"Need to be quick about this, Celestine," he said.

"I've never seen you so tense, Synjon Wise." She turned to him then and laughed, her blue eyes and oval face framed by long black hair.

"I've got a serious problem, or haven't you heard?"

She smiled, her teeth and fangs the color of the moon over their heads. "I know whom you seek, and why. This *paven* is a difficult one to locate."

"Yes, I'm starting to realize that."

"However," she said, still holding her newspaper aloft, "difficult does not mean impossible."

Syn lifted one eyebrow. The woman may have appeared soft and gentle, but she was a tiger with terrible claws when she needed to be. "What can you tell me? Do you have the location of his laboratory?"

She leaned in closer, her breath scented with cinnamon and cloves. "I will give it to you with a warning. In this hunt, you may go looking for the thing you think you want, yet end up with the thing you hate."

The way she spoke, the language of prophecy, had never bothered him before. Probably because her predictions had never been aimed at him before.

But he didn't have time to heed her warnings—if that's what they were. Bronwyn was out there, waiting for him to come to her rescue, and he was growing more apprehensive by the moment that he wouldn't succeed. Just as he hadn't succeeded with the last female who'd needed his care.

He stood. "The location now, Cellie dear. I must fly."

Bronwyn was careful to remain close to the guards when they landed in the middle of a wild and beautiful countryside under the bright light of the moon. Somewhere in the distance, she heard the sounds of the sea and she wondered just where the Order had planted them.

"They've got to be kidding," she heard Lucian growl, his voice filled with ire as he attempted to turn his pain-laced frame around, but was halted by the shackles that connected him to one of the guards. "I'm going to ring their ancient necks the moment I see them again."

"What's wrong?" Bronwyn asked, taking in the site before her, trying to see what was so vile to him. But she didn't. The area was rural to be sure, with vast lands and heavily dotted with mature pine trees that stretched to the sky, but it was undeniably lovely, scented with earth and forest and clean life.

To their right, a dirt path stretched out like a garden snake before them, going so far into the distance the moonlight was no longer sufficient at showing her the way. But in this serene oasis, Lucian could see nothing beautiful. The poor *paven* vibrated with agitation so deep that he snarled both at her and the two guards bracketing him.

"This isn't going to happen," he said, his eyes wild, his fingers clenched and curled as a breeze picked up around them, sending his white hair across his chiseled face. "Take me back. Now!"

"This is the safest place for you, sir," one of the guards said, his tone without sympathy.

"That is complete bullshit, Bel," Lucian raged at the male. "I cannot imagine a worse *credenti* to drop my soon-to-be Breeding Male ass in. If you don't take me back, I'll have her do it." He nodded at Bronwyn.

The black-haired, black-eyed guard said nothing, just stared at his employer, waiting for him to act or give an order that he could actually follow without risking the wrath of the ancient rulers of their breed. After all, the Order had given into Lucian's demand, and agreed to allow the Romans' own guards to accompany them, just as long as Lucian was contained, chained.

"What's wrong with you?" Bronwyn asked him, totally confused by his hatred of their surroundings. "This is beautiful, and completely isolated."

"Oh, nothing's wrong, Princess," Lucian muttered sarcastically, gripping his stomach. "It's a perfect spot. It's just great to be home."

Bronwyn's eyes widened. "Home? You mean ... this is where ... "

He cursed again. "That's right. Where I took my first steps—where I took my first fist to the head and fangs to the neck. Welcome to motherfucking Banchory, Scotland."

"Oh dear," Bronwyn said, then turned to the guards. "What is the Order trying to prove with this? Did they tell you when they prepped you for the journey?"

Bel, the one guard who seemed to be the designated speaker explained. "According the Order, there is a natural defense against being found if you are in the *credenti* of your birth. According to the Order, he will be more protected here than anywhere else."

Lucian grunted. "Bullshit."

"The Order said they can anchor him here," the guard continued, undeterred by Lucian's ranting. "Where his body, his cells began."

A hand reached out and grabbed Bronwyn's wrist, and she gasped, but it was only Lucian. His eyes looked ghostly and desperate in the pale light. "Flash me back to the caves, Princess."

Bronwyn stilled, her eyes locked with his. She hated seeing him like this, begging and so deep in pain. She hated seeing the past in his eyes. She knew his request had nothing to do with getting back home, getting himself caught and going after Cruen. This was about memories he had no desire to relive.

It was no shock to her that his early years had been rough ones, unhappy ones. With the stigma of who and what his father was, the teasing and torment from the "normal" *balas* must have been overwhelming. That was how it was for most Breeding Male offspring, she knew. And yet she was going to refuse to help him escape this new prison. It was ugly and unfair, but it was for his own protection. She wouldn't let him be hunted, not like this—not defenseless. Alexander and Nicholas must have known where they were headed, and if they believed their brother was better off in the *credenti* of his birth, she would trust that.

She shook her head. "No, Luca."

He closed his eyes and groaned. "Don't call me that. Not if you're going to deny me."

She wouldn't let him change her mind. "I'm denying you only this, the sure path to your demise. It's only for a few days."

"Come. Your cottage is this way," Bel said, his hand close to Bronwyn's back as he intended to get them moving.

Too close to Bronwyn's back apparently. Lucian struck out at the male, his arm slashing, his fangs extending.

"Touch her again and I will rip the head from your body," he snarled wildly. "No one touches her. Not you." His eyes shrank. "Not me."

Regret mingled with relief in Bronwyn's blood. She wasn't sure what awaited them during their stay here, but her fear didn't stem from his attack, the Breeding Male's attack. Not yet. Or perhaps not ever. It was the flash of heat in his eyes, the memory of his touch. And the acceptance and understanding that it would never happen again. Frustrated, she could only say, "Lucian, please." And motion for him to walk with her. "Let's go."

The four of them pushed on, moving along the snake-shaped

path, then up a hill and over as Lucian's breathing sounded far too labored for her comfort.

"This is more isolated than I was hoping," Bronwyn remarked drily, worried about Lucian's state of health as he endured the change. "Are we still in the *credenti*?"

"The outskirts," Lucian uttered, moving slowly and arduously, shaking his head every few minutes, perhaps to clear his vision. "Do *they* know?"

"Who?" Bronwyn said. Did he mean his family, the members of the *credenti*? Her concern for his mental stability jumped. It had to be devastating to come to this place as the reviled Breeding Male.

Lucian sneered at Bel and the other guard. "Do they know? Did the Order inform my kin I'm coming?"

The guard nodded sedately. "Yes."

Cursing, Lucian stopped and doubled over, catching his breath. "Why the fuck don't we flash closer?"

"The Order has put charms around the property that stretch far. We can only go by foot until our blood is given at the gates."

"Fine," Lucian said, clearly in pain. "How much farther, then?"

"I can carry you if that would be more comfortable, sir," the guard said.

Lucian jerked upright, defiance radiating from his gaze. "No fucking way, Bel. Just keep your trap shut and your feet moving."

They continued on for another few minutes and from the way Lucian groaned and gasped every step, Bronwyn knew he was near collapse. Her poor *paven*, she thought, then quickly realized he was not hers at all, and never would be. Her *paven* was missing, no doubt searching for her. Lord, she'd wanted so much to leave word for Syn with the Order, with her parents—and yet she couldn't. Not if they were going to keep up this ruse and not attract suspicion.

A white fence appeared to her right, glowing brilliant and comforting under the moon. It stretched far into the distance, and they followed it all the way to a large clearing. It was lovely and ethereal in the evening light, and if it were any other moment in time, Bron would hope for fairies to appear, to rise from the field of thick, sweet-smelling grassland.

But the magic of the moment was vampire-made only, and when they came to a stone pillar shooting out of the ground, the guards were the first to stop and begin the ritual.

"We must use our blood to enter," Bel informed them. "As the Order instructed."

Each guard bit into their wrists and ran their red blood over the top of the pillar.

"Mistress Kettler." Bel gestured for her to come forward. "If you please."

"What about me?" Lucian rasped behind her.

"You do not need to bleed to enter, sir." Bel bowed his head just a fraction. "The Order said it is your birthright."

"My birthright," Lucian said caustically. "I don't want it. No choice in coming out of my dam here, no choice in coming back in."

Bronwyn did as she was instructed, bit into her wrist and let the blood flow before pressing it over the cold stone.

"Oh," she gasped as before her eyes the gates parted and a blanket of mist swirled, then evaporated in thin air. A few acres of grassland sloped to a hillock, and on the top sat a lovely one-story stone cottage. Torches were lit in several spots around the property, alighting the rustic home and the small loch in the distance.

Bronwyn glanced over at Lucian to see if he too was seeing what she was seeing, the charming little house on the hill. But his face was a mask of pain and disgust. Clearly the only thing he saw was his past coming back to haunt him.

The guards moved forward with them, and they crossed the large expanse of grounds, entering the cottage fast and furious. It was cold and dank inside, but there was plenty of firewood stacked in one corner of the moderately spacious room. Bronwyn had expected the place to be updated somewhat with all the amenities of the twenty-first century, as most homes were these days, but it wasn't. Everything was ancient, from the furnishings to the homemade candles to the windows and their coverings. Granted, she had lived in a *credenti* that was more on the modern side, but she understood and respected the communities that embraced the old ways.

A massive fireplace took up one wall, and before it a long table and several chairs.

"He must remain tethered," Bel said to her, nodding toward the corner by the fireplace.

It was a dark corner she hadn't noticed before and as she walked toward it, she saw that the cottage was indeed a living, breathing thing from the past. There on a stone wall behind the hearth were two sets of chains and shackles.

Bronwyn covered her mouth. Was this really his fate? She had known in the abstract that this was what they had to do to keep him contained and safe and unable to harm anyone until help could be given, but to see the actual chains made it so horribly real.

"Yes, tie me up," Lucian called behind her like a drunken man. "Tie me up and never release me."

Turning, Bronwyn addressed the guards. "Perhaps we can wait until he ... "

"Until I what, Princess?" Lucian interrupted blackly, stumbling over to the mantel and holding on for dear life. "Until I drag you beneath me and fuck you senseless ... not stopping until you're swelling with my seed?"

She shook her head at him. "Do you have to be so crude all the time?"

"Fuck yes!" he returned, then sucked air through his teeth. "It's all I have. All that makes me *me*—still me ... " He cursed and grabbed his belly. "My eyes aren't clear. My head too ... " He groaned. "My fucking head is breaking."

"It is important that he is contained now," Bel said to her. "He knows it."

"Yes, he does," whispered Lucian, his eyes flipping up and his foggy gaze trying to hold on to her, trying to hold her captive. "He knows what's coming for you, for all of you—"

He went down like a stone, his body crumpling into a ball at the base of the fireplace.

"Lucian!" Bronwyn screamed. She ran to him, knelt beside him. Goddamn it, this was wrong, all wrong. He was a bastard, an asshole—a warrior. Not this male being tortured from the inside out. Not this *paven* who was being taken against his will ...

She touched his face, patted the cold, clammy skin of his cheeks, but there was no reaction. He was completely passed out now, the pain no doubt having gotten the best of him.

"It's better this way, Mistress Kettler," Bel said softly. "He won't fight us or his bindings now."

"He wouldn't have fought," Bronwyn said, but she knew that wasn't true—even though he may have known it was the right thing. Lucian was the epitome of a fighter.

The guard who had said nothing on their journey went to the fireplace and picked up Lucian, carried him over to the chains.

"Go, mistress," said Bel, his eyes urging her not to remain and watch. "Find your quarters while we ready the room for him."

"I ... " She shook her head, but her eyes were fixed on his still frame. "I can't ... "

"He will be all right. We have a pallet for him to lie on, and he will have the constant warmth of the fire here."

Her eyes broke with tears. For Lucian, for his future ... and yes, for herself. Her life's work ... a foolish pursuit to avoid this very moment—a moment that she had walked into so freely. She had to look at herself now, and her lifelong hatred of the Breeding Male: all stupidity and fear, and a refusal to investigate further. God, she'd never realized that the creature she had reviled had once been a *paven* whose life had been ripped from him, his body and mind forced into an animalistic state. In truth, wasn't he just as much a victim as her sister?

Perhaps it was time for her to use her work in a different way. If she could find a way to help him, use her results, her skills ... use the research and information she had already gleaned from her private client—from Cruen ...

"It is best to get him shackled now, mistress, please," Bel said, interrupting her thoughts. "When he wakes, he may have completed the change."

The guard's words sank deep into Bronwyn's mind, her heart, her guts. Perhaps it wouldn't be the best thing for Lucian to see her when he woke, if that was the case. She didn't want him hurting himself further.

She nodded and left the living area, headed down the hallway. Perhaps it would be a mistake to see him after the change, to get too close—but she, and her body, had unleashed this beast inside him, and she would care for him until she knew if he would ever have the chance to be a *paven*, her pain-in-the-ass *paven*, again.

Alexander and Nicholas stood at the mouth of the cave in the Hollow of Shadows. Letting their brother go, to be taken to his despised homeland where he would be chained and force-fed blood, while they searched for the monster who had turned him into the Breeding Male before his time, had made them both so angry, so vile-tempered, so on edge, they knew they'd better wait to venture home to their mates. Wait until their control returned.

"He will be all right."

Or, Alexander mused, perhaps they needed to unleash some of that ire on the one who deserved it. Whirling around to face the ancient *paven* who had orchestrated the safe house and the transport to Scotland, Alexander snarled, "Will he? Will he be 'all right'?"

Titus nodded, though his eyes were uneasy.

"And by all right," Nicholas said, following his brother to stand before Titus and entering in the question-and-answer portion of their tirade, "do you mean he will go easily and gently into the Breeding Male state? Or is there more of this pain coming, long and arduous?"

"Pray, step back." When they did no such thing, Titus sighed. "The pain is a curse, but it is not brought on by my hand."

"No, not your hand," Nicholas tossed out. "More like your cock."

A low growl sounded from Titus's throat. "There is no call for this, my son—"

"No." Nicholas stuck a finger in the ancient one's face. "Don't you dare."

"I was made into the Breeding Male," Titus defended, his back close to the mouth of the cave. "I had no choice. I had no choice when it came to the females who were put before me. Your brother will understand this—"

"Our brother," Nicholas said tightly, "will understand nothing when the gene completes its hold on him—and you know it."

Alexander lifted his chin, asked, "Why didn't you tell him, Titus?"

"I did tell him," Titus said defensively, almost emotionally. "He knew the risks if he bedded the *veana* who had drunk from him."

"No. Not that," he snarled, fighting to get enough control to even speak. "Why didn't you warn him of how this transition would be? The pain? The ongoing, tormenting pain?"

That made Titus pause. Alexander watched as the question went through the old *paven*'s mind, watched his eyes appear suddenly grieved; then he said softly, "What would've been the point?"

"He had a right to know!" Nicholas raged. "We all had a right to know the hellacious agony we would have to see him endure! There is no more point than that!"

Titus shook his head. "I didn't think—"

"No, you don't think," Alexander said, moving closer, moving in. "I'm starting to believe you don't really care either."

"That is not true."

Even if it had been only a fraction, they had begun to trust this *paven*, and now Lucian was paying the price. "I'm starting to think your motivations for helping him aren't even remotely pure."

Titus took a step back. "You can't understand."

Undeterred, Alexander kept at it. "The fact that your assistance seems to be inconsistent at best is suspect." He cocked his head in his brother's direction. "Don't you agree, *Duro*?"

Nicholas nodded. "Abso-fucking-lutely."

Titus found his voice. "I do what I am able to do."

Nicholas snorted with derision. "Well, what you're able to do isn't cutting it, *Dad*."

Nearly on top of his father now, Alexander asked, "Why are you a member of the Order?"

Lifting his chin, Titus warned, "Have a care, *Paven*."

But Alexander was undeterred. "Perhaps the better question is, *how* are you a member of the Order?"

"I am one of the ten, one of the Eternal Order," Titus said brusquely. "And that is all the answer you will be given."

"Wrong. I need to know how the hell a Breeding Male defies his cursed gene, gains a sane mind and control of his body to ascend to the Order. That is what I need to know." Alexander watched Titus's eyes widen. "Did they cure you of your need to fuck anything in a skirt? Does this antidote really exist?"

Right beside his brother in both space and thought, Nicholas added, "And if it does, why the hell haven't you given that magic pill to Lucian?"

A flicker of panic lit the ancient *paven*'s eyes before they went cold and dead. "I know of no antidote."

Alexander leaped on the evasion. "But Cruen does, doesn't he?"

Titus lifted his chin. "The Order has no idea where Cruen is. It is why we recruited your help—"

"This isn't about the Order, Pops," Nicholas said with venom. "This is about you. Do *you* know where Cruen is?"

Titus looked away, but his voice was level. "Ridiculous. If I did, I would inform the Order."

Alexander sneered. "See that, *Duro*? The way our father won't look us in the eyes?"

"He's lying, covering his ass," Nicholas said with a bitter

chuckle. "He doesn't give a shit about Lucian. Never did. Or he'd tell us where to find Cruen."

Alexander pinned Titus with his glare. "Maybe it's time we go to the Order with our suspicions. They might be interested in helping us learn what he's hiding."

"I'm all over that," Nicholas said with a false bright smile. "And hey, we're right here at the Hollow. No time like the present to send Daddy dear down the river like he did Lu—"

"Fine! You want Cruen so badly," Titus interrupted fiercely, his eyes too large, his fangs dropped low, "why don't you ask your little friend Dillon to take you to him?"

The moment the words were out of his mouth, Titus went as white as the small patches of snow still littered in the grass at their feet.

Alexander grabbed him by the throat. "What did you say?"

"I . . . must go."

"You're not going anywhere!"

But Titus was gone in an instant, flashed away from the Hollow of Shadows, flashed out from under Alexander Roman's vise grip.

"Duro . . ."

Alexander whirled around to face his brother, whose black eyes were heavy with confusion and concern.

"What the hell is going on?" he said. "What did he mean by that?"

Alexander shook his head calmly, but his insides were a raging sea of anxiety. Why would Titus mention Dillon? How would he even know her name? "Let's get back to our mates."

"D."

It was the last thing they uttered before flashing from the caves, the Hollow, and the memory of their brother's face as he went to his fate.

15

Dillon rarely slept anymore.

If she did, if she managed even a thirty-minute down for the count, there was no true rest in it. Problem was, she dreamed. And it was the heavy, awful kind—and always the same. A black forest, so thick with trees she couldn't see five feet in front of her face. Even her keen eyesight and sense of smell were lost there in suck-ass dreamland, and all she wanted to do was run. At first the sprint would seem pointless; as if she were after nothing, or running from nothing. Then everything shifted. The trees would begin to sway dauntingly, the color of the forest would fade to a deep purple, and in her cells and her veins, a feeling, a sensation so concentrated, would creep up her legs, her stomach, her chest and neck.

It was the sensation of being prey.

In the moment when the feeling hit her tongue and nostrils, her eyes would pop, her skin would shake, and her speed would go almost bionic.

She always outran the unseen monster, but every step of the way, every inch, an unseen voice warned her to stop, to hide, to give up before it was too late. Instead, she woke up, breathing heavy, distrusting everyone and wishing she could go back to sleep in peace.

Kind of like now.

Like this very moment.

If she could just sink deeper into the mattress, closer to the warm body beside her, and drain her mind of all thought, she would know contentment. But instead, she sat up and grabbed her clothes off the chair beside the bed.

"Where are you going? Don't go."

The warm body had a warmer voice, and Dillon was quick to respond. "I have to meet him."

The mattress creaked. "Where?"

"The airport." Dillon glanced down at the clothes in her hand, attempting to mentally shift gears, from lover to bodyguard.

The sigh behind her was audible and spoke volumes about its owner's disappointment. "Are you both staying here at the house tonight?"

Dillon stood up and put on her pants. "The senator will be here."

"I could insist that you stay as well."

Dillon tried not to react, tried not to pause or flinch at the sweet, almost pathetic sound. Senator Bisset's wife, Abigail, could be a dictatorial bitch at times, but right now her words weren't a demand; they were a question laced with longing. To Dillon, longing was an altogether vile and unattractive emotion—especially when outwardly displayed. She needed to take off, like, now.

"Hey there."

Her shirt over her head, Dillon yanked it down and glanced over her shoulder. "Yeah."

Abigail grinned at her. She was a beautiful woman—no

151

doubt—but it wasn't her features that drew Dillon to her. It was never looks that got Dillon's rocks off with either male or female lovers. It was a quality, something rare, something she found devastatingly attractive and impossible to deny herself when she encountered it.

The lure of someone else's property.

She grinned. The adrenaline rush of having something that didn't belong to her made Dillon feel alive and impossible to touch. A total high. An addiction she never deviated from. Well, except for the one moment of idiocy that she engaged in with Sara's brother, Gray, a week ago on the night she rescued him from the Paleo and the fangs of the Order. But hell, that was just amped-up adrenaline and maybe a teaspoon of concern for the Impure's sister—shit, how would Sara feel if her little brother came home blood castrated by the Order?

Dillon was able to help him out and she did. No big deal— not the rescue, not even the lip-on-lip, tongue-in-mouth action they'd shared in the shower—or the blood she'd let him suckle right out of her neck before she told him to get lost.

Her hand went to the spot on her neck where the imprint of his fangs still subsisted in its way ... the tiny holes still open.

Lounging on the bed she shared with the senator, Abigail's baby blue eyes beseeched her charmingly. "You'll be safe out there?"

Dillon nodded. "Sure."

"Because that's all I want for you, darling," she said, rolling to her back, the covers over her breasts. "To be safe, to come back to me."

Dillon wondered if the woman meant it in any other way but sexual. Then again, did that really matter?

Wasn't that the point?

Her cell buzzed on the bedside table and she grabbed it,

stared at the readout. Alexander. Again. Why couldn't the Romans get the message already? She'd paid her debt—she was out, done. And though she would always have a soft spot for Sara, they weren't her family, no matter how many times the thought had crossed her warped mind. She had no family. Only conquests.

Grabbing her bag, she slung it over her shoulder. "I've got to go."

"Wait a second."

Only slightly irritated, Dillon raised an auburn brow. Of course there would be a demand. "What?"

The grin was slow and seductive as Abigail dropped the sheet covering her naked flesh and moved catlike to the edge of the bed. "Kiss me good-bye."

Dillon leaned in and was about to kiss her on the cheek, but Abigail turned her head and laughed. "No, no—not like that. Like this." Her mouth was soft, her kiss not exactly hungry, but in it there was a point to prove. A predatory point as she ran her tongue across Dillon's fangs.

Dillon pulled away. She didn't have time for this, wasn't going to play the vampire game with Abigail right now.

She headed to the door. After all, it was time to go and protect the woman's husband.

Lucian had only one thought as he came to—finding relief for his painfully hard prick. He had never felt such a base need to screw something, anything, in his life, and the scent that hovered near his nostrils made him growl and lunge forward.

Female heat.

Attack.

Take.

Fuck.

But he felt the bite of steel dig into his skin. Fury blasted through him; he couldn't get to it, get over it, sink inside of it. Why couldn't he get to it? He couldn't reason it out; he needed to sink his cock into some slick female heat.

He dropped his head back and keened. It was as though he could smell the female's very insides, her bones, her tongue, the tight passageway of her cunt . . .

And he wanted it, wanted to consume it—fill it.

"Lucian?"

Shudders rippled through him at her voice. He gasped in pain, and his cock swelled.

"Can you hear me?" she asked. There was a pause. "Do you think he can hear me?"

"I don't know, mistress," came another voice.

Male.

Lucian surged forward, his mouth open, his fangs bared. He would kill that male, rip out his voice box and feast, but something contained him, held him back.

His head twisted and turned. He couldn't control it, couldn't control anything.

Where was the female? He wanted her. Only her.

"What can I do?" she said, her voice so pained. "What should I do?"

"Nothing to do now. He has turned." The male again. Lucian growled, something dripping from his fangs—what was it . . . blood?

"Just try and keep him calm," the male continued. "He seems to respond better to your voice than to mine. And if he will take the blood that's been given that should help."

"The blood is from the Order?" she asked.

"It should tame him some."

Kill.

Lucian's whole body spasmed, racked with the need to fight and leap and taste and maim. Why couldn't he move? Why couldn't he reach that male and tear into his flesh?

"Lucian?" It was her again. Her voice moved through him, making him hungry and lustful—yet she made him able to breathe. "If you can hear me, please open your eyes."

Sensation moved through his veins, pulsed, ached—then something happened without his consent. Light assaulted him. Not daylight, but active, moving. He squinted against it.

"That's right," she said encouragingly. "Look at me. Can you see me?"

He blinked, blinked back the terrible light. It was like seeing the world through a kaleidoscope of blazing color, and it was painful as hell. Like he'd been born again into a frame he didn't recognize and couldn't escape.

A face shifted into his line of vision. Dark eyes, long hair like an animal's . . . "Do you know what's happened to you? Lucian, do you know where you are?"

It happened without his thought, again without his consent—but it couldn't be helped. The scent . . . the scent was too good to resist.

He reached out, grabbed her arm, and pulled her in.

"Lucian! No!"

But it was too late. His fangs had hit skin, then vein, and her hot, sweet blood was cascading down his throat like a waterfall. Her whimpers did nothing to halt him, yet did everything to raise his pulsating cock to new heights.

Stunned and still shaken up, Bronwyn blew on her wrist for the fourth and final time, then sat back against the wall—the wall the guards had dragged her to when Lucian had gone mad with bloodlust a few minutes ago. Inside her, everything was shaken up, loose, even her skin didn't feel connected to her bones and muscles.

She closed her eyes for a moment, saw the battle that had raged when Bel and his partner had attempted to free her from Lucian's iron grasp. The guard had nearly been killed, while his partner had been tossed like a rag doll against the door. The poor male was unconscious on her bed, suffering from several broken bones and a deep gash in his neck.

"I did warn you, Princess. Now do you believe me?"

Her eyes flew open. Lucian. He was awake. After Bel had knocked him out with a strike to the head, he'd lain there on the floor, unconscious, her blood dripping from his full lips. And now, here he was, sitting up, alert, his almond eyes almost ... almost—eased? Was it possible? Did he actually appear alert? Concerned?

"Lucian?" she whispered, his name feeling different on her tongue somehow.

"Yeah. I'm here. I don't know how, but I'm here. And I feel like a bastard."

"You feel?" She leaned forward, keeping her voice low so she wouldn't wake Bel, who slept near the fire. "What do you mean, you feel?"

He opened his mouth to speak, then shook his head. "I am a Breeding Male. I know this, and yet ... something has calmed inside of me."

He still wore the clothes she'd fetched for him at the house in SoHo, but they were pretty tattered now. The shirt was torn open in the front, the buttons gone, no doubt scattered about on the floor somewhere, his chest revealed to her gaze. She swallowed tightly, the smooth, pale skin stretched over hard, tense muscle momentarily reminding her of their time on the island, of his chest, his belly against hers. Her gaze lifted, hoping his eyes didn't hold the same fire, but his face, even with all the hard angles, appeared the calmest she'd seen him in a while.

She asked, "You don't feel the hunger, the lust anymore?"

"Not like I did." He regarded her with a solemn look. "Not as a rabid animal would."

She wanted to get closer, look deeply into his eyes, but she didn't dare. Not yet. Not until she was sure he was stable. "Is that even possible?"

"I don't know. Shit, I don't know anything, except—" His gaze slammed into hers. "Except that I hurt you, that I scared the shit out of you. I should be gutted for such an act."

"No," she said, shaking her head. "You were not ... you."

For a long moment, neither one of them moved, just sat there across from each other as Bel snored near the fire and the sound of night birds landing on the nearby loch stole in from the open window.

"Do you think this sanity will last?" Bronwyn asked, breaking the thoughtful silence with the hopeful sound in her own voice.

"I don't know," he said, shifting his position as much as the chains would allow.

The questions that flashed inside Bronwyn's mind were almost too many to contain. Perhaps the *paven* before her wouldn't have to be chained forever; perhaps he was not the beast he had been minutes ago. A seed of hope lodged in her chest. "What could've prompted the change?" she asked, glancing around the room as she thought out loud. "The hit on the head, or maybe it's your natural body chemistry—maybe it's rejecting the gene?"

"Your blood."

She lifted her head and found his gaze burning like it had when he'd taken her blood on Cruen's reality. "My blood?"

He nodded. "On the island, after drinking from you I felt . . . a surge of power. Feels the same way now."

"In what way?"

"I have strength," he began. "In body and in mind . . . I feel supported somehow. It's hard to explain, but it's there, deeply embedded in my cells."

"For a Breeding Male, blood from a *veana* should make the urge to breed even stronger," she said, her brain spinning from such a possibility. "It shouldn't take it away."

He shrugged, said softly, "Just telling you what I'm living, breathing. Your blood felt like sweet sanity running down my throat."

Bronwyn shook her head against the words, the incredible suggestion. As a scientist, as one who knew the genetic makeup of a Breeding Male, his reaction to her blood should've been the opposite of what he was claiming. And yet crazy feelings of hope and pride bloomed within her. To be the one to sustain his sanity long-term—be the only one who could feed this captive beast after taking it from him in the first place?

God, she wanted that. She wanted it to be her blood that was his magic potion.

Just her blood.

Then a thought entered her head. A scientist's thought—not a *veana*'s. "What about the Order's blood? Maybe you should try that, see if it would have the same effect?"

"The Order's blood will have no effect," he stated flatly.

"Why would you say that? You have no idea—"

"I know. Fuck. I just know. It will do nothing but send me back into the mind of the Breeding Male."

Lucian felt a sudden shift inside himself. A shift in the room too, and the black night outside the window. His eyes narrowed on Bronwyn, and a shot of nausea so tremendous he had to swallow repeatedly came over him. Something was way off, something was terribly and uniquely wrong. He drew in a breath as a volatile shot of misery moved through him.

Like a tidal wave.

To his very bones.

But it was not the misery of the Breeding Male—no, that side of him had been pure madness, unstoppable lust, untamed hunger. This, this feeling coming over him now was the sickness of a *paven* who had done something so vile, so unforgivable that he wished for his end.

Panic gripped him.

But what was it?

What was wrong with him now? Maybe he did need the Order's blood? Maybe he needed to consume a member of the Order whole . . .

He suppressed the bitter laughter hovering on his tongue. This was complete bullshit. The Order and their blood—neither would do anything for him but feed him. It would not soothe his beast, quell his lust, or tamp down his rage.

Not as Bronwyn's blood would.

As it had minutes ago.

Fuck, there it was again. The strange sensation, and yet within the waves of continued nausea, he could still feel those wisps of lingering calm that tasted exquisitely of her.

He closed his eyes, searched his mind, his insides—his blood to find it, this beautiful sensation, this unbelievable calm. Ahhhhh . . . there. Once again, he felt her blood rush through his veins, soothing, supporting, easing. It hadn't taken much, but the amount of blood he'd managed to barbarically extract from her had been enough to feel her.

Enough for him to hear her . . .

He froze at the thought, confused, careful—stunned.

Bronwyn was a Pureblood *veana*—there were no beats of life inside her blood. He would feel her, yes—but hear her? Never. And yet the sensation, the sound was there. The steady, even beats of life—the rush of another in his veins.

Oh, God.

Lucian's soul died right there on the floor of the cottage.

There was only one reason for Bronwyn's blood to have a rhythm, a movement ...

A child.

Oh, God.

His child.

Shock waves slammed into his mind.

No! Fuck no!

His head began to pound, his skin burning as though he lived in the center of a forest fire.

Fucking hell! He didn't ... shit! He didn't do that to her—saddle Bronwyn with a *balas*!

"Lucian?" she said, her voice threaded with concern. "What's wrong?"

He stared right through her with unseeing eyes ...

"You're so pale," she continued, truly distressed now. "Are you in pain? Oh, God, is it coming back?"

Calm down, asshole, he warned himself. *Calm the fuck down now! Agitation will only bring back the Breeding Male, set off the hunger and lust and uncontrollable violence.* His head spun. Maybe it was a mistake, maybe he was only hearing himself—*his* new beginnings of life.

He slammed his eyes shut and felt for it again, searching his blood for her and for ...

No. God, no ...

What had he done?

His lids lifted, slowly, sadly, and he stared at her, horrified.

There was no mistaking what every cell in his body knew and cried out with animalistic pride. Bronwyn Kettler was in *swell*. The one thing she'd feared above all else, and he had done it to her.

Lucian Roman.

The Breeding Male.

16

As he sat at the long table of judgment listening to his fellow Order members discuss new provisions for the inmates at Mondrar, Titus felt the shift in his son—the shift into Breeding Male status. A wave of sadness moved through him, a sadness he could feel only because he was no longer the Breeding Male. The irony was not lost on him. Now that he could care about the children he'd created, they wanted nothing whatsoever to do with him.

It was not as if he could blame them really. And they didn't know or understand how he had shed his Breeding Male chains—they didn't know, could never know how he'd bargained with Cruen for his seat on the Order—and his step into sanity. The blood Cruen had given him had rid him of his animal-like desires and ways, and in return he'd allowed Cruen to take all the samples of his Breeding Male blood that he required.

And he'd never asked why.

Perhaps he should have. Perhaps his son was now paying for his father's mistakes once again. Whatever Cruen was cooking up in that secret laboratory of his had everything to do with Lucian, and Titus would do everything in his power to stop him.

A slam of raw pain stuttered through Titus then. The connection he had with Lucian was unlike any he had ever had with one of his children. He could communicate with the *paven*, feel his deep feelings and fear, and shift his physical body—beyond what his Order powers allotted him.

It was no doubt the Breeding Male bond.

But Titus couldn't go anywhere near Lucian—not now, not yet—not when the *paven* was just at the height of his change. Without Cruen's blood to keep him even, keep him in the Order, there was a possibility that Lucian's change could bring back the change in Titus.

He wouldn't risk it.

"Do you not agree, Order Member Titus?"

The words of his neighbor thrust Titus back into the present, into the world he never wanted to leave, and he nodded sagely. "Wise course of action. Yes."

The provisions he'd agreed to were lost on him, but his Order status, his mental and physical capabilities were not, and he would do anything to keep them secure—anything to keep his Breeding Male beast secure inside his unbeating heart. For he loved his son, cared deeply about his son, but he would never join him in the hunt, or in that devastating state of pain and pleasure, again.

"We're wasting time." Alexander dropped from the last step in the tunnels and walked with his brother and their mates down the hallway toward the weapons storeroom. "If she won't answer my calls, then we're going to have to pay her a visit."

Sara tossed him a sideways glare that screamed, "Are you insane?"

He was holding her hand, and with a quick movement of the wrist, he flipped his arm so that it was wrapped around her waist. "I play games with only one female in this life," he growled.

"And I am grateful for that, *Paven*," she said, her brows lifted. "But Dillon has always been intent about keeping her private life, work and otherwise, separate from the personal one she shares with us."

"She hasn't shared anything with us in weeks, Sara."

She cocked her head to the side and gave him a soft smile. "Awww, the big, bad vampire misses his verbal sparring partner."

But Alex wasn't playing. "This is more than concern over a friend's whereabouts. This is Luca's life, his future. D's being a pain in the ass. She'll just have to deal with the upset. Don't you agree, Nicky?"

Nicholas held tight to his *veana* as they turned down another lap of tunnel. "I do. But you stand in her line of fire when you tell her that, cool?"

Alex snorted. "Chickenshit."

Nicky didn't even growl. "Only when it comes to that *veana*. She's scary."

Kate laughed as they entered the storeroom. "Nicholas Roman, afraid of a girl. I never thought I'd see the day."

Nicky snarled playfully, then turned to his true mate quickly and gently pressed her up against the wall. "Watch yourself, *Veana*," he warned.

Her eyes sparkled. "Or what?"

He leaned in, so close their breaths mingled. "Or I may have to put you over my knee."

"Promises, promises," she whispered against his mouth, then pulled back slightly. "Hey, aren't we here for weapons, *Paven*?"

Grinning, he kissed her, slow and hungry, then said, "If I say I have your gun right here, baby, will you think it crude or pleasing?"

She arched her back. "Mmmmm ... Both. But I like it both ways."

He kissed her again. "Then maybe you should undo my fly and check your weapon, make sure it's—"

A knife whizzed past Nicholas and hit the wall five feet left of his ear.

"Hey," Nicholas grumbled, glancing over his shoulder.

"The next one will nick your neck, *Duro*," Alexander warned, already balls deep in weapons. "Spawn on your own time. We have work to do."

"I should've been an only child," Nicholas grumbled, backing away from Kate and heading for the weapons stash.

Kate laughed. "What fun would that be? No one to give you shit—no one to pull you out of shit."

"Well said." Smiling, Sara leaned against the table that housed over one hundred guns. "Though I'm still waiting for my brother to pull me out of shit. Maybe someday ... "

Alexander cupped his mate's neck and dropped a kiss to her lips. After a devastating fire that Sara had accidentally set when she was just a child—a fire that claimed the life of her father and irrevocably damaged her brother Gray's hands and his mental state—she spent years with her nose in the books, becoming a psychiatrist. All for one purpose: to bring her brother out of his mentally unreachable state. But now that he was out, recovered and cognizant of the hidden secret of their mother, that he and his sister were Impure vampires, the male had made it clear he had little or no time for his family. He was on some mission—Impure rights or some such bullshit—and refused to take the time to call or see his sister.

Pissed Alex off, but he wasn't about to let Sara know it. She needed his support not his anger.

"What about trying to find Gray?" Nicholas asked, pulling a Beretta 96 from the shelf. "He and D did have something . . . a friendship, or maybe it was more of a mutual hatred of each other."

"My brother has also been unreachable for weeks now," Sara said, the worry evident in her blue eyes. "He's involved in some kind of ritual with a couple of Impures."

"Ritual," Alexander muttered, forgetting his vow to keep silent on the Gray front. "Can't wait till that bullshit begins. Another push for an Impure uprising. And what now? Gray Donohue instead of madvamp Ethan Dare at the head?"

"God, I hope not," Sara said sedately. "But he does seem determined to support 'his' people."

Alexander snorted. "As if we don't have enough to fight without a new war being waged." Suddenly he noticed Sara digging in the stockpile and asked, "What are you doing, my love?"

"What does it look like?" she said easily. "I'm coming with you, so I figure I should be packing."

Nicholas glanced over at Kate and grinned.

Sara held up a small gun. "Packing light."

"No." Alexander said the word as though it was all he needed to say to have Sara reverse her action and her choice.

"Did you just say 'no' to me?" Sara turned and eyeballed Kate. "Did he just say that?"

Trying to suppress a laugh, Kate said, "I believe he did." Then, eyeing a particularly shiny Glock, she added, "Hey, you know I'd be all over this if I didn't have Mr. Ladd to take care of."

Choosing another tack, Alexander put down his weapon and

pulled his mate close. "My love, I don't know what we're going to encounter. Could be dangerous—"

"We're going to encounter Dillon," Sara said tightly. "And she's a friend; she trusts me."

"Sara—"

"I get the danger. I really do. But I'm a part of this family and I can offer something here. She'll listen to me, Alex. And if you're trying to get information out of her that is buried, information she doesn't want to share, you're going to need me." She lifted her brows. "So. Deal."

She broke away from him and placed her gun in the back of her jeans. "I'm no warrior like the two of you," she said, looking up at both Alex and Nicholas. "But I've gained some skills since I've been here, and I'm ready to try them out."

As always, Celestine had come through for him—this time with the location of Cruen's laboratory. For Syn, flashing into the small ski town and hiking up into the mountains hadn't been an issue. The problem was, the compound itself was a right bitch and a half to get into. The grounds alone were hardwired with some serious Grade A magic, and as Synjon stalked the perimeter like a cat, he surmised that getting into the area where prisoners were held was going to be pretty sodding beastly.

But he would. If Bronwyn was in there, he would get to her and get her out. He wasn't losing another female, love of his life or not.

Under the spotlight of the moon, his lips lifted, his fangs extending. And after he rescued the *veana*, he'd return to rip the skull off the bugger who'd nicked her in the first place, then drop his sorry carcass at the feet of the Order.

A sudden tingle of warning licked at his skin and . . .

Ah! Bollocks.

He slammed back, fell on his arse. Damn it, too close to the magic. If he wanted in, he was going to have to find a break in the magic pulse somewhere around the perimeter, then endure the unbearably hellish pain of near electrocution for as long as it took to bypass the invisible fence.

Leaping to his feet, he flipped down the shades of the high-powered night-vision specs he'd had made last year. They were the perfect spy wear for vampire vision, getting up close and personal over real long distances.

Slow and steady, he moved, testing the pulse while checking for guards—hidden and not. He tried not to think of Bron. It didn't do any good to think, to worry about her. He'd get there, find her and bring her home. Failure was just not an option for him, ever. He was not losing another *veana*—not unless she was dead.

Then there was nothing he could do. He'd learned that lesson the hard way.

The snarl that played about his lips was short-lived as he spotted guards in the distance. He counted them up right quick. Six in all and every one of them decked out in weapons.

He squinted. What were the blokes doing? Walking with something. Something in white ... white robes or a nightgown or some shite like that.

Syn hit the button on his specs, amping up the zoom so he could see what the guards were guarding. Shape was female. Could be Bronwyn. His unbeating heart stuttered, and he pushed through the high grass bordering the perimeter. If it was Bron, he was going straight through this barrier, permanent damage to his insides and hardwire or not.

His vision cleared then, and what he saw killed the breath in his chest.

He came to stop, his hands slowly closing into fists at his sides.

It wasn't Bron.

It wasn't bloody possible.

He ground his molars as a low growl escaped his throat. Surrounded by six massive males, a *veana* with hair the color of copper, so long it curled under her backside, walked through the yard. There was only one female he'd ever met in his life who had hair that color.

His female.

The love of his sorry cock-up life.

And she was dead.

Day broke in a vision of color, and as Bronwyn dug in the cold earth under the growing morning light, she was so thankful Meta didn't take away a *veana*'s need to live in the sun, as it did for *pavens* who go through morpho.

She had been outside for more than an hour now, digging up a patch of dirt near the house, breathing in the stark Scottish air in that strange, ethereal light before dawn. Perhaps, under normal circumstances, she wouldn't have been out and to work so early, but these weren't ordinary conditions. These were strange times with unpredictable characters, and Bronwyn had never done well in the unpredictable. She appreciated concrete and foreseeable outcomes. Two things she wasn't getting sitting across from Lucian, watching him sleep, watching his beautiful chest rise and fall as she waited for any sign of the Breeding Male to return. After a couple of hours, she had been quickly driven to the brink of madness.

She had wished for her equipment, her computer, something to keep her hands and brain busy, but there was nothing. Nothing but the earth outside. After wrapping herself in a blanket, she'd found a small trowel near the stacked firewood and had been creating the rectangular-shaped bed ever since. She didn't know how long they would be here. Could be a few days, a week ... But this was planting season in every *credenti* she knew of, and the work was hard and good for her insides. It would keep her out of the house, her hands busy. Unfortunately, it did nothing to quiet her thoughts of Lucian.

Her trowel met with a rock and she circled around it, dug it up and pitched it toward the shore of the loch. Much as she had pitched Synjon from her mind these past days. She crumpled inside then. As much as she wanted to, or wanted to want to—she could no longer pretend she had saved even a small part of herself or her virtue for the *paven* she had mated. He wasn't her true mate, of course, but he was the one she had chosen, committed herself to in front of her family and the Order. He was the one who had given up so much to take her on, and God help her, where was her loyalty to him now? Would he be able to look at her when she returned and told him everything? Would he be able to forgive her?

Would she be able to forgive herself?

A heavy breath left her lungs, and she brushed her hand over her sweaty forehead. How was it that the very thing she had married him to avoid had come to pass? Her body had been taken by a Breeding Male—or as near to one as you could get—and it had been by her own choosing.

The trowel hit another rock, the impact vibrating up her arm, and she attacked it, digging it up and pitching it. This time it landed against the side of the cottage with a soft chink.

Her gaze followed it, even lifted to the window to see if the noise had disturbed anyone inside. Holy God ... She gasped—not in shock, but in wonder, in appreciation, in approval. Lucian was standing, nude, perfectly framed by the window. Someone—probably Bel, as he was the least injured of the two guards—had brought the claw-foot tub over for him, and he was bathing near the fire, the red and orange flames licking at his powerful thighs. Her mouth began to water, her fangs began to drop, and her breath came quickly in and out of her nostrils.

One wrist remained shackled to the wall, and Lucian used his free hand to pour a wood bucket of soapy water over his head. The water rushed down his frame, wide shoulders, and chest to tapered waist. The garden all but forgotten, Bronwyn's gaze clung to his skin, moving with each droplet of water as it followed the gravitational pull downward, over his belly, hips, between his legs, where his cock hung relaxed against his thigh.

On that island, under duress, she had offered her body to him. If given the opportunity, would she do it again? she wondered. Would she do it again without any threat or coercion upon her?

At that very moment, Lucian looked up and caught her watching him. His eyes darkened and his mouth thinned, and as they stared at each other his cock stirred. Bronwyn dropped her gaze, watched as his heavy prick slowly left the haven of his thigh and began to rise hard and thick toward his belly.

Oh, God ... Her breasts tightened, her cunt too ...

Hadn't she broken enough vows, she thought bitterly, without adding *covet* to the list? Blood pounding in her veins and her face, Bronwyn ripped her gaze away and returned to her earth and her trowel.

His cock was stone, nearly leaking at the tip, and he did nothing to cover the sight.

Her eyes had returned to her work, but what she saw, what she had created, had to be imprinted in her brain. Her gaze— just her gaze had sent his prick to his belly. Did she even fully grasp the power she had over him?

Shit, did he?

171

He knew it wasn't merely the sweet orgasmic power of her blood—there was more, too fucking much more. Maybe something about her brains and the way she seemed to give a shit about him. He didn't know. He didn't want to know. What he wanted was to despise himself for tasting her to begin with. On the island. Starting that circle of madness, not holding out for Cruen the Dickhead to give up and make an appearance at his little display of theatrics. If Lucian had done that, he wouldn't be in this mess—and she wouldn't be either.

Fuck, he didn't even want to say the words in his head anymore.

I'll say it, asshole.

You put a balas *in her womb.*

It was the Breeding Male talking now—he was the one with the gifts—impregnating, deciding the sex of the *balas*, and right where Lucian was now—not just able to hear the new life in Bronwyn's blood, but scent the *balas* within her. Bile rose in his throat, but as usual his mind kept up the onslaught of torment and abuse.

And now her blood, the blood of your kid, could be the key to keeping you sane—keeping me at bay. How's that for a nice kick in the cracker jacks?

Despite the heat of the fire, cold air moved over his wet skin and he ground his teeth together against the coming shivers. He'd been thinking about it for hours. What other explanation was there? One moment, he was the Breeding Male, the monster, his mind and reasoning gone, and seconds later when her blood entered his system he was purring like a goddamn pussycat.

The weight of all he knew and the impact of revealing it to Bronwyn was crushing. What would the outcome be to such an admission? And with her history— Jesus, her twin fears of being taken by a Breeding Male and being impregnated by one. Would she hate him? Shit . . . Or worse—would she hate the *balas*?

His wrist strained against the shackles that Bel had refused to let him remove—even for cleaning himself. At least the Impure had removed himself from the living quarters and allowed Lucian to bathe without an audience. The guard had gone off to tend to his partner, the sorry Impure who still remained in a coma in one of the bedrooms. That unfortunate situation was sure to be a problem for them all.

His gaze narrowed on Bronwyn working the land outside the window. Her lovely shoulders were hunched, her gaze focused downward as if she wanted him to see her determination not to look at him again.

He wasn't the *paven* who wanted offspring, never thought about *balas* in any way other than how to keep his seed from spreading so he wouldn't have any. And yet the life inside the *veana* outside his window not only interested him, but made the protective instincts he never knew he had flower.

Lucian sank into the water, keeping his shackled arm out. If Bronwyn found out about the babe would she run from him? Would she take his salvation with her and leave him to rot in the dark madness alone and unfriended?

He had to have time—time to figure out the truth of her blood. And she needed time for the visions of him as the untamed and treacherous monster of a Breeding Male to ebb in her mind. Maybe then, she would, at the very least, not spurn the child before its arrival.

17

Inside his private quarters at the laboratory, Cruen had gathered his adopted children to him. The four *mutore* he had paid the London flesh seller barely a farthing for nearly two hundred years ago stood shoulder to shoulder before him, no longer terrified *balas*, but grown *paven*, each hovering between their moderately attractive vampire form and their horrifying beastly one. It was how they felt most comfortable. But today, Cruen cared not for their comfort. He was in a foul mood, his anger so fierce, the energy of it filled the room.

"The female is ripe in three days," he said, his eyes narrowing on Erion, the one he trusted above all the others. "And I have no male for her to lie beneath."

Erion nodded, his black hair falling in unkempt waves around his scarred lion face. "They have been moved by the Order. They remain under their protection. It is intense and heavy magic. It is taking time to defuse that magic, locate their whereabouts."

"But you will."

"Of course, Cruen."

Cruen tried not to show his distaste for being called by his name rather than "Father," but he allowed his lip to curl a fraction.

"We did not expect the Order to champion this cause," Erion said, his gaze shifting momentarily to Lycos, the wolflike Beast with a heavy head of streaked blond hair who stood beside him, before returning to look at Cruen. "It is unfortunate that they learned of it before we could get control of the Breeding Male and the *veana*."

The quick glance at his brother wasn't lost on Cruen, and he lifted his brow. "I wonder, my son, if it is possible that you have developed sympathy toward the Roman brothers?"

"Never!" Erion returned with a charged snarl.

Around Erion, his brothers, Lycos and Phane, agreed with this in their low, growling way—while the third, Helo, remained silent.

"I can see how this would happen," Cruen continued thoughtfully as he walked toward them, stopping directly in front of Erion, like an army drill sergeant challenging his cadet. "Though they were born the perfect Pureblood vampire from the same Breeding Male's seed, and you were considered trash to all but me, they are in fact your blood."

Erion's jaw worked, and Cruen saw the Beast's fury flash in and out of his diamond eyes. "My one true family is here."

Feeling smug with the predicted reaction, a grin tipped Cruen's mouth. "As is your loyalty, I hope."

"Always, Cruen." But the words didn't hold the same passion as the ones he'd used in defense of his feelings regarding the Romans.

Interesting, Cruen mused as he left Erion and began to walk in a circle around the foursome. Interesting, and worrisome. The ancient and the keeper of all dark magic in their breed always

175

suspected anyone and everyone he came in contact with. And yet with his "children" he had never felt even the smallest fragment of cause to suspect their devotion.

After all, they owed them everything.

A home, blood, warmth, a decent place to sleep—and a master—a father—who never looked upon them as an abomination to their breed. He had watched them grow with the warm and soft eyes of a parent. Granted, he had no heart, but there was something inside him that would break if his children, his Beasts, turned on him—turned away from him.

As the one had done ...

He paused behind his favorite son, the Beast who towered over him by at least a foot and a half. He put a hand on the *paven*'s massive shoulder and whispered a heavy-sounding, "Find them, Erion."

Erion glanced over his shoulder, looking every bit the fearsome thing, and yet he placed his hand over Cruen's. "I will, Father."

"Enough." Cruen snatched his hand away, waved at him to go, to leave. When Erion was out of the private chamber and back to his work, Cruen stepped in front of the one who remained a wolf more often than not. "Watch him, Lycos. Watch him closely. I fear he is slipping away."

Lycos shook his head, his dark blond hair, which was streaked with gray and brown, kissing the edges of his muzzle. "My brother would not betray you, Father." His ice blue eyes were sure and even. "He knows what was given to him—and that is deeper than blood, I assure you."

"I hope you're right," Cruen said, waving them all away, just as he had Erion after the *paven* had granted him a moment of affection—the first affectionate touch the favored Beast had ever given his father. It was truly suspect. "For I would hate to have to show him the fate of an unprotected, unloved Beast."

"Well?"

Sitting against the wall that contained him, Lucian looked up from the cup in his fist, the cup that held the Order's blood. "It sure as hell ain't yours, Princess," he grumbled.

Bronwyn shut the front door and sighed. "I know that, but is something wrong with it?"

He glanced down at the remaining blood and snorted. "It's cold."

"Lucian—"

"And then there's the aftertaste . . . "

Her brows came together as she walked over to him. "What aftertaste?"

He ran his tongue over his fangs in a mock attempt at contemplation. "It's like a cross between ancient, piece-of-shit bastard and foul, motherfucking liar."

She narrowed her eyes. "Not funny."

"Come on. It's a little funny." But Lucian wasn't laughing—he was way too freaked out to laugh. The difference in swallowing the Order's cold, unappetizing swill compared to the sweet, fragrant blood of Bronwyn's was night and day, heaven and hell—and yet he had hoped that by some miracle, it would work, that it would calm and soothe the pissed-off beast within.

It didn't.

It had been twenty-four hours since Bronwyn's blood had entered his veins and sent the demon Breeding Male to hell to wait. Now he could feel it scratching at the walls of its cage, trying to get out, get between the next female's thighs and plant more of his seed.

"Try it again," she urged him, her concerned gaze running

over his face, perhaps looking for something, some change of mood or pain in his countenance. "Just to be sure."

"Fine," he grumbled, as much to himself as to her. In actuality, he did want this to work, to be the answer to his massive problem.

The shackle rattled as he lifted the cup to his lips once more. There was nothing in the world he wanted less, but he shut his eyes and drank it down like a good little *paven*. Soon as it cleared his throat, his nostrils flared and his tongue protested. Gahhh ... *Metallic Ass d'Order*. And though he felt mildly stronger in body, he also felt the newly familiar rain clouds moving over his mind and mood. *It* was returning.

He threw the cup at the door and growled. "This is bullshit."

"Must you get violent?" Bronwyn scolded, though her dark eyes betrayed fear as she stood over him. She knew something had changed in the past hour or two. She knew it was coming back, and that the Order's blood wasn't doing a damn thing to quell his monster.

"The Order always makes me feel violent," he said, his eyes trained on the rug he sat atop. He wasn't looking at her, shouldn't look at her—not with the Breeding Male clawing at his belly, his throat, his fangs—his cock.

"The Order didn't turn you, Lucian."

"Not directly, no, but they are responsible for this whole fucking thing."

"It was Cruen," she said hotly—too hotly. "From beginning to end."

His gaze lifted and he tried not to breathe too much, too much of her into his lungs. "Cruen was the Order, Princess. Who do you think hired him to do the job of creation way back when?"

She dropped into the chair behind her, her eyes the darkest he'd ever seen them. "I'm not defending the Order. I'd never defend those creatures. With my misguided parents' consent, they sent my sister to her death. I'm just saying that Cruen was the one who made the weapon. He ..." Her gaze trained on him, her expression changed to one of concern. "You're panting."

"I know." His control was slipping again, the fog of uncensored lust shoving his mind into a corner where it would be locked down, forced to watch in helpless rage as he did things that belonged only in nightmares.

Bronwyn scrambled down from the chair and came over to him, sat before him on her knees.

"Not so close!" he roared, shooting back against the wall, knocking his shoulder into the metal bolt that held his chain. He cursed. "We have no Bel, no guards—no one to help you if I cannot."

The guards were gone, headed to town and to a vampire doc in the *credenti*. The guard Lucian had tossed around wasn't improving, and Bel thought it right to bring him in. Until they returned, Lucian thought he and Bronwyn needed to remain far apart. Hell, he should send her outside into the coming evening. She could work on her garden under the moonlight while he gave in to the change, transformed into that fucking Breeding Male monster again.

"You need to go," he said tightly. "Go. Outside or in your room, just get out of my sight."

But Bronwyn was heeding nothing—as usual.

He flashed her a weary, yet feral gaze. "Why is it you refuse to listen to me, *Veana*?"

"Force of habit, I guess." She moved closer to him. "Perhaps when you say something interesting, I will."

"You're being a foolish little shite," he muttered, her scent inching up his nostrils.

"No, that wasn't all that interesting either." She rolled up the sleeve of her shirt. "You know you're starting to use a brogue. Being home has its effects on you, doesn't it?"

"No." He started panting again, like a fucking dog. "I'll work to remove it from my voice."

"Don't," she said, looking up at him, her eyes so bright with fear and concern. "I find it quite handsome."

"Oh, *Veana*," he uttered on a sigh, his gut clenching like there was a hand fisting inside of it. She was so near, so goddamn pretty—her skin, her pale, scented skin moving closer to him. Why couldn't he just have her, take her for his own? Just for a moment?

Unbidden, his hand—the very one that was chained to the wall behind him, the very one that was shaking like a human adolescent male—lifted, and he touched her face. The skin was so soft, like the petal of a rose. "Princess ... "

For a moment, one extraordinary moment, Bronwyn leaned in to him, in to the curve of his palm. They were close, too close, but Lucian was beyond hope now and he told himself to screw it. To screw caution and let her look at him that way, let her breathe in and out, back and forth against his face, his mouth. Then the pain struck, deep, like a hundred knives stabbing into his organs all at once and he clamped his eyes shut and groaned—groaned like a fucking gutted animal.

Bronwyn pulled back and her expression shifted from soft to serious in seconds. "Do it, Lucian," she said. "Do it now. Drink from me. Whatever the reason, my blood calms you."

His nostrils flared, jacking her scent into his lungs as the pain continued, pulsed, quicker and quicker. He knew the reason her blood drugged him so thoroughly, knew that it couldn't be from her—from a *veana* alone—or every Breeding Male who took the blood of the female they bedded would be "cured." No, this had to be from the *balas* inside her, and yet he refused to say the words out loud. He couldn't say it . . .

Shit, he was a worthless *paven*—and a truly worthy Breeding Male.

"Stop thinking!" she commanded, her tone somewhere between resolute and pleading. "This is your one and only solution—don't be a fool. Take it!"

He looked up, into her forest green eyes, his vision starting to blur. "I could rip your arm from the socket. I could attack you. I just don't fucking know—"

"You're doing this now," she said with deadly calm, "while I know you're still in there, that you won't hurt me. Because once you lose control, I'm not going to be within reach."

Hunger raged within him, the uncontrollable kind. He feared himself in that moment. "You are mistaken if you think even the sedated Lucian Roman is not to be feared. I need your blood, crave your blood, but there will always be an unrelenting desire to get you on your back again. A desire that has nothing to do with the Breeding Male." He swallowed, his breathing growing even more labored as he fought for sanity. "You felt that good, Princess."

Bronwyn felt her body kick and hum and heat with awareness. Even as she sat beneath that hungry, animal-like stare. It wasn't an easy thing to admit, but she and this *paven* were linked in more ways than just a choice of survival she'd made on an island. He couldn't stay sane without her. And, God help her, she would never allow him to go hungry and feral again—even if it meant risking her own safety, her own life.

Without another word, she reached up, cupped his neck, and slammed his head down upon her wrist. Then she waited, one second, two. "Do it!" she cried. "Take me, take it. Now!"

She gasped as his fangs plunged into her wrist, straight into her vein, deep inside where her blood flowed raw and heavy. But the pain was quick, and soon the nearly sensual pulls of his hunger found a rhythm. She released the breath she was holding and tried to cool the pulsing heat that nipped at her breasts and squeezed the walls of her cunt.

Her body coiled around him like a snake, and as she listened to the sounds of his suckle, his feed, the erotic swallows of him draining her life force, she fought the urge to lean down and kiss the top of his head, scent his hair, connect with him as she wanted to—in a way she'd always wanted to connect with a lover; something beyond desire, beyond lust, something monumental, yet peaceful and true and abiding.

As if he sensed her thought, Lucian's eyes drew up to meet hers and Bronwyn held his gaze. But his gaze wasn't soft, wasn't satiated, it was confused. As though he were trying to work something out in his head. Losing the battle with herself, attempting to comfort whatever was worrying him, she brushed his hair out of his eyes and touched his face, his high cheekbones with their empty circle brands, the curve of his ear, the roughness of the skin around his mouth and chin, then down to his neck. His growing power, his visible strength made her smile with satisfaction, as did the feeling of his throat as he swallowed her blood in hard, hungry gulps.

How was this possible? she wondered dazedly. That her blood could control the Breeding Male? And if so, could it control all the potential Breeding Males? In her work, she'd never heard of anything like it.

Her head began to feel heavy and dizzy from the blood loss, and as if sensing this, Lucian pulled out of her and sat up. His eyes locked on to hers and held. "You are like the sweetest drug imaginable."

Bron inhaled, loving and hating his words. "Once a day,

then," she began, watching his tongue dart out to lap at a few stray drops of blood on his lower lip. "You will feed from me. Then perhaps we could remove the chains."

He cocked his head. "Drugs can become addictive if they are taken too long."

She shrugged, seeing his eyes grow heavy as they blinked up at her. "I see no other choice, do you?"

"No," he whispered.

"You're tired. Sleep." She started to rise, but he caught her arm.

"Lay with me." His eyes flared with strength and heat, but behind his gaze that same wonder, same confusion glistened. "I took much of your blood; you need rest too."

Her entire body shivered. "I cannot."

"I won't touch you."

No, she thought, her gaze drifting downward to where his manhood strained against the fabric of his trousers. *But I may touch you, and I won't stop there.* "I have given my body and my blood," she told him with as much earnestness as she could manage. "The intimacy I must save."

"For your mate?" The words weren't tainted with bitterness as she would've expected, but with an ease that surprised her.

"Please don't," she said.

He dropped back against the wall. "What about when your true mate shows up someday? What are you going to do then?"

"I will have to explain to Synjon that—" she began, but he cut her off.

"No, Princess." He lifted one pale eyebrow, and the look of confusion that had lingered behind his eyes only a moment ago now flared with something far more worrisome. "Your *real* true mate."

18

Lucian's words—his accusation—hit her like an iron pole to the head, and at first didn't exactly register. Then, slowly and awfully, she felt the blood, the little amount of blood left inside her, drain from her face. How could he possibly know? Maybe he was just baiting her ... Maybe this was all his idea of a joke.

"You still wish to play this game?" he asked.

Or maybe not.

"I—I have no idea what you mean," she stammered stupidly, coming to her feet.

He snorted. "Guess that's a yes."

"You should rest, Lucian." She went over to the window and lifted the curtain. Night was coming in waves of blue and gray with strokes of purple streaking across. She wanted to run, run away from his accusations. How the hell could he know the truth? Was it written in her blood?

"I'll rest when I'm dead," he muttered behind her.

"You are dead."

"No, I'm the undead," he called out with a touch of sarcasm.

Then he released a heavy breath and his voice softened. "Come here, Princess."

She turned, looked at him—his ungodly, beautiful face. All hard angles and full lips under a heady rush of white hair. He sat on his pallet against the stone wall like a prisoner, a beautiful, fearsome angel prisoner.

"I'm fine," he said, flashing that charming, boyish, wolfish smile her way. "The beast is dead—for now. My belly's full."

Didn't he get it? This wasn't about fear of him attacking her. It was the raging, desperate feelings of desire running through her body that wouldn't calm down. It was about him knowing her truth and her refusing to acknowledge it, admit it—admit anything that could tie herself any closer to him than she already was.

"You look pale," he said, his expression grim, overly concerned. "If you're not going to come to me, then sit down at the table."

The table. The cold, hard table.

Was she a fool to walk back to him and sit beside him on the floor near the wall? Absolutely. It could lead to nothing but trouble. Yet trouble of the sweetest kind. And so she bypassed the cold, hard table and the equally cold, hard chairs and returned to his side, sat on her heels, and let him take her hand.

He held it gently, then studied her thumb for a moment. "It's quite a mark."

"I think so." She tried to take her hand back, but he didn't let her go.

He looked up into her eyes. "And yet he won't come for you."

"He can't," she said tightly. "He can't find me."

"No. I suppose not. He would need your blood inside him at the very least. As I do." In under a second, he pulled her onto his lap and cradled her in his arms, the cuff and chain at his wrist knocking together in the movement.

He smelled wonderful, like peat and the Scottish air outside as it grew to evening, and she had never felt so safe in her entire life. She nearly laughed. Safe—with the Breeding Male. And yet it was the truth.

His face was just inches from her now, and he lifted her hand, lapped at her thumb with his tongue. "So, what is it, ink?"

She gasped at the feeling, hot and dangerous. Why couldn't he leave this alone? Forget what he thought he knew? "You enjoy tormenting me."

He chuckled softly. "I do at that."

"I really should hate you." She shook her head.

"Why?"

"Your attitude. Your arrogance. Your foul mouth."

He grinned with that mouth.

Her eyes lifted and she whispered almost desperately, "I wish I hated you."

His mouth twitched. "Yes, it would make things easier all around." He lowered his mouth to her hand again and ran his fangs over the mark. "Shall I remove it for you?"

She snatched it away. "No!"

He growled at her like she was his, his mate, his property. And, Lord, maybe she was. Maybe with her gifts of body and blood, that was exactly what was happening. Yes, he was the Breeding Male and would never have a true mate, but the way she was feeling about him, the need she had to be close to him, the deep care she had for his well-being—well, that could mark her as his in its own way.

The overwhelming realization of that truth sent panic running through her at a frantic pace. Was she really this kind of *veana*? Mated to one *paven*, yet bound to another?

Yes ...

She scrambled out of his arms and got to her feet, went over to the front door and grabbed the handle. But where was she going to go? Seriously? The wilds of Scotland in the growing darkness of night ... Maybe into the *credenti*?

"So, why the lie, Princess?" he asked behind her. "I can't say that I'm not thrilled you don't belong to that British bastard, but—"

"Don't." She leaned against the door, let her head fall against the wood. What was the point of keeping a secret that was clearly no longer a secret? "How did you know?"

He sniffed. "I think I knew back when you were taken by the *gemino* and Brit Boy couldn't find you. True mates—real true mates—are bound together by more than blood or sex—no matter what anyone says."

"Syn and I are bound," she said, trying to defend something that didn't requiring defending. Their friendship, their commitment was more than blood, more than sex.

"Your mark," Lucian continued as though her words had no effect on him. "After the Veracou took place, that mark should have repelled me, just as my blood should make you gag. Does it? Does my blood make you sick?"

Miserable, she shook her head against the door. She couldn't look at him, couldn't see his eyes.

"But I knew—definitively knew—just now, when I took your blood."

She whirled around to face him. "How?"

He dropped his chin, stared up at her through his pale lashes. "I could taste the ink. It has moved into your blood. I wouldn't be surprised if it begins to fade soon with my new and rigorous feeding schedule."

Her throat dropped into her belly.

"Tell me why, Princess."

She just stood there, staring at him; then finally she shrugged. "Self-preservation. You understand, I'm sure."

He didn't answer right away. Then after a moment, he sighed. "So, all this to avoid the Breeding Male."

"Yes." She nodded, to herself, to the wood door. "To avoid the Breeding Male, avoid the fate of my sister. To have that monster forced on me, forcing himself on me … You must understand, Lucian. That monster is the only Breeding Male I know. The only one in my memory, my nightmares."

"You don't have to justify or clarify, Princess. I get it." But his voice sounded raged, tortured to her ears.

"To be treated in such a way," he continued. "And then to have a *balas* forced on you. A *balas* of *his* … Yes, anyone would run from that fate."

"No. I don't think I could ever feel that way, but—"

"But you would be reminded always," he finished.

If it was only that simple, she thought. She tried to explain, "When I looked at the child—"

"You would see its father."

Her gaze reared up. "Please. Let me say this in my own way, my own words."

"It is understandable, that's all I'm saying." He shrugged nonchalantly. "My mother felt that way. It's why she sent me away the moment I was old enough."

Bronwyn's chest started to constrict. "Where did she send you?"

"A lovely little rat hole called Creglock Academy." His eyes were dead with the memory. "Really top-notch military school, you know, for obnoxious shitheads whose families want to get rid of a growing problem. It's about sixty miles from here. I walked it once."

"Sixty miles?"

"Everyone was going home for winter break, and I was getting real sick of always being left behind, so I took off. Got forty miles before the school officials caught up with me, dragged my puny ass back. Gave me the beating of a lifetime." He grinned, but there was no humor in it. "She had given them strict instructions to keep me there."

Bronwyn couldn't believe what she was hearing, the cruelty of the school—but worse, his own mother. And yet she couldn't help but wonder if her sister would've felt the same, would've hated the sight of her two *balas* and sent them away. And would it have been an understandable reaction?

She noticed the fire was low. As evening was coming on and the cold would soon come rushing under the door, she went to the hearth and began pitching logs onto the fire. Anything to keep her hands busy and her body active. "Were they awful to you, Luca? The other children?"

He was up in a flash, the length of his chain just reaching her side. "Here. Let me." He took the heavy logs from her arms and placed them on the fire. "They couldn't help it. As they aged normally, I did not. I was a weak runt, and though it may be hard for you to believe, I had one smart mouth on me."

Bronwyn smiled. "Impossible."

He smiled too. Such a rare, beautiful sight, she wanted to bottle it to have for her bedside table always.

In the light of the crackling fire, Bronwyn looked at him. "She was cruel for sending you there. It wasn't your fault that she was forced ..."

"Doesn't matter," Lucian said, cutting her off.

She grabbed his hand, her tone fierce. " 'Course it matters."

His pale eyes searched hers, for what she wasn't sure, but the intensity between them was as hot, if not hotter, than the blaze at their feet. Lord, she was so caught up in raw emotion when she was near him that she could hardly figure out what to think or know or believe anymore. And where were the guards as the night settled in? Where were the two Impures who not only served to protect her against the one she wanted no protection from, but who also acted as a barrier, as a reminder that he was not to be touched.

She released his hand and stepped back. "I should retire."

"You sure you don't want to come down here?" he asked, returning to his pallet, stretching out like a canine. "Fire's made it damn comfortable."

Her gaze trailed over his long frame covetously. "I'm sure."

Then she started to move past him, and his voice, rough and sensual and near impossible to resist, called out to her, "Princess?"

She released a breath. "Yes."

"I know you're not going to lay beside me tonight, but ... do you want to?"

She closed her eyes and held on to the wall. "Yes."

"Fuck." He uttered the one word as if it were made up of true pain, true desire, and the truest of all disappointments.

Yes, indeed, she thought, leaving the heat of the living area and its resident, and heading for her cold, unremarkable bedroom. *Fuck*.

Seated across from the sharply dressed, perfectly coiffed senator from Maine in his black stretch limousine, Dillon tried to get it into his thick brain that his evening plans sucked bull cock.

"That isn't acceptable, sir," she said.

He fiddled with his iPhone, texting at a rapid pace. "Dillon, you know I don't always do the acceptable thing."

"This route isn't safe," she said for the fourth time. "I can't allow it." She rapped on the privacy screen behind her with her fist. "Marvin! Get back on the highway now!"

"Can't allow it?" The senator chuckled, glancing up to pin her with his watery brown stare. "If anyone else spoke to me the way you do ... "

"You'd have their ass canned," she said with aplomb. "Yes, I know." She pounded on the privacy window for a second time. "Marvin, get back on the fucking highway or I'm going to have to come up there and stick those car keys up your ass."

"He's been instructed to ignore you."

Dillon turned back to face her boss, eyebrows raised. "Really?"

"Just for tonight." His eyes swept over her—from her black boots up to her black leather coat. "You sure I can't take you out sometime?"

Ah, shit, Dillon thought. *Really? We're gonna go here again?*

"I know a great spot in South Burlington," he said, his smile brilliant and camera-ready.

"I remember." Dillon nodded. "You took that hooker there back in July. Comfort Inn, wasn't it? Or maybe it was the Sheraton ... "

His smile died a quick death and he sneered. "She wasn't a hooker."

"Right," Dillon said drily, thinking how good it was going to feel to pound on Marvin the limp-dicked limo driver later. "They call them escorts. I keep forgetting."

He frowned, dropped his iPhone in his suit jacket pocket.

"Look, Senator," she said, nice and easy with a hint of kiss ass because she really liked the job and wasn't all that keen on looking for another, "I don't give a shit what you do or who you do it with—bang the whole cabinet and the escorts who walk the back alleys of Ebony Row, for all I care. I'll just be making sure no one has a clear shot on you when you're doing it."

"No." He sat forward, his chin resting on his hand.

"Sir?" But Dillon had her eyes on what was going on outside the limo. They were rolling through a sketchy part of town. Marvin was so getting his ass kicked.

"No," the senator said again. "That's not acceptable."

She was barely listening to him, her hackles up. "Where are we going? Even if you're trolling for 'escorts,' this isn't the way." Her gaze returned to him, hard and unflinching. "Talk. Boss." She said the last word with only a trace of respect.

He smiled, but it was not a kind or friendly one. "You've known me for quite a while, Dillon. When I want something, I get it."

Bor—ing. She mentally rolled her eyes. She liked this gig, was good at this gig—but fanning egos and spreading her legs for overinflated politicians would never be her thing. The senator had come on to her a few times over the years, but had always backed off. It was going to be a real downer if she had to teach him some manners on this trip, but she'd do what she had to do.

She gave him one last opportunity to play nice. "You keep this up, Senator, and you'll need to look for a new head of security."

His eyebrows shot up and he inquired as innocently as a snake, "And where does one go looking for another talented bloodsucker?"

Dillon stilled. *This* she hadn't expected. *This* was a problem.

For a moment, she thought about denying it—wondering how the hell he had found out. Then she got it, real simple and real stupid on her part. The little missus . . .

"Now," he said as the limo slowed to a stop under a bridge in the very center of Shitty Town. "Everything can stay the same. No one has to know anything. You have your job and I have mine. After years of pretending you don't fraternize with the ones who pay your salary, I think it's only fair to have a taste of what my wife has been enjoying for the past few weeks."

Dillon scooted forward in the seat. "Oh, you want fair?" she said. "Okay." She smiled ever so brightly, then hauled back and punched him in the face.

19

Weapons strapped to his chest, Erion ran at top speed, almost unseen to anything that could not decipher a blur. It was his preferred method of transport—Lycos too. The wolf *paven* kept pace with him over the rolling Scottish hills as they neared the *credenti* it had taken two slit throats and a near drowning to find out about. Of course, they had to flash over things like massive bodies of water, but other than that they used their legs, their incredible lung capacity, and their animalistic need to hunt.

A Beast was a Beast always.

And for Erion, no amount of sympathy and curiosity regarding certain blood relatives would ever change that. Just as the rest of the Pureblood vampire race thought him and his brothers gutter shit, no doubt the Romans thought so too, and the sooner he released any thoughts of bonding, any hope of a life similar to theirs, the better off he would be.

His loyalty was with his father. Had to be with his father. The new Breeding Male was coming back with him, and if he had to torture the *veana* the *paven* was with to get his pale ass moving, he would.

Reaching inside his pack, Lycos took the arm he'd severed from a Pureblood herder they'd found in one of the fields they'd come through a few minutes ago—the nasty bastard had been nearly ready to mount one of his sheep.

Sick fuck had a worthwhile purpose dead, Erion mused, watching his brother bite into the *paven*'s wrist, then run his still warm blood over the lock.

The *credenti* gates creaked open and before another breath was taken, the Beasts were off.

Bronwyn sat up in bed and clutched her stomach. The empty feeling had been gnawing at her belly for over an hour, but she'd stayed where she was. She'd fed so well from Lucian on the island, she hadn't expected to be hungry—this hungry—for another day or so.

Slipping from the bed, from the cold, dank room, she stepped out into the hallway. All was quiet except for the low crackle of the fire. She padded down the hall, not wanting to wake him, yet knowing she must. It wouldn't do for her to get sick, too ravenous to feed from him properly, gently.

Not that Lucian was ever into gentleness.

But he wasn't asleep. In fact, he was stretched out on his pallet with a book in his hand, reading by the light of the fire as though he were on vacation. Bronwyn's gaze swept over him with a covetous pinch in her chest. He looked so beautiful, so intimidating, even with the shackle on his wrist. He wore no shirt. It sat on the floor beside him, shredded from the scuffle with the guards and all the wear and tear he'd experienced becoming a newly born Breeding Male. As her gaze continued to peruse him, an uneasy thrill coiled in her belly. With the bulk of muscle on his arms she wondered if he could rip the bolt that held him from the wall if he wanted.

If there was something before him that he wanted badly enough ...

She tore her gaze from him and quickly searched the room—the empty room.

"Have the guards returned?" she said, remaining at a safe distance. If there was such a thing anymore.

He looked up over the top of his book, his eyes heavy, reminding her of the moments following their encounter on the island, the moments after she'd given him her body, the moments after they'd both climaxed.

"They have left us fairly unprotected, it seems."

"Us?" she said.

His eyes flashed with amusement. "You."

She inhaled deeply, trying to convince herself of the words she was about to utter. "That's not good."

Lucian just lifted a brow, but neither agreed nor disagreed with her statement. "So, what has you up, lass? Checking on the Breeding Male in training?"

"I couldn't sleep." She wrapped her arms around her chest, the thin fabric of her white nightgown allowing every bit of cool air to caress her skin. "Bed's too hard, room's too cold."

"I did offer." His brows lifted. "Though meager, my pallet is soft and there is much heat down here by the fire."

A shiver moved through her that had nothing to do with air now. It settled deep in her belly and threatened to fall lower. "And it was a good offer. I'm just looking for a different one."

He put his book down, his eyes glistening with sensual curiosity. "What do you need, Princess?"

She shook her head and sighed. "I'm hungry. Far more than I should be. Must be all the activity, stress ... "

The heat in Lucian's eyes was quickly replaced with concern.

He sat up, motioned for her. "Come, Princess. I have what you need. Always."

She melted a fraction. Why did he have to say things like that? And in that way—his voice growing huskier with each syllable. It was cruel—cruel to her unbeating heart and her foolishly willing body.

"I'm worried," she said, though she took a few steps closer to him and to the fire, "about stripping you of blood right now. It may activate the gene. I just don't know. I can't predict what's going to happen."

He shrugged. "Neither one of us can predict what's going to happen." His voice grew firm, determined. "But you must feed."

She licked her lips. She could practically taste him on her tongue. Which in turn sent coils of awareness through the lower half of her body, squeezing the muscles of her cunt. "There is the Order's blood," she considered, though that was supposed to be for him, only for him.

"And you are welcome to it." Lucian said the words, but every inch of him clearly despised the idea.

She sighed. "I hate the Order's blood."

His lips twitched with amusement. "Your veins, your belly, they deserve better than cold, thick swill."

Did they? she wondered. At this point, she wasn't sure she deserved much of anything with her wanton behavior and broken vows—and the thoughts, the desires that she never stopped or tamped down. Wouldn't it be better, smarter to take that cold swill and keep herself at a distance from this *paven*? Not to mention that it may risk Lucian's mental state to bite him and consume from him right as he battled against his own demons.

"Get over here, lass," Lucian commanded. "We will take it slow and I will let you know if the beast threatens to emerge."

His command pushed her forward just as his eyes, his wicked, wicked eyes, hypnotized her. The firelight and its warmth seared her skin as she moved, as she came to sit on the center of the pallet near his feet. "It is so lovely and warm down here," she said, trying not to look at his chest, at how the firelight played with each hill of muscle, and the enticing bones of his hips.

"Warmer now," he said, catching her eyes on him. "And if your gaze falls upon my cock it will become like a forest fire down here."

She made a piteous attempt to rebuke him. "Your crudeness—"

"Turns you on." He laughed at her shocked expression. "Come on, you like it. In fact, I'm willing to bet you more than like it. Admit it now, Princess. Make a *paven* happy."

She shook her head, unable to quell the smile tugging at her mouth. "Perhaps I do. Perhaps I like many things about you, Lucian Roman."

"I knew it," he said with a roguish grin, but his gaze was all caresses and promises, and in that moment, she wanted so much more than just his blood.

Her insides trembled with the danger of the situation she was in—that she was putting herself in. She could have chosen to remain in her room until the guards returned. She could've chosen to drink the Order's blood and keep her insides sustained. And yet she couldn't stop herself from seeking him out, living and breathing under his gaze.

She exhaled. So, what did that make her if she didn't care about her fate or her sins—if she pretended nothing outside this cottage existed so she could have him all to herself for a while?

He opened his arms then, giving her access to his body, to his scent—an invitation to heaven. "Where do you wish to tap the keg, Princess?"

"What?"

He laughed, his eyes glittering at her. "The neck or the wrist is where you'll get it hard and fast. But if you'd rather go slow and easy, there are other spots on my flesh that may appeal to you."

Her mouth watered. Again. He was a beast, even without the Breeding Male crouching within him, waiting to spring up and seize control of the *paven* that housed it. Her gaze ran over his skin and she inched closer to him. Oh, how she would love to taste him, every inch—feel his hot flesh on her tongue, against the tips of her fangs.

"The wrist is fine," she said, disappointment filling her. She was a coward, a *veana* who knew what she wanted and yet refused herself.

Lucian stretched his arm out to her. "We will start there, then."

As she had done before, in his bed in SoHo and on the island, she gripped his wrist with her hands and lowered her head. The anticipation was nearly the same as when his solid cock had hovered at the entrance to her body. How strange, she mused, her eyes locked on to the long, pulsing vein on his inner wrist.

And how delicious.

She gasped and closed her eyes as her fangs sank into his flesh. Deep, deeper, until the hot, wet, crimson gold flowed like the sweetest river. She drank like a *veana* who had never tasted blood in her long life, and every swallow urged her forward, to take more, take her fill. She'd never felt so needful, so overwhelmed by every sensation—taste, scent, the feel of her fangs penetrating him. She never wanted to release him.

Was this how a *paven* felt when he sank his prick inside a

female's body? Was this how a true mate felt for her other half when that connection was found and tied for an eternal life?

She prayed not.

She hoped so.

Lucian fell back suddenly, onto the pallet, chuckling softly. He uttered a husky, "The princess is hungry," but Bronwyn barely heard him. She was trying to understand his movement, wondering in her blood haze why he was pulling away. Then suddenly she realized it was her that had driven him backward. Her aggression, her hunger—and she was straddling him, her thighs on either side of his hips. How had she gotten there? she wondered like a drunk fool. And yet the questions went unanswered as she continued to feed from his wrist like a starved creature.

The rush of blood quickened, and just as she was about to swallow, she felt him—his cock, hard and straining against his jeans. Her mind brought forth images—images of him inside of her, his hands gripping her backside, guiding her back and forth as he hit every sensitive spot within her tight cunt.

She coughed and sputtered, blood shooting down her throat, but also into her lungs. She tried to breathe ... God, she wanted him—didn't care about breathing, living, feeding—she wanted what she felt against the thin barrier of her undergarments right now.

And then Lucian was lifting her off him, pulling her to his side, and rapping her back gently. "Easy, Princess. Easy. There is always more. Whenever you need it."

Breathing heavy, her throat raw from choking, yet her body warm from the feel of his and his potent blood, she looked up at him. He was lying on his side, facing her, his gaze an odd mixture of heat and gentleness.

"You okay?" he asked.

She nodded, whispered, "What about you? Are you all right? Do you feel … anything?"

"I feel fucking amazing," he said with a grin.

"Don't say 'fuck,' Luca," she scolded halfheartedly, curling deeper into his embrace.

"Why?" he whispered against her hair. "Because it's crude or because you want to?"

She was too satiated and delirious and turned on to lie. "I suppose it's both."

He inhaled deeply and wrapped his arms around her. "Oh, my princess …"

She lifted her head, looked at him through her wonderful blood haze. "Will you kiss me, Luca?" She shook her head. "I know no good can come from it, but I don't care."

"You're wrong about that," he uttered, his eyes blisteringly hot now. "So much good can come from a simple kiss." He tightened his grip on her, his mouth closing in as he whispered, "I'll see to it."

Bronwyn closed her eyes and melted as his lips touched hers. The combination of hard and soft turned her inside out and she moaned contentedly. She could remain this way forever, or for as long as she was allowed. Holding her against him with a possessiveness she found deliriously arousing, Lucian kissed her as though he knew her more intimately than anyone else, knew what she liked, knew her pace, her penchant for nips of pain on her lower lip and a slow, deliberate suckle on her tongue. Pressing her hips to meet his cock, she inhaled him, breathed his scent into her lungs and felt every inch of her body flare with heat and want. Lucian must've felt it too because he made a low growling noise and pulled her impossibly closer, his chest so hard against her chest, his jean-clad thigh locking over her hip as he thrust his tongue deeply into her mouth.

Her body went limp at his delicious assault, yet inside a fire blazed. How did *veanas* exist without this, this exquisite pleasure? If she would've known how it felt to be consumed, taken, adored in this way, she would have forced herself on him sooner, begged him to kiss her sooner.

"Bronwyn," he whispered into her mouth, against her lips. "Bron ... "

Somewhere in the back of her mind she heard him, heard him calling her. But it wasn't the same as before and she dropped her head back, abandoning his mouth for one brief moment.

"You called me ... "

"Bronwyn." He claimed her mouth again in a quick, intense kiss.

"Yes," she said breathlessly, "but you've never called me by my name before."

He shook his head. "I could not."

"Why?"

"I suppose I felt it wasn't my right. Maybe like the shrinks say, I didn't want to get attached." His gaze lifted to hers, the pale brown flickering with sudden intensity. "Or maybe I didn't feel as though you'd ever belong to me."

Her heart, the one that never beat, moved so profoundly in that moment she almost believed herself mortal. "Do I belong to you now?"

"I'm afraid so."

His mouth captured hers again and their kiss was frantic and passion-filled, and Bronwyn wished with everything inside her that his words, his declaration could be true. She wished her entire past away, wished for nothing but him and this.

She wrapped her arms around his neck, her belly tingling with heat. His mouth took hers with such exquisite force she lost her breath and her sense of self for a moment, and she was but a feeling—a single strand of happiness. As she met him kiss for kiss, she abandoned the realities of their situation and just let go, let herself be his.

Lucian nipped at the corner of her mouth, kissed her cheek, the spot at the corner of her eye and then nuzzled deep into her neck. Bronwyn gasped as his lips suckled the ridge of muscle, the softness of vein.

She wanted to cry out—tell him to bite her, drink from her there, right there, in that sensitive spot that was making her breasts swell and her nipples harden and tingle. But he had his hands on the top of her nightgown, easing the pliant fabric down, over her shoulders, down, over her breasts, until it lay just beneath, at her rib bones.

There was a quick urge to cover herself, her modest upbringing and the shame attached with nudity under the eyes of anyone but her true mate filled Bronwyn's senses for a moment. Especially when Lucian lifted his head and took her in.

"My princess ... " Bright, greedy eyes roamed over her, flashing with a hunger her blood could never feed. "You are so beautiful."

Her own eyes glistened with thankful tears as his hand moved down her shoulder, his thumb tracing the curve of her right breast.

"I have thought about this," he said, his fangs descending, "thought about you—touching you, tasting you, for as long as my memory will hold."

"So have I," she uttered, her hips pressing forward, trying to get at him, get closer to what her body craved.

He laughed softly. "In your bed. I remember."

"That was not for you to see."

"That was *only* for me to see." He lowered his head and licked her nipple.

She gasped as the feeling shot straight down through her belly to her core.

"And I will not apologize for it," he said, his breath on her nipple causing it to swell and beg for him. "For my covetous stare. For watching, panting as you touched yourself, your hands moving down your belly. Your fingers sliding through the lips of your cunt to find the hot, aching clit beneath."

She could barely breathe, barely rasp out the words, "Bad *paven*."

Chuckling with satisfaction, Lucian bent his head and pressed his lips over her nipple. He drew it so deeply into his mouth, Bronwyn cried out with the pain/pleasure of it. The wetness between her thighs said everything, said yes, Lucian Roman had claimed her. She was his. Truth or a lie, she didn't care, and she brought her hands up and thrust them into his hair. She wanted him to suckle her deeper, take her under him and bury his large prick inside her where he could truly declare ownership.

Her gaze slipped down to watch him, his head to her chest, his white hair bracketing her breast like a cloud, his harsh, demanding mouth, wet and stroking. Oh, God ... Her core clenched, releasing more moisture against the thin fabric of her underclothes. The agitation, the need—the need to be filled was making her writhe, her legs moving, her hips lifting—she just wanted her panties off, wanted to feel his hips against hers, feel his long, thick rod pressing against her nether lips, begging entrance to the hot, wet sheath it craved.

Or demanding it.

Lucian's hands slid to her nightgown again and down it went—over her belly, her hips, down to her knees. She was nearly completely exposed to him—all that remained was the strip of white cotton that covered her. The soaking wet strip of cotton.

His nostrils flared then, and he lifted his head. "Oh, God,

204

Princess. Your scent. As much as I would love to see you work your cunt again, up close and personal this time, I must have you, taste you. Fuck, I want to drown in you, bury my face in your pussy and lap up every drop."

His words had her moaning, moaning his name—she sounded so desperate. His hands were on her belly now, moving down—his head too. Bronwyn wanted to feel embarrassed, maybe even momentarily startled by his direction, his course of action, but she felt only the electric pangs of passion and the provocative urgency of a *veana* who wanted everything her *paven* had just described.

"You have my blood inside you, Bronwyn," he said, his chin resting just above her pelvic bone as he stared up at her.

"And you have mine." Her gaze locked with his, so beautifully fierce, so tight with desire.

"I want to taste more than your blood." His fingers closed around the waistband of her panties. "I want the very essence of you inside me." He looked at her through his lashes and grinned. His eyes were the darkest she'd ever seen them. "I want to show you just how good a simple kiss can be."

Her stomach fluttered, her core releasing more moisture, and before she could stop him, Lucian bent his head and ripped her panties from her hips with his fangs.

Her hips jerked and her breath hitched in her throat.

"Part your legs for me, lass," he commanded on a growl. "Wide, so I can go deep, drink deep. Fuck your sweet cunt with my tongue."

Bronwyn licked her lips. She felt a quick shudder of nervousness as she stared down at him, his gaze so viciously hungry, so dark and excited with his lust. She knew how wet she was, how it rained from her, relentless. What if she didn't please him, what if—

His growl turned into a stream of curses as his gaze took in the sight before him. "Ah, lass, this is torture—this is the real torture. You, my princess, are the most delectable thing I've ever seen in my long life." One hand, the shackled hand, grasped her knee and drew it back. "Hot-pink and so wet. Crying for me." He lifted his eyes to her. "You have the sweetest pussy, Bron. And it's mine. All mine to taste, to suckle, to devour."

He lowered his head and lapped at her with his tongue, running it straight through her slit, then up over her clitoris.

Bronwyn's hips jerked like a wanton, like a *veana* who wanted more, wanted deeper and quicker.

Lucian spread her pussy lips with his fingers and groaned. "Yes. Fuck yes, there you are. That's where I want to go." Then he dropped his head and slid his tongue inside her.

Bron gasped and writhed beneath him. The feelings running through her were savage and untamed. Electric pulses hit every muscle, every cell. Never had she felt such all-consuming pleasure, never had she wanted something, someone, so much. And as he worked his tongue in and out of her like his prick had done on the island, she melted, died, ached, but with absolutely no relief. Not that she wanted relief. God, now she didn't want this to end, ever. She wanted the pleasure of his tongue, his teeth on her forever.

"Ahhhh, yeah," she heard him moan between her legs. He gripped her hip bones, the long chain stretching, slapping gently against her thigh as he slid up to her clit. "It's begging for me, Bron. It's so red, so full. Should I lick it nice and slow or suck it into my mouth and make you come?"

"I can't come," she cried, her ears filled with the sounds of the fire crackling behind her and screams of pleasure coming from her body, her skin, her core. "Not yet. Please, Luca, not yet."

He chuckled softly, his lips, his breath so close to her clit. "Tell me what you want, lass."

"You're doing it," she uttered. "It's perfect."

"Tell me," he urged. "Tell me to lick you."

She shook her head, her body on fire, her nipples so hard it was painful. She couldn't. She couldn't ...

"You must," he said wickedly. "Say the words. Say the words and I will lick your sweet clit so softly, feather-light strokes until you fall apart under me."

"Oh, God," she cried out, her hips jerking, shaking. She was desperate, so desperate for him she'd do anything, say anything he asked of her. "Lick me—"

"Lick my tight cunt, Lucian," he corrected, dropping his head and giving her pulsating clit one soft lap. "Say it, Princess."

She pulled in a breath, her lungs so tight she thought she might die from the pressure. "Please, Lucian," she begged. "Lick me, lick my tight cunt."

His head disappeared between her thighs and his tongue went to work on her clit. Slow, gentle circles as his fangs grazed the flesh surrounding. It was too much. Bronwyn felt herself slipping away, her mind unhinged, perhaps dead now—dead and gone. All that remained were the sounds of him as he fed from her. She arched her back, moaned, gripped his head, his scalp, his white hair with her fingers until he hissed.

"Oh, yes," she called out, riding his mouth as the heat began to build inside her.

No! She wasn't ready. She wanted him all day, for hours. She wasn't going to come.

But as his tongue moved quicker over her clit, as the heat and the pressure collided into a mass of uncontrolled sparks, she knew holding on was impossible.

And then he slid two fingers inside of her and she lost all

control. Her skin went tight, her head buzzed, and she felt herself cream all around him.

"Ah, you have the sweetest taste any *paven* could wish for," he whispered, his breath moving tantalizingly, achingly over her wet, sensitive lips. "I will lick every last drop from your pussy, lass; then I will hear you scream."

His mouth closed around her clit and as his fingers played inside the hot, wet channel of her body, he sucked.

Bronwyn's hands left his hair and fisted around the pallet, her breathing so ragged she couldn't keep up with her own movement, much less the hope that she could prolong her climax. It was too much, too wonderful, too perfect, and so she let go, let his fiercely passionate suckle on her clit, his fingers moving inside her like a piston, drive her over the edge.

Without the thought of his earlier command, she screamed— loud and long and without care. A shower of sparks had erupted inside her and she could do nothing but take them and cry and pump and die under his mouth.

Her blood—or was it his?—rushed from her veins toward his mouth, his tongue, and she came, tumbled over the edge, her legs shaking, her hips spasming as she rode the waves of pleasure, rode his mouth and fingers until exhaustion struck her down.

"Oh, God," she uttered, unable to breathe, to think. He'd destroyed her, and yet given her life in the process. She lay there, trembling, wanting to move, wanting him, but unable to move. Tears fell from the corners of her eyes, but not from sadness, from the purity of release. She'd never felt so boneless, so heavenly, so deeply relaxed, and she wanted to remember the feeling always.

Lucian was beside her in an instant, pulling her into his arms. "Come, my tired one."

"Your blood is a drug to me," she said, burrowing into him where it was warm, safe.

"As yours is to me," he growled.

"But your body," she murmured, unable to think properly . . . "Your hands, your tongue . . . "

"I know. Fuck, I know."

"I want to touch you, Luca. I want—"

He kissed her temple. "Not now. Now, you rest."

Her breath was gone, her words too. All she wanted was him, all she wished for was to stay in his arms forever—for the pure true mate love she had longed for since *balashood* to be real. But what was the truth? She burrowed deeper into his flesh to avoid answering, even silently. Yet it was there . . . He could have no true mate, and in the blink of an eye, his safe arms could become weapons to hurt her—her perfect fantasy into her most ultimate nightmare. Conflicted down to her soul, she whispered, "What are we going to do, Luca?"

"Sleep," he said, his jaw tight, and yet his hand on her back was so gentle.

"Not that," she said, utterly wiped out now, the warmth of the fire lulling her. "About us. What is the future for us?"

Too late, she wished she could call the words back. Future? Us? She was a fool. How could there be a future?

"Not tonight, Princess. Tonight you must rest." He turned onto his back and took her with him, let her fall easy against his chest. "I will read to you, shall I?"

"Hmmm," she breathed, "that would be lovely."

Her eyes closed then, and as he read *Treasure Island* to her in a soft, husky baritone, she drifted off into a sound, gentle, and very warm sleep.

Lucian, however, remained awake.

Something was happening. A sound he knew touched his ears,

a feeling of foreboding pulsed through him. Then, on the stone wall before him, moving in those slow, easy waves he both recognized and despised, were letters carved with an unseen hand.

Beware, my son. Cruen and his mutore *advance. They will not stop until they have you caged. They will kill whomever they must to get to you.*

Including Bronwyn Kettler.

The only words in the message that had Lucian's fangs extending were the final ones. He pulled Bronwyn closer to his side and growled a word of warning himself . . .

Mine.

Synjon's insides felt as though they'd been stuffed through a meat grinder. But he didn't give a donkey's arse. He needed to see her again. Up close. Know that what he'd seen through those razor-sharp specs had been complete bollocks—that his mind was playing tricks—bloody cruel tricks.

Couldn't be his love, his *veana*. It was impossible. She was dead. And though her body had been stolen before he'd ever had a chance to give her over to the sun, he'd seen her murdered. He'd chased her killer into the woods near their home until the coward had flashed away with her body in his arms.

Syn had never forgiven himself for being a premorph and unable to flash, and his body, his veins, had never stopped craving her. Never would.

On the rock ledge facing one window in the compound, Synjon raised his blade and cut through the glass, popped it out, then expertly slid through the opening.

He'd be quick, unseen like the ghost he was named for, and he would find this imposter who tortured him with a hope he could not have, did not deserve. And once he revealed her identity, he could get back to work.

He had to find the one who truly waited for his rescue.

Bronwyn.

The *veana* he would never let down.

The *veana* he would never fail.

With the memory of his father's warning still very much imprinted on his brain, Lucian flexed his muscles in frustration. "If you'd free me, I could help you with that."

Bronwyn was warming water on the stove for the bath, but glanced over her shoulder to answer him. "I don't have the key. One of the guards has it and, as we both can see, they haven't returned yet. It's why I need to go to town. Find those males and bring them back."

Yes, the guards—where were those bastards? Screw his own protection; how the hell was he to protect Bronwyn?

"I should be going with you." Not chained to the wall like a dog, unable to bite if any problems should arise.

"Agreed," she said, carrying the water over to the tub and pouring it in. "But unless you're capable of ripping down the stone wall and taking it along, then you're sort of stuck here."

He watched the steam rise from her nearly full tub. He didn't want to overreact to what Titus had written on the wall and scare the *veana* before him, but he needed to find a way to calmly talk her out of this journey. "You don't know your way."

"I'll be fine," she argued, returning to the stove and the final pot of heated water. "I have a very good sense of direction."

Leaning against the wall, his arms folded across his chest, he grumbled, "I don't like it."

"What is it you don't like exactly?"

Oh fuck, did he tell her? Lucian thought, grinding his molars. Did he tell her about the warning or that he hated the idea of her leaving at all, walking out the door, taking her scent and her smile with her, leaving him alone with his thoughts and the possibility that while she was gone he could change back into the monster?

Shit, no. He wasn't saying any of that. Not yet.

"You will be meeting *credenti* members," he said instead, "speaking with them."

She laughed, her back to him at the stove. "I hope so. It's the only way I'm going to get some information on our guards."

"Screw the guards! I don't need them anymore. I just need you."

She brought the last of the hot water toward him, toward the tub. "Well, that's very sweet, in a volcanic eruption sort of way, but I'm worried about them." She smiled at him, her green eyes flashing like emeralds. "You? Not so much."

He pushed away from the wall and headed straight for her, only stopping when the chain wouldn't allow him farther. Even then, he yanked on the thing, seeing if he in truth could rip the fucker off the wall. Damn the Order! Damn his father. Damn his head for all the thoughts of her, his tongue for wanting to taste her again and again . . .

She poured the last of the hot water in the bath and was about to remove her nightgown when she suddenly realized he was in the room and unable to leave it. She glanced up at him, her brow lifted.

Lucian rolled his eyes. "I've seen you naked, remember?"

"I don't care," she said with too much calm, too much embarrassment. "This is . . . different."

"What? Standing before me in the light of the fire as opposed to lying beneath me in the light of the fire?"

"Shut up." Her eyes narrowed and a blush crept up her neck. "And yes."

He grinned and his cock knocked at the door of his zipper

again. Poor fucker needed some attention ... "Since I can't get this leash off and take myself for a walk, what would you suggest, baby?"

She lifted her chin. "That's Princess to you."

He snorted. "Maybe stab my eyes out with the fire poker?"

"Hmmm," she said, her eyes roaming over him, his chest, his zipper, "not a bad idea."

God, he'd love to take her right now—rip that white scrap of nothing off of her once and for all. Let her walk around naked all the time. "Or perhaps I can turn around and face the wall like a good dog?"

Her lips twitched. "Even better."

Wicked thing, he mused, backing up until his back hit stone. Forget tasting her. What she needed was a good slap in the ass. And he was just the ass*hole* to do it. "Or perhaps I could watch you bathe and comment as crudely as possible about everything I see and wish to touch?"

She swallowed, her neck turning a pretty pink as blood rushed toward her face. "That would be true to your nature."

He looked at her through his lashes, his voice going savage. "You know, with your blood inside me, I would be calm and gentle—fit to assist you."

"What are you suggesting?" she asked, her eyebrow lifted. "Touch, but don't look? Is such a thing possible for you, Lucian Roman?"

His cock pulsed. It wanted her, wanted between her legs, wanted up and inside her cunt. "It would be a supreme effort, Princess, but I believe I am up to the task."

"Perhaps I could blindfold you," she joked, holding up the dish towel she'd used to wipe the stray droplets of water that littered the side of the tub.

The seductive humor dropped away from Lucian's mood and

countenance and was replaced with a tight jaw and eyes narrowed into two slits of predatory lust. "I would like that."

She tilted her head. "Stop it."

His brow arched in challenge. "Blindfold me, baby."

Her cheeks colored prettily. "No look. No touch."

"Well, what the hell else is there?" he growled with annoyance.

She walked toward him, waving the piece of fabric, her grin widening with each step.

"You will make me a *credenti veana* with that wrap," he uttered, but beneath his grouch, his body was aflame and pulsing, thinking about her containing him.

"Fine," he said as she placed the towel over his eyes. Anything to keep her here, keep her close. "Have it your way, but I will be listening."

She reached up, fitting the white fabric to his eyes. "Consider me warned," she said, as she moved behind him, her breath on the back of his neck. Then slipped away, cool air filling the space.

He stood there, his chain and shackle hard against his wrist, digging into his flesh. But he didn't give a shit. His ears strained for any sound it could manage to pick up on. Hands rising, the hiss of fabric as it fell down the body.

This was fucking torture! "What are you doing?" he demanded.

"I have just removed my nightgown," she said.

He ground his molars, his hands clenched into fists. "I knew it."

"You peek, you die, Roman."

"I'm already dead, remember?" he growled. His cock jerked, his balls tightened. "You said so yourself, lass."

"No, you're the undead. Remember?"

He never got a chance to answer because he heard the sounds

of water moving, rushing, greeting beautiful, white skin. *Fuck*. His nostrils flared. This was completely unfair. He wanted to see—using his imagination was complete and total horseshit!

He heard her hiss and started.

"What?" he said, his hand reaching for makeshift blindfold. "What it is?"

"Hot," she said with a sexy little growl.

He about lost his mind. "This is bullshit!"

"Wait, Lucian!" He could almost hear her covering up all the good parts with her hands, her thigh crossing over to meet and protect the other in a continuation of splashes. "We agreed—"

"I agreed to nothing," he uttered tersely, his body on fire. "I don't follow rules. No matter who makes them." He ripped the fabric from his eyes and threw it into the fire, then let the sunlight assault his vision. "No one will ever keep me from looking at you, Princess. Understand? Not even you."

She stared up at him from the center of the white claw-foot tub, her green eyes emerald bright. Her dark hair was loose and falling over the back edge like a waterfall of chocolate. He was no artist, but she was sure as hell a painting.

His eyes roamed over her in the water, and as they did, she let her hands fall away from the places and treasures they were hiding.

"That's right, lass," he said, his tone as fierce as his intent. "What you have, what you are, belongs to me now. No more pretending, remember?"

Her eyes closed and she inhaled. "I don't know how this happened ... It wasn't supposed to happen."

His hand went to the waistband of his jeans, flipped off one button, then another. "Does it matter? Does anything matter anymore? We are both doomed to our own particular brand of hell."

Her eyes opened and she turned her head toward him. "I wish you could come in here with me. Water's warm. I'm warm."

His lip curled. "Too far, but how 'bout I come right here."

She bit her lip and her gaze dropped to the waistband of his jeans.

His hand was almost to his cock when a loud rap on the front door halted him. In under a second, he had his head down, his eyes up, and his fangs bared.

20

Bronwyn stood up so quickly water splashed like a tidal wave over the sides of the tub. She looked around for her nightgown, spotted it on the floor in a discarded puddle of white cotton.

"No," Lucian uttered, the word exiting his lips with a grave snarl.

Naked and dripping wet, Bronwyn's gaze shot to the *paven*, who one moment ago had had his eyes on her skin and his hands hovering near his cock. Now his gaze was pinned on the door, his growl for the one behind it.

"It has to be the guards," she said, stepping out of the tub, grabbing a towel. "The magical barriers the Order put into place wouldn't allow anyone else to pass."

"The scent of Impure is weak," he said, suspicion lacing his tone. "I don't like it. Don't want you anywhere near that door."

"You'll like when we have the key." As she quickly dried her limbs, there was another knock on the door, harder this time, more insistent.

"Get lost or get bitten!" Lucian shouted at the wood.

"Stop that now," Bronwyn scolded as she grabbed her night-gown and pulled it over her head. She wasn't altogether dry and the thin cotton fabric clung to every hill and valley she possessed. That would not do, she mused, grabbing a blanket off the chair near the fire and wrapping it around her shoulders.

"Stay where you are, Bron," Lucian said darkly, straining at his chain, his eyes still locked on the door, "Cruen is trying to get to us, to you."

Bronwyn laughed, wrapped the blanket tighter around herself, and headed for the door. "Do you really think Cruen or any of his recruits would come knocking on our door to capture us?"

She had a point. "Not unless they were incredibly stupid," he said with deep irritation and heat.

"Or wanted to borrow a cup of sugar." She glanced over her shoulder and smiled at him. Him with his sculpted chest, piercing eyes, and hard, beautiful features.

He softened a fraction and whispered, "Don't open it."

"You're acting as though I'm taking away your freedom instead of trying to give it back to you," she said, her brows lifted. "The key to your release awaits, Vampire."

"You are the only key to my release," she heard him whisper as she opened the door.

Her body felt heavy and inflamed by his words, but the sight that greeted her outside the wooden door cast those feelings away like a stiff breeze. No guards waited expectantly, but a *veana*. She was a striking *veana* of about Bronwyn's height and her mother's age, and she stood there with her hands in the pockets of her blue dress, her dark green eyes cast in the shadow of her mood, curious and concerned. She was long and willowy and had the most beautiful hair Bron had ever beheld. Hundreds of perfectly shaped ringlets fell around her face and kissed her shoulders in a color that could not be forced; it was as if the afternoon had found its most perfect shade of dappled sunlight.

"I apologize if I'm disturbing ye, lass," she said, her voice as soft and pretty as her hundred ringlets. "Would ye be Bronwyn Kettler, then?"

Before Bron could answer, before she could even ask if the *veana* had come with news of the Impure guards, Lucian growled behind her and called out, "Fucking hell."

The *veana* blushed, the color soaring up her high cheekbones, making her green eyes glow with fire and with fear.

"Do not step foot in this house, madam," Lucian shouted, his tone so vicious Bronwyn wondered what in the world this *veana* had done to make him act so.

Tears sprang to the *veana*'s eyes, and she said to Bronwyn in a soft voice, "It's good to hear his voice even if he doesna want to hear mine."

A slow roll of understanding moved through Bron and yet she still asked, "Who are you?"

She smiled gently. "His ma."

The opposing emotions inside of Bronwyn in that moment nearly tore her apart. She stood in the doorway, gripping the wood for support, knowing this *veana* was telling the truth, as only Lucian's blood could find its way here, through the Order's barriers and charms. She cared for Lucian more than she wanted to admit, even to herself, and the impulse to protect him against a *veana* whom he'd told her was unloving, uncaring, and had tossed him into a torturous school situation for her own convenience was strong. And yet this *veana* with her blond curls and anxious expression appeared anything but callous.

"Tell her to go," Lucian snarled behind her. "Tell her never to come back here if she values her life."

Bronwyn hesitated. She wasn't sure what to do. She wanted

to honor Lucian's wishes, but she also wanted to find out the truth. Clearly Lucian's account of the past wasn't the complete one. This was no monster standing before her. Of course looks could be deceiving—she knew that all too well.

"Perhaps another time," Bronwyn said to the *veana*. "When he's more—"

"Perhaps never!" Lucian shouted.

The *veana* glanced past Bron and called out, "I only wish to see ye for a moment, *Balas*."

"*Balas*," he spit out.

"See if ye are well," she continued quickly, almost desperately.

"You want to see if I am well, Mama?" he roared, the chains that held him rattling in the background as he surged forward. "Fine! Open the door, Bron. Let my *mother* come inside and inspect me."

Bronwyn eyed the *veana* seriously, knowing that this was a volatile situation and would no doubt turn uglier if she took another step farther. "I think another time would be better, don't you—" she began.

But Lucian cut her off. "Let her inside, goddamn it!" he snarled. "Let her see the monster she created!"

The chains of his birth held him captive in both body and blood, and as the *veana* walked through the door and entered the cottage his world went from warm and pleasant and safe to all darkness, all brutal despair. Her eyes were heavy with sadness and guilt and, God help him, love, as she closed the distance between them, but all Lucian could feel was the weight of the *credenti* on her, of the community that had both seen his entrance into the world and had found a way to make him unwelcome and abhorrent in it every day afterward.

220

Shit. He wanted to look away, look down as she stopped in front of him, her gaze roaming over him, her hands twitching at her sides. It was the *balas* inside him that felt the shame, the wee one who had learned very early on who he was, who he had come from and who had knowingly brought him into the world.

But the *paven* he had become, the pureblood Breeding Male that he was now, refused to drop his gaze.

"Is this a proud moment for you, Mama?" he asked, his fangs descending over his lower lip as he stretched out his arms and let her take a good look at what she'd wrought on the world.

Her gaze started at his shackles and traveled the length of him. Horror, sadness, fear, regret all glistened in her evergreen eyes, and she shook her head. "I am not proud of this, surely." Her eyes lifted to meet his own. "But of ye."

He laughed, though buried deep within himself was an adolescent wish for her arms around him. "Don't pretend you care," he uttered.

"I pretend nothing, *Balas*," she said fiercely.

He inclined his head, spoke through gritted teeth, "I am no *balas*. Not anymore."

"Stop, Lucian." Behind his mother, Bronwyn closed the door. She came to stand beside his mother and spoke clearly and gently. "Can I get you something? To drink? A chair?"

"She's not staying," Lucian stated flatly. "She's seen her little circus freak and now she can go."

Bronwyn turned to him then, her eyes as fierce as his own. "You need to calm down before you say something you'll regret."

"Not possible."

"Or do something you'll regret." She lifted her brows. "Like implode."

Lucian growled at her and turned, headed for the wall. He wasn't going to sit around and watch her entertain his mother with tea and tales.

"What is your name?" Bronwyn asked.

"I was born Maidan, but I have been called Mai for nearly as long," she said, her tone relaxing a hair. "And ye are Bronwyn Kettler."

"Yes."

"Sounds like a right good Scottish name. Where do ye hail from, lass?"

"Boston," Bronwyn said. "But I am part Scot."

He could practically hear his mother smile. She would not make an ally here, not from her—not from his Bron.

"And a very pretty Scot ye are," she said, a touch of the sadness leaving her tone. "Our Luca has brilliant taste, does he not?"

"There is no 'our,'" Lucian said, whirling around, his ire once against provoked. "There is no conversation with my *veana*—you will be no friend to her. You need to leave now before the Breeding Male returns." His brow arched. "Or perhaps that is why you came. Too witness my descent into madness. Did the Order contact you directly, let you know your piece-of-shit *balas* has returned with the disease you forced upon him?"

"Lucian!" Bronwyn said, shocked.

"'Tis all right, lass." His mother kept her eyes down as she walked to the door and opened it wide. "I know ye wish me not to bother ye again, and I'll try to honor ye, but it willna be easy. I do love ye, *Balas*."

The blood inside Lucian began to churn, the blood of her, the blood of Bronwyn, the blood of his father. His veins felt tight and constricted, as if all the oxygen were being sucked out by a force he couldn't see or control. Then everything hit at once, the hunger, the lust, the anger, the pain, and as his mother walked out his door into the day, his head fell back and he let loose the mournful wail of a *paven* who truly had no life, no love, and no chance for either in his future.

Maine was fucking cold.

Witch's tit kind of cold.

After stuffing the driver's pockets with cash, Alexander jumped inside the sleek black town car that hovered in the circular driveway and grabbed the seat opposite Nicky. Sara remained in the front, her weapon at the ready in case the male driver decided to get greedy. All three of them had just received the brush-off from the senator's staff, and Alex hadn't thought it wise to get physical with that many witnesses inside the politician's home. They were able to get one piece of needed information, though—Dillon was on detail with the senator.

Now, all they needed to do was find the man.

Alexander scented the human woman before she even had a stiletto inside the car.

He nodded to Nicky, who moved in, close to the door, ready for the woman to step all the way inside. She barely had her ass to the leather before the door slammed shut and the car took off.

Mrs. Senator gasped and dropped back against the seat, looking like she'd just shit an icicle. Her chest rising and lowering at a clipped pace, she looked from Alexander to Nicholas, then to the driver and Sara, her knuckles white as she clutched her purse to her chest.

"Please don't scream," Alexander said easily. "The driver's paid not to hear you, and I will be far friendlier if you remain calm."

"What do you want?" she asked, pure terror in her tone as her gaze caught and held on Alexander's facial brands. "If it's money, my husband won't pay. Can't. Negotiating with kidnappers or terrorists isn't done in American political families these days, or haven't you heard?"

Nicholas chuckled softly. "We're not here to terrorize or kidnap you."

"Then what do you want?" she demanded, her pulse pounding against the vein in her throat.

"Information," Alexander said simply, watching her press herself back into the seat as far as she could go. He was across from her, knees splayed, arms resting on the back of the seat with absolutely no interest in making her feel comfortable in his presence. "Where's your husband tonight?"

She swallowed hard, shook her head. "I have no idea."

"You're wasting our time," Nicholas said, leaning toward her. "Please don't do that. We have a tendency to get irritated rather quickly."

"I rarely know where my husband is these days," she said disdainfully. "He was picked up at the airport by his bodyguard—"

"His female bodyguard, right?" Alexander interrupted sharply.

Her expression changed dramatically. From one brand of fear to another. "Yes. Why?"

"She is the one we seek," Nicky said, as the world rushed by outside the window. "What airport? Public or private airstrip?"

The woman didn't answer him. Her lips were pressed tightly together and her face was a mask of concern. Far more concern than she'd shown when they'd asked for the location of her husband, Alexander mused drily.

"What do you want with Dillon?" she demanded. "How do you know her?"

"She's a friend," Alexander said, feeling Sara's growing anxiety in the front seat. "We need to speak with her immediately. We can't get ahold of her. Haven't for quite some time, and we're ... concerned."

Going for the sympathy card was the right move, Alexander realized as Mrs. Senator leaned forward, her hand to her neck.

"You think she's in danger?" the woman said, fear threading in her voice. "She's so strong, so tough. He wouldn't hurt her; he—"

"What?" Alexander said, cutting her off. "He? Who is 'he'?"

Her lips parted, but nothing came out. She glanced down, at her left hand—at the band of diamonds encircling her finger.

"Are we talking about your husband?" Alexander pushed, his skin tightening. "Why the hell would he hurt his bodyguard?"

She shifted in her seat, bit her heavily painted lower lip.

Alexander leaned forward and snarled, "Speak, woman."

She gasped and the words came out in a rush. "It's nothing. My husband had someone watching me—watching us. But it's impossible. I'm sure she's fine. She can't be hurt. Not with what ... she ... is." Her eyes flipped up, locked with Alexander's.

Fuck me! Alexander growled inwardly. And he heard Sara and Nicholas tossing off a few choice curses as well as they got wise to what the woman was saying. Unbelievable ... Dillon had told this woman what she was. *Stupid* veana*! Shit.* How could that horny little vampire be so fucking foolish?

His eyes narrowed on the woman in front of him. "Your husband's cell number. Now."

She rattled off the number, and as she did Alexander eyed Nicholas.

"Take the memory from her—all of it."

Nicholas nodded.

"I'll get a location."

Nicholas moved toward the woman, his fangs extending. "Won't hurt a bit, female. In fact, after what you just told us, you may even enjoy it."

21

Bronwyn closed the door with more force than was necessary, the action indicative of her mood. Nostrils flaring, she turned to face the albino *paven*, her hands on her hips. "What's wrong with you?"

Pacing the floor, his shackles clanking angrily, Lucian spat out, "I don't know, Princess. Perhaps I'm just an asshole. Is that what you wish to hear?"

"Yes," she said, her gaze following him, watching as the skin on his naked chest pulled against the hard muscle. "And arrogant and foolish and cruel and—"

"When you're done running down the list of my less esteemed qualities"—his head turned and his eyes lanced through her, rabid with heat—"I need you."

A momentary wave of fear rushed at her. Was it back—the claws of the Breeding Male? Or was this something else? Desire? Anger?

"Your blood," he said, stopping and reaching out for her. "I need it." He growled low and irritated. "She riled me up."

Bronwyn took a deep breath, attempting to channel some

patience. No, this wasn't the Breeding Male. She saw the control in his eyes. This was about his mother, his anger, his resentment. This was about Bronwyn giving him comfort, drowning the memories of his past with her blood.

"No," she said evenly, calmly. "Not yet."

He looked shocked and displeased. "What do you mean, not yet?" he ground out. "I need you, Princess."

"Tough shit, *Paven*."

Lucian's brows shot up.

She pointed a finger at him. "I have something to say to you first."

"Can you say it in my arms?" he said, his eyes softening with a gentle lust. "Lying beneath me? With your blood fusing to mine?"

She released a loud, frustrated groan. "You lied, Lucian. You lied. To me—to all of us."

Her words killed the lust in his eyes and he walked forward, as far as his chain would allow. Bronwyn didn't move, though her insides clenched, waited. He stopped a foot away from her, his chin tilted up. She could feel his tension, his trauma. It was as if the sun had suddenly gone running to the clouds for shelter, leaving only gray streams of light to enter the cottage windows.

"All of us?" he ground out, his lips lifting into a daring sneer.

"I'm assuming your brothers think you had a horrible mother and *balas*—"

"Don't assume, Princess," he growled. "As I said, *I'm* the ass here."

"I don't get it." She shook her head. "Why would you do it?"

In that moment, his gaze moved over her face, her chin, her cheeks, her eyes, her mouth. He looked almost capable of confiding in her. Almost. Then he uttered, "My business is my own."

"Wrong answer if you want my blood."

His fangs descended and he cursed. "I have a horrible mother, Princess. Whether you want to believe it or not."

"That *veana*"—she pointed to the door—"who was here a moment ago didn't seem all that horrible to me."

"Your opinion," he returned.

"In fact, she seemed rather lovely."

He snorted.

"She seemed kind, and nice, and grieved over your—"

"That's enough."

"She seemed like a mother."

"She's a whore!"

Bronwyn gasped. Truly gasped, because she couldn't have heard him correctly—she prayed she hadn't heard him correctly. She knew Lucian was capable of saying all kinds of things, the worst of the worst, but this—this was about his *mother*. A body, a soul who had given him life. She never thought he'd go that far. She never thought the *paven* she had come to care about so deeply would go that far.

She stared at him, her eyes wide, praying he'd take it back so she wouldn't have to stop caring about him as she did. But he just returned her stare, defiant as the first day she met him, looking down at her from the library balcony in SoHo. "That is ... God, Lucian ... How could you even say something like that?"

"Because it is truth," he answered, passion in his tone now—the passion of one who hates. Perhaps he didn't like what he was saying, but he sure as hell believed it. "She lay with the Breeding Male. My father, the animal, the monster, the rapist."

"So did many," Bronwyn countered fiercely, ire replacing any thread of melancholy as she thought of her sister—her poor sister. "They had no choice. My sister had no choice. Would you call *her* a whore?"

He slammed his body forward, and the chain pulled. "No!"

"Why not?" she demanded. "Why is your mother any different?"

His lip curled into a sneer, but he didn't answer—refused to answer.

Bronwyn wanted to slap him, hard and several times in succession. "You should be ashamed of yourself," she said, despising him, loving him, not understanding him in the slightest. "Who are you to judge her? Her reasons, why she felt she—"

"She liked it, okay?" he snapped, his face contorted into a mask of hatred and pain and the worst kind of despair. "Christ!"

Bronwyn stood there before him, frozen like a statue, except she could feel. She could feel the heaviness of shock, the weight of disappointment, the dread of more questions on her tongue— and the blind idiocy of wishing the past hour hadn't happened. She closed her eyes and inhaled. "What did you just say?"

He cursed. Then again. "She liked it, Princess," he ground out. "She liked it so fucking much, she went back for more!"

"No," Bronwyn said, shaking her head.

"Don't tell me no," he said. "Fuck!" He reached for her hand, clasped it. "I need your blood," he said, impassioned. "I need you! Right now, goddamn it!"

She let him pull her into his arms because she was weak and confused, and, God, it felt so good. "Where would you hear such a thing?" she asked him, feeling almost drunk, her head spinning, her skin aflame in his arms. "Someone in the *credenti*, someone awful and spiteful, someone who probably had a grudge or—"

"Stop it, Bron," he urged, almost pained, his hands on her arms, his eyes locked hard on hers. "I heard it from her. I heard it straight from her."

Bronwyn shook her head, but he persisted.

"She wanted him, Bron," he continued, his tone pained now. "She kept wanting him."

The weight of his words, the implication of his words battered her insides. She almost couldn't speak, and yet she had to. "I gave myself to you. On the island, here beside the fire. I gave myself to you and I liked it. What does that make me, then?"

Lucian stood motionless, his breath coming heavy, his nostrils flaring as he stared down at her. He couldn't answer—he didn't have an answer.

"What does that make me?" she pushed him, her tone almost frantic.

He looked up, away. "Goddamn it! It makes you different."

"No." She shoved him away. "I'm no different." She turned away from him.

"Where are you going?" he demanded.

She needed to get out, get away from him and this house, the fire and his warm pallet, and figure out what she was doing. "I'm getting dressed; then I'm going to town. Perhaps we need the guards more than I thought we did."

He cursed. "With your blood inside me, you have no need of protection and you know it."

"Yes, Luca," she said, heading for the hall, "but what about when my blood's not inside you anymore?"

"You won't go without me, goddamn it!" he called after her.

"Watch me!" What was she doing here? She had a life—a whole life outside of this cottage—and a future. Why was she protecting him? Saving him?

She heard him snarling, heard his chains clanking loudly as he tried to yank them out of the wall and free himself.

Why did she care if he turned into the Breeding Male for good? She dropped on the bed, put her head in her hands. Perhaps because she had become an even bigger fool than he

231

was—perhaps because she had fallen hopelessly and desperately in love with him.

Synjon Wise could remain still as stone for longer than any *paven* on earth—or so he believed. It was one of his skills, his strengths—total control over his body and mind. Problem was, in Cruen's laboratory from hell, he'd stood unmoving for over thirty minutes now while the *veana* he had believed dead for over a year sat nude and shaking in a cell barely twenty feet away.

It took supreme control not to run at her, tear down the walls of the cell with his teeth, and snatch her away. But if he did, neither one of them would be getting away alive.

There were guards, several of them—and the Pureblooded tossers were heavily armed.

Syn hadn't believed it was her—even as he'd slipped inside the compound, moved silently past the guards, tunneled through pipes, even when he'd emerged into the lab's epicenter. Even then, he'd thought his mind had conjured her image. He'd thought he was an even bigger sod than he'd believed himself to be. And then ... *Fuck!*—and then, a scent so raw, so delicate, so unmistakably *her*, had snaked its way toward him, slowly drifting up into his nostrils, until it all but encased him.

Juliet.

His Juliet. The love of his crapper of a life. Bloody hell, he'd had that scent infused inside him from the moment they'd met, then imprinted on his mind when they'd shared their blood, and again when his body lay beneath hers, holding on as she'd rode him into beloved oblivion.

Synjon's teeth ground together as he stood frozen in his hiding place. Once he'd recognized her scent, he'd run, vigilant as ever, but unbearably desperate, toward it, stopping only when he'd met with a circle of guards—where he now remained unmoving.

Pain and need shot through him as he watched her writhe against the floor of her cage. His poor *veana*. She was hot, her cunt so wet he knew every male in the room could scent it. She was in heat, desperate for a *paven* to climb atop her and put her out of her misery. His insides shuddered with a need to protect her, bring her back home with him where she belonged. How had he not felt her? How had he not known she still existed in this world? No, they weren't true mates, but wasn't love—deep and returned—just as strong a bond?

Maybe it was Cruen's doing. Yes. That had to be it.

A low growl rumbled in his chest. What *had* that piece of shite done to her to not only dampen her scent, but send her into this state of sexual frustration and desperation?

Whatever it was, that ancient cock-up would die by his hand, slow and with grave, long-lasting pain. Then, after taking what belonged to him and any innocents who remained, Syn would plant explosives in every crevice of this laboratory and blow the sodding thing to bits.

Juliet moaned then, a sexual moan, a need so painful and frantic, his own body inflamed, his cock, hard and anxious to get out of his jeans. Bloody hell, he had to help her, had to take her pain somehow. Bugger the guards—he'd kill them all—and yet he knew he had to be thoughtful if he wanted her to live, to come home with him.

His soul ached, she looked so broken, so far from the *veana* he had known. Guilt swam in his blood at the thought of how he'd failed her. His mind ached for her, to hear her voice—see her face, her eyes locked with his. He hadn't been able to give his life for hers until now.

"She's a beauty, ain't she?"

The gun pointed at his temple didn't worry him. Didn't even cause him to flinch. No, it was the anger, the feral anger that was spiraling inside of him at the moment—out of control—that concerned him. Not only would he kill this guard, but he might very well rip him to pieces, then eat his Impure heart.

In under a second, Syn was on his feet, the gun was on the floor, and the bastard's chest was gutted.

She'd dreamed of going to Scotland, the land of her ancestors. In fact, she'd even contemplated traveling there for her mating trip—when she finally found her true mate, that is. Then her Meta had hit, and she'd had to cease thinking romantically and had to start thinking practically.

As blue sky fought with white clouds for space in the heavens above, Bronwyn trudged up the hill, the world so green around her even in early spring. It was a warm day, with a light breeze, and as she came down the other side of the rise, she breathed in the fragrances of the beautiful wildness of the Scottish Highlands. The air smelled so fresh, so new it should have renewed her spirit as it entered her lungs, taken away a trifle of the melancholy she had left behind in the cottage with him. But it didn't. Lucian's words were too deeply imprinted on her mind for solace to take hold.

She wanted him. She kept wanting him.

The length of Bronwyn's strides increased, her breath coming in heavy gasps as she leaped over a thin stream and made her way down the hill into the valley where the *credenti* had their village, hidden from view as they all were. Lucian could've been speaking of her with those words. She wanted him—the Breeding Male. She still wanted him. Did that make her a whore in his eyes?

A cloud covered the sun then and bathed the surrounding farmland in a peaked, gray light. What did it matter? she thought, moving through the tall grasses. What did his opinion matter? She didn't belong to him, did she? They could play all they wanted, say what they wanted in the throes of climax, but she was Synjon's.

Synjon . . .

She stopped in front of the *credenti* gates, a stutter in her thoughts, a reality check in her mind. Syn may have been able to forgive what had happened on the island, what they'd had to do to escape. But there was no way he was going to forgive what she'd allowed, what she'd wanted and begged for since. And she was fooling herself if she thought otherwise. The truth of her future, of her choices, was a life lived in censure now. Not unlike Lucian's.

She bit into her wrist; the pain she felt was not for herself, but for the loss of a lifelong friend.

All for the love of a hypocrite *paven* who no doubt thought her a whore.

The blood ran from her bite marks down her wrist and she lifted it to the gate, ran it across the lock, and waited.

She would find the guards, bring them back to the cottage, and . . . and what? she thought as the gates opened with a rousing creak. Leave? Leave Lucian to the fates, to a downward spiral back into madness again? Groaning, she walked past more farmland toward a grove of trees, a stream, and finally a single lane with homes and businesses on either side. She could no more do that than stop loving him. He had sacrificed himself and his life to get her out of Cruen's reality, and no matter where this all ended up, she would do no less for him.

The center of the *credenti*, of the small village, was charming and rustic, so different than her home in Boston, and she fell in love with it instantly. Every *veana* she passed and every unmorphed *paven* waved hello and wished her a good day.

Even the Impures appeared happy and well cared for as they worked side by side with their masters on the land, in the shops, and in the open markets. Spying a bustling food cart situated between a blacksmith and a potter, Bronwyn headed that way with her questions regarding the guards. But just as she approached, a voice called out from behind her.

"Bronwyn Kettler?"

Bron turned to see Lucian's mother walking down the road toward her, her hand in the air in greeting. Bronwyn waved back. The *veana* was still in her plain blue dress, but under the glow of the sun, she looked anything but plain. With all her honey blond curls and full, pink lips, and that welcoming, open demeanor, she seemed like a goddess on earth. As she approached, Bronwyn couldn't help thinking about Lucian's statements and beliefs and opinions. Was it true? she wondered. Had Mai actually told her son that she liked the Breeding Male, had wanted the Breeding Male—and still did? And if so, why? Why would a mother tell her child such a thing?

"It's good to see ye again, lass," she said, a trace of grief in her green eyes. "Is my *balas* all right?"

Bronwyn nodded, her throat suddenly tight. She knew horrible people, wicked people who knew nothing of love. This *veana*, this one who stood before her with unchecked vulnerability in her eyes, was not a mother who didn't love her son. "He's fine. Stubborn, but fine."

She gave Bron a soft smile, then asked, "What are ye doing in town, then? Can I help ye find something?"

"I'm actually looking for the guards we came with. One was ill, and was brought to town to see the doctor. We haven't heard from either of them."

Suddenly wary, Mai stepped closer, her tone dropping to a whisper. "I'm afraid yer guards are no longer here."

Bron's gut tightened. "What do you mean?"

Mai bit her lip. "They were at the doc's up until last eve," she said, glancing around to see if she was being overheard. "This morning, she found their cots empty. No one has seen them since. It was assumed they went back to ye."

The air around Bronwyn suddenly felt flat and her chest constricted as if she wasn't being allowed to breathe properly. What did this all mean? Did the guards run off? And if so, why? They knew they had a job to do, and commissioned by the Order, no less. No vampire, Impure or Pureblood, would deny the Order, save the Roman brothers.

This wasn't good ... No one to protect them from Cruen—nothing to keep her and Lucian apart.

"Are ye all right, lass?"

Bronwyn glanced up, saw the concern in Mai's eyes, and forced a nod. "Fine. Just concerned. For Lucian ... "

Mai smiled, her fangs so white they nearly glowed. "We have that in common. Please. Sit with me for a spell." She led Bronwyn to a nearby bench that overlooked the winding stream Bron had jumped over earlier. It was far thinner here and felt the water flowed at a gentler pace.

Folding herself onto the wood bench, Mai sighed. "It pains me that I cannot reach him, cannot make him understand."

Though Bronwyn's head spun with concerns over the guards, it also spun with questions about Lucian, and she sat beside his mother and prepared for the intimacy of their discussion. "How could you make him understand? Anything?" she added plainly. "He won't let you explain, and the moment you try he says awful, cruel things."

"Don't feel bad, lass. He has his reasons for feeling and acting the way he does."

"His reasons are shite," Bronwyn said suddenly, then felt

237

embarrassment creep up into her cheeks. "If you don't mind me saying so."

The *veana* smiled. "Don't mind at all. I see yer ire comes from the same place as my grief. The love of our Luca."

Our Luca.

Bronwyn's entire body melted at those two words, swooned over their significance and weight, and she felt tears behind her eyes.

Mai covered her hand with her own. "Lucian had a difficult time of it in the early days," she explained, looking out at the water moving downstream at a slow, bubbling pace. "My feelings about the Breeding Male were revealed to one friend who didna keep my secret, and the word spread like a plague through the village. Lucian was a wee *balas* then, and the other bairn in the village picked at him like a bunch of hungry hens."

Bronwyn shook her head against the image in her mind; she could see a little white-blond child wanting to run from his tormentors, but standing his ground. She could see a little blond *balas* attempting to defend his mother, but wondering in the back of his mind if it were truth his bullies were spewing.

"There's a part of him that canna make sense of his birth, his existence," Mai continued. "Breeding Males are to be reviled, feared, despised, and exalted at the same time." She opened her bag and rooted for something inside. "A child of the Breeding Male is already reviled, and his mother is pitied. Yet Lucian's mother—me—I wanted the monster. He didna feel like a monster to me." She laughed softly. "I know it's impossible for anyone to understand such a thing."

"No," Bronwyn said, squeezing Mai's hand. "It's not."

Mai looked over at her and smiled. "I chose the sex of my *balas*, ye know."

Bronwyn stared, shocked, yet fascinated. "He let you choose—"

"No," she said quickly. "I asked."

"You asked the Breeding Male for a boy?"

"Aye." Her eyes, her exquisite emerald eyes, sparkled. "I wanted the *balas*. I wanted him so much—just as I wanted the *paven* who gave him to me. The Breeding Male, *my* Breeding Male, was not forced upon me. I wanted to mate with him, lie beneath him, and whenever he was brought to our *credenti* I sought him out again. I will defend my desire for him." Her eyes clouded over. "But I didna think at the time how it would affect my wee one. I didn't—I *couldn't* imagine him becoming a Breeding Male. If I had … " She shook her head, tears in her eyes. "So ye see, lass, he has good reason to hate me. But I'll keep trying to gain his forgiveness."

Bronwyn's emotions were riotous and plenty, and she wasn't ready to stop the discussion with this *veana* who had explained so much. "His brothers … their mothers either despised them or used them, and Lucian—he has a mother who loves him—"

"His brothers had more simple, understandable outcomes to their conception and births," Mai pointed out, swiping at her eyes. "Lucian's is far more complicated."

"The school you sent him to …?" Bronwyn began, an unfinished question.

Mai sighed. "The *balas* in the *credenti* were so ruthless, so cruel. I thought it better to send him away to school, with human males who knew nothing of who and what he was." She shook her head. "It was not. I have made many mistakes, and Lucian is paying for them. But"—she paused and locked her gaze to Bron's—"one thing I am certain of. Luca is no mistake."

Bronwyn could hardly take it all in, understand the divide—

the choice Lucian was making to hate this *veana*. He had to know all of this, had to know Mai wanted him, loved him.

"Would you care for a seedcake?" Mai offered, taking a handkerchief out of her bag and unwrapping it. "I make them myself from the garden behind my cottage."

Bronwyn took one of the small cakes, though she felt no hunger inside her, only thirst for more stories of Lucian. "Thank you. I'm trying to start a garden near the cottage."

"Ah, that's lovely, lass. If Luca wouldn't be opposed to it, I'd be happy to help," Mai said kindly. "After all, ye shouldna exert yourself overmuch."

Bronwyn smiled, confused. "Why not?"

"Keeping yer feet elevated above yer fangs ain't just an old *veana*'s tale." Grinning broadly now, Mai's eyes dropped to Bron's midsection. "So ... how far along are ye?"

"With what?" Bronwyn asked, a little harder now, her eyes narrowed.

"Yer *swell*, lass."

Bronwyn's smile died and she stilled. "I'm not pregnant."

Mai's expression went dry and a bit worried. "Oh dear. Oh my. I thought ... "

"I'm not pregnant," Bronwyn said again, rising from the bench, her seedcake dropping on the ground.

"Bronwyn. Lass." Standing, Mai attempted to explain, attempted to calm her. "I thought I sensed something back at the cottage ... I thought I scented myself in yer blood. Lucian too ... I thought ye were here because ye wished to talk ... "

"I came here to look for the guards," Bronwyn stated, her breathing uneven and quick.

Mai looked worried now. "My dear, I didna mean to upset ye. I'm so sorry."

Bronwyn waited, shock buzzing in her ears, her mind

tumbling with confused thoughts. "It's fine," she said, her hand shaking as she lifted it to brush the hair out of her eyes. "I'm fine." She eyed the older *veana* directly. "I'm not in *swell*, Mai. He would know. Lucian would know if he'd . . . done that."

"Only if he was a Breeding Male when it happened."

The buzzing got louder. Bronwyn's eyes widened. He hadn't been the Breeding Male . . . not then—not on the island.

Mai looked utterly bereft now. "Lass . . . "

This was insanity. Just the suggestion. A *balas*? *Swell*? No! That was her sister's fate, not hers. Breathing heavy now, Bronwyn glanced over her shoulder, looked all around. The square seemed crowded all of a sudden. Everyone looking at her, seeing her lose her mind right out in the open. "He would know now though. He would scent it now." Her gaze shifted back to the older *veana*. "Right?"

Mai swallowed tightly. "Aye. He would."

She had to go, had to run. "Thank you for the cake," she muttered stupidly. "I have to get back." She turned around and started walking.

"Lass, wait," Mai called. "Please! He has become the one thing he never wanted to become," she shouted after her. "Perhaps he didna tell ye because he was afraid ye would hate him for it."

Numb, eyes wide as a frightened animal's, Bronwyn kept walking. She looked at no one, acknowledged nothing as she walked out of the square, past the farmland and trees, her head down, tears in her throat.

Or perhaps he didn't tell me because he doesn't want me, she thought wildly—*or the* balas.

Because that would certainly make her hate him.

22

Dillon couldn't flash. Hell, she could barely move. Every bone in her body felt broken, her muscles felt pulled or torn apart. The senator and the six or seven bastards—she'd lost count—he'd hired had done a bang-up job of teaching her a lesson. Like, a) You don't punch a politician in the face without expecting to be punched back. And b) You don't punch a politician in the face after refusing to give him the same ride as you've given his wife.

Not if you want to keep your bones unbroken and your skin intact, anyway.

But Dillon had always had a problem with authority, especially when that authority became a total dickhead. She didn't lie down and take it from anyone—unless they beat her so badly she couldn't help it, unless her body couldn't help it and gave out without her permission.

She tried to move her arm, close her fist, but ended up sucking air into her lungs, the pain was so fierce. No quick blow job was going to fix these wounds. Her hand, it felt so heavy. It hadn't felt that heavy in a long time, not since ...

Sudden fear pummeled her, mixing with the acute pain running up and down her frame. No ... Fuck no ... Not now. Not ever! She needed to feel her—no! She needed to *see* her face. Gathering every ounce of strength left inside her, she fought to peel herself off the ground, off the stinking, ice-cold cement. *Get up, you stupid bitch! Get up before they come back and see you.* Shit, maybe they already had—when she'd lost consciousness.

Her fingers tore into the concrete, but she had nothing left in her. She let her head fall and her hands go limp. Maybe she could just curl up and disappear. Curl up and die. Right here, bleed out on the concrete like roadkill.

She heard something then—inside her bloodied ears, or was it in her brain? She couldn't sense where anything was coming from, or even what position she was lying in. But there it was again. A male voice. It was coming closer, she could feel that in the rise of the skin on her arms. *Shit.* Her fingers dug in again and she pressed her torso up. *Come on!* Goddamn it. She had to get up, get out, before anyone saw her.

"Took you long enough," the male voice said with deep aggression and concern. "Where is she?"

The scent of Impure blood shot into Dillon's nostrils and she flinched. *Have to get up. Have to fight.* But her muscles refused her, rejected her. Assholes, she thought dazedly.

"Oh, shit. You didn't tell me it was this bad." She felt hands on her back and the voice again. "Easy, D."

D.

The name ... barreling through her mind as she fought to make sense of it. Who called her that? Not the senator, not his bastards for hire. Oh, God.

The Romans.

Someone was lifting her—the male—so gently it felt like slow motion.

"No," she mumbled between torn-up lips.

He cursed, whispered, "Who did this to you?"

Couldn't be the Romans. No scent of pure blood. She shook her head, or tried to.

"I want names," he said fiercely, but his voice wasn't soft anymore. It traveled, maybe to whoever was there with him. "I want to make sure I kill the right people."

"You got it, Gray," another male said.

Gray.

"Where ... taking ... me?" She barely got the words out. Her throat was so tight, as if she'd been choked.

"Home."

"No ... home ... "

"You're coming home with me. Don't try to fight me, D, 'cause you've got no fight left in you anyway."

"I can't ... Impures. They ... won't want me."

"I want you."

Her brain was going fuzzy. She was going to lose consciousness soon. "Fuck. Gray ... "

"Shhh," he soothed. "Don't talk anymore, baby. Just rest."

Always hated that word, "baby." But not today, not right now.

She felt his grip on her shift, scented leather and gasoline; then she was tucked against his chest, his heart beating hard and strong against her cheek.

"You can't let anyone see me," she uttered, her throat so pained, but she had to get this out. "Not like this."

"Don't worry, baby," he said, gripping her tighter. "I've got you. No one's going to hurt you again."

"Gray," the other male voice called out.

"Yeah?"

"They're coming."

244

Dillon started, her fingers flinching against Gray's chest. "Who?"

"Romans," Gray told her, moving quickly now.

Shaking her head against that awful truth, Dillon clung to Gray as he climbed into the backseat of a car. "How ... did you find me?"

"Your blood."

"What?"

"That night I drank from you. Remember? You rescued my nearly blood-castrated ass from the Paleo?"

He slammed the door shut and Dillon groaned. Did she remember it? The shower, the kiss, the bite? Or had she blocked it out like she did everything good that happened in her life?

A car screeched to a halt beside them, doors opened.

"Go," Gray commanded.

The car lurched forward, took off at high speed.

Dillon felt herself shutting down, but before she gave in, she whispered, "Did they see ... me?"

"No," Gray uttered. "But they saw me."

The words entered her ears just seconds before her brain shut off and she succumbed to the blackness.

Lucian had loosened the bolt on the wall.

Around the metal fastener, stone was breaking off in small, dusty chips, falling onto the soft pallet by his feet. It hadn't been a picnic in the park to make that happen. He was pretty sure his motherfucking shoulder was dislocated, if diabolical pain in that area was any indication. But it didn't matter. He had to get to her. He had to see her face, shield her from the *credenti* that had nearly destroyed him, and, if his father's words were true, protect her from a mad vampire and his Beasts. He had to know she was breathing and unhurt and that the life he'd put inside of her continued on. It was illogical, instinctual.

He lifted the chair again, yanked it high above his head, then sent it falling back down against the bolt, pounding the shit out of it like a hammer to a nail.

"Arrrr," he groaned, the vibration ricocheting up the chain, into his shackle, and through his entire system.

Fuck. The pain sucked ass, but more chips of stone dropped away, loosening the bolt a little bit farther. He grinned, growled his appreciation, and again brought up the chair and again slammed it down on the bolt. This time the chair's arm smacked the shackle on his wrist and he felt the bone crack.

He screamed a curse and pitched the chair across the room.

"What the hell are you doing?"

His head came around so fast it took his eyes a moment to adjust. But he didn't need his eyes; he had his nose—his scent. *Bronwyn.* She stood in the doorway, her eyes narrowed with a mixture of shock and fear as a light rain dropped behind her. Relief poured through him, but all he wanted to do in that moment was laugh, sneer. His *veana* thought he'd turned Breeding Male, when all he'd really turned into was a fucking idiot.

"Afternoon, lass," he called through gritted teeth, the pain sucker punching him with every breath. "Did you bring the Impures back with you?"

"No." She closed the door. "They're gone." She came over to him, stopped a few feet away, her gaze running from the chair near the wall to the bolt in the stone, to his ripped jeans, to his dirty, sweaty chest and shoulders. "Is this the Breeding Male or just you?"

"Just the asshole trying to get to the princess," he said, breathing heavy, nostrils flaring as he locked eyes with her. "Where are the guards, Bron?"

"I don't know," she said, dropping her damp sweater on the table near the fire. "No one knows."

He studied her. Her expression had changed since entering the cottage a moment ago. She wasn't fearful anymore, but there was something there—something dark, like anger—or worse. What was it? he wondered. Had she been attacked, chased—

"I saw your mother," she said, remaining near the table.

Or worse.

Lucian felt his face go rigid, and the pain in his broken wrist no longer registered. "Why would you do that?"

"Doesn't matter," she said quickly.

"Like hell it doesn't."

She shrugged. "Maybe I just wanted to spend some time with someone who understands, you know? A *veana* I have something in common with."

He chuckled bitterly, the movement sending shock waves of pain through his system.

"Don't laugh at me, Lucian," she ground out.

"Why not? That was damn funny, Princess."

She pointed a finger at him, her green eyes brutal, and hurt. "And don't call me that anymore. You don't get to call me that anymore."

The Lucian Roman of a few weeks ago would've walked away from a conversation like this one, wouldn't have given the time, energy, or care to fight for a female. But Bronwyn Kettler wasn't just any female. She was his. All his. Every inch, every breath, every movement—it all belonged to him. It wasn't a pretty package of a reality—her falsely mated to another *paven* and him the goddamn Breeding Male, but there it was. He had claimed her. He had claimed the shit out of her!

He strained against the chains and snarled, "What's wrong with you? What did that *veana* say to you?"

"That *veana* is your mother!"

"I know exactly who she is! What the fuck did she say?"

"Just the truth," Bronwyn answered, crossing her arms over her midsection. "Which is more than I can say for you."

His jaw twitched. What the hell was going on here?

"When we were together," she said slowly, softly, "on the island."

This time, instead of his jaw, his cock twitched. "Yes."

Her chin dropped, her eyes fixed him with a menacing stare. "Did you put a *balas* inside me?"

Lucian froze, legs apart, chain held straight and tight as he pulled air into his lungs through nostrils so flared they ached from the stretch. "How the hell . . . "

She swallowed, her eyes suddenly frantic. "Did you?"

Goddamn it! His gaze locked to hers.

"Answer me, *Paven*!"

Fuck. "Yes."

"Oh, God." Her hands dropped and she clutched her belly. She shook her head.

Lucian despised her panic, her disgust—but he'd known it was coming. To bear a Breeding Male's *balas* was a blight on a *veana*'s soul, but to *this veana* it was the ultimate living nightmare.

He tried to reach her. "I wasn't the Breeding Male making that choice, Bron. It wasn't intentional."

Her face dropped and her eyes filled with tears. "It was a mistake. This whole thing was a mistake."

His gut clenched, mixing with the pain in his bones and muscles to form a shitty-ass cocktail. "Princess, please don't—"

"Don't what?" she interrupted, starting to back up toward the door. "Were you ever going to tell me? Or were you just going to wait until we got back to our lives and let Synjon take credit for . . . " She trailed off as she saw the look on his face.

Lucian didn't have a mirror in front of him, but he was pretty sure he looked confused, maybe even thoughtful for a second. Whatever it looked like, she took it as confirmation and cried out, "Oh my God."

She whirled back and grabbed for the door handle. "I've got to get out of here."

"Bronwyn!"

But she wasn't listening, or if she was she didn't give a shit. She wanted away from him. She took off into the rain, leaving the door open, leaving Lucian staring after her, his mind fast framing her face, her eyes, her mouth, her belly—his *balas*.

In that moment, when she was lost to his gaze, Lucian Roman ceased to exist. He became an animal—a feral animal—and without a care to his already shattered bones and ripped skin, he slammed himself forward over and over until at last, he ripped the chain from the wall. Broken, battered, and bloody, he went after her.

Bronwyn ran like a young *veana*, without thought or direction, just a desperate need to flee, to get lost forever. Rain fell from the sky, pelted her face, her hair, and body, but she barely felt it. If anything it fueled her movement. She ran in the opposite direction of the *credenti*, hoping to get lost, hoping she could find a hole to crawl into and weep, as she used to do against her mother's breast—as she'd wanted to do against Mai's an hour ago.

A *balas*.

Her mind spun. It couldn't be. She couldn't have spent a lifetime protecting herself from this exact situation only to have it come to pass. What the hell was wrong with her? She could've studied anything, become anything—clearly, it didn't matter because this had been her goddamn destiny all along.

She ran up a gentle slope and straight into a vast field of thick grass. Out of breath now, she stopped for a moment and put her head down between her legs to make her lungs stop aching. Rain dropped on her back, poking at her with accusatory fingers. *You slept with him—no protection, no nothing,* it screamed at her. *You took every risk there was, foolish* veana, *and now you have a Breeding Male's* balas *inside you. How much of it was out of your control and how much of it—down deep, down deep where your unbeating heart beats for Lucian Roman—was something you wanted?*

No!

She ran again, through the field and into a stretch of woods. It was darker here, the heavy shroud of trees giving her a modicum of protection from the rain. God, she didn't want this. It would be insane and wrong and a scab on the memory of her sister to want this. Her sister—her innocent sister who was a victim—her life taken by one such as him.

Him.

Her pulse slammed against her veins as her ears picked up something behind her. But the crunch of leaves and the snarl of a bloodthirsty *paven* came too late for her to react. She was down on the ground, whipping around to her backside and crawling like a crab toward the nearest tree trunk as he moved over her. It was like slow motion: naked, wet chest, sopping jeans gripping muscular thighs, an erection so thick it tented his zipper, and a severe, erotically handsome face slashed with hard angles and tight jaw, all hovering over her.

His mouth was inches from her own, his hair hung down, licking the sides of her face, making a curtain of privacy in the cool, wet woods. "You won't run from me," he said, dipping his head and kissing her mouth possessively.

Growling, Bronwyn bit his lip until she tasted blood, until he pulled back. "You won't tell me what to do. Ever."

He pressed his hips down so she could feel the hard length of him. "You belong to me, Princess, right or wrong—lie or truth. You belong to me and I belong to you."

Her wicked, thoughtless core shuddered with awareness as she raised a brow at him. "The whore and her bastard, eh?"

His eyes narrowed, minimizing the look of pain that crossed his face. "I am bleeding, *Veana*. Inside and out."

She ran her tongue over his bottom lip, took the drops of blood she'd called forth with her quick bite into her mouth, then blew on the tiny wound. "That's all the healing you get from this *veana* tonight. Feel better?"

"No. Not better outside, not better inside. Not better until I lick your pussy again, have you come in my mouth again." He snarled over her. "Not better until I'm inside you, so deep you can't breathe." He grinned. "But that's okay, my princess. Because I can breathe for the both of us."

She lay beneath him, her skin on fire despite herself, her anger, her feelings of betrayal. "Do you think you deserve to be inside me, *Paven*?"

"Fuck no," he said, leaning in, lapping in her ear with his tongue. "But does that matter to you or your pretty pink cunt?"

Panic jumped inside Bronwyn. He had a power over her, her body, her mind. He wanted to take her, consume her, rid her soul of all its anger and leave only the lust and, God help her, the love.

He licked the inside of her ear and she gasped.

"My cock is in heat, Princess," he whispered, his mouth trailing hot, yet achingly soft kisses down her jaw, "and you have too many clothes on."

She arched her back, in heat, in need. "You want me to give myself to you, Breeding Male?"

He lifted his head, his eyes blazed down at her with the fire

251

of a *paven* who knew he had no need to ask, no right to want, no future to give. "You can fucking punish me all you want, Bron," he said, his voice rough, "as long as you do it with your mouth on mine and your legs spread."

Her hands found his back, his hard, smooth back. "Maybe I'll do it with my hand around your cock."

"Yeah, I'd like that."

"Or my fangs on your co—"

"Don't say it. Oh, shit." His eyes were fierce, inflamed. "I'll come in my jeans."

"Maybe that's what I want," she said, her nails gently digging into his skin. "Maybe that's all I want."

He laughed, hissed, his eyes savage with lust. "Tell me you don't want me inside you, don't want my cock sliding home, kissing every inch of those honeyed walls of yours. You tell me that and I'll get up off you and walk my broken ass out of these woods right now."

Bronwyn opened her mouth, ready to speak—ready to jump at the offer the Breeding Male had just given her. But she couldn't do it. As the rain beat down on the trees above them and Lucian pressed his cock against the top of her pelvis, she cursed. She cursed, dark and lustful and defeated.

Grinning like the arrogant bastard he was, Lucian dipped his head and, with his teeth, drew her shirt all the way up to her neck. "Tell me you don't belong to me."

Bron gasped as the cool air hit her skin. "I don't belong to you."

He kissed the curve of her breast, then down to her belly. "Oh, lass, the scent of your wet pussy says different."

She moaned helplessly at his words, at the truth inside them, at her core so hot it begged for release.

He had her shirt and bra off in seconds, his chin resting on

252

her belly as he stared up at her, sniffed at her. "I want to eat you again, Princess. Inside and out. Press my tongue so far up your cunt you'll come all the way down it."

"Oh, God," she uttered, her hips lifting, her mind giving itself over to her body.

"Say you're mine," he whispered, his fangs raking gently against her belly.

"No . . . I can't."

He hooked his fangs on the waistband of her skirt and yanked it down. "Do I have to lick the words from you, Princess? Suck the words from you?"

Bronwyn's skin was on fire. She was so hot, she wanted to run to the rain, get on her hands and knees under its spray while Lucian took her from behind.

"Or do I have to fuck the words out of you?" he uttered, his mouth so close to her cunt, his breath, warm through the thin cotton of her underwear.

"Yes," she uttered, her hands reaching for the last bit of clothing that separated her from him. She fumbled with the edges of her underwear, trying to get them off. "Help me, Lucian," she begged. "Take them off. Take them off before I burn up, before I die."

"You're not going to die, Princess," he whispered, sliding the bit of cotton from her hips and down her ankles until she was free. "I'd never allow it. Never. You belong in life, breathing and smiling and cursing me with that pink mouth of yours."

Then he was on his knees, his jeans unbuttoned, his fly down, his cock out—so heavy and hard it was nearly purple.

"And I belong inside you," he said, lifting her up and slipping her shirt beneath her. "My tongue, my cock—it all belongs to you if you want it, Bron."

Moaning now, keening, baying into the empty woods,

Bronwyn grabbed at his chest, her hands fisting his pecs, her hips lifting in silent invitation.

Lucian hissed at her grip on him, but his eyes, wide and savage, were on her mound. He growled, "I'll take your glistening pussy as a yes, shall I?" Then he drove his cock inside her, groaning as her hot, tight muscles welcomed him, then sucked him in deeper.

Bron gasped at the feel of him, the heaviness of him, the deep pleasure that his cock wrought on her body. It was the most perfect sensation in the world. Nothing was better—nothing—except the movement, the slow pistoning in and out of her.

She arched her back and wrapped her legs around his waist, rubbing her wet core against his pelvic bone and his balls, circling, using her hips and her cunt as her body liked, as it silently instructed her. It was instinct, all instinct. Taking what she needed, what she'd always needed from him but never had the guts to ask for.

Well, perhaps now she did—she would.

"Lucian," she uttered, beautifully pained, "go deeper, deeper inside of me. Fuck me so deep I can't breathe or see or do anything but come."

"Oh, God, Princess," he whispered softly. "I need you to tell me—tell me you belong to me, that I've claimed you inside and out."

Bron shook her head, her breath heaving, making her breasts quiver. She couldn't. She wanted to, but she couldn't—he could never claim anyone, not in love, not in heart.

He left her, pulled his cock from her, and she cried out. Then he moved down, quick as lightning, and buried himself in her curls, licked up her soaking slit until she screamed into the open air. Her head thrashed from side to side and her hands found her breasts. As he nipped her clit, she tugged and played with her nipples.

Just as she was about to come, about to scream, die, he rose up, the head of his cock an inch inside her entrance.

Still tugging at her hard nipples, Bronwyn cried out, "Lucian, please!"

Her eyes opened and she saw him above her, staring down at her with a gaze unlike anything she'd ever seen, his Breeding Male brands—the empty circles nearly glowing. "I want to hear you say it," he said in a savage, pained voice. "Fuck, I need to hear you say it."

He inched inside her.

She gasped.

"You want me inside your cunt ... "

"Yes!" she cried out.

"But not inside your heart."

She gasped, then cried, "God, fuck you, Lucian." Tears glistened in her eyes as she stared into his tortured, hungry gaze. "This is cruel."

Another inch inside her. "I am cruel. I am savage. I'm the worst—no good for any female, and yet I am the *paven* who wants to hear that the mother of his *balas* cares about his sorry ass."

"I do care. Please," she whimpered, tears falling down her cheeks.

"Do I own your heart, Princess?"

"It doesn't beat, Luca."

"It beats for me," he said, his hand tunneled between them, his finger trailing up her sensitive slit, "just as this sweet little clit does."

Her hips slammed up, trying to get at him, get all of him. But he lifted himself just enough to escape her as his finger flicked the swollen bud, then tapped it gently with his thumb. "You hold me captive, Bron."

"And you me!"

He leaned down, lapped at her tears with his tongue. "I won't take you, make you come until you tell me you belong to me because otherwise I'm just the Breeding Male again. Don't you understand that?" Her eyes locked with his. "Don't you understand that I love you. Me. Not 'it'—me."

Her body was on fire, her mind gone, but her unbeating heart could only call out, cry out to the one it had no right to claim. Lucian Roman. "Damn it! I love you too, you bastard."

He grinned down at her, his eyes shining. "Asshole." Then slid an inch deeper inside of her.

"Arrogant prick!"

"Say it, my princess."

"I . . . am yours."

And with that, he slid all the way home.

23

The reality of Titus Evictus Roman's choosing lent itself well to reflection. Here within the travertine walls of the Colosseum in Rome, on his podium overlooking the arena where many of his brothers had once battled, he could think, could connect deeply with his son. He chose a crowd of five hundred, all shouting in anticipation of the battle ahead. The intense noise blocked out everything superfluous and allowed him to focus on the emotions and fears within the Scottish *credenti*.

He could not be harmed inside his own reality.

"Feeling weak, Titus?"

No matter who chose to enter it.

His eyes opened, his gaze searching the massive space for the form attached to that voice.

"Or hungry?"

In the very center of the arena stood Cruen. He was still wearing his Order robes, the hood pulled back to reveal those startling blue eyes and the black circle brand around the left.

Titus lowered the level of crowd noise within the reality and stood. "You have no right to be in here."

The *paven* grinned up at him, his fangs long and curved and bloodred. "I apologize for intruding on your time-out. But that is what happens with you run away like a scared little *balas*."

"You would know, wouldn't you?" In one thought, Titus was on the ground before him.

"Impressive," Cruen said. "You know, if you weren't so depleted, if you weren't the half-assed Breeding Male you used to be, I'd have *you* lay with the Breeding Female. Payment for the blood you will always require. She comes from another line, after all."

"I will never lay with that female," Titus said darkly. "And neither will my son."

His blue eyes as calm as a steady ocean wave, Cruen nodded. "We'll see about that. Hunger, power, and the desperate need for sanity forces us to make difficult choices sometimes, does it not?"

A low growl rumbled through Titus. Maybe he wouldn't escape the binds of his blood master here, but Lucian would never be taken. Never. "Stay away from him, Cruen. My son will have nothing to do with you or your schemes."

"Your son," Cruen mocked.

With barely a thought, Titus had the crowd on their feet, had them jeering at Cruen.

Shaking his head, amused, Cruen shouted over the din, "Honestly, I don't know who your son despises more—me or you." His eyebrow lifted. "But if you wish to remain as part of the Order, you will not interfere again."

Without another word, Cruen disappeared, leaving Titus alone with his thoughts, his fears, and a crowd of five hundred strangers who had all suddenly fallen silent.

The day had aged thoroughly by the time Lucian carried a beautiful and worn-out Bronwyn through the woods toward home.

The rain had gentled somewhat, and its soft, wet pings to his skin felt good and refreshing after such delicious labor. She hadn't said much to him, only releasing from her throat three cries of climax beneath their tree on the forest floor, then the coos and heavy breaths of a satiated and perhaps thoughtful *veana*. And he hadn't pushed her. His declarations, his demands during lovemaking had been enough for them both. He had said what he felt, what he'd felt for a while now, and its repercussions would be dealt with soon, he imagined.

The cottage stood quiet and empty, the loch beside it higher and darker with the heavy rain, the rain that didn't still as they reached the door.

Bronwyn stirred sleepily in his arms and he placed her down ever so gently on his pallet, then got to work lighting the fire and heating water on the stove. Drowsily, she watched him as he filled the bath, higher and higher until the steam hovered inches above the tub's rim. Then he came to fetch her, lifting her nude body and placing her in the water.

She gasped at the heat, then sighed and unwrapped her limbs, her knees bobbing up toward the surface, her arms drifting to the sides of the tub.

Lucian went to sit beside her, watched her as she let her head fall back and once again sigh with pleasure. In that moment he understood the drive and the wish to care for a *veana*. It was a strange, overtly tender feeling that made him want to simultaneously touch her and run to the fields to gather her a bouquet of wildflowers. He wanted to call himself eight kinds of asshole—he didn't appreciate soft emotions or grand gestures, but for her he was pretty sure he'd grow those fucking flowers himself if she wanted him to.

Pussy.

He grinned, shook his head.

"What are you smiling at, *Paven*?"

His head came up, eyes too, and focused on the water nymph with blackest hair, eyes the color of the verdant loch at midnight and lips heavy with the stain of his kisses.

"You." He took a breath, cursed, because well, he was still him, and said, "I'm sorry, Princess."

She sat up just a fraction. She regarded him seriously, but without malice. "Why didn't you tell me?"

The fire crackled hard and harsh behind him. "Besides how you feel about me, about the Breeding Male—about what happened with your sister?"

"Yes."

"You will hate this *balas*." His gut constricted with so much pain he couldn't breathe for a moment.

Pussy.

"What?" She sat up, water splashing over the edge. "No—"

"You will hate this *balas* because of how it was conceived— who conceived it with you." Goddamn, the pain in his lungs was fierce as fuck.

"Never." She shook her head. "I could never hate a child, my child."

Why was it he could barely hear her—or was it believe her . . .? "Then you will hate the babe's father for what he is and what he will become."

"Lucian."

"The *balas* will be ashamed." He was on a roll, a shitty, nonthinking, every self-loathing thought he'd ever had kind of roll.

"Stop, please."

He was staring at the floor, at his feet. "The kid—and fuck, I've never wanted a kid, mostly because I always had the feeling I was destined to be the Breeding Male. The kid is going to look

260

at me like I fucking ruined its life. If it ever looks at me, speaks to me, thinks I'm anything but a goddamn monster."

"Lucian!"

His head came up, his fierce eyes fixed on her. "I couldn't bear it. Do you understand?"

"And I will love this *balas*. Do *you* understand?"

Every muscle in his body clenched at her words. Not because he believed them, but because he'd wished, prayed when he'd realized what he'd done, that he'd planted the seed of life inside her womb, that she would say such a thing aloud. He was on his knees, leaning over the tub, his arms in the water, his chain, still attached to one wrist, lying across her belly. "Stay here, Bron," he begged. "With me. In this ancient cottage in this dreary, old-fashioned *credenti*. Forever." His hand trailed in the water, down her thigh. "Keep me tied up like a dog, feed me scraps, and let me lick you whenever you're unhappy."

Her eyes closed and for a moment she said nothing. Then a sigh and, "I wish—"

"That things were different?"

She nodded.

"They're not. Never will be."

Her eyes opened. "I have mated, Lucian."

"Me," he said fiercely, possessively. "You have mated me. In every way that matters."

She shook her head. "A Breeding Male cannot have a mate—"

"Don't," he warned, his eyes suddenly fierce. "Don't tell me what I can't have. I am a Breeding Male now and still in control, able to reason and choose. With your blood—"

"I don't think it's my blood," she said, though her eyes had gone heavy and her hips lifted, sending her core closer to his palm.

261

"What?" he rasped.

"You must've thought about it, Lucian. I know I have. In my work, it would be my first thought, my first educated guess knowing what I know. Breeding Males take blood from the *veanas* they lie with—not all the time, but it's not uncommon. The community, the Order, would know by now if *veanas*' blood had such an effect on the Breeding Male. At the very least, it would be spoken of in scientific circles. It hasn't. Ever." She swallowed tightly. "But a Breeding Male never goes back to the *veana* he has impregnated. They'd never know if *balas* blood— or the combination of mother and *balas*—spurred on such a reaction."

"No." He released her, pushed himself away from the tub, stood over her.

She stared up at him, her eyes pained, yet heavy with desire. "If we're speaking truth, it can't be just the truth we wish to hear." She reached for his hand. "I don't think it's my blood that's keeping you sane and controlled."

Lucian's jaw tightened.

She sat up completely now. "And if that is the case, what happens when I bring this *balas* into the world?"

"Well, I suppose I'm good and fucked," he uttered, turning away, heading for the hearth, his pallet, his corner of the world.

She said nothing for a moment. The room fell silent except for the fire, its snaps and pops orchestrating a terrible sound track for the scene in which they found themselves.

"Perhaps your brothers will find an antidote," she said behind him, her voice filled with a doomed sadness.

"Perhaps," he muttered, feeling the heaviness of the shackle around his wrist for the first time since his escape. Yes, perhaps his brothers would find a cure for his coming madness. "But if not," he uttered aloud, "I will become what I am meant to

262

become, and seconds afterward, I'll force one of them to end my miserable life."

In an abandoned hut forty miles outside the Banchory *credenti*, Erion stood in the center of the darkened room, his hand curled around the neck of Lucian Roman's number one guard. The other was dead and buried already, his wounds from the Breeding Male attack too severe to keep his Impure heart beating. If he'd been raised to feel and exhibit compassion, Erion might have given the dead male's associate here a moment to grieve.

But he wasn't raised to feel anything save blind loyalty to his father. It was enough that he had experienced a few lapses in that stalwart devotion as of late. That momentary error had passed.

"You will take us to where your master and his *veana* are hiding," he said with absolute calm, absolute confidence.

White with terror, the guard shook his head. "The Order has protection on them," he stuttered. "Heavy protection on their dwelling."

"Of course they do." Lycos stood a foot away at an old beat-up table, sharpening his blade. "And is it just on the dwelling, Impure? Or the whole fucking *credenti*—because when we were inside fetching the two of you, we could barely breathe at times. What is it? Pockets of magic?"

The guard's gaze was locked on Lycos, who as usual appeared as near to a wolf as a *paven* could get, and whimpered. The Beasts were the stuff of nightmares, the ghost stories told round the *credenti* campfire.

"Do not go mute, Impure," Erion said flatly. "Unless you have a burning need to join your friend belowground."

The guard gasped. He shook his head. "The magic exists

263

inside the *credenti*, but around the property and cottage in which my master and his *veana* dwell, it is as thick as these stone walls with the Order's magic." The guard swallowed, his gaze running over Erion and the scars on his face. "Your genetic structure will never allow you to get close."

Erion growled at that and dropped the male near the back of the cottage. "Just get us back inside and headed toward their dwelling. We will take care of the rest."

Bronwyn stood up in the bathtub, her eyes narrowed and her voice deadly. She'd never been so angry at anyone in her entire life. "How dare you!"

Lucian turned away from the wall, his expression changing from confusion to lust as he caught sight of her stance—naked, wet, pink.

"Please," he uttered hoarsely. "Return to the water, Bron." His gaze ran down her body, following every drop of bathwater. "It is unsafe for you, for the *balas*—"

She heard nothing, just shook her head at him. "How dare you tell me I am yours," she said tersely. "Tell me you love me, force me to admit my feelings for you, then say you're going to have your brothers kill you."

"I cannot live as a monster, Bron. Would you want to see me that way—know I was fucking anything and everything that crossed my path—without their consent?" She winced, and he narrowed his eyes. "Would you want our *balas* to know me that way, know the Breeding Male as a father?"

The question didn't have an easy answer anymore, and as Bronwyn stood there with water dripping down her skin, growing colder by the moment, she felt the instinct of her mind and soul and the one inside of her speak, guide her to the one who held her heart. Gingerly, she stepped out of the tub, didn't

264

bother with a towel as she went over to him and wrapped her arms around his waist. "Call me a fool a hundred times over, but I believe I want you any way I can have you."

"Oh shit," Lucian whispered, his mouth to her hair, his arms tightening around her. "We're the most fucked-up pair of bloodsuckers on this earth."

She smiled against his chest, the warmth of him infusing her senses. "I know. Ain't it grand?"

He chuckled. "Ahh, this poor kid."

She looked up, her brow lifting with humor. "If he or she turns out to be as bad as you, at least we'll know he or she will be loved."

A shadow, small and worried, crossed his features, and he pressed his lips together as though he fought against speaking. Then his hand moved from her back and tunneled between them until his palm lay flat on her belly. "She."

Bronwyn stilled, her breath caught in her throat. But she managed to utter a soft, "What?"

His eyes warmed, warmed like she'd never imagined they could. She had seen them cold and heavy-lidded, angry, and filled with lust, but she'd never seen them ... cozy, emotionally supple. He gave her one gentle kiss before answering. "We are having a wee *veana*, Veana."

Bronwyn could barely breathe, could barely believe what she was hearing. She reached up, took his branded, beautiful face in her hands. "How?" she whispered. "How do you know? Did you choose that?"

"No," he said quickly. "I had no sense of it until after becoming the Breeding Male. Then I wasn't sure of what I was feeling, sensing ... if it was you or ... her."

"But now you know."

He nodded.

265

"A little girl?"

"Yes." His face softened, though his eyes were fearful, concerned, perhaps even a bit hurt. "Does this please you, Bron? You can tell me the truth."

The truth. She closed her eyes. What was the truth anymore? Did she even know? Did she even care? The whole of her world had just exploded brilliantly, and comically and beautifully before her very eyes. For all of a sudden she was no longer the Bronwyn Kettler of the Boston *credenti*, the *veana* who would do anything—had done everything—to stop this very moment from becoming her reality, her now, her future.

She pulled his face down to hers and kissed him, kissed him with everything she was and felt, everything she couldn't say— maybe could never say. Then she opened her eyes and placed her own hand over his on her belly. "I love her."

Lucian's eyes grew wide, disbelieving, yet so hopeful it hurt her insides.

"I swear, Luca," she said breathlessly. "I swear. I love her. Always." She tried to stop the tears, but they came heavy with her words. "Just like you."

Lucian pulled her close and took her mouth under his, giving her kisses that were both passionate and grateful, loving and melancholy. For now ... for now they had this, each other, a moment in time, a moment of perfect pleasure that they were both going to enjoy for as long as they could.

Bronwyn gripped that thought tightly as Lucian gathered her in his arms and carried her down the hall, into the back bedroom, the one she'd never seen, the one that had gone unused. The one that they would claim as theirs for however long they had together.

Bronwyn hugged him, so tightly that when he placed her on the bed, he came along for the ride. Her face tucked into his shoulder, her mouth near his ear, she whispered, "Feed me, Luca. Feed me and your *balas*."

Lucian sucked in air as she nuzzled his skin with her nose, let her fangs rake across his thick vein. She could taste him already, his spicy, delectable blood. And then his hands came around and slipped under her backside. He gripped her tight, kneading her flesh, pressing her up and against his thick cock, trapped inside the confines of his jeans.

"Do it, Bron," he rasped. "Fuck me with your fangs. Go deep, drink deep."

Her core swelled with arousal and she bared her fangs and struck.

"Christ!" he called out, then with a deep, guttural snarl, he flipped them over so that he was on his back, his mouth tucked into her neck.

Bronwyn's fangs never faltered as he struck her vein, and as she drank from him he drank deeply from her.

Lucian had always hated feeling any sentiment, any sweet emotion, the beginnings of connection with anyone but his brothers. But this time, with this *veana*, he couldn't help himself. He wanted her, all of her, every inch of her skin, every muscle and bone; her mind and her laugh, her cunt and her sighs. He wanted to please her, give her anything her unbeating heart desired, make her the happiest she'd ever felt. He wanted to be worthy of the love she'd given him and the love she felt for him.

He felt her hands on his hips, tunneling between them, tugging at his button, sliding down his fly. She worked his jeans down over his hips until his cock sprang free, until it found its way between the wet folds of her cunt, until it pressed hard against her clit.

She moaned against his neck, the sound of her deep, hard sucks making his muscles clench, making his mind frenzied, making her blood cascade down his throat at a frantic pace. Finally, he couldn't stand it any longer. He left her throat and dipped his head. He wanted her breast, wanted to suckle her nipple until it rose up hard and heavy against his tongue.

His mouth left a blood trail down her collarbone, and Bron followed his movement, still suckling, still drinking, her hips lifting and lowering as she silently told him her pussy needed to be filled.

"Mmmmm," she murmured when he finally captured her nipple, sucked it deep, then flicked it with his tongue.

He pulled back, she did too. They stared at each other, their mouths, their lips, their fangs, bloody and hungry for more than just blood to feed them.

Goddamn, Lucian thought, she was the most beautiful thing he'd ever seen; her eyes, blazing down at him, her neck with his deep puncture wounds; her breasts, coated in her own blood; and her belly, humming with the growing life of his *balas*.

Her hand came up, her thumb brushing the excess blood from his lower lip. Before she could pull it back, he turned his head and captured it in his mouth. He suckled it, his fangs raking over the one spot that still belonged to another.

"Say it," he whispered, his tongue lapping at the mark. "Say yes."

Her eyes widened. She hesitated.

"Fuck, Princess!" He suckled on her finger. "It doesn't belong on you anymore—it never did. Let me take it from you as you come. Let us all be free."

Before he said another word, she sat up, her knees bracketing his hips, her eyes trained on his cock. Shit, he was so hard, the thing looked like an immobile pillar, a slab of burning-hot marble that wanted only to be suckled by the sweet, wet walls of the *veana* above him. And then she moved, dove, sat down

268

right on top of him, her drenched cunt swallowing him up inch by inch until he was completely hers.

"I have taken you, *Paven*," she said, completely impaled by him now, her eyes hot and heavy with passion. "You must have everything of me."

She placed her thumb in his mouth, pressed the spot where her mark lay right up against one razor-sharp fang. "Take it. Take it while I take you."

Lucian needed nothing else. He pierced her flesh and as she held on to his hip with one hand, she rode his cock. She rode him so hard and fast as he pulled the ink from her, he thought he was going to come. It was her eyes, black and savage as she gazed down at him, as she fucked him—this *veana* who was once tamed and tamped down and scared of her past, present, and future. She was living now—really living, taking what she wanted with no fear, not even a trace of it.

The way she clenched around him, her walls fisting him as though he were home, as though he belonged in her—just her ... Shit, he was going to lose it.

He lifted her up, off his pulsing shaft that shone with her arousal and yanked her forward, set her down near his mouth. "I need your wine, lass. I need the sweet milk of your pussy on my tongue."

Bronwyn stared down at him, breathing heavy, watching him.

"Yes, lass. Watch me. Watch as I spread your pink lips, watch as I drink every drop of you. But first." He turned his head, his fangs extended, and bit into her inner thigh.

She cried out, reached behind herself and gripped his chest, her nails digging into his flesh. As he suckled and drank from her vein, he slipped two fingers inside her trembling cunt. As she moaned and writhed above him, her body calling out how close she was to orgasm, he groaned at the way her body hugged him, how her wet and tight core fisted around him.

He hated to do it, to leave her, but hunger and desperation called.

He stopped drinking her blood, and eased his fingers from her body, shiny and slick. Oh fuck, he was going to die from wanting ... With a groan of hunger, he pushed his tongue inside of her, let her heat, her cream slide down his tongue to where it truly belonged.

"Oh, God, Lucian," she cried out, watching him with heavy-lidded eyes, her fangs dropped and pressed against her lower lip. "Whenever I thought of you, I touched myself." Her fingers gripped his nipples, rolling them between her fingers, making his cock pulse and bead at the tip with cum. "I imagined your tongue on me, your cock in me."

Her cunt clenched, spasmed against his mouth and he felt her cream against his chin.

Fuck, he wasn't going to hold on for long, not with the way she was rubbing herself against him, the way she flicked his nipples.

He lifted her up, came with her, and flipped her around so she was on her hands and knees facing the window. Outside the sun shone down on the surface of the loch, the water slow and smooth.

Bronwyn arched her back, pressed her legs apart, showing him the pink mounds of her buttocks and ruby-red opening of her cunt.

"Lucian, please," she called. "I need you. Now!"

He needed no more invitation than that. Lucian mounted her and sank his rock-hard cock deep inside her.

Bron didn't gasp. She sighed, and her cunt suckled and fisted around him. Madness gripped his brain as he thrust into her, over and over as she cried out, keened, screamed for him to work her harder and deeper and faster. And then without thought, his fingers slipped from her hip and began to play with her ass, with the sweet, soft pucker in the very center.

"Yes," she said, slamming her hips back. "Yes, touch me there."

Surprise registered within him, but didn't hold him long. He had promised to give her the greatest pleasure, whatever she wanted, however she wanted it.

Sliding his hand down until he found her hot, wet core, he lubricated his fingers with her juices, then gently slid one finger inside her anus. It was tight, so delectably tight, and the farther he went the more his brain succumbed to madness, the more his balls tightened, and the more his cock begged for release.

"Oh, God, yes!" Bronwyn milked him, arching her back, swinging her hips as arousal leaked from her body and snaked down her inner thigh.

Lucian kept his touch inside her anus gentle, but his thrusts inside her cunt fierce. As her walls spasmed around his cock, signaling how close to release she was, he kept the pace, kept touching her. Sweat broke out on his brow and he pummeled her flesh, his hips slamming against her backside, making it move, making it grow pink to match her cunt and her anus.

And then she screamed. She screamed so loud, he had a moment of worry. But her hips continued to slam back against him and her cunt flooded his cock with cream.

Goddamn, nothing felt so good as being inside of her; as holding her, moving with her—loving her. He wanted no other, would take no other, would drive his cock into no other but her.

He'd die first.

He'd die.

He could feel the cum rising to the head of his prick. It

271

wanted inside her, wanted to coat her walls, mark her. "Oh fuck!" It was too much, the sensations, the rockets going off inside his brain and her sweet walls gripping him like a vise. "Bron, my beautiful Bron," he called. "Princess, I'm done for."

A growl ripped from his chest and he dropped onto her back, reached around, and cupped her breasts. He pounded into her, calling her name as his hips shook and he took his climax.

His *veana*.

His.

He must've made a sound, something plaintive as she shuddered around him, because she gripped one of his hands with her own, one of the hands that held her breast. "What? What's wrong?"

A soft curse escaped his dry throat. He kissed her back, slow and seductive, and whispered against her skin, "I don't think I can give you back, Princess."

"I can stay ... I can stay ... "

"Only for a short while," he said, the pain of his words nearly debilitating. "Until she is born." He pulled out of her and lay down on his side, easing her back against him like two spoons.

This time he didn't say his thoughts aloud.

When the wee veana *comes into the world I must leave it.*

24

Synjon woke with a bastard of a headache and an unclear need to reach his weapon. But when he groped for his back, he found nothing but the waistband of his jeans. Bugger and blast, he thought, his brain filled with static, his eyes refusing to open. He moved, felt something hard beneath his face. Concrete? Stone? Bloody hell, he was beat up and tossed ... but where?

He forced his eyes open, and despite the gripping pain, was on his feet in seconds. Bloody right, he'd been flogged, many times, by many wanker Impures, and his vision was rubbish. Shaking his head a few times, he attempted to focus. A wall of stainless-steel cages—the cries of both male and female.

Shite.

It took about three seconds for everything to come back, and when it did he pushed the pain back and went on high alert. Metal floor, bars all around. He was in a cage too and across from him, to the right ...

"Fuck, Jules," he hissed, his eyes going fierce. He would take that bastard Cruen apart piece by piece for this.

The love of his miserable life lay nude and writhing on the

floor of her own cold, dank cage. She lifted her head when he called her name. Despite the world in which she was chained to, she looked beautiful, wild, inflamed, but her eyes—her exquisite lavender eyes were nearly dead.

Synjon gripped the bars of his cage and forced himself to remain calm. It wouldn't do to amp up her fear and anxiety any more than it already was.

Panting, Juliet locked on to his gaze and shook her head. "Syn? Syn? Is it really you?"

"Yeah, sweetheart. It's me."

"Oh, God ..." She started to cry. Not just heavy tears, but great sobs of misery. "No. No ..."

His unbeating heart shredding as he watched her, Synjon pushed against the bars of the cage. "Don't cry, Jules, please."

"I'm so sorry for leaving you, Syn," she wailed.

Fuck! This was not happening. "It's all right, love," he told her, trying to make his tone comforting instead of what he truly felt like doing—shouting, screaming, raging, threatening— killing. "Everything will be all right."

As several others in cages around them began to shift and murmur, Juliet turned her body, so she was on her stomach, gripping the bars. "I thought I was dead, Syn," she cried out. "I thought he'd killed me. Until I woke up here. In this cage."

The anger raging inside Syn churned dangerous and hot, but he wouldn't let her see that. "I'm here now, love. It's all over. No one will hurt you again."

"He doesn't want to hurt me," she cried. "He wants to mate me."

Syn's fingers tightened around the bars. "What?"

"I never told you. I never told anyone—didn't want anyone to know. My father was a Breeding Male." She shook her head, her eyes the saddest he'd ever seen them. "I didn't know, but I

274

have the gene, this rare gene that gives me all the same powers, same hellish needs as a Breeding Male."

"A Breeding Female," Synjon uttered.

Tears welled in her eyes. "Cruen took me, made it look like my death, only to grant me this ... life. Lying beneath the Breeding Male—he wants to create a master race of vampires."

Synjon could barely contain the fury that raged inside him. The one thing he knew was that Cruen would be creating nothing but his own funeral.

Juliet started to cry again.

"Please, Jules. No." He didn't give a shite, not for any of it. They could sort it out later, make sense of it later—when he took her from this miserable place. "I have you back. That's all that matters."

"I've thought about you," she uttered, a shudder of pain rippling through her, and she gasped.

"Fuck, Jules!"

"I've thought about us," she whispered, "every moment I've been here."

His jaw was so bloody tight it might crack in two. "I'll get you out of here, Jules."

"Syn, please ... " she begged as another wave of whatever it was moved through her.

He pounded the bars. "I swear it."

"You swear it?"

Syn tensed at the words, at the voice, instinctively reaching for his weapon. Wasn't there. Wasn't goddamn there.

"That's an ambitious statement from someone surrounded by iron bars." Cruen stood in the laboratory doorway. He still wore his Order robes, still had the black circle around his left eye, still sported a pair of red fangs, but the rest of him—his skin, his eyes, his movement—had aged a hundred years at least.

He walked to within a foot of Synjon's cage and sneered. "Synjon Wise. I always thought you were overprized by the Order. A second-rate spy, at best." He turned and glanced at Juliet, his smile brightening. "That is, until I realized what you truly possessed. *Who* you possessed."

Feral rage suffused Syn's tone. "My *veana* will be allowed to walk free."

Cruen's eyebrows lifted. "Which *veana* are we talking about? The one in the cage here who will never have a true mate, or the one who is hiding out with Lucian Roman?" He stepped closer to Juliet and grinned. "You know the one I mean, Synjon—the *veana* you pretended was your true mate, gave your vow to in a Veracou ceremony not long ago."

A gasp escaped the confines of Juliet's cell, and Syn's gaze locked on to his love—his one and only love. His soul died at what he saw. Pure misery deadened her orbs, and she dropped her head and cried.

Gripping both sides of the metal bars, Synjon growled at Cruen, who merely clucked his tongue and said with deep, deceptive sympathy, "She didn't know, then. She didn't know that you betrayed her, betrayed your love—that you found another's legs to lie between."

"Fuck you," Syn snarled, knowing this mad vampire before him was going to die so slow and painfully he'd beg for the blade across his throat.

Cruen turned to Juliet and spoke softly. "News like this is difficult at first, my dear, but you will feel better when the Breeding Male is here, when he holds you in his arms and takes you as only a Breeding Male can—deliciously rough. Or so I am told."

Synjon growled, slammed against the bars of the cage. "I will remove every organ from your body with a toothpick.

276

Everything but the voice box." He ground his molars. "I want to hear your screams, Cruen. For hours, days."

Cruen laughed. "The only one who will be screaming will be this lovely one, this beautiful rare creature—this Breeding Female. And it will be screams of pleasure." He cocked his head and smiled at Syn. "But I'll tell you what, Mr. Wise—how about I let you watch?"

Maybe he was the one who deserved the slow death, Synjon thought wildly, slamming his body against the bars over and over to no avail. He was the one who had lived in a riotous sea of his own making, a sea of anger and bitterness, while the love of his heart—this innocent one—had existed in a cage, her fear taken only by the sick, twisted, crushing shock waves of an unending arousal.

As day slipped away and gave in to the cool comfort of evening, Bronwyn cuddled deeper into the strong arms of her lover, pretending that life outside their cottage didn't exist. But the sounds of the birds landing on branches and rocks near the slowly melting loch snaked their way through the open window, defying her daydreams. Life was happening all around them, and soon they would have to face it. Soon they would have to make decisions about where and when and if.

"Stop thinking."

The command was quick and all male. Bronwyn raised her head. "What? Me?"

Lucian snorted and gave her backside a soft slap. "I can feel it."

"Oh, come on."

"'Tis true, lassie," he said, rolling to his side, his white-blond hair dropping against his high cheekbone. "I can feel your thoughts in my blood. I can feel you everywhere. Sense every feeling, every want—every need."

"Mmm, how convenient."

He grinned.

She aimed for innocent. "And what am I thinking now, *Paven*? What am I thinking to bring about ... this?" She reached down and palmed his cock, stiff as the stone cottage that enclosed them.

His grin widened like the unabashed rogue he was. He leaned in, his lips inches from hers. "You are thinking about pulling your knees back to your tits so the rod you hold in your hand can find its way home right quick."

Smiling, she shook her head as she cupped his. "No, my crude *paven*. Not what I was thinking."

He groaned. "Disappointment's such a bitch." His nostrils flared as she stroked him. "Tell me, then."

She licked her lips and his in the process. "I was thinking about *you* pulling my knees back to my tits so the rod you hold in your hand can find its way home right quick."

His eyes widened and he broke out laughing. She followed, then squealed as he came at her growling playfully, his hands encircling her ankles, pushing her knees back.

"Prepare to be mounted then, lass," he called, and was nearly inside her when the sound of horses' hooves stayed him.

Bronwyn had never seen anyone move so fast. Lucian was up and off the bed, pulling on his jeans in under five seconds. "If I ask you to remain here, you won't listen to me, right?"

"Something like that," she said, grabbing the quilt from the bed.

"Stubborn *veana*," he muttered, leaving the room and heading down the hall.

Bronwyn followed, wrapping the quilt tight around herself, wondering who could be visiting them, who had access. She wondered if it was the guards, finally the guards—then hated herself for praying it wasn't.

When she reached the living area, the front door lay open. She ran out into the cool, moonlit evening, and saw a horse and rider at the gate, unable to pass with the enchantments. Lucian was heading straight for him, no shirt, no shoes.

"Master McCrary?" the rider called out.

Bronwyn continued down the path. McCrary? The rider obviously had the wrong place, wrong inhabitants. But when Lucian didn't correct him, just stood there and sneered, she began to wonder.

"What do you want?" he asked brusquely.

"I've brought an invitation from yer ma," the male said, holding out a pale yellow envelope.

"Well, you can take it back again," Lucian said with menace. "Now get off this property."

Bronwyn wasn't sure what was happening, but she hurried forward and spoke directly to the worried-looking messenger. "Here, you can give it to me."

Lucian tried to intercept, but Bronwyn threw him a dangerous look, and the Breeding Male cursed and backed off.

The Impure nodded, smiled. "Thank ye, lass."

"You gave your letter," Lucian said, his arm going around Bron as he turned back to the cottage. "Now, off with you."

The male nodded. "We hope to see ye both there, Master McCrary."

"I hope you all fuck off and die," Lucian stated flatly. "But I doubt I'll get my wish either."

As the horse's hooves pounded the earth behind them, Bronwyn gripped the letter and said to Lucian, "That was lovely, really smooth—very mature."

"I thought so."

She shook her head. "So, McCrary? Who is that?"

"'Tis my true surname."

Bron stopped, stared at him. "Really? What about Roman?"

As the wind picked up, Lucian's pale hair whipped around his handsome face. "My brothers and I took that name together, when we became a family—our only family."

"It is the Breeding Male's name," she said, confused, though highly interested in the explanation. "Your father's name. I'm surprised you chose to use it, considering . . ."

"Considering what?" His brow lifted. "Considering that we all despise him?"

"Yes."

He took a deep breath, and as he released it, he pulled the blanket closer around her shoulders. "We have all been treated as Sons of the Breeding Male for as long as each of us can remember. We decided to be what we are on our own terms. Simple."

Hardly, she thought, but didn't press it.

Lucian nodded at the letter. "Toss that into the loch, if you please."

She looked down at the paper, the pretty writing, the request for their presence. "It's an invitation."

"Fine, you can toss it in the fire when we return to the cottage, then. I am not keen on littering."

Her gaze moved over the words. "Tomorrow eve there's a festival at the *credenti*."

"Or better yet, let's burn it in the stove."

"A spring festival, looks like." As the wind jostled their hair, entwined the black and the white tresses, Bronwyn slipped her arm through his and tugged him toward the cottage. "It sounds fun and I'm going. I'd love it if you were my date."

He laughed, bitter and harsh, like the Lucian she used to

280

know. "What are you suggesting, Princess? Put the Breeding Male on a leash and escort him through town like prize livestock?"

"No."

He snorted. "Fucking right."

"I don't need a leash," she said, grabbing the remainder of his chain as they reached the door. "I've got this."

His eyes darkened, and he moved her in front of him, pressed her back against the wood. "Perhaps we should tie *you* up, Princess. See how you like it."

"I think I may like it very much." Grinning with sensual heat, she let the blanket drop, let his eyes feast on her for a moment. Then she fisted the chain once again.

"What do you say, lass?" he asked, letting her reel him in like a fish.

Grinning, she dropped the invitation and yanked him to her. "I say let's tear this chain in two and make me a lovely pair of handcuffs."

Dillon lay on a bed she didn't recognize, in a room she didn't recognize, and listened to a voice she did.

Gray.

In the short time she'd been here, wherever it was she'd landed—another compound with another group of Impures readying themselves for war—this Impure male, the brother of Sara, the one she had saved from the Order's blood castration ritual, hadn't left her side.

She wished he would.

He sighed above her. "You need to blow on your wounds, D."

She shook her head slowly.

"You don't care if you bleed out? Get an infection."

No. She didn't care.

She didn't care about anything.

"Fine," he said tightly, resolutely. "I'll have to keep cleaning them the old-fashioned way, then."

Something rubbed against her arm, and maybe in the back of her mind she felt something, a quick sting, a flash of pain, but it barely registered. She just wanted to stare at the wall, let her mind shut off, shut down.

"Wish we had a goddamn Pureblood female here," Gray said, his hand on her shoulder as he cleaned her neck. "And I wish I could hear your thoughts."

I wish they had just killed me.

A growl sounded, harsh and fearful, and echoed through the room, and for a moment Dillon wondered if he had heard her thoughts. "Why the hell is it that I can hear everyone around me, but not you?"

Her head turned; her eyes lifted to him.

Gray sat beside her on the bed, his gaze fierce, intense as he stared down at her. "That's right. Every single human, every vamp. But not you. I don't get it."

Dillon stared at him for a moment, wondering if it was really him, really Gray—the Impure, the once-catatonic brother of Alexander's mate. It wasn't that he looked different exactly. He was handsome, wide in the shoulders like the Romans, a mouth that liked to tease sensitive body parts, and those hands, those scarred, fire-ravaged hands that only a short time ago had pulled her into the shower at her house, gripped her waist as he'd kissed her—gripped her shoulders as he'd bit into her neck. It was all there, but there was something else too ... a supreme confidence or control ... a quiet power.

His brow lifted. "Any idea why that would be?"

She turned back to the wall. "Fuck off."

"Yeah, that's the D I know and find irritating," he said, a forced lightness in his voice.

Where she once would've verbally sparred back at him, now there was little motivation and zero tenacity. She closed her eyes. She was tired.

"The Romans are acting pretty desperate to get at you," he said to her back. "They're all looking for you. Sara too."

Blank. White noise. Happy white noise.

"They're looking for the location of an ex-Order member."

The white noise waned and Dillon's fingers curled around the sheets.

"He used to be their leader," Gray continued, "but has gone rogue. Cruen."

Dillon's entire body flooded with anxiety as she fought to keep her head clear of thoughts.

No. No. No. No.

"Hey," Gray said, his hands on her back, his tone worried now as she began to shake. "What's wrong? What the hell is it? Do you know where this guy is?"

"Get out," she uttered.

Gray cursed. "Don't lose it, D. Don't lose your mind over this. It's not worth it. I'll swear to that."

"Get the fuck out of here. Now!" Slowly, she turned to him, her eyes wide, her entire body trembling. "You heard that, right?"

Gray didn't say anything for a good five seconds; then he nodded and stood up. "That I heard, *Veana*."

She returned to her wall.

"You need anything," he said, "just pick up that phone on the table behind you. I'll be here before your next breath."

She said nothing, thought nothing.

Then she was alone.

283

Her mind free.

But her body, not so much.

Bronwyn's hands moved over the smooth skin of her belly, still flat, yet beneath a life was growing. A life she had sworn to love: to him, to herself—and to the *balas*. And she would. She would with everything that was in her no matter what came her way. And there would be much coming her way after she left the wild beauty of the Scotland *credenti*, the calm protection of the cottage and the not-so-calm protection of the Breeding Male.

She released the grip on her belly and reached for the shirt she'd laid out on the bed. In a wave of sweet-smelling cotton, she dropped it over her head and pulled. Evening was coming on now, and as it had always been for her, contemplation bloomed in the night, like jasmine. Loving her *balas* was not the question or the concern that plagued her heart now. What worried her were the things surrounding her announcement of her child. And she would announce it, to her parents, to Syn, to anyone who asked—for she was not ashamed, would never be ashamed of her child. And to that end, she would make certain her daughter knew the pride she felt for her.

Bron reached for her skirt and stepped into it, then put on her shoes. Synjon, her dear friend, would no doubt offer to remain by her side if she wished, stay with her out of duty and loyalty, maybe even offer to claim the child as his own. But Bron would never do that to him. She would never do that to him or to her child.

Her *balas* had a father, and though he would be an unreachable, impossible force someday, it didn't change the truth.

Just as it didn't change the way she felt about him, the depth of her love for him.

It wasn't unreasonable to think that her parents would reject her for lying to them, shaming them, but that would be their shame alone. She was no longer the fearful *balas* of the *credenti*, the child who had only cared for a planned and safe future. She was a *veana* now, grown, passed through into her Meta and come out the other side someone who understood true love. That would sustain her—that and the vow she'd made to her unborn *balas* to be a strong and capable mother.

Dressed and ready, she left the room she now shared with her lover and ventured down the hall and into the living room. There she paused and let her gaze rake over the very fine specimen standing near the fireplace.

"Well, well, Lucian Roman," she said with appreciation, yet undisguised confusion. Black jeans encased his long muscular legs, and the thick black sweater that stretched across his wide chest made his white hair glow and his pale, savage eyes smolder. She had to swallow before she continued. "Don't you look nice this eve."

"Thank ye, lass," he replied in the Scottish brogue that was becoming standard in his speech now. "But it's nothing to how fine you look."

As his gaze moved over her covetously, she smiled. "So, did you dress up for our farewell, or are you headed out like me?"

He looked suddenly annoyed, then grumbled, "I've decided to accompany you to town."

"Really?" she said, surprised—knowing she'd heard him correctly, but not believing it.

"I suppose the dog must follow its mistress." His eyes narrowed.

As did hers, but not on his face—on his wrist. "Yet the dog seems to be without his chain tonight."

"I smashed it against one of the rocks down at the loch.

Finally broke the piece of shit off, but I may have broken my wrist right along with it."

She went over to him, took his wrist in her hands—so thick and strong, like another part of him, she thought wickedly. Her eyes lifted. "Does it hurt?"

He caught her wicked glare and the corners of his mouth lifted. "Unbearably so, *Veana*."

She blinked once, twice. "Shall I blow on it for you?"

His gaze went hot and heavy-lidded, and he inhaled deeply. "How 'bout you blow me, I blow you, and we blow off this bullshit in town."

Though her skin tingled, and her core clenched in the memory of just such an action earlier that day, she shook her head.

He growled. "Fine."

"Come on, now. We'll have fun."

He snorted. "What we'll have is weapons. I have two blades hidden on my person right now."

"I'm sure that will go over well in town."

"We must be vigilant, Bron. Always."

"We are protected here. The Order's magic is very strong."

He looked utterly unconvinced. "And then there is the small issue of how unkindly we may be treated. You understand what might go down there, right?"

She sobered somewhat. "I do."

His chin dropped, his eyes darkened. "Do you also understand how I will react if they do? Or God help them, if they say anything to hurt you?"

"I understand," she said, holding out her hand for his. "Ready?"

He looked down at it and barked.

Her laughter echoed through the cottage, and when he swept

up her hand in his own and she gently blew his pain away, they left the safety and comfort and seclusion of the cottage and walked out into the cold evening air, completely unaware of the three words being carved into the exterior stone wall of the cottage behind them.

Beware the Beasts.

25

"While Dillon continues to refuse us," Alexander said, his tone heavy with frustration as he walked the tunnels below the SoHo house with his brother, "Whistler never does."

Nearly as on edge as Alex, Nicholas snorted with derision. "Where there is only a price to be met, things are far simpler."

"The Eyes are the only simple path we tread these days." Alexander checked his weapon ... just in case. "Luca is contained, and though I hear reports of his well-being, I grow in concern."

"As do I."

"Bronwyn's mate has not only been impossible to locate, but refuses to keep in contact with us as he seeks Bronwyn—the one vampire whose location is known to us. Ladd still has no father—you still have no *gemino*, and we have no Cruen or antidote to the Breeding Male gene."

Nicholas released a weighty breath. "Let us see if this one can shed any light on our smorgasbord of troubles, shall we?"

Up ahead, at the very end of the tunnels, where stone wall met iron stairs leading to the subway, Kate and Sara were waiting with a very familiar member of the Eyes.

Alexander went directly to his mate, while Kate met Nicholas halfway, then returned with him to the nervous-looking Eye.

Nicholas offered no pleasantries to the Impure, just a demand for information. "Do you have a location for us, Whistler?"

The male shook his head. "No one can get to Cruen. Not even the Eyes. Not even with the kind of currency you're willing to put out. It's been attempted, but the only ones who can find their way in and out of his laboratory are his children."

"Children?" Alexander repeated, his brow furrowed. "That piece-of-shit member of the Order has spawned?"

Whistler shook his head. "They are not from his body. They are foundlings, what he calls his Beasts."

"The *mutore*," Kate said, her gaze first on her true mate, then on Alexander. "Sara and I spoke with Whistler before you arrived. It seems Cruen has several *mutore* in his compound."

Nicholas stiffened beside him.

"That bullshit legend again," Alexander sneered, his gaze narrowing on Whistler. "How much are we paying you for these lies?"

"*Mutore* is no legend, I assure you," Whistler told him, his eyes as serious as the Romans had ever seen them. "More like a nightmare. A living nightmare." He paused, then glanced at Nicholas. "The *balas*, your twin, was born with this mutation."

"So I've heard," Nicholas uttered through clenched teeth.

"And he is one of them. One of Cruen's adopted pack."

Both *veanas* gasped, while Nicholas remained composed, though his tone was cold, steely. "This is insane."

"And impossible," Alexander added quickly. "There is no such thing. No one has ever seen one, no one—"

"They are seen at birth only," Whistler said, every inch of him looking as truthful as a saint. "They shift immediately into their Beast state when air enters their lungs. Understandably,

289

when this happens, the mothers are horrified. They want nothing to do with it, and get rid of it as quickly as possible."

"Get rid of it," Nicholas repeated, a bristle of ire coating his words now. "How do they manage that?"

Whistler shrugged. "Sometimes the mother will suffocate it, drown it—sometimes the father will drain it of blood." He glanced at both Kate and Sara, who had begun to utter words of horror, shaking their heads. "You must understand, a *mutore* is a bad omen on a *credenti*. The parents, family, all would be ostracized by the community—singled out by the Order as a *veana* or *paven* who produces the mutant gene. They might even be killed themselves. To most, these are soulless beings, wrong, beneath even the lowest of animals."

"I don't believe this," Alexander said, though he didn't feel altogether certain of his opinions anymore. Would that truly happen? A mother killing her *balas*? He cleared his throat, wondering for a moment if his own mother had wished to do such a thing to him when he'd exited her body. Only stopped because the Order deemed a child of the Breeding Male of higher value to themselves.

Beside him, Nicholas remained on one direct path. "I know my brother wasn't killed at birth."

Whistler nodded. "No."

"What happened to him after he was born?"

Whistler's gaze faltered. "Some *mutore* are thrown out like trash after their breath has been extinguished; some, only a few, survive—"

"You mean survive their botched execution," Nicholas said blackly.

Whistler nodded. "They are sold into a slave trade."

"Oh God," Kate uttered, gripping her mate's hand.

"For what purpose?" Nicholas said.

Whistler shook his head. "Anything the vampire who buys it wants. Sex, servant, toy."

Nicholas growled. "Call him an 'it' again and you will feel the wrath of my fangs, Whistler."

Ready to give in, give up his belief and his rant that *mutore* were nothing but myth to be feared, Alexander asked, "How many are there like this?"

"It's impossible to tell. *Mutore* are very uncommon. Death is still the preferable way to deal with them. The ones who survive must be low in numbers, to stay undetected."

"The Order must know about them."

"I would believe so, and they would be killed outright. They cannot be allowed to exist, much less reproduce. Though they are Pureblood and descendants of the Breeding Male, they aren't *paven*—they aren't worthy of breath and life."

"Cruen was a member of the Order," Kate said, watching her mate's horrified expression. "And he had these *mutore* from infancy. Clearly the Order did nothing to harm them."

Whistler shrugged. "Cruen has done many things the Order has no knowledge of, yes?"

Pacing the floor of the tunnel, Nicholas said, "You said my brother is with Cruen—you called him Cruen's child."

"From what information I could gather, Cruen bought five *mutore* infants from a flesh seller in London and brought them home"—Whistler shook his head, as if this was an odd thing he was saying—"and raised them."

"As his own *balas*?" Nicholas asked, his black eyebrows lifted.

Whistler nodded. "That, and as weapons, as soldiers."

Stopping, Nicholas turned and eyed Alexander. "Cruen may send these weapons to fetch the prize he wants so much."

Though his gut clenched, Alexander shook his head. "Lucian

is protected in the *credenti*. No vampire can get past the Order's charms."

Whistler made a sound, a soft, uneasy sound that made them all turn to face him. "Remember, *mutore* are not just vampires," he said. "They have a very different genetic structure. The Order's magic may or may not keep them out."

The *credenti* of his *balashood* was a dark, cold, miserable village that scented of animal shit and housed a community whose stares and jibes about his sire had made his young belly ache every minute of every hour of every day. As Lucian walked through the gates and down the path toward the center of town, he had very little belief that what he was about to walk into would be any different. But this time he didn't care. This time he wasn't looking to be accepted or welcomed. In fact, he almost hoped they'd try something ... just a little something so they could see what he'd turned into—what their unfeeling, ungenerous ways had helped him become.

Unfortunately, that looked as though it wasn't going to happen.

Fuckers.

Immediately upon entering the town square, Mai rushed up to them, her skirts long and blue, and waving prettily in the gentle breeze, just like her hair. She laughed a rolling laugh as Bronwyn quickly smothered her with a hug.

Lucian rolled his eyes. Fucking *veanas*.

Mai turned to him then and offered him a hint of a smile, a tentative thing that no doubt was supposed to bring him around, make him forgiving, perhaps even cordial—shit, maybe even jovial.

Wasn't happening.

He nodded. "Mother."

"Ye came!" she said breathlessly as though it was her greatest wish in the entire world, and maybe it was—then she calmed herself and lowered her voice. "I'm so glad. It's so good to see ye both." Her gaze moved over her son, her eyes shining. "And ye look well, *Balas*. Very well."

"Pray do not get emotional, Mother," Lucian said flatly, though his insides were doing some kind of bullshit dance of softness that really pissed him off. "Asshole feelings" is what they should be referred to as. "I have enough of that from my *veana* here."

Mai smiled at Bronwyn, who squeezed Lucian's hand before leading him forward. They followed Mai through groups of Impures and Purebloods mixing soil and compost, some carrying trays of seedlings, their expressions happy and excited under the mixture of torchlight and moonlight. Lucian couldn't understand excitement over a few plants and a couple of buckets of shitty-smelling earth, but to each his own, he supposed.

"Here," Mai said, pointing to a patchwork blanket near the river. "I saved ye the best spot."

"Thank you," Bronwyn said, her tone so damn kind he almost wondered if she was faking it. He guessed not. "It's lovely." She elbowed him then. "Isn't it lovely, Lucian?"

"It's precious," he said tightly. "As precious as pig shit."

Bronwyn turned to him and glared, but Mai laughed, a damn pretty sound that brought him back a few years, maybe more than a few. He didn't want to go back there. Didn't want to acknowledge the good or the tolerable, only the heinous and the suckass. Only the debilitating fact that his mother welcomed the rutting, unfeeling monster of a Breeding Male into her bed and her heart and turned a blind eye to the torment that it caused her son. It was easier to hate that way.

A loud sound—some kind of pop—electrocuted the air. A

shot of lightning or burst of sound. Then again. Lucian came alert, his nostrils flaring as he scented the air. "What is that?"

Far from alarmed, Mai smiled. "Some of the *balas* get ahold of firecrackers this time of year. Ye remember."

"Fuck yes, I remember." He turned to Bronwyn. "I believe one of them placed a particularly nasty blaster in my school bag."

Bronwyn's eyes softened and she leaned in and whispered, "May have been why your mother sent you away, huh?"

"Stop trying to make sense, *Veana*," he growled, seeing his mother move down to the stream out of his peripheral vision. "I'm not in the mood."

She grinned. "What are you in the mood for?"

"I don't know." He released a weighty, tired breath. "Perhaps for you to tell me you love me."

Bronwyn's brows lifted. "Really? In front of all these people? All these townsfolk who treated you so foully?"

He lowered his chin. "Especially in front them."

She smiled. It was like sitting inside the goddamn sun it was so brilliant. "Come here."

When he leaned forward, she kissed him, so softly it hurt his empty heart. Then she whispered, "I love you, Lucian Roman."

There was another blast, a crack of sound, then something that resembled a soda bottle opening.

"Little shites," Lucian grumbled, standing up and offering her his hand. "Come. I want to show you something."

Making their way between couples and families, both Pureblood and Impure, along the gentle river, Lucian led her up a rise and into the center of town.

"Where are we going?" Bronwyn asked.

"You will see, lass."

He led her past the market carts and around the blacksmith's shop until they stopped in front of a tree. *The* tree. It was a massive birch with a sturdy trunk and thirty arms at least, stretching every which way. It had been Lucian's one place of comfort, of respite from the bullying *balas* of his youth. Carved into the wood were the names of nearly everyone who had lived in the *credenti* during Lucian's life there.

He watched Bronwyn draw her hand over the wood, over the carvings. "It's beautiful."

"It is more than that," he said, leaning back against it smartly. "As long as I stood close to this tree, no one could ever, or would ever, hurt me." He grinned. "They thought this a magic tree, believed that if they disturbed it in any way, stood beside it, touched it—they would be cursed."

"Why would they think that?"

"The names of everyone in town were carved into this tree by an unknown, unseen force. Morning dawned, a new name. A walk in the square after evening meal—a new name." He looked past her at the town and its inhabitants. "The names of the *balas* who tormented me went up first."

"They never knew it was you, did they?"

He found her gaze and grinned widely. "Fuck no." Then he reached in his pocket and pulled out a crude knife, the only thing the cottage had in terms of weapons. "It's time for my name."

"Nothing to fear from the *balas* in town," she said. "Not anymore."

The wood gave easily as he carved. It felt good to put his name there, release it all into this living thing. He was nearly to the final letter when the crash and pop of another set of fireworks went off.

"Those little shites are really asking for it," Lucian griped, his back to Bron as he worked.

"The *balas* are a good distraction," a deep voice said. "For the Beast."

Lucian whirled around to find Bronwyn in the arms of the *mutore*, of Nicholas's twin, of what could be his brother, her back to his chest, her eyes wide and as fixed on Lucian's as the glittering diamond ones of her captor.

"Flash, Bron," Lucian hissed, though his gaze never left the *paven* holding her.

He regarded Lucian without vitriol. "She cannot."

Out of the corner of his eye, Lucian saw Bronwyn nod imperceptibly. Fucking hell. Whatever magic the *mutore* had was rich and solid. He would have to think quickly to get her out of his hold.

He pushed away from the tree and said evenly, "You won't take her."

"I will have you both, Lucian Roman."

Forcing his body to calm, Lucian's mind worked hard and fast. Did he get physical with this bastard? Could he do that without injuring Bron? His fingers played with the blade in his hand. The possibilities were few, but he circled on one and landed. He stepped closer, his knife in his fist. "She is in *swell*, *Gemino*, and the *balas* is mine."

Bronwyn made a sound like the last thing in the world she wanted was for this bastard to know such a thing.

The *mutore*, the *gemino*, raised one black eyebrow. "Cruen will be most interested in your offspring, Son of the Breeding Male."

"I'm certain of that," Lucian uttered. "Though he may try to hurt the child."

The *paven* nodded. "It is possible."

Lucian's fangs descended. He couldn't help it, couldn't stop the instinct of protection. Through gritted teeth, he said, "Understand something, *Gemino*—if my *balas* is hurt, yours will be as well."

The *mutore* sneered. "My *balas*. I have no *balas*."

"Unfortunately for the boy, you do." Lucian moved closer. "Remember the *credenti veana* you bedded? The one who thought you were Nicholas?"

Deep in the *gemino*'s gaze, there was a shudder. "I remember. But passing my seed is not possible. I am not able to sire."

Lucian chuckled. "Well, it looks like your pecker was working just fine that day, *Brother*. The *veana* you hold in your arms at this very moment is a genealogist and the very one who tested your son. He doesn't belong to Nicholas, as we first believed— he belongs to you." He took another step. "Now release my *veana* and I will go with you nice and quiet and easy."

"No!" Bronwyn yelled, the sound rushing down the town road to the ears of the other *credenti* members.

The *mutore* looked unconvinced, yet affected by Lucian's words. He signaled to Lucian. "Come. Now."

The switch was quick, and left no time for Bronwyn to fight. Right before Lucian was flashed away, Alexander and Nicholas landed in the square.

"Take her home!" Lucian shouted, praying that his command, his last request for Bronwyn's care, made it to the ears of his brothers.

As Dillon sat on the window ledge outside the room Gray had given her in his compound, her legs dangling down over a good eight stories, she ignored the thick, pale wrist that had been shoved under her nose a second ago. Not as an offer, but a demand. He wanted her to flash her fangs and feed off his Impure blood. And she just wanted him to fuck off.

Gray took his arm away, leaned against the window frame, and made a sound that confirmed his growing frustration. "I know my weak swill doesn't tempt your refined palate, but you need something."

Dillon didn't answer, just stared out at the lights of the city, let the cold air numb her skin.

"Do you want me to contact the Romans?" he asked.

"No."

"What about Sara?" The strain of bitterness was barely hidden beneath the surface of the question.

She inhaled, closed her eyes. "All I want is to be left alone."

"So you can flash out of here?"

She turned to look at him. "You're kidding, right?"

His gaze moved over her. Not as it had a few weeks ago when he'd pulled her into the shower and kissed the shit out of her. No ... this was a pity kind of gaze.

"I'll leave you alone, D," he said. "No problem. But you're not leaving here without me knowing about it. Understand?"

"Don't manage me, Impure. I'm not a motherfucking fool, okay?" She opened her arms—not to invite an embrace, but to show herself to him fully. "Where exactly would I go looking like this?"

His jaw worked hard. "You need to feed. You don't want it now, fine. But I'll just keep asking till you do."

He almost didn't get that last word out before Dillon grabbed his wrist and ripped into him with her fangs.

"Fuck!" he cried, but he didn't flinch.

She drank. She drank hard and fast and just to shut him up. Because she needed to think, plan, devise. She wasn't jumping out the window tonight, maybe not even tomorrow or the following day. But it was coming. Her revenge. That was the blood she wanted flowing down her throat. That was the blood that would make her strong again.

Sweet, satisfying senator's blood.

26

Alexander and Nicholas left Lucian's bedroom with a heave of a sigh and with all the invisible scratches and dents to their *pavenhood* that either one could stand. Outside the door, they stopped and looked at each other, shook their heads in amazement and exhaustion. It was an understatement to say that Bronwyn hadn't wanted to go with them—hadn't wanted to leave the Scottish *credenti* or the memory of Lucian, or the company of his mother. And it had taken every ounce of explaining and coercion by both himself and Nicholas to get her to even agree to talk with them about it.

Alexander headed for the stairs, Nicholas behind him. Unfortunately, talking had led nowhere, and with only Lucian's plea to guide their actions, Alexander and Nicholas had ended the fruitless negotiation and just flashed her home to SoHo, getting her inside and upstairs before she could flash back out.

"I'll get Evans to watch the door," Nicholas said. "Can't have her getting out, going right back."

"Lucian would kill the both of us if we let that happen," Alexander put in as they hit the bottom step and headed for the library, ready to plan their next move. First they were going to get through to Titus, see what their father really knew. Then, if that didn't work, they were going to the Order. If it got them to Lucian, they were going to bow down at the ancient feet of those nasty bastards and beg them for help.

"You think he's still breathing, *Duro*?" Nicholas asked, heading down the hall.

Alexander stopped at the door to the library and gave Nicky a quick smile. "I think it'll take a hell of a lot to bring our brother down."

"Hope you're right." Nicholas's cell rang and he yanked it from his pocket, answered it with a quick, "Yeah." He stiffened, looked up at Alexander. "Here." He held out his phone. "It's Dillon." His brow lifted. "She says she knows where he is."

Lucian sat inside a metal cage with a naked *veana* and tried not to breathe. A few minutes ago, he'd been hauled into this room, some kind of lab facility, heavy on the cages and inside them Pureblood and Impure life—one of which was the very *paven* who'd mated his princess.

Not surprisingly, Synjon Wise hadn't acknowledged him from the dark recesses of his small cage. Sure, he'd seen Lucian, even had offered him a momentary flare of anger as he'd been tossed into the cage with the naked *veana*, but that had been that. Ever since then, Brit Boy had offered him nothing, no explanation, no questions about Bron—just silence as the *veana* across from him stared into his cage with desperation in her eyes.

Lucian didn't have a clue what was going on here, but it didn't look good. None of this looked good.

"Your Breeding Female, Lucian Roman." Cruen entered the room in his Order robes, followed by the *mutore* and three of his friends. "Beautiful, isn't she? Irresistible, she will be."

Lucian heard Syn growl behind him.

"Not going to happen, asshole," Lucian stated flatly. "I'll never take this *veana*."

Cruen laughed. "You think you have a choice?"

Lifting his chin, Lucian said with a clear voice, "Fuck yeah."

Arrogance fairly bled from Cruen's ancient pores. "You don't. Your seed belongs in her womb, and your *balas* will be the pride of a new vampire regime—the beginnings of a new class of elite vampires." As the female across from Lucian moaned, Cruen moved closer to their cage. "Know this. Until you send her into *swell*, you will both remain where you are."

Lucian glanced at the *mutore*, narrowed his eyes, then returned to the master. "You really are a fucking fool, Cruen. You think the Order will ever accept this new regime of yours? They want only the purest of blood—they think only the purest of blood is worthy."

He sniffed. "As do I. And this *balas* is pure—pure Breeding Male blood. And with me by its side, it will rule us all."

"And anything not worthy of the new regime?" Lucian asked.

"Will be eliminated," Cruen stated simply.

"Like Impures."

"Yes."

Lucian pressed his advantage before Cruen caught on. "And *mutore*."

"Of course." Cruen froze, realized what he had said, and hurried to put a Band-Aid on the wound. "Not my children." He turned and looked at the four Beasts. "I do not speak of you, you know that."

Three of the *paven* stood there, nostrils flared, eyes narrowed, while one remained expressionless.

The Beast Lucian knew as the *gemino* spoke first, his gaze

hard on his father. "You would not eliminate us, but others like us?"

Cruen stared at him. "You and your brothers are special, Erion. You are my sons."

Erion, Lucian mused. So the *gemino* had a name.

"I am your son," Erion said tightly, "and yet you have lied to me."

"You will not speak to me this way," Cruen began with a low snarl.

"I have been told I have a *balas*," he said, the Beasts around him turning to stare at their brother with shocked expressions.

Baring his red fangs, Cruen spat, "By whom? Lucian Roman? You would believe the word of a stranger, of a nothing, over your own father?"

Erion walked toward him, his massive size and scarred face making him look like a demon in the electric lights. "You told me, told us all, that we cannot breed. We are incapable of it."

Cruen was unafraid. "I did."

"Is that the truth, Father?"

"You had all your needs met here, Erion. Every one of you has had your pick of females to bed—females I blood castrated myself—and yet you would go outside these walls when I forbid it!" Tipping up his chin, Cruen added, "Breeding is not meant for ones like you."

"For a *mutore*." Erion's eyes shuttered. "Neither is any real sense of living, I suppose."

Cruen's eyes widened as he saw something, one of the cages— empty. "The *paven*—Synjon Wise—he is gone, escaped." Cruen raised his hand to one of the *mutore*. "Go. Go and find him."

Not one of the Beasts moved.

"Don't stand there, gaping!" Cruen raged. "Move, you fools!"

"So that is all we are truly meant for," Erion pushed. "To be little more than your guard dogs?"

"No!"

"To be lab rats, then?"

"Find that fucking *paven*," Cruen ordered, low and slow. "Or you will find yourselves caged and hungry and hurting like the rest of them."

Lucian cursed. "Listen to him. Christ. He lied to you! Used you! All of you. Get it through your heads, *brothers*. You are not worthy of reproducing, of anything but remaining in the shadows like worthless pieces of shit." He chuckled. "The last thing in the world this Pureblooded bastard—your *daddy*—wants is more freaks running around, and when he's done using you, you'll be eliminated right along—"

Cruen flew across the room within a second and hit the bars of Lucian's cell. The Breeding Female cried out as Cruen's hand shot through and curled around Lucian's throat.

Barely able to breathe, Lucian grinned. "Do it. Take the breath out of me, the life from me. It would be my pleasure."

"If you weren't such a perfect cock for hire, I would," he snarled, his pale blue eyes flashing hatred. "I'd love every second of it."

Lucian struggled to breathe when Cruen's fingers suddenly slackened around his throat. Then he crumpled to the ground, revealing Erion behind him. The *gemino* eyed him. "That wasn't for you."

Gripping his bruised throat, Lucian nodded. "Good. Glad to see you have some balls, Brother. I was beginning to wonder if we really did share the same blood."

Erion unlocked Juliet's cell, but the other Beasts remained where they were. Lucian could tell by their eyes they weren't going to trust anyone but themselves. Wise bastards.

Lucian hustled out of the cage as Erion carried the nude *veana*, who continued to moan in pain. They left the lab and hurried out into the hallway. Lucian followed the Beast down several corridors, both of them moving as silently as they could manage.

"This way," Erion called back, moving swiftly, the *veana*'s legs bobbing against his forearms.

Then, from out of nowhere, it seemed, Synjon moved directly into their path. His face was a mask of death and the gun in his hand was expertly trained on Erion. "Hand her over, Beast."

"Easy," Lucian warned him. "This *paven* just saved her life, Brit Boy."

"Good," Syn said flatly. "Maybe I won't kill you, then." He motioned to the floor with his gun. "Put her down and walk away."

Erion did as the *paven* asked. "Your lover is unharmed, but she needs care."

"Lover?" Lucian hissed, his eyes flashing to Synjon. "What the hell?"

Synjon didn't answer, but regarded Lucian with a hard stare. "Bronwyn?"

Goddamn, just hearing her name made his gut hurt like hell. "She's fine," he said, then added, "And she's mine."

For one brief second, Synjon held Lucian's gaze, something silent and understood passing between them. Then Erion interrupted with a terse "You must go," and Synjon scooped up the *veana*.

"Follow this corridor to the right," Erion continued. "When you reach the wall of windows, smash out the center one and you will be able to jump and flash."

"Windows have already been smashed."

The voice came from behind Syn, and Lucian nodded at the

304

familiar faces, so goddamn welcome right now. Alexander and Nicholas jogged toward them, stopped at the semicircle of *paven* and *veana*. Nicholas stared at Erion, his gaze running the length of the *paven*. "It's true."

The Beast nodded. "The *mutore* exist, yes."

"No, that you exist, my brother." Nicholas asked him curiously, "Are there others?"

Erion nodded, his eyes softening just a touch as he stared at his twin. "They are back in the lab."

"You have a *balas*," Nicholas told him. "Did you know that?"

"My father swore to me I would not be able to father a *balas*. It is the only reason . . ." He looked up, diamond eyes gazing into black. "I dreamed of him. The boy. Once. But I was awake."

"His name is Ladd," Nicholas told him. "He's been under my protection. Where he will remain until I can be sure . . ."

The Beast released a heavy breath, almost a pained one. "There is nothing to be sure of, nothing to change or alter or smooth. I have no *balas*, and we are not brothers. My brothers are back in the lab."

For a moment, Nicholas said nothing. Then he nodded, his eyes suddenly blank with feeling. "My brothers are here and I need to get them out."

"No one is going anywhere."

Cruen appeared behind them, the rest of the Beasts at his side. His gaze narrowed on Synjon and the female. "Release her."

Syn snarled. "Never."

"Then you will die."

Cruen raised his hand, gave the order to attack, and the Beasts rushed forward, leaped at them in sudden attack.

Alexander slammed his fist into the face of the first one, the sound of cracking bone fueling his battle rage. Hyperaware, he saw Nicholas take down a male with a ball-busting groin kick, and on his other side, Lucian launched himself at Cruen, reaching for the ancient one's weapon.

But the ex-Order piece of shit flashed away, vanishing before Lucian could even reach him.

Fuck!

Had to be trick. Nothing this dickhead liked better than a trick.

Every one of Alexander's senses fired up to red alert. And a split second later, Cruen materialized in front of Syn, shoving his weapon against the *paven*'s temple.

The Breeding Female, cradled in his arms, wailed in distress and jacked upright.

The sound of a gunshot exploded throughout the corridor.

As the echo died away, they were all shocked to see Syn still standing. And in his arms, he held the limp, bleeding form of the *veana*. Alexander cursed into the blood-scented air. The *veana* had taken the bullet meant for Syn.

They all fell silent, the only sound breathing and the *veana*'s blood dripping on the floor.

And then a cry so wretched it ripped apart Alexander's gut shot from Synjon Wise's throat, making them all freeze, making them all stare at the beautiful *veana* lying dead in his arms.

"Not her," Cruen said from behind them, his voice hoarse with shock. "Not her."

Before another breath was taken, Synjon shifted the *veana* to one arm, snatched a dagger from one of the Beasts with the other, and flung it straight for Cruen's neck.

The blade hit the wall with a deadly smack.

Cruen had vanished.

The aftermath of Cruen's bloodletting clung to each of them, but to Lucian there had been something earth-shattering about watching Synjon Wise break into a million pieces over the dead body of the *veana* he loved. An innocent had been killed, had been taken again from this *paven*, and Lucian could see in the male's eyes that he desperately wanted to follow her.

As Erion and the Beasts left them in the corridor, in search of the one who had betrayed them, Alexander, Nicholas, and Lucian moved down one hallway into another until they reached the wall of windows.

Synjon stared into the black night, quiet as he held his dead *veana* in his arms.

Alexander touched the *paven*'s shoulder, but Synjon snarled at him.

"What can we do?" Alexander asked him.

"Anything," Nicholas said, the weight of the *paven*'s devastation hanging in the air oppressive and contagious.

The blood of his beloved *veana* infused into his skin, into his clothing, Synjon moved toward the window, the *veana* crumpled against his chest. Then he stopped and without turning said, "There will be a day when I will come to you. There will be a day when I ask you to help me find and dispose of the garbage that stole her life from me."

It was all he said, and Lucian was the one who answered him, who stepped forward and said in the clearest and most resolute voice he could manage, "We will wait for that day, Brother."

Lucian watched him move through the window, watched him disappear in a flash, the remaining shreds of life, of devastation and horror following along behind him. There were many things Lucian was capable of in this life, many things he didn't give a shit about that maybe he should have, but one thing he knew for certain, he was not going to allow Bronwyn to feel what Synjon Wise was feeling. She would not cry over his dead body or bury him in the ground, pine for him for years, then settle into a life of regrets.

He was going to lose the battle he had waged with his Breeding Male self—it was just a matter of time.

He turned to his brothers. He forced emotion out of his voice and infused practicality and immobility into it.

"I can't return with you."

Nicholas's nostrils flared, but he said nothing.

"We have a cage, *Duro*," Alexander said firmly. "You will come home and we will care for you."

Lucian shook his head, his chest tightening. "I won't be anywhere near her. Can't."

"Then send her home," Nicholas spat out. "She doesn't belong to us, to you—"

"She carries my *balas*, *Duro*!"

Nicholas paled. "What?"

"And I believe I love her."

Both his brothers just stared at him, as if neither one of his admissions could be possible.

"Where are you going to go?" Alexander asked, finding his voice. "Run away somewhere, get lost—never see us, never see your family again? Your child . . . ?"

Lucian's lip curled, but inside him the turbulent emotions and hopes and wants of a father churned. "I won't be able to control myself much longer. Even now, I feel it coming over me, like having my insides filled up with paint. Soon I will be blind to my actions. Do you think I will ever allow myself within a foot of my daughter?"

Nicky looked like he was going to lose his shit. "A *veana* . . ."

"Swear to me you will treat Bron as my mate should be treated, and my *balas*—"

"Stop," Alexander said harshly. "There is no need for your request. You know our hearts, unbeating though they are."

Lucian nodded. He took one final look at them, knowing it could be the last time, and jumped from the window.

27

Six months later

Bronwyn felt the sudden jerk in her belly and groaned into the lens of her microscope. "Easy there, little *veana*," she said, giving her stomach a pat. "Let's wait until you come out for the soccer game kicks, all right?"

Laughing, Sara set a seedcake down beside her on the desk. "I think she's trying to tell you something, Mama."

Studying the blood samples, Bronwyn didn't even raise her head to ask, "What's that?"

"That maybe you should give the microscope and yourself a rest."

Bronwyn narrowed her eyes on the sample, cursed, then switched it with another slide.

"Bron."

"Yeah."

"Can you stop for a second, look at me?"

Bronwyn closed her eyes and exhaled. She didn't want to talk, or look at anything but her blood samples; the ones of her own and Lucian and the ancient samples of Breeding Males before him. She'd promised herself she'd take every last bit of research she'd performed for that bastard Cruen and use it to help her *paven*, her child, and her new family.

"Do I have to go all doctor on your ass?" Sara said. A hint of humor threaded her tone, but for the most part it was serious threat time.

Bronwyn turned away from the microscope and swiveled her chair to face Sara. She'd had all her things brought to Lucian's room, turned half the space into her own mini lab so she could work night and day.

"Talk to me," Sara said, her blue eyes heavy with concern. "Tell me what's happening here."

"Nothing's happening here," Bron said with frustration and more anger than she wanted to reveal. Why couldn't they all just leave her alone, let her get back to work? "Every time I feel like I'm close, it's a dead end."

Sara took a breath and released it, then said calmly, "I know this isn't something you want to hear, but have you thought that perhaps there is no way to fix him, no cure?"

"No." Time passed all too quickly now—an oddity, as she'd expected it to move slowly and painfully—but as she researched, as she tried desperately to find an antidote for the Breeding Male gene, she knew that Lucian was somewhere slipping away. Without another word, she turned back to her work, flipping open her computer.

"Your real true mate will come at some point, Bron—"

Bron shook her head, her insides jumping now. "Maybe. Maybe not. I'll deal with it if it does, but I'll never mate with anyone else. My choice will always be Luca."

"Bron, please, I know this is painful as hell and impossible, but you've got to—"

"No! What I have to do is get back to work. Get back to finding . . . " Bronwyn froze, her mouth filling with saliva.

"Bron? Bron, what is it?"

A sudden shock to her system had Bronwyn ratcheting up, then doubling over in pain. She began to pant, gripping her belly, the pain centering below her pelvic bone.

"No," she uttered, feeling a gush release from her core. "No, no ..."

Sara was beside her, holding her up. "Your water broke."

"Oh, God. It's too early." *And you're not here. Goddamn you, Luca, I need you here!*

"Early or not," Sara said calmly, "she's coming."

Bron glanced up and whispered through waves of debilitating pain, "Without her father."

"He will know her, Bron," Sara said, her eyes strong and resolute as she helped her to the bed. "Let's get you settled and call for Leza."

He was lost inside his mind, had been for longer than he knew. Both his arms and his legs were shackled, his neck too. When they'd brought him here, his mother and Titus, Lucian had made them swear to see it done, and both, through their tears, had given him his last cognizant wish. Without sight, without knowledge of the days or hours, he existed on blood rations and bouts of both hysteria and manic sexual hunger. But he would hurt no one.

He scented his mother before she even walked into the room, and when she did, he let his eyes lift a fraction to follow her movement. She went straight to his father, to Titus, who had been at his side every night until dawn hit. She put her hand on his shoulder and nodded sadly.

"I don't know if you can hear me, son," Titus said, his voice strained. "Your *balas* has been born."

"She is well and beautiful," Mai continued softly. Something in her voice changed then, just a quiver. "Her mother, too."

311

Lucian didn't know where it came from, but a feeling long buried flickered in his chest; then it grew, flowered, spread, warmed, and after a moment, a tear wound its way down his cheek, over his chin, and onto his chest.

He felt his father's hand over his, and for the first time in his long life, he didn't want to pull it away. The *paven* understood; the *paven* would help him

It took every effort to move his lips, but he had to. The time had come, blissfully. "You . . . kill me now."

28

Bronwyn walked the same dirt path she had many months ago, but on this day, this beautiful September day in the Scottish Highlands no cold winds kissed her cheeks, no patches of snow lay bride white on the ground. The hills bracketing her were coated in a brilliant purple heather blanket and the sun was warm and welcoming to an old friend.

She followed the fence line until it gave way to the gate. Biting into her wrist, she let the blood flow, then swiped it across the lock. Her skin vibrated with equal parts pleasure and fear. There was nothing in the world she had wanted more than to see this day come to pass. She had nearly collapsed with joy when Alexander and Nicholas revealed his where-abouts to her—only when it had been finally revealed to them. Saving her tears, she had flashed from SoHo to Banchory within minutes.

The property looked so beautiful, so lush and green and well tended, and beyond the cottage, the loch sat blue and steady. As she drew closer, she noticed that the plot of dirt she'd raked and readied and planted had also been tended in her stead. The beans and berries were tall and heavy, water and sun and the breath of life obvious within their solid green limbs.

"Everything has grown and flourished here, lass."

Bronwyn glanced up, gasped, and ran at the *veana*, falling into her open arms.

Mai held her tight to her bosom and rocked her. "It is good to see ye too, Bonnie Bron."

For one moment, Bron let her head rest on the *veana*'s shoulder and breathed her in. When Alex had revealed to her that Lucian had gone home again, home to Scotland, allowed his mother to finally care for him, love him as she'd only wanted him to do, Bron had been so relieved. But the Romans had also warned her that Lucian wasn't there to reconcile or reminisce. He was there to die.

She lifted her head. "Where is he?"

"Follow me." She led Bronwyn inside the cottage, everything the same as when she'd left it. "He won't know ye, Bron. Ye must prepare yourself. He is much changed."

"Doesn't matter, Mai." She held tight to the bag over her shoulder, all that she needed. Her *balas*—their *balas* was at home with her aunts and uncles, being cared for and cooed over.

Mai led her into the room he and Bronwyn had shared, had made love in, where they had held each other and listened to the birds on the loch. She stepped aside, let Bron go forward to the bed; then she put her hand over her mouth as Bronwyn gasped. The sight of her beloved Lucian made her want to both vomit and cry. Every inch of his pale, painfully thin body was chained so completely he could no doubt only move his fingers and toes were he conscious. His eyes looked fused shut, his lips were cracked and blue, and the only thing that looked the same on him were the two empty circle brands on his gaunt cheeks.

"He has refused all blood now," Mai said, tears in her voice.

"He made me promise to keep him this way, keep him alive until he knew if ye and the *balas* were well and safe. Now he just wants to die."

Bronwyn opened her bag, done with pity and pain. She was here to fight for Luca, her Luca, the only *paven* she ever loved, would ever love. She wasn't allowing him this way out, not until she saw with her own two eyes that there was no other choice *but* death.

"Don't," Mai cried, reaching for Bron as she moved toward the bed. "Don't go near him."

Determination steeled her spine and her words. "It will be all right," Bronwyn told her, taking the vials from her bag.

"No, it won't. He could kill ye, Bron. He doesna know who ye are. Who I am. Hasn't for some time."

"This *paven* sacrificed all for me and my babe," Bronwyn told her, as she sat on the bed, looking at her beloved. "I would do the same for him, for the chance to free him from this fate— to give us a chance to be what we were meant to be."

"Oh God . . . " It was all Bronwyn heard from behind her, her mind and her love completely focused on the nearly dead *paven* before her. "Lucian," she whispered.

Nothing.

"Lucian, it's me." She opened the vial, her movements precise while her heart reached out to the *paven* of her dreams, of the future she wanted so much to see with him. "Lucian, hear my voice. Know it in your heart."

Her hand holding the vial trembled. He was so still. He lay so still. Perhaps he was dead already. God, perhaps there was nothing . . .

Gripping the vial, she brought it to his lips. With her other hand, she forced his mouth open and poured the entire tube of blood down his throat.

Unconsciously, she swallowed as she saw the slight movement of his throat. Staring at him, she waited, waited for some sign of life, of movement.

"Bron, lass, please," Mai whispered behind her. "No more now."

Bronwyn refused to listen. Her eyes were on her beloved, his face, his eyes, willing him to move—any small movement.

"He's not coming back, Bron," Mai said through her tears. "He can't. You, me, the *balas*—we must let him go—"

A hand shot up out and grabbed Bronwyn's wrist. She jumped, gasped, but didn't move. *Lucian. Lucian.* She heard Mai behind her. She was saying something about getting up, moving on, but Bron pushed her away. "No. Go away. Get out." She dug in her bag with her free hand and grabbed another vial, ripped off the stopper with her fangs and held it to his lips again.

"Open your mouth, Lucian," she ordered fiercely. "Open your goddamn mouth!"

A growl started low in his throat, and though his eyes wouldn't open, his upper lip lifted, curled, and he bared his fangs.

"Bronwyn!" Mai screamed. "Get back!"

It was good, just enough to get the blood into his mouth and down his throat.

"He'll kill ye, Bron, please! Think of the babe!"

"Get out! Now!" She couldn't spare sympathy for Mai, not when she was fighting for the soul of her Luca, for the father of her *balas*.

She snatched up another vial, ripped off the top, and poured the red blood into his mouth. Fear ripped through her, but she pushed it away. It had to work. Had to. It was all she could do—all that was left.

She did it again and again, over and over, ripping the tops off the vials and pouring blood into his mouth, watching it go down his throat, watching as his nostrils flared and his back arched, staring, praying as he fought the chains, as he howled, as he snarled, spit, and writhed, and cursed his way back to life.

"That's it, Luca," Bron cried out. "That's it. Come back to me, goddamn you!" She watched him struggle with the animal in him, praying the real *paven*, the true *paven*—*her paven* would win.

And then suddenly he stilled. The world too, so quiet inside the cabin, the room, she could hear only her breath.

Several moments passed where Bronwyn wasn't sure what was happening, if she'd failed, if her theory had been no more than the foolish wishes of a *veana* in love. Had she truly lost him? Would her *balas* have no father? Her throat tightened, and her chest filled with dark, shattering pain.

Then, out of that debilitating darkness came light. It was as if the sun suddenly shifted from behind the clouds and the world brightened. Lucian's eyes squeezed and fought, and finally, opened. He blinked, stared at the ceiling, as every second that ticked off his skin began to change from gray to sickly pale, to vampire white.

And then he turned his head, his eyes struggling to focus. "No! No!" he wailed, thrashing against his chains, but not as the Breeding Male. He was a *paven* now, angry, desperate. "No, damn it! I was nearly dead, gone, free, and now ... the *balas* blood has brought me back to this miserable life—"

Bronwyn's tears streaked down her face as she stared at him, at the miracle of him. It wasn't possible and yet it was. "Lucy," she whispered.

He blinked up at her. "What?"

"Our daughter. Her name is Lucy."

"Oh God, Bronwyn," he cried out, hoarse, yet so moved. "My beautiful princess. Why did you bring me back to life? To torture me with all I can never have?"

She was crying hard now, tears she'd held on to for months, when she didn't have time to give them flight—when she had time only to believe and fight for her love. That single hope had kept her sane through her *swell* and through the most abject loneliness.

She crawled onto the bed, curled up beside him in the chains, her arms going around him.

"Oh God, my love," he uttered. "It won't last long, I know. I know, and yet I'm so thankful. I'm glad to know about her. My Lucy ... Tell me about her. Talk to me of her for as long as I have left." His voice broke. "Is her face like yours? Is her hair dark and lovely like yours?"

"She has my hair, Luca, but your eyes—your beautiful, soul-gripping eyes."

Tears spilled from those eyes onto her shoulder. "I love you. I would have loved her too."

"You *will* love her," Bronwyn said with deep determination and feeling. "Forever, and ever."

"The babe is gone from your belly." He turned to her startled. "The blood—"

She lifted her head, gazed down at him with the love of centuries, an impossible, improbable love that would help them both through times of pain and suffering and questions ahead. "It is my blood, Luca."

His brow creased.

"It was my blood. All along. This, what you have just consumed, was my blood. It wasn't Lucy's blood that sustained you before. I tested it—tested it with the blood of your father. Her blood changed nothing in his cells. Then I tried my blood—still nothing, but I couldn't walk away from what happened here in this cottage. You were changed by my blood. It caused me to hope that perhaps you and I were different, that just as your blood sustained me mine might sustain you. And it did. Look at you. I don't know how or why, but my blood was always meant for you."

"No," he whispered, his gaze moving over her face. "Only a true mate ... I don't understand. I cannot have a true mate."

"And perhaps that's not what we are," she told him. "Perhaps we are something more, something unholy, something genetically wrong—and yet perfection." She brought her wrist to her fangs and bit down. The sting from heaven. Felt so good, so right. "Take my vein, my love. Drink from my wrist, then from my neck, and soon—maybe in a few weeks' time, when you are happy and whole again, you will take me."

"My love," he whispered almost desperately, almost hopefully. "My princess. My savior."

Lucian's fangs elongated as she brought her wrist up to meet him, to let her love, her life, her one and only captive feed. And when his fangs pierced her flesh and suckled, Bronwyn knew the sweetest and truest pain.

Epilogue

"And you thought we'd never need this, Luca."

They all sat around the massive dining table, looking like the oddest collection of vampire family in the world—and perhaps they were. Alexander and Sara, Nicholas and Kate, Lucian, Bronwyn, and their *balas*, Lucy, the four feral-looking Beasts, and Ladd.

After several weeks of recovery in Scotland, Lucian had returned home with his *veana* and his *balas*, and just a day later, the four Beasts had shown up on their doorstep. They'd claimed their stay would be for only a short time, until they decided where they wanted to go. Still unsure about these savage new-comers, but recognizing them as family, Alexander and Nicholas had told them they were welcome to stay for as long as they liked.

Lucian had not been so courteous.

Seated beside the albino brother, Erion was working on a bite of Bronwyn's seedcake and trying like hell not to make a face.

"Good eats, eh, *Gemino*?" Lucian asked, his eyes narrowed on the dark-haired *paven* with features resembling a lion.

"Very good." Erion glanced at his wolflike brother, Lycos, and grinned. "What do you think, Ly?"

Without answering, Lycos shifted his gaze to massively tattooed and skull-shaved Helo, who was just staring at the thing, cursing to himself.

"Well, I love it."

They all turned to look at the final Beast, Phane. The long-haired *paven* was all kinds of badass, but he had a mouthful of seedcake and was grinning like a fool.

Bronwyn laughed. "There is always more, Phane. Whether it is wanted or not."

He took the whole plate and grinned. "Appreciate that, ma'am."

Bronwyn turned to Sara and Kate and grinned. "More Roman brothers. What in the world have we gotten ourselves into?"

Before anyone could answer, the doorbell rang. They all looked at each other in wonder. No one ever came to their door.

"Trick-or-treaters?" Alexander said, grinning.

Nicky nodded. "Right. It's Halloween."

Lucian grinned broadly. "Should we really give them a good fright?" He jerked his chin at the Beasts. "Hell, we got these four things now. Let's use them. Shift into your ugly forms, *Paven*—oh wait, already done." He chuckled to himself.

Erion's nostrils flared and Phane growled. "You want to see a show, do you?"

Lycos grinned. "A little four on one?"

Taking his baby daughter from her mother's arms and giving her kiss on the neck, Lucian snorted. "Not into males, but if I was I wouldn't be going anywhere near the four of you with all that seedcake in your teeth. Christ, get a toothbrush!"

"Don't you mean a 'fang' brush, Uncle Luca?" Ladd said, laughing at his own joke before stuffing another seedcake inside his mouth.

The hard rumbles of laughter were interrupted by Evans, who rushed into the room followed by Gray. They hadn't seen Gray in so many months, they almost didn't recognize him. He seemed larger, more imposing, completely self-contained. There was something in his arms.

"We have a problem," he said, his eyes steely and concerned.

Alexander was already on his feet. "Is that Dillon?" Nicholas and Sara crowded around Gray too. "What the hell happened?" Alexander asked. "And why has she been unreachable? Why have you kept her from us?"

"I did as she asked," Gray said, his jaw tight. "I will always do what she asks. Seems I'm wired that way when it comes to her. It's why I'm here. She wanted to be brought to you."

Alexander shook his head. "Why?"

"She killed someone. A human."

Nicholas cursed, "Fuck." Lucian too.

"The Order—" Alexander began.

"Will be on her the moment they find out," Gray finished. "But not just for the killing."

"Oh, Jesus, what now?" Lucian muttered, his arm stealing around his *veana*, pulling his *balas* closer.

Gray looked only at Alexander. "She wasn't in this form when she did it."

"Form?" Alexander repeated.

"Dilly." It was Erion, and he was standing and staring at what was in Gray's arms. He motioned for the other Beasts to come take a look.

Nicholas stared at Erion. "You know her?"

322

"She was with us as *balas*," he said. "She left our father … Cruen, when he got too rough."

His eyes wide and sharp, Alexander looked up, looked at Gray. "She's a … "

"*Mutore,*" Gray finished for him.

And before their eyes, Dillon shuddered, screamed like a jungle cat, and shifted into a Beast.

Acknowledgments

I've said it before, but it must be said again—publishing a book takes a village. A very talented, supportive, creative, and generous village. And sitting in the mayor's seat (the hot seat) is none other than my extraordinary editor, Danielle Perez. Thank you so much, Danielle, for not only working as hard and as long as you do, but for giving the Romans, and the series as a whole, your love and care and support. You are truly one in a million.

Thank you to my village champion, my backbone, Maria Carvainis—and to the entire MCA crew. Your hard work and attention to detail are so very appreciated!

To my friend and critique partner in the writing stockades, Jennifer Lyon: For all the hard work, endless reads and rereads, and those gentle pushes I always seemed to need throughout this book, I thank you! You, me, and Lucian, right?

Thank you to the entire NAL family—a village I am so honored to be a part of.

And the village wouldn't look nearly as beautiful—or as hot—without an amazing team of artists. Thanks to the NAL art department for their brilliant Mark of the Vampire covers! Better and better, baby.

To my homegirl and the extraordinary artist, Tricia Pickyme Schmitt: Thanks so much for the support and the beautiful artwork you've given me and the boys. And to my homegirl authors, Larissa Ione and Nalini Singh: Thank you for the support and friendship.

And last, but most important, my family. Daniel, Isa, and Lucca, thank you so much for your support, love, and daily, "You can do it, Mommy!" I love you all so much!

Do you love fiction with a supernatural twist?

Want the chance to hear news about your favourite authors (and the chance to win free books)?

Keri Arthur
S. G. Browne
P.C. Cast
Christine Feehan
Jacquelyn Frank
Larissa Ione
Sherrilyn Kenyon
Jackie Kessler
Jayne Ann Krentz and Jayne Castle
Martin Millar
Kat Richardson
J.R. Ward
David Wellington
Laura Wright

Then visit the Piatkus website and blog
www.piatkus.co.uk | www.piatkusbooks.net

And follow us on Facebook and Twitter
www.facebook.com/piatkusfiction | www.twitter.com/piatkusbooks

piatkus